BALANCE
POINT

Baen Books by
Robert Buettner

Overkill
Undercurrents
Balance Point

ROBERT BUETTNER

BALANCE POINT

This is a work of fiction. All the characters and events portrayed in this book are fictional, and any resemblance to real people or incidents is purely coincidental.

A Baen Books Original

Baen Publishing Enterprises
P.O. Box 1403
Riverdale, NY 10471
www.baen.com

ISBN: 978-1-4767-3644-0

Cover art by Justin Adams

First Baen printing, April 2014

Distributed by Simon & Schuster
1230 Avenue of the Americas
New York, NY 10020

Library of Congress Cataloging-in-Publication Data

Buettner, Robert.
Balance point / Robert Buettner.
pages cm. -- (Orphan's legacy ; 3)
"A Baen Books original"--T.p. verso.
ISBN 978-1-4767-3644-0 (pbk.)
1. Life on other planets--Fiction. 2. Space warfare--Fiction. I. Title.
PS3602.U344B35 2014
813'.6--dc23

2014000099

Printed in the United States of America

10 9 8 7 6 5 4 3 2 1

NOTE TO READERS REGARDING THIS VOLUME'S CONTENTS

Robert Buettner's short story, "Mole Hunt," is included in this volume after the end of *Balance Point*. "Mole Hunt" was originally published electronically, as a Baen Free Library short story in 2011.

Readers need *not* have read "Mole Hunt" first in order to fully enjoy and understand *Balance Point*. The events detailed in "Mole Hunt" are summarized where, and in as much detail as, necessary in *Balance Point*.

However, the events detailed in "Mole Hunt" occur in the *Orphan's Legacy* series time line before *Balance Point* and after series book 2, *Undercurrents*.

"Mole Hunt" is placed in this volume after *Balance Point* because "Mole Hunt" was written as a stand-alone short story, differs radically in style and viewpoint from *Balance Point*, and depicts no characters who appear elsewhere in the *Orphan's Legacy* series.

CONTENTS

For Emily, and for Rob

Most students of superpower relations know that the balance point between detente and Armageddon is a razor's edge. Few realize how often that edge has been as slim as the survival odds of a single spy.

—Vladimir Yefimovich Semichastny,
Chairman of the KGB
throughout the Cuban Missile Crisis
of October, 1962

BALANCE
POINT

ONE

The pilot on my left tapped my shoulder as his voice crackled in my headset. "Captain Parker? There, sir!"

I looked where his gloved finger pointed. Twenty degrees right of the tilt-wing's nose, five miles distant, an oily black rope writhed between the ground and the sky. The smoke tied together the South Georgia swamp below us and the low cloud ceiling beneath which we raced.

"Fire? Why the hell is there fire?"

"Flame thrower, sir. Apparently the animal doesn't like 'em."

I shook my head and swore. Of course "the animal" didn't like 'em. No being in its right mind liked burning alive. "What idiot thought that up?"

"I just fly the bird, sir." The pilot banked the tilt-wing toward the smoke. He had never overflown this place before and knew only what he'd been told through his headset during the last two hours. His tilt-wing was a regular Army trainer that had been diverted in flight from Ft. Stewart, a couple hundred miles northeast, because it was the only available vertical take-off and landing aircraft near enough to pick me up in a shopping center parking lot, then drop me off, that was also clearable into restricted airspace.

The pilot leveled the ship and settled it toward a landing pad. The pad was just a rectangle where the scrub had been scraped back to expose bare soil. At one corner an orange wind sock flapped from a pole. A ground-level breeze now carried the smoke from the fire across the pad like a shroud four hundred yards long.

Two turret-variant hellcats idled at the pad's edge. Each 'cat's roof was stenciled "OCWTRS," an acronym for "Okefenokee Chemical Weapons Test Range Security." Of course, the eighty-three square miles of muggy Federal scrub woodland and restricted airspace that surrounded the pad had never seen a chemical weapon, unless you counted that flame thrower.

But the skull-and-crossbones signs on the barbed wire fencing and the overflight restrictions advisories on aerial maps discouraged the curious. The 'cats with their turret guns, and automated triple-A 'bot batteries along the range perimeter, discouraged the more-than-curious.

Half hidden in the trees bordering the pad, a boxy command and control hovertank hunched like a plasteel porcupine, its roof bristling with swept-back antennas.

On the pad another tilt-wing, like the one that was delivering me, but spook-black, already squatted on its landing gear alongside the vehicles. A command-and-control communications pod bulged from its back like a tumor.

"Looks like there's some brass on the ground already, sir. Guess you could ask them about the fire."

The tilt-wing's props were still blowing at landing pitch when I dropped through the belly hatch and ran, eyes slitted against the dust and smoke, to the command slider. The air smelled of seared wood and jellied gasoline.

As the tilt-wing that had hauled me in lifted off, a personal security detail corporal, posted alongside the slider's rear hatch, recognized me, saluted, then jerked his head at the command vehicle. "The Old Man's waiting for you in the slider, Captain Parker."

Inside the red-lit command slider only one person sat, back to me, hunched at one of the flatscreen consoles.

The rest of the consoles were dark and unattended. "Where is everybody, Howard?"

General Howard Hibble, AKA The Old Man, AKA The King of the Spooks, didn't turn around, but in the reflection of his face off the screen I saw his gray eyebrows flick up. "Inauguration Day's a federal holiday. If you hadn't been moping around for the last week you'd know that, Jazen."

Howard Hibble was the longest-serving general officer in the history of the United States Army, but not because he was conventional. He had been a professor before the Slug War, was commissioned as an intelligence officer during the Blitz, and had run his spooks his way ever since. His way included being called by his first name by everybody, and an every-day-is-casual-Friday dress code that would choke any drill sergeant. Howard's way also included knowing more about the personality balance point between the two individuals who made up each of his officer pairs than a marriage counselor knew about her clients.

In fact I *had* taken accumulated leave to mope after Kit left. Not just because I missed waking up beside her. Case officer pairs, whether het or monogender, typically bond closer than married couples, but separation is a job requirement of military life. The trouble with this particular separation was that Kit's job required her to spend two weeks in Paris without me, because the man in charge of the trip preferred I disappear from her life. And he happened to be her father.

I said, "It's my leave. I can mope if I want. I've still got more time accumulated than I can use."

With a bony hand Howard twisted the handlebar of the little scooter he rode around on—they didn't call him "The *Old* Man" for nothing—and faced me. "It is, you can, and you do. I assume you're seeing her this weekend."

"If I can still rent an outfit. You kidnapped me in the tux shop parking lot before I got in the door."

He adjusted the old-fashioned wire rimmed glasses that hung on his wrinkled face and stared at my jeans. "Wear your dress whites instead."

I eyed his wrinkled flannel shirt. "What do you know about the dress code for black-tie parties?"

"As little as a man who's survived four decades in Washington can. But I know you. You'll be less intimidated in your own skin." Howard shrugged as he spun back to the console and tapped up the screen image. "I didn't send that tilt-wing so I could give you relationship counseling."

I peered over his shoulder.

The screen showed a crowbot overhead, real time, visible light, displaying two hundred by two hundred yards. Dismounted infantry, probably the squad that normally patrolled the range's perimeter aboard the two parked hellcats, were deployed on line, prone behind the cover of a shallow ridge at the screen's left, west, edge.

I guessed that when things had gone bad they had been pulled off perimeter patrol. The command slider probably had been rolled out from The Barn on auto and rendezvoused with Howard's hunchback when it landed.

The infantry were all armored up in full Eternads, and two of the GIs had flamer tanks strapped on their suits' backs.

Fifty yards to the squad's front, brush and scrub burned. The smoke plume now drifted south, forming a concealing barrier at ground level between the squad and anything beyond the smoke that depended on visible light to see. The Okefenokee is damp terrain, even around its edges, and the fire looked to be burning itself out.

On the other side of the smoke screen, the hovering crowbot's feed highlighted three biologics among the trees.

The first biologic, twenty yards beyond the fire, was another GI in Eternads, lying face up. Fifteen feet from him lay a twisted metal lump that had once been the tanks and hose of a back-mounted flamer. Just beyond the trashed flamer were two larger lumps. They remained barely recognizable as a utility-variant hellcat and its flatbed trailer, both now mangled and overturned, impellers to the sky.

The GI lay motionless, and at first I assumed he was dead. But his suit vitals shimmered in orange digits displayed on the screen alongside his image. They were normal, except for elevated heart rate and respiration, which were hardly surprising considering his circumstances.

I nodded to myself. Playing dead was a logical strategy.

His circumstances were defined by the other two biologics on the screen. The first, according to the vitals displayed alongside it, was a newly dead, but still warm, truck-sized animal carcass. One of its six legs had been torn off and lay alongside the limp body, and its neck had been wrenched so that its rack haloed its head like a spiked wreath.

I pointed at a shredded harness that had tethered the recently deceased animal to the trailer. "I assume that's his Christmas turkey woog?"

Howard nodded, then frowned. "Normally, that makes his day."

I nodded back.

Woog were more-or-less antelope, but six-legged, bigger than elephants, and not native to South Georgia. Very not native. Downgraded Earthlike 476, known to everybody except its tourism bureau as Dead End, was about as far from South Georgia as the human race had gotten so far.

Dead End harbored a Carbon 12-based fauna so biochemically dissimilar to Earth's that feeding an Earth animal's flesh to a Dead End carnivore was like feeding sand to a lion. So, in order to nourish OCWTRS' one and only guest, Howard's xenobiologic nerds had bred, here on Earth, a herd of woog.

The nerds found that the docile, Earth-bred woogs provided dandy nourishment, but failed to offer the "robustly combative dining experience" provided to a grezzen when he chased down a natural-born wild woog back home on Dead End.

The Army has its faults, but it spares no expense to give remotely deployed GIs a taste of home. You may get your Christmas turkey dinner in a bunker, but you *will* get it. So, on each federal holiday, one of which was the inauguration day of the United States President, the Army, driven by force of habit, imported one live free-range woog, all the way across the ten jumps between Dead End and Earth, as a dietary change of pace for South Georgia's most voracious tourist.

I squinted at the third organic on the screen, which was the intended beneficiary of the Army's generosity. Unlike the possum-playing GI game warden who had delivered the woog, the grezzen was very much in motion. As I watched, the grezzen uprooted a thirty-foot cypress with a paw swipe that spun the tree through the air as if an eleven-ton, six legged ochre grizzly bear had swatted a salmon out of a stream. The grezzen spun like a dog chasing its tail, sprang twenty yards in a single bound to another cypress, then splintered it, too.

"Howard, what's got up his ass?"

Howard shook his head. "Don't know. That warden lost his helmet audio before he could elaborate."

"He's lucky he didn't lose his helmet and the head in it. He knows better than to use his flamer. Does that relief squad know enough to hold *their* fire?"

"Well, I hope so."

I blew out a breath. A dithering professor *hoped* his students knew what to do. A four-star general made *sure* they knew, then motivated them to do it. Intelligence was an unconventional business, and Howard's resumé spoke for itself, but there were times when running a military organization like a Socratic-method graduate seminar was idiotic.

I stepped to the hatch. "I'm going over there, Howard."

"Take the hellcat on the left. There's an Eternad suit in your size in the right-hand seat."

I had already slid behind the hellcat's control yoke when I realized that, for a dithering professor, Howard Hibble excelled at motivating people to risk their lives without even asking them to. At least the gullible ones. Who never seemed to learn.

"God *damn* you, Howard." I shifted the 'cat into drive and steered toward the smoke.

TWO

Ten minutes later I left the hellcat idling at the base of the ridge, and low-crawled up alongside the squad leader where he lay in the middle of the line. Howard had radioed ahead that I was coming. The sergeant's visor was up, and when he turned and saw my civvies, his eyes widened.

He shouted to be heard over the grezzen, which bellowed beyond the smoke. "Where's your armor, Captain Parker?"

I shook my head. "I've seen grezz claws cut main battle tank armor. There's no point." The sergeant was new, and it was as much of the truth as he needed to know. "What do you make the range now, Sarge?"

He glanced up at his visor display. "Three hundred yards, sir. The animal's moved farther east since we got here. Running out of trees to punch, I guess."

I squinted at the smoke and saw nothing. Maybe I should have armored up just to access the snoops and visor data. "The warden out there. It's Buford? And he's still down?"

"Yes, sir. I suppose he's waiting until the animal gets farther away before he makes a run for it."

I shrugged. This squad leader was on duty because the experienced security troops had holiday passes. A grezz can cover sixty yards in a bound and sustain seventy miles per hour across open country. There was no making a run for it, and the warden and I knew it even if the newbie didn't.

I levered myself up, stood and brushed damp soil off my civvies while I stared into the smoke.

The squad leader's eyes widened again. "Sir?"

"I'll walk over there and have a look."

He frowned, shook his head. "Sir, you can't. The animal's berserk. And they say nothing short of a hovertank main gun can take a grezz down."

"They say right, Sarge. But work with me on this."

He swallowed. "Yes, sir. One fire team to maneuver with you and the other to provide covering fire?"

I shook my head. "No. I'll go alone. Nobody fires, covering or otherwise. Have your squad safe their weapons. I don't want to get shot or fried by friendly fire. Especially while I'm on leave."

He shook his head again. "Sir, may I suggest—"

"Safe 'em, Sarge. And everybody stays put. Period."

Pause. "Yes, sir." He thumbed the safety lever on his carbine, then spoke into his helmet mike.

I waited until he had confirmation back from every member of his squad, then I walked down the ridge's front slope and skirted the fire around the upwind side.

Ten minutes later I got to ten yards away from the warden, then I knelt and hissed. "Buford!"

Nothing. But I could see that he had drawn his sidearm and laid it across his belly, and his visor was open. Buford knew better than to bother firing a pistol at a grezzen. He had also seen the grezzen eat many times and probably preferred a bullet in the mouth to ending his life as a dismembered canapé, if it came to that.

But if Buford was that jumpy, I didn't want to sneak up on him and get shot.

"Sergeant Buford!" This time I yelled loud enough to be heard over the fire.

He turned his head, saw me, and twitched his free hand in a half-ass wave.

I low-crawled to him and peered down. His face inside his helmet was so shiny with sweat, and so rigid, that he looked like a black marble. "You're okay, John?"

He nodded, wrinkled his forehead. "Captain Parker? Sir, you're on leave."

"Life's a bitch, Sarge. What happened?"

He turned his head toward the grezzen, which was screened from our view by brush. Buford paused, then, when the bellowing and the flying shrubbery didn't change in intensity, answered. "I trailered the holiday woog out here, sedated like usual. I cut it loose, dumped it off the trailer and shot it with wake-up juice. Then I backed off in the hellcat. The woog was up and wobbly after five minutes, frisky after ten. Then the grezz showed up."

"Showed up how?"

Buford shrugged. "Trotting on all six, like usual. The woog made a couple good runs, a pretty strong threat display—it was a big bull with a good rack—the grezz ran with him, back and forth. When the woog's head finally came down . . ." Buford pantomimed chomp-chomp with his free hand's gauntleted fingers, then shrugged. "'Nother day at the office."

I nodded. "But you stuck around?"

Buford nodded back. "Like I said, it was a big bull. I figured there might be some leftovers worth freezing. The grezz really prefers wild meat, even dead and cold."

I glanced up. In the distance, the tantrum continued unabated. "You must have done something."

Buford shook his head so hard that his helmet neck ring squeaked. "Not one goddam thing, Captain. I swear! I was just sitting behind the wheel, reading the news on my handheld. The grezz had torn off the first drumstick. Then I heard him growl. Different. Angry."

"Then?"

"He was on the 'cat in two bounds. He took it in his forepaws and shook me out like I was cereal in a box. Then he trampled the 'cat like it was cardboard." The range warden shook his head. "Sir, he's never done anything like that. Ever. He goes to The Barn when the tech nerds arrive, like he was a big dog. Wags his tail, usually. I think he likes the company."

"The flamer?"

"It fell out of the 'cat when I did. It's, you know, for absolute last ditch deterrence only, sir. I know the animal's valuable. But the way it was going, I figured I was in the last-ditch, you know?"

"I understand."

"So I just triggered a burst. Not even at him. Just into the grass between him and me, to back him off. He hopped the fire like it wasn't there, cuffed me once, with the back of his paw, not the claws. Knocked me face-down. Then he tore the flamer off my back and pounded it like a biscuit." Buford raised his head six inches like he was afraid it would fall off if he raised it higher. "Since then he's just been chewin' the scenery like this, sir. And I been holdin' still 'til he wears out."

"What were you reading?"

Buford squinted. "Sir? Why would that matter?"

"Humor me, John."

Buford reached into his armor's thigh pocket, tugged out his 'puter and unrolled the screen. He clicked a bookmark, then drew a trembling finger across the displayed page. "Ah . . . Cold day for the parade. Inaugural Ball. Bla-bla. Outgoing pardon scandal. Bla-bla. Tycoon freed. Bla—"

I grabbed his wrist, turned the screen toward me, and read. "No!" I closed my eyes, then opened them and watched a tree trunk spin as it arced beneath the clouds. Then I sighed and held up the warden's 'puter. "Mind if I borrow this a minute, John?"

He wrinkled his forehead and sat up when I stood. When I walked past him, toward the grezzen, he grabbed for my arm. "Sir!"

I jerked my head at him. "Don't worry, John. Get back behind the ridge."

"It's not my 'puter that worries me, Sir. I seen men commit suicide by walkin' into a mine field. Whatever's been bothering you—"

"Is my problem. Do I have to make it a direct order?"

He shook his head, stood and backed in a slow crouch toward the relief squad.

Ten minutes later I had left Sergeant Buford behind and was crossing a muddy clearing that ended at a tree line fifty yards to my front. Then the grezzen's bellowing and tree ripping stopped, like the sound had been cut off with a knife. For a moment, the only sound was the distant crackle of the fire, and, I was sure, my heart pounding.

I stood still, and ten seconds later trees crashed again. The treetops nearest me swayed as something big came toward me. The grezzen's head poked out of the tree line, sixteen feet above the ground. Its three red eyes, set in a line across its great, flat face, glared above a mouth large enough to swallow a man whole. Two curved black tusks walrused down from the grezzen's upper lip, and dripped saliva the color and texture of oatmeal.

He rumbled a growl that shook the mud in which I stood.

I swallowed. "Oboy."

THREE

The grezzen peered out across the clearing at the human, as tiny as Buford, who brought his meals, but pale. Unlike Buford, this one was uncovered by the stiff shell in which humans normally wrapped themselves before they came close to him.

Even unshelled like this one, the little bipeds were visually indistinguishable. Even their sexual dimorphism was unobvious, unless one peeled away the artificial integument in which they wrapped themselves. And that was scarcely worth the energy expended because, at least according to those of his race who had sampled humans, the females were as bony and tasteless as the males.

He flexed his limbs until his belly brushed the ground, then peered at this one. No tiny mammaries pushed against its ventral integument, which was patterned in multiple colors. Its lower jaw was smudged, a recurring condition the humans called "five o'clock shadow" for incomprehensibly complex reasons. Male.

The human extended one forelimb behind himself, with one digit extended, toward the smoke and the human shell the grezzen had trampled. "Not exactly a people person today, are we, Mort?" The human audibilized the thought, tiny mouth opening and closing as though eating, but the grezzen understood without the auditory cue.

The grezzen also felt the human's inner fear, of which the little biped gave no outward sign. The fear was understandable. The grezzen's current intemperate rage created the very real apprehension that he might kill any human who came near him.

The grezzen responded to the human without sound. "I have not eaten people in years. Ha-ha."

His response relaxed the human, as intended, and the little creature audibilized, "Not funny. Better. But your joke-telling skills need more work."

"I felt it was you, Jazen."

"You've made a mess here, Mort."

"You know why. I felt you communicate with John Buford."

Jazen tilted his head forward and back. The grezzen understood that this indicated agreement. Humans communicated by patterned sound, but also by body displays, much like prey animals did.

Jazen raised a tiny white leaf in front of his eyes with one hand while he pointed at it with the other. "You eavesdropped on Buford while he was reading the news on his handheld. But Mort, when the news is bad, you can't just kill the messenger."

The grezzen rocked back on his third legs, a pose humans used to communicate affront. "And I did not! John Buford tried to burn me with the fire stinger, so I removed it. That is all I did."

"All? You know what a hellcat costs?"

The grezzen dropped back onto all six. Cost. Grezzen had no need for tools, much less a system by which to value them. Humans, however, valued the tools they communally created and shared, like the hellcat. Only by community and tools had a species so tiny and fragile survived. It was but one reason the little creatures fascinated him. "Perhaps I over-reacted."

Jazen swiveled his head, pointed his foreclaw at the vast expanse of spoiled and burned vegetation that surrounded them. "Ya think? And you scared John shitless."

"Such news would have upset any individual of normal intelligence and sensibility."

"John doesn't know you have intelligence and sensibility! To him you're just a big dog."

The grezzen extended his forelimb and pointed a claw at the leaf. "Read the rest for me. Of the news that John Buford was learning from the leaf."

Jazen crossed his forelimbs, shook his head. This indicated both displeasure and intransigence. "You're a goddam telepath. Go find a mind that's not pissed off at you and read it yourself."

"You know it does not work like that."

How it worked, in fact, was that Dead End's entire grezzen population, the tiny apex atop that planet's predation pyramid, were telepathically connected in real time, cousin-to-cousin, like 'puters wired to a single server. Mort accessed his grandfather's memories as easily as his own, and saw, heard and smelled what any other grezzen experienced whenever he chose.

But with other species, Mort couldn't rummage through individuals' memory banks. He could only see, hear, feel, sense what any individual did, in the moment. As if that individual wore a head-cam with earpiece, and Mort could access the feed anytime he wished.

Grezzen attacked and defended using sight and sound and smell when convenient. And fell back on their gift when they chose. Evolution had upgraded them from physically dominant predators to lords of their world.

However, when eavesdropping on aliens in an alien world, Mort's gift underperformed.

"Jazen? Please?" The grezzen stroked the old scar tissue on his face where the kerosene rain had burned him. "If not for me, for the memory of my mother."

Invoking his dead mother, killed by humans, was a tactic he had learned from the humans. They used it to induce sympathy in another. Although neither party moved in any direction, it was called a guilt trip.

Jazen expelled breath, indicating reluctant assent. The humans called it a sigh. "If I do, you'll calm down?"

The grezzen lay on his back, laced the claws of four limbs across his belly, then remained motionless, like an inanimate vegetable. "There. I am as calm as a cucumber."

"Cool. Cool as a cucumber."

"As you prefer."

Then Jazen raised the leaf again, drew a foreclaw across its surface, and spoke.

"Turn in Tale of Tarnished Tycoon. Once the fourth richest man on Earth, and majority shareholder in its largest communications conglomerate, Bartram Cutler was serving the second year of a twenty-

two-year sentence after conviction on criminal charges that remain sealed on national security grounds. That changed yesterday when Cutler's name appeared on the outgoing administration's list of midnight pardons—"

The grezzen raised one foreclaw. "I came here only because you and Kit told me that Cutler would be restrained because of his misdeeds. You, and so I, have just learned that you said that which is not."

Jazen pointed a foreclaw at the grezzen. "We didn't lie to you! Being wrong about the future's not lying. Just because telepaths don't know how to lie doesn't mean you can't understand the difference. You know humans by now."

The grezzen did indeed know humans, at least his humans, now. He did not know when, precisely, he had begun thinking of Jazen and Kit as "his." Nor did he know when he, a being who lived his adult life, save for mating, apart from others of his kind, came to enjoy proximate interaction with these two frail creatures.

Jazen made another tiny exhalation. "You think I like it? You felt my anger when John read it for me, didn't you?"

The grezzen nodded. "I did. However, I have left my home and come to this place in reliance upon what you said. I have remained here because of what you said. I have endured bland food and miserable climate and the poking and prodding of the nerds at The Barn." He stroked his old scar tissue again. "To say nothing of the attempts to burn me alive." The grezzen turned his mouth up at its corners. "Ha-ha."

Jazen's tiny facial muscles mimicked the grezzen's in response. "I was wrong. Your sense of humor's improving. But remember, if you hadn't come to Earth with us, Cutler would have killed half your cousins by now. Just like he killed your mother. And he would have enslaved the rest of you. He's a bad human. Unfortunately, we have lots of those."

The grezzen raised and lowered his chin in a human nod. "And so I have been content to endure the nerds. But now Cutler is unrestrained. He killed my mother and now he is out there somewhere." He raised up on his back two and stared toward the distant perimeter fence, invisible beyond the trees. "That should not continue."

Jazen's small eyes widened and he raised both foreclaws and turned their inner surfaces toward the grezzen, as though he were pushing against a tree trunk. "Don't even think about it!" He pointed with a foreclaw at the boundary which could not be seen from here. "Mort, you cross outside that fence and the villagers'll go torches and pitchforks on you."

The grezzen stroked his face again, where the kerosene had burned him, then shook his head vertically to punctuate. "Yes. Villagers. I understand. Humans acting together are even more dangerous than a human acting alone."

"More powerful, yes. More dangerous? Not usually. Mostly, when humans act together, it's to do something good. You like the London Symphony."

"I do. But the Yavi act together. The nerds who study me act together. Unlike the musicians of the London Symphony, the Yavi and the nerds wish to kill the other not for food."

"War brings out the worst in both sides. Some Yavi are very bad. But I was raised on Yavet. Most Yavi have nothing to do with what makes the others bad. And maybe a few of the nerds are bad. But most of them are like Kit and me. They just want to protect your race and understand your gift, not weaponize it."

"If Cutler and the bad Yavi acted together, they would be very dangerous."

The corners of Jazen's mouth turned up again, and he shook his head horizontally. This signaled indulgent disagreement. "Cutler's a Trueborn. The bad Yavi hate Trueborns. Especially rich jerk Trueborns. And even jerk Trueborns like Cutler hate the Yavi." Jazen pointed a foreclaw at the woog, dead and warm in the distance. Already a cloud of scavenging local insects rendered its outline indistinct. "Mort, if Cutler and the Yavi ever act together, I'll eat a rotten woog, flies and all."

FOUR

"Relax your forward hand, Mr. Quartermain. Let the rifle's gyros do the work and you'll kill him clean." As Carl Otto, Hospitality Vice President of the Bank of Rand, whispered, he laid his own mittened hand on his depositor's coveralled forearm. The two of them lay prone on a rock ledge in the High Rand Range, within a firing position that the guide hired by the banker had scooped in the snow.

Quartermain peered through the stabilized rifle's optics across a glaciated valley draped by late afternoon shadows, then shrugged off the banker's hand and snarled. "I don't pay you to touch me!"

The depositor kept squeezing the forward stock so hard that the rifle's muzzle quivered visibly as the man outfought stabilizers whining at their limits.

The depositor's name wasn't really "Quartermain," of course. Outworlders who visited Rand typically assumed aliases, because they came less to take the mountain air than to manipulate money they weren't supposed to have. In fact, the Rand Tourism Bureau offered an online alias list to arriving passengers.

Most of the Bank of Rand's sealed accounts were assumed to belong to Trueborn Earthmen, because, among the Human Union's five hundred planets, Earth was where the money was. But the assumption was further supported by the Trueborns' insistence on picking their false names with the same self-referential carelessness by which they dismissed the banker's home world as "Switzerland with bad travel connections."

This particular depositor had chosen the name of a storybook Trueborn hunter. He wasn't the first to make that choice, and it gave him away as obviously as spoor steaming in snow gave away a trophy animal.

But if the Trueborns' privilege and arrogance insulted the Rand, the Trueborns' benign mercantilism made Rand, and worlds like it across the Union, prosperous and kept them independent. The banker's family had lived well for generations by catering to pompous Trueborns even worse than this one. Outworlders said that it was easier to take a Trueborn's money than it was to take a Trueborn.

The banker sighed, withdrew his hand and stroked his neat, red beard.

Four hundred yards across the valley, atop a sheer, windswept spur, a trophy sized, stationary rock goat bull balanced on all six hooves as solidly as though it was part of the mountain. The goat's grown-out mating coat blazed scarlet against the snow, and he emanated musk so strong that the banker's experienced nostrils caught a whiff of the scent on the breeze that blew toward them.

The rutting male stretched his neck and trumpeted, for the benefit of a hundred as-yet-unmet girlfriends.

Before the trumpet's echoes died, the depositor fired.

Blam.

The animal lurched and thrashed in an explosion of snow, and within three heartbeats bled buckets. The bull's masculine trumpet dwindled to a piteous bleat.

The banker closed his eyes to shut out the mess, and swallowed. Like most Rand born to wealth, he had since childhood hunted big game among the High Rand's peaks, and not every kill had been sporting. But he had rarely seen worse than this. "Quartermain" had pissed up an unmissable kill shot, and struck the bull not in the thorax but the hindquarters.

The hired guide, who lay alongside this Trueborn's guest in a similar blind a hundred yards away, whispered in the banker's earpiece. "Sir, should I let Mr. Hickok put him down?"

The banker cocked his head.

"Quartermain" had chosen his guest's alias, a name that referred to a Trueborn wild-west sheriff. But "Hickok" had a Yavi accent so thick that he couldn't be Trueborn. That made "Hickok" not only a Yavi, but a liar, and as bad a liar as Quartermain. However, Hickok could scarcely be as bad a shot.

The banker winced as the bull's bleats echoed off the valley walls. "Let him try. Pelt's spoilt anyway."

Two heartbeat's later, Hickok's shot cracked across the col. It struck and nearly severed the bull's right forelimb. Hickok may, like his namesake, have been some sort of sharpshooting sheriff in real life. But Yavi weren't accustomed to the recoil of gunpowder rifles. "Hickok's" shot struck the bull above the midshoulder, bloody, painful, but not immediately fatal.

However, a meat axe still cuts, even if two butchers have to swing it repeatedly.

The bull stumbled, its chin tusk furrowing the snow, toppled off the spur and tumbled a half mile through the air, its echoing bleats diminishing as it fell. Finally, the carcass bounced off the scree apron that angled out from the sheer valley wall, then the bull slid across the glassy valley floor, leaving a hundred-foot-long blood trace atop the ice.

Quartermain pounded the heated mat on which he lay. "Damn it! That was *my* goat!"

"Ah . . . it wouldn't have made a trophy, sir." The banker bit his lip, glanced at the sky. Shooting light was gone for today. He radioed for the pickup skimmer, then shivered in silence as they waited for it.

He couldn't bring himself to soothe this idiot, whose stubborn incompetence had caused the bull gratuitous agony. To say nothing of what the bull's potential lady friends would now be missing. But scolding a Trueborn wasted breath, and scolding *any* depositor would bring Bank Board discipline.

A half hour later the skimmer, with the banker, the guide, and the two offworlders aboard, settled on the Lodge's arrival pad. Autumn twilight arrived abruptly in mountain valleys, as though a tapestry had dropped across a window, and the pad's landing floods sparkled the powder-snow fog that roiled up from beneath the skimmer's skirt.

The banker and the guide tied down the drone in the gloom while the depositor and the depositor's guest disembarked. The Earthman and the Yavi stalked shoulder-to-shoulder, heads down, hands in pockets. They passed the two Rand without a word, much less the customary tip for the guide.

The Lodge's door minders held the twelve-foot-high double doors open, and yellow glow silhouetted the clients for a heartbeat. Then they disappeared into the lodge where brandy, tobacco and warmth waited.

The guide cocked his head at the closed doors. "What's their business, do you think, sir? Drugs? Slaves?"

The banker rubbed his beard as he turned to the guide, whose cheeks were bare as a girl's, then poked the boy's chest with a mittened finger. "First rule of Rand hospitality. A client's business is his, not yours!"

The boy stiffened, wide-eyed. A guide position for the Bank of Rand was a scarce opportunity, and the boy didn't want to lose his.

But good guides were scarce, too. The kid had simply asked aloud what had puzzled and annoyed the banker, himself.

The banker touched the boy's shoulder as he shook his head. "Not drugs. Not slaves, either. The gangsters, they always tip big to make a show. A show's the last thing those two want."

The boy wrinkled his forehead. "You *don't* think they're criminals?"

The banker smiled in the dark. "There are criminals, there are serious criminals, then there are politicians." He jerked his head toward the Lodge. "Those two are used to traveling with advance parties that see to tipping the locals. They didn't stiff you. They just assumed someone down the line would take care of you. And I will."

"Politicians, sir?"

"Or tycoons. And important ones, whichever they are. Middling crooks couldn't wangle bull permits this time of year."

"But one's an Earthman and the other's a Yavi!"

The banker rubbed his beard again, narrowed his eyes. "That *is* a sow in the parlor, isn't it, boy?"

The Trueborns said—they had sayings for everything, whether outworlders cared to hear them or not—that politics made strange bedfellows. But a powerful Yavi and a powerful Trueborn meeting face-to-face was beyond strange. Cold War II had grown so frigid that

Earth and Yavet conducted no politics with one another at all, in bed or otherwise. Even here in the most exclusive and discreet hideaway among five hundred planets.

The kid whistled. "Making peace? Or plotting war?

The boy had a knack for perceiving the obvious, which was ninety percent of what the rich paid others to do for them. He would go far.

The banker bent and tugged the drone's tie-downs a final time, as though their solidity would soothe the discomfort that swelled in his belly. "War and peace is somebody else's business. Your business is tracking goats. Stick to that."

The boy tramped on ahead to his guide hut while snow crust crackled beneath his boots, echoing across the darkness. Like whispers in the banker's head that wouldn't quit.

Peace between Earth and Yavet? That was unlikely. But the Cold War between the Human Union's two nuclear superpowers turning hot? That was unthinkable.

Only the Trueborns had starships. So they could rain nuclear bombs down on Yavet, or any other planet, with impunity. The Yavi had nuclear bombs in plenty, but no way to deliver them in strategic quantity.

So Cold War II stayed cold based on counterbalanced assumptions. The Trueborns were assumed to be too self-righteously moral to destroy even an enemy as evil as the Yavi, if doing so would kill billions. The Yavi, on the other hand, were assumed to be quite immoral enough to lay waste to worlds, as they had to their own, if they ever obtained the means. But the Trueborns assumed they could prevent the Yavi from obtaining the means by incremental containment: a patchwork of alliances, a mixed bag of surrogate, brushfire, and clandestine military adventures, and espionage.

It seemed to Otto a balance as ludicrous as it was precarious. But it was the only balance this agglomeration of civilizations had.

So despite a code of secrecy that had bound his family, and all the great banking families of Rand, for generations, Carl Otto had long ago chosen sides. And he would do whatever he had to in order to preserve the balance.

Inside his parka, the banker shivered, and watched until the boy disappeared inside his hut. Then Otto turned and walked toward the communications shed.

FIVE

The tuxedoed *maître de hôtel* behind the polished wood rostrum of the High Rand Lodge's dining room shook hair as long as a woman's into place and smiled. "Good evening, Mr. Hickok! Successful day on the Cols?"

Maximillian Polian, Director General of Internal Security for the Unified Republics of Yavet, let his mute stare melt the man's grin. Polian knew that his Yavi accent didn't match his Trueborn alias, and had no desire to further advertise an already obvious lie.

The man made a small bow. "Yes, sir. If you would be so good as to follow me?" The *maître d'* swept a hand toward the open double doors that led to the private salon on the opposite side of the chandeliered dining room. The place was empty during mating season. Shooting animals that were about to swell their population was bad policy here. Polian thought that perverse.

Max Polian didn't roll his eyes at any of it until the poof turned away and snaked through the silent shoals of linen-draped tables. As Polian followed, he sawed a bony finger between his throat and the stiff collar of the tuxedo shirt that had been hung in his closet for his use. The thing threatened to strangle him. His police mess-dress uniform collar was actually even tighter, but Polian would gladly have traded.

As he swiveled his head back and forth, Polian ground his teeth at three annoyances. First, poof tuxedos were not just uncomfortable, they were Trueborn fashion, rather than Yavi. Every detail of this overwrought palace of a hunting lodge, from the heavy table silver to the chandeliers glittering beneath the high ceilings, copied Trueborn opulence. Like most outworlds, Rand borrowed its cultural cues from Earth. Second, Polian's host chose a Trueborn alias for Polian. As a Yavi first and last, Polian chafed beneath the alias worse than beneath the stiff shirt. Third and worst, this entire meeting was mere playing at espionage. It fooled not even these outworlders. Any ten of the thousands of Yavi criminals Polian had spent a lifetime bringing to justice created more credible lies than this overprivileged Earthman had fabricated.

As the *maître d'* ushered Polian into the private salon, Polian's host stood, crossed in front of the crackling hearth. Like Polian and the dining-room staff, he wore black-tied evening dress. Unlike Polian, his host looked at ease in his Trueborn skin. He shook Polian's hand with the overt familiarity that marked a Trueborn as clearly as the pearlescent perfection of the man's smile. "Mr. Hickok!"

Polian squeezed up the corners of his mouth up beneath his moustache. "Mr . . . Quartermain."

Max Polian, like most members of Yavet's martial services, had been selected over generations and stood a head taller than the civilians they ruled. But the eyes of Polian's host were level with his own, and set in a tanned face symmetrically handsome even by Trueborn standards.

Polian turned his gaze to the fire laid in the great stone fireplace that warmed the private dining salon until he heard the double doors click shut behind them. Once the *maître d'* bowed out, the only sound in the room was the blazing crackle of logs, which would defeat listening devices. "Mr. Cutler, I understand Trueborns love their melodrama. But can we stop playing spies?"

Bartram Cutler smiled, nodded. "Sure. It was mostly to make you comfortable anyway. I've trusted the Rand all my life."

Polian didn't doubt that. Like any good cop, Polian had done his homework. Bartram Cutler, third-generation owner of Cutler Communications, was the fourth richest man on Earth. Or he had been. Two years ago, Cutler had been imprisoned by his own government for publicly undisclosed crimes. The scandal had cost Cutler not only control of the family business but, presumably, the fortune that business had created. Presumably.

Polian covered a smile with a cough as he glanced at the padded, silken wallpaper.

Smart criminals hid a nest egg. Cutler's nest egg was obviously proportional to his family fortune, and just as obviously hidden in an encrypted account here on Rand.

From a bottle in the table's center, Cutler poured amber liquid into two glasses, then handed one to Polian and raised the other. "To the Rand. Where I come from, we say that the Rand can keep a secret."

Polian grunted, didn't drink. He wasn't in the habit of drinking with crooks, or of trusting them, especially failed Trueborn crooks. "Where I come from, Mr. Cutler, we say that three can keep a secret. If two are dead."

Cutler threw back his head and laughed. "I take your point. Director, I asked to meet you here precisely so that we could speak face-to-face. Rand's the most discreet and secure venue in the Human Union. But as you see, I dismissed the clerks and jerks. Any secrets we share will be between us. No middlemen to reveal our business."

"Our business? Mr. Cutler, you and I have no business." Polian pulled his fingers back from the glass on the tablecloth and sighed. "And you have no business at all these days, from what my people advise me."

Polian read the frown that flicked across Cutler's smooth face. Bart Cutler still had a great deal of money, even by Trueborn standards. But money without influence was almost worthless to someone born to both.

Polian frowned back. "My sources are unclear about what crimes you committed. But we have it on good authority you were pardoned only because you hired clever lawyers. Who in turn hired an even cleverer elected official."

Blood pinked the Earthman's cheeks. "And neither the lawyers nor the outgoing bitch in the White House came cheap. Director, I was the victim of a power play and trumped-up charges."

Polian allowed himself an eye roll. "A policeman's heard that one before."

"You doubt that my government would persecute an honest man?"

Polian smirked. "Now it is my turn to get *your* point. A crime committed against Earth hardly bothers a Yavi. But I don't know how I can help you."

"Not you personally, perhaps. But Yavet can."

Polian wrinkled his brow. "I carry no portfolio for Yavet, sir. I am here as a private citizen on medical leave." It was true. The old fools on the Central Committee were always ready to believe that someone nearly as old as themselves had medical problems. If they knew the truth of this they would suffer strokes, themselves.

Max said, "Yavet can help many people. But why would she?"

Cutler leaned forward. "How did you get to Rand?"

Polian snorted. "Sir, if you expect a candid conversation, don't answer a question with a question. Especially one to which you already know the answer. You arranged my passage, to conceal our meeting."

Cutler nodded. "Even so, like every Yavi, like every interworlds traveler in the Union, you were booked aboard a Trueborn starship. Even more unjustly, although you represent the most populous planet in the union, the nuclear and economic co-equal of Earth herself—in fact *because* of your position—you had to pretend you were a common tourist. Because Earth presumes to dislike the way Yavet runs its own society."

Polian's hands wrinkled the tablecloth as his fingertips whitened. "You pander to a Yavi's pride. But you're right. Your government's patronization of Yavet insults our people and our principles. A great society has the right to the principles that made it great, and to gift lesser societies with them."

Cutler hesitated, as Trueborns always did at self-evident truths with which they disagreed.

Then he said, "First, Director, it isn't *my* government any more. Looking out a cell window for twenty-one months changes a man's world view. Second, Yavet's problem isn't obtaining the *right* to expand, is it? Your problem is obtaining the *means*."

Polian felt himself nod.

Cutler smiled. "And right now you're dead in the water on that."

Polian's nod froze.

Cutler leaned forward, lowered his voice, even in the empty room. "Six months ago your people conducted a covert military operation on Tressel. Yavet came away with enough propulsion-grade cavorite to fuel a fleet of cruisers."

Polian's eyes widened a millimeter. The wretched business on Tressel. His eyes burned, moistened, at the mention, even now. But he swallowed and said nothing.

Cutler stabbed a finger into the tablecloth. "But starship fuel without starships is useless to Yavet, isn't it? So you tried to steal a C-drive unit."

Polian blinked. "I don't know what you're talking about."

Cutler cocked his head, sat back. "Of course not. But I'll speak hypothetically, as a man who knows industrial espionage. I'd say that even if you had managed to salvage a Scorpion fighter's C-drive unit from some wreck, reverse engineering a small interceptor's engine into a strategic fleet of jump-capable cruisers would have taken decades."

Polian forced his face blank. Cutler might have lost much of his influence, but he still knew how and where to buy accurate information. And he knew how to draw accurate conclusions from that information. Max Polian was not, however, about to concede an inch to a Trueborn.

He shrugged. "Time favors the righteous."

Cutler poured again into Polian's half-full glass. "Sure it does. But wouldn't the righteous prefer to get keel-up starship technology delivered to them on a silver platter, instead?"

Now Polian sat back, narrowed his eyes, even as he felt his heart skip. "Assuming—purely for the sake of argument—that Yavet *were* interested in acquiring, as you put it, Trueborn keel-up starship technology on a plate, why bring your offer to me? I'm just what you call a flat-footed cop. My responsibilities are internal. Stealing external secrets isn't a simple policeman's job."

"Director Polian, if you're just a simple policeman, I'm just a simple salesman. Did you know that my father made me start at the bottom at Cutler, as a field salesman? He said he wasn't going to turn the business over to a rich bum." Cutler shifted in his chair. "But tough love taught me plenty. Before I made a sales call on a big client, who do you think I always contacted first?"

Polian made a show of shrugging again, but he didn't turn away. "I have no idea, and less curiosity. Peddling disinterests me."

"I approached the guy on the inside who I figured had the best reason to buy. Because if I got to him face-to-face first, and sold him, he'd sell the rest of management for me."

Max Polian waved his hand at the glittering room around them, snorted. "You think this frosting can sell me? Or buy me?"

"Bribe you with a hunting trip? My father didn't raise a fool." Cutler paused, softened his voice. "And you didn't raise your son as one, either."

The old man stiffened, stood. "My son?"

Cutler paused a heartbeat, then said even more softly, "Director, how much do you know about the circumstances of your son's death?"

The old cop narrowed his eyes. "What do you know about—?"

Cutler raised his palm. "I know he died a hero. And I know the power of the bond between a father and a son."

Polian swayed, silent, for ten seconds, then whispered, "It's my turn to answer a question with a question. Why do you bring up my son's death?"

Cutler inched Polian's glass toward him again. "Sit down. It's real single-malt. I brought the bottle out from Earth myself."

Polian sat, lifted the glass and sniffed.

After Ruberd's first off-world posting, Polian's son had brought home a bottle of Trueborn whisky, purchased duty-free at a hub layover, for the two of them to share. But they had argued on the shuttle down from the Ring. He could no longer remember about what. Max Polian had found the bottle, still unopened, among his son's effects, when the service had delivered them.

Max Polian sipped, and the scotch—he was sure it was the scotch—made his eyes water.

Polian blinked back the tears and peered at his host.

It seemed to Polian that Cutler was now watching him with the same expression that the Earthman had worn two days before, while he watched a snow leopard taste a bait. Moments later, Cutler had killed the animal with a shot so clean that it tore the trophy's heart out.

Cutler nodded. "Here's what I have in mind."

SIX

The uniformed guard, one hand on the gunpowder pistol holstered at his waist, stepped out and blocked Max Polian's path up the starship's embarkation gangway. The guard raised his other hand, palm out. "Hold it right there!"

Polian froze, held his breath.

Polian could, if it came to it, claim diplomatic immunity. However, a cabinet-level Yavi reduced to traveling from Rand to his own homeworld incognito aboard a Trueborn starship would be a gross embarrassment, even though the practice was the worst-kept secret in the universe.

But—had Cutler been a Trueborn Intelligence plant? The meeting a set-up? No ruse was too petty for the shadowy Hibble's legions. A cabinet-level Yavi caught spying would be beyond embarrassing, it would be a propaganda coup for the Trueborns. To say nothing of the reaction of the Central Committee.

The guard, wearing the chevrons of a Trueborn Marine Lance Corporal, pointed at Polian's gut. "Turn 'em out."

"What?"

"Your vest pockets, sir. Would you turn 'em inside-out for me? Please?"

Please? Polian stifled an eye roll. When, as a young vice cop, Polian had been in the kid's position, there would have been no "please," just an order. And a mailed fist to the jaw if that order wasn't immediately obeyed. Hibble's minions aside, trusting these people with the fate of five hundred planets was like allowing a child to conduct a symphony.

Polian reached slowly into the waist pockets of the souvenir leather Rand hunting vest the Lodge had provided, with its crest on the left breast. Polian had worn the thing to flesh out his tourist image. He plucked the linings and tugged them out. With them came a half dozen large-bore cartridges that Polian hadn't realized were there. Polian left his hands in the fabric so that the guard wouldn't notice that they quivered.

"Hunters forget leftover ammo all the time, sir." The Marine pointed at an open bin alongside his boot. "If you dump no-carry items here, no sweat." The kid smiled, jerked a thumb at the scanner arch ten paces up the gangway. "If the scanner catches them, there's paperwork. Strain for you, strain for us. Sorry."

Polian exhaled, managed a smile back, dropped the cartridges into the indicated bin. "No apology needed, Corporal. An old man already strains enough."

The Marine guard's earpiece chirped, and the kid turned away, hand pressed to his ear, nodding. He had already forgotten the forgetful old fool in front of him.

Before he continued aboard, Polian looked up at the vast cruiser within which he would begin his circuitous voyage back to Yavet. The vessel, with the others that comprised Earth's fleet, connected the five hundred worlds of the Human Union. And—he clenched his jaw at the thought—allowed Earth to dominate mankind in general and Yavet in particular.

He had seen cruisers before this trip, drifting at orbital mooring, tethered to the Ring, two hundred miles above Yavet. They resembled skeletal, mile-long white whales, and their projected power intimidated him.

Max Polian, like any vice cop who had worked the downlevels, understood physical intimidation. A head, and usually much more, taller in his armor than the little people, simply raising a mailed fist had usually been enough to get any question answered.

But here on Rand, one of the worlds where cruisers like *HUS Emerald River* actually descended from space and hovered at the surface, the enormity of a C-drive star cruiser, the simple reality of a movable object so vast, didn't merely intimidate, it overwhelmed.

To his left, the conical C-drive booms tapered down to tips that ended eight hundred yards aft of the vessel's midpoint. In front of him the vessel's midsection rose, windowed with thirty-six midpoint bays that had once harbored a full wing of interceptors, ground-attack ships, and transports. To his right, the great tube of the cargo and passenger spaces tapered forward, ending another eight hundred yards distant, in the blunt crystal tip of the forward observation blister.

With such ships, Yavet would be more than equal to the Motherworld. Without them, Yavet would always be shackled.

After Polian cleared the embarkation sensors he passed an entry hatch that led aft. A pair of Marines stood guard there, in full Eternad armor with automatic weapons unslung. What lay aft remained a mystery to Yavet's external intelligence services despite decades of effort. Nano remotes, recruited human agents, open-source research, nothing had unlocked the secrets.

He looked away as he passed rather than be reminded of his own frustration. Continuing through the vast ship's decks and sectors to his cabin, he lay rigid on his bunk and stared at the ceiling.

Ruberd had sacrificed his life to end the Trueborns' dominance. At least to begin the end.

Max Polian clenched his teeth. No, his son had not sacrificed his life. It had been stolen from him by Trueborn assassins. And now Cutler had presented Polian with the opportunity to punish the thieves.

After the great ship lifted, she hung above Rand while her crew prepared her for the nearlight voyage to the first of the Temporal Fabric Insertion Point transits through which the ship would jump. The jump across the TFIP, from one limb of a fold in space to another, connected points that were otherwise centuries of travel apart, even for light itself.

Polian made his way to the ship's centerline passage, where rotational gravity was effectively zero, and swam forward through thin air to the observation blister. He emerged into a crystal hemisphere eighty feet in diameter, its inner surface spiderwebbed with handrails at which passengers floated like fish crowded in a bowl.

The world they were leaving behind filled half the blackness of the view that entranced them. Like most seeded Earthlikes, Rand was a blue and green ball frosted with white cloud swirls. Unlike most seeded Earthlikes, it was a satellite. Beyond Rand glowed the uninhabitable, streaked orange gas giant around which Rand orbited.

Polian hung in the air, staring. The sight awed even him.

He found a vacant space along a rail, alongside a group of five outworlders. At least he assumed they were outworlders. Two adults with three children could only come from a place where the problem was underpopulation. The man in the group floated alongside the boy, the woman between the girls. Both adults pointed out features visible on the globe below, compared them to the place to which they were bound.

Polian rested both hands on the rail in front of him. He had, after all, no one for whom to point out sights.

On inspection visits to the Ring he had often looked down on Yavet from near space. Yavet had, perhaps two hundred years before, resembled the blue, fleecy ball below him. Today, clouds rendered her a burnished gray, an enhancement wrought by industrious purpose and unified government.

Even the Trueborns conceded that, but for the interruption forced on Earth by the Pseudocephalopod War, Yavet was what Earth would have become. He smiled into his reflection in the crystal. Leave it to the Trueborn historians—no, propagandists—to paint Yavet as ruined, instead of vigorous.

What did the Earthmen say? History was written by the victors.

The Trueborns had won the final victory against the alien civilization that had once kidnapped and enslaved the Trueborns' paleolithic ancestors. Then that civilization had sprinkled those ancestors across the universe like seeds before it returned and tried to destroy mankind's motherworld. And why had the Pseudocephalopod Hegemony returned to destroy Earth? Only the Slugs knew that. And now, no one would ever know. Because the Trueborns had ended hostilities by some still-undisclosed treachery that had annihilated their opponent without so much as a body left behind.

But the history of the ongoing struggle within mankind between the motherworld and the seeded worlds like Yavet remained to be written. Polian had lost his son to the struggle. History would never, Max Polian thought, be allowed to forget that.

Inside the ship's gravity cocoon, the separation from the orbit of Rand and subsequent rapid acceleration brought with it no sensation of motion. The change was perceptible only because Rand, and even the planet around which Rand orbited, vanished, replaced by blackness salted with cold starpoints. Undistorted by atmosphere, the stars didn't even twinkle.

The outworld children whined at the suddenly monotonous experience of floating in the fishbowl, and the family disappeared aft, first among many.

Thirty minutes later Polian pushed back from the rail and let himself turn slowly through three hundred sixty degrees. The vast chamber had emptied, save for a single figure floating at the rail on the hemisphere's opposite side, fifty feet away. No longer shielded by the discretion of the Rand, Polian and Cutler had boarded separately, and would limit their overt contact during the voyage now underway which would end at the Mousetrap. At the Mousetrap hub, each man would board a ship bound respectively for Earth and Yavet.

Polian regrasped his railing and pulled himself along until he and Cutler drifted side-by-side at the rail, staring out at the flat lit stars.

Cutler didn't turn his head. "Well? Are you in, Max?"

Polian glanced around the empty space again, more from instinct than any real concern about eavesdroppers.

The Trueborns were a conflicted paradox. They continued to maintain themselves as individual nations on their own planet, and even now fought among themselves. Yet those charged with maintaining order handcuffed themselves with absurd rules. On an Earth ship, as on Earth, "privacy," like being born, was a "right." Nonetheless, Polian scrolled his wrist 'puter display to sweep, then waited in silence until the display winked green. This fishbowl was clean of listening devices.

He said to Cutler, "You're sure your information is reliable?"

"If I can buy a presidential pardon, I can buy a junior officer's personnel records. It's all there for you, right down to his psych profiles."

Polian nodded. "I don't doubt that you've learned what the man did. But whatever the psychologists claim, predicting what a man will do is less simple."

"You forget, I know this man. He's as predictable as water flowing downhill. I've given you the concept, and all the information that can be developed from my end. From here on out, it's your operation."

"And if Yavet succeeds, what do you get out of this?"

"When Yavet's got its own starships, you'll establish a sphere of influence within the Union. I want the exclusive communication franchise within the Yavet sphere. And a free hand over commercial development on Downgraded Earthlike 476."

"Dead End? It's worthless. Jungle and bloodthirsty monsters. Why?"

"It's the place where my troubles started. Call it unfinished business."

Polian shook his head. "I can try to get you your price, but I can't promise it. The Director General of Internal Security is just a local cop."

Cutler rolled his eyes. "A *cabinet-level* local cop, Max."

"Your concept would require cooperation from the Directorate of External Security. That's not my jurisdiction. And only the Central Committee could approve the rewards you want."

Cutler's fingers whitened as he gripped the rail. "Independent directors! They'll knife an innovator through his heart before it beats twice. Then steal his birthright. Max, you get starships for Yavet and you won't be a cabinet-level cop anymore. You'll be *on* the Central Committee."

Polian stared straight ahead, face as blank as he could manage. If anything, Cutler was understating Polian's potential reward. Max wouldn't be *on* the Central Committee, he would be running it. "General Secretary Polian." The astropolitical upside for Yavet and the career potential for Max Polian almost outweighed his thirst for revenge. Almost.

He said to Cutler, "It's not a simple plan."

"It's simple enough, Max! To catch the biggest fish, use a smaller fish for bait. And to catch the bait, use a smaller fish still. But it all starts with you. If you can't find the small fish . . ."

"It's been thirty years. And the woman, if she's even alive, isn't in a fishbowl. She's in an ocean along with thirteen billion other fish."

Cutler smiled. "But Max, that ocean and all those fish *are* your jurisdiction."

Polian nodded, smiled in spite of himself. "True."

"Then we have a deal. You take it from here, Max." Cutler patted his shoulder, drifted back and left Max alone at the tip of the enormous ship.

Polian knew he wouldn't see or hear from Cutler again until and unless the plan succeeded. So very Trueborn. Cutler cajoled someone else to do the heavy lifting, then would step in to rob the spoils. Or keep his distance if the weight collapsed and crushed the gullible unfortunate. But the spoils for Max Polian, and for Yavet, were worth the heavy lifting and the risk.

Polian stared into the blackness, as though he could see the first jump, days away even at the unimaginable speed at which they already moved. Beyond that jump lay seven more jumps, and a transfer at the Ring to a downshuttle, before he reached home.

Even weightless, he felt sore and tired. Yavet to Rand and return was a long journey even for a man half his age. Just as well, though. He needed time to plan his fishing trip.

SEVEN

Three days after *l'affaire* Mort, I slid down the electric's driver's side window and waved my invitation toward the gate guard, who didn't stand up inside his stucco box when he saw me. To my left the orange Sun sank into the Gulf of Mexico. Ahead, a half-dozen private tilt-wings nested on the ground between the wrought-iron fence and the main house, and beyond them row upon row of parked limos gleamed black on the emerald lawn.

The gray-haired guard peered in through the Florida twilight at my dress whites and medals and whistled. "HSLD, Captain Parker!"

I smiled at him. "We'll see, Leon."

"High Speed Low Drag" was the buttoned-down configuration adopted by terrain-independent extralight armored fighting vehicles when maximizing forward progress. Applied by one hovertanker to another, the acronym implied a sleek appearance likely to maximize progress with the opposite sex.

I eyed the sea of tilt-wings and limos.

Their male passengers had surely arrived dressed not in brass-buttoned uniforms worn by persons for hire, but in tuxedos. And not tuxes rented from some storefront next door to a fried chicken place, at that.

Leon wrinkled his nose at the bugs spattered on my four-year-old electric's windscreen. HSLD my Chyota was not. "The Colonel's Dad would have sent the plane for you, Captain. Or at least one of the cars."

"Tankers drive themselves, Leon."

Especially if the alternative required me to accept an act of *noblesse oblige* from Edwin Trentin-Born. The Trentins and the Borns had been *oblige*-ing the less-fortunate classes since long before the hard freeze that followed the Blitz had chased Philadelphia's society main line permanently to Tampa.

Not that Kit's father disliked GIs. On the contrary. Leon hadn't stood when I pulled up to his guard box because he had lost both legs to an Iridian IED, back before subabdominal regrows.

Edwin Trentin-Born simply liked GIs who knew their place. Which was in his guard boxes and mowing his lawns, albeit for above-market wages and benefits. But since Edwin's wife had died and left him only with Kit, one place a GI didn't fit was alongside Edwin's daughter, except in a professional capacity.

Ten seconds after I slid out of my car beneath the *porte cochere*, a bow-tied valet I didn't recognize chirped my clunker's tires and sped it away to invisibility around the side of the house.

He wasn't regular staff, because this wasn't a regular evening with my significant other's family.

The fine print on my invitation disclosed that the valet, and everything else about this event, was paid for by The Bradley Weason Initiative. This event was nominally a welcome-home party for a diplomatic mission of which Kit, and Bradley Westphal Weason, had been a part.

But it was really a campaign fund raiser for Weason, Florida's brand new junior Senator.

I should explain. Florida is one state within the United States of America, long Earth's most powerful and influential nation. America is to the rest of Earth as Earth is to the rest of the Human Union.

That is, Americans are richer than the rest of Earth, and they think they got that way because they're morally superior and work harder. The rest of Earth believes the Americans got that way because they had the perverse luck to win, and win the spoils of, a long and terrible war that engulfed Earth during the 1940s. The rest of Earth therefore resents Americans, although it follows Americans' pop-culture fashions like a dog follows bacon.

And the rest of Earth continues to look to the Americans, like the Human Union's outworlds continue to look to the Trueborns, to lead the bleeding and cough up the treasure when really bad stuff threatens.

Tonight was about American politics, an engine of such peculiar complexity and apparent contradiction that it beggars the complexity and apparent contradictions of C-drive. About both of which I know only that they exist, and they work, and the less said the better.

Inside, the Senator himself stood in the house's foyer, sleek and handsome at the base of the great staircase. The burble of two hundred conversations mingled with a live band somewhere beyond the foyer. Weason radiated a thousand-watt smile, pulling a stream of paying guests past himself one handshake at a time.

I looked past him and stretched my neck, straining to find the only guest who mattered amid a sea of of bobbing gray heads and sparkling tiaras.

I saw her hand first, waving at the end of her tan, bare arm as she dodged through the rich and famous toward me.

Kit squeezed past the last captain of industry that stood between us and planted one that, if it had continued another ten seconds, would have gotten embarrassing.

I held her back by her shoulders at arm's length and stared. The first day I saw Kit Born, she was sweaty and dusty and wearing bush shorts and field boots. I thought she was the most beautiful woman in the universe. The years and the scars, inside and outside, never changed that for me.

Her blonde hair was still practically short, her eyes as vast and blue as the Gulf that twinkled beyond the windows behind her. Her earlobes and a band that embraced her neck glittered with stones that would unquestionably appraise for more than my car's trade-in value.

I raised my eyebrows at her dress, which was black and tight in the best places, and sparkled.

She smiled, turned for me. "I picked it up in Paris."

I raised my eyebrows higher. "There's no back."

She faced me again and smiled.

I said, "Not much front, either."

Her eyes twinkled like her diamonds. "Jazen, the right thing to say is that it's graceful. Or elegant."

I eyed the guest of honor, who was still showing shiny teeth to a procession of donors. "I suppose Weason said the right thing."

I clamped my jaw too late.

She rolled her eyes. "Really? Jesus, Jazen!"

I needed a subject change like a man on fire needed water. "You heard about Mort?"

My heart thumped twice while she looked away and shook her head. Finally, she turned back to me, nodding, brow furrowed. "He found out about our friend?"

I nodded. "Yeah. But Mort's okay with it for now."

"Our friend" Bart Cutler had plotted to enslave half of the only other remaining intelligent species in the universe, and to exterminate the other half. He had also been responsible for the death of Mort's mother, and of my best friend, and in the process had left Kit and me for dead in a jungle full of monsters. Kit and I needed to talk about what Bart Cutler might be up to now that he was out of prison. But neither of us dared mention him by name because, in this crowd, the mention of one of their own might have attracted an attentive ear. "Mort," on the other hand, sounded like just another boring human.

Which, of course, he was not. Mort was the only living representative of his species ever to leave his planet, or even to accept the reality that his cloud-shrouded planet was not the entire universe. He was the only one who had ever revealed to a human that his species, which the xenobiological nerds had named *Xenoursus nutritor mortis* (roughly, "alien bear who brings death") were more than just apex predators. Grezzen were, in fact, the sole remaining intelligent species with which man shared the known universe.

After Kit and I had persuaded this grezzen to come to Earth with us, Kit and I had started calling him "Mort." Not so much to preserve his race's secret of its intelligence, or the even bigger secret that grezzen could read minds. And not because he had ever needed a name. Telepaths don't use names. We named Mort, and he accepted the name, because he was an individual who had become a friend.

Friendship hadn't come easily among the three of us. It hadn't yet come at all to most of mankind and grezzenkind. Actually, the xenobiologists of the Downgraded Earthlike 476 First Colonial Expedition had named the species before Howard's nerds had. However, Mort's ancestors had eaten the invaders before they could publish, so *Xenoursus nutritor mortis* became his species' official name.

By whatever name, Mort's ancestors slaughtered the Second

Colonial Expedition, too. But that time the humans took some grezzen down with them. Hard feelings remained on both sides.

Kit smiled at me and slid her fingers up and down the lapels of my mess jacket. "You don't wear full dress enough. You look gorgeous." She narrowed her eyes as she traced my medals with one finger. "And I've never seen you wear these. Ever."

I frowned. Medals were just ways that armies hid their mistakes. I hated mine.

Kit leaned close and breathed in my ear. "I could rip 'em off your chest with my teeth."

Maybe my anti-medal bias bore reconsideration. And our discussion of Cutler could wait.

Kit took my hand and towed me through a sea of tycoons and holo producers to the grand staircase.

Kit's father, the ringmaster of this black-tie circus, now stood alongside his guest of honor like they were a pair of penguins.

Kit tapped Bradley Weason's shoulder and he turned away from some guy wearing a sash. "Brad, this is Jazen."

Up close, the golden boy looked tanner and more square-jawed than his holos. "Captain Parker! An honor to meet you at last." He shook my hand and somehow made me believe that the pleasure really was all his. Which, come to think of it, it was.

The annoying thing about really good politicians is that they actually make whoever they're talking to feel like the most important person in the room for forty-five seconds, then manage to drop the sucker like a spent magazine without disappointing anybody.

Senator Weason unwrapped one finger from the glass in his left hand and pointed at the Star of Marin, probably because it glittered brighter than the Earth medals. Then he leaned close and lowered his voice. "Was that for saving Kit's life?"

He laid his right hand on my epaulet and stared into my eyes like he was ready to cry. "We all owe soldiers like you so much. But I'm especially grateful for that on a personal level."

I would have been grateful to remain unreminded that there had ever been a personal level between Kit and Brad Weason. Kit had assured me it was totally over, just dating during undergraduate school. Under hovertanks at armor school was the highest formal education I ever had, so I wasn't assured.

I said, "I never got a medal for that." Which was true, though I had saved Kit's life more than once. Most of what Kit and I did never happened, officially. But it was nice of him to mention it.

The Senator raised his eyebrows at Kit. "Kitten? Did you misspeak?"

Kitten. Just when I was starting to not hate his guts.

Kit's father wrapped an arm around the Weasel, one patrician to another. I think the Weasons fled Philadelphia aboard the same refugee yacht as the Trentins and the Borns. "Brad! You know Catherine can't be specific about her work."

Same mud, same blood, Edwin. It was *my* work too, thank you very much.

But neither could Edwin Trentin-Born be specific about *his* work. Which tonight, political fundraising aside, consisted of hooking his daughter up with a mate of better breeding and prospects than some mutt officer three ranks her junior. Brad Weason was on his way to becoming President of the United States. President of the United States is like King of the Earth, but with an expiration date. And Edwin Trentin-Born wanted his daughter to be queen. At least that was how I saw it.

A fat man wearing a thin blonde oozed up to The Weasel.

Kit's father lit up. "Ernesto! Shake hands with Florida's newest senator!"

The Weasel excused himself from Kit and me and picked Ernesto's pocket for the next forty-five seconds.

Kit took my arm while she tapped her father's elbow. "Daddy, we're going down to the boathouse to check on Daisy. I bet her bright work hasn't been polished for a month."

Daisy was a boat Kit had sailed since she got it as a ninth birthday present.

Her father nodded without glancing back.

The Trentin-Born boathouse stood on pilings above the waters of the Gulf, at the end of a two-hundred-foot-long pier that was lit by flickering kerosene lanterns. The night was still, and the two of us walked alone, listening to the waves lap the pilings as distance faded the sound of the band and the crowd.

When we got halfway out along the pier I said, "Your father still hates me."

It was cooler out over the water. Kit hugged my arm tighter. "No, Daddy just hates my work. Two administrations ago Daddy was Secretary of freakin' State, Jazen. The most civilized public servant in America can't accept that his daughter serves the public by doing unspeakably uncivilized things."

I shook my head. "No. He can't accept that you do them *with* somebody who's unspeakably uncivilized. Kit, my only family was a downlevels midwife who delivered me illegally."

"Your parents are still alive."

"If you believe Howard Hibble. But not even Howard knows where they are now. Compared to people like you and Weason I've got the heritage of pond slime. Weason even has a silver medal."

"Equestrian? Jazen, that's more poof than the one I got for sailing."

I shrugged. "I thought Trueborns were proud of their Olympics."

Her eyes widened. "Omigod." She poked my chest. "That's why you wore these!"

"No."

"Yes!" She stood back, rolled her eyes. "God, you're so insecure."

"It was Howard's idea. So I *wouldn't* be insecure."

She smiled. "Jazen, I don't care rat shit for Brad Weason. Or whether your parents are A-List."

"Your father does."

"You think I care rat shit for what Daddy thinks?"

I tucked my hands into my pockets and shrugged. She had a point. "If you did care you'd stop shooting bad guys for a living."

Demure as Kit looked with her diamonds glittering in the moonlight, I had watched through a spotting scope while she exploded a bad guy's head at twenty-two-hundred yards. Then did the even-badder guy crouching next to him without a hitch in her breathing. Daddy couldn't have envisioned *that* when he tickled her, pink and naked, in the delivery room.

We walked on to the boathouse. The house recognized her, unlocked, and turned on the lights. Daisy hung from ropes and pulleys attached to the ceiling, her hull dry and gleaming beneath the floods and her bright work securely wrapped against corrosion.

"God, I missed you, Jazen." Kit turned, pressed herself against me and kissed me. "Checking Daisy" was code that Kit and I had shared before, and it had nothing to do with boat maintenance.

There was a suite at the far end of the boathouse that had been designed for a caretaker, but never occupied. The suite had a view of the Gulf, which was nice, and a bed, which was nicer.

Later, we sat naked side by side on a platform at the base of stairs that led down from the office to the Gulf and dangled our feet in the warm water. It was, in fact, so much later that the band had quit and the main house and outbuildings were dark except for the downlights of the security 'bots circling above the compound's roofs. The Moon had risen and now hung high in the silent sky. Whatever the condition of Daisy's bright work, after two weeks separation, Kit's had required *lots* of polishing.

"Did Weason even know why you were along on the trip?"

My view had been that Kit's father had steered her onto the mission to Paris with Weason because it might reignite Kit's feelings for a man Edwin Trentin-Born saw as a suitable match for his daughter. However, the last few hours had temporarily mellowed my anxiety.

"Mostly the trip was to pump up Brad's foreign-policy credentials. He knew I was along to notify other governments that we've certified an intelligent species under the Intelligent Species Protection Act. And that we promised the grezzen race that the ISPA notifications would be delivered confidentially."

"We could have told the French that in a Cutlergram."

"Jazen, diplomatically and philosophically, contact with another intelligent species is the biggest event that's happened to mankind since End of Hostilities. Civilized nations deliver news like that in person."

I loved Kit with every fiber of my being, I knew that my birth parents were Trueborns, and I had come to believe in Trueborn democracy, with all its warts.

Nonetheless, there were moments when anyone raised on an outworld saw a certain irony in the way Trueborns perceived the universe and their place in it. Which was that everything revolved around perfect them.

I kissed a half-moon-shaped scar above her clavicle, which her dress had barely covered. I had dug that bullet out myself.

Then I answered her. "Civilized nations don't end hostility by exterminating the only other intelligent species in the universe." Even though the Slugs had started the war by killing sixty million Earthlings, Orion had raised me to believe me that two wrongs don't make a right.

"Which is exactly why we passed ISPA. So what happened between mankind and the Slugs wouldn't happen again."

"ISPA or no ISPA, we can't even get along with ourselves."

Kit straightened her back like the self-righteous Trueborn she was. "Cold War II's Yavet's fault. What kind of civilization pollutes and overpopulates its world so badly that killing babies at birth is virtuous?"

I raised my palms. "No argument, lady. Remember, I was raised an Illegal."

We sat and listened to the waves lap the pilings. Then she nudged me with a bare shoulder. "Illegal. I *like* bad boys." She shoved me off the platform, dove in behind me, then wrapped her thighs around my torso.

"Can we get off underwater, Parker?"

She dunked me, then I clawed to the surface and coughed salt water. "Dunno. We can drown there, though."

"We'll cross that bridge when it collapses underneath us."

It wasn't until the next morning that I realized that we had never discussed what rat bastard Cutler might be up to. I thought about poor Mort's concerns and smiled. At least whatever Cutler was up to didn't involve the Yavi, who were even bigger rat bastards than he was.

EIGHT

Max Polian floated weightless in the Trueborn cruiser's forward observation blister. The ship again drifted within sight of an inhabited world, but virtually nothing else remained the same since his conversation with Cutler.

Cutler had transferred at the Trueborn-controlled hub at Mousetrap to an Earthbound vessel, as had most of the passengers. And the world ahead was coming closer, not receding as Rand had been.

The sight of home after the long journey caused Polian's throat to swell. Yavet hung against the blackness of space like a soft, gray pearl, girdled at the equator by the thread-slender silver band of the Ring, twinkling in the sun as it turned slowly around the planet. Yavet's clouds and the Ring, both symbols and products of mankind's triumph over the environment, seemed to Polian more meaningfully beautiful than the Trueborn's blue marble, smudged with uncontrolled smears of white and complemented only by a pocked and lifeless natural moon.

The purser's voice echoed through the blister, and the other six passengers in the blister turned in the direction of the speakers as though there were something to see. "Ladies and gentlemen, it will take us another hour to match and moor with the Ring of Yavet, which marks our closest approach to the Unified Republics of Yavet, as well as the terminus of our outbound voyage. All passengers are required to disembark at Ring Station, and once disembarked, cannot reboard. The Ring is officially part of Yavet and not affiliated with the Human Union Transport Authority. Downshuttle passage and baggage claim are entirely controlled by Yavi Customs and Immigration. So please be sure to gather all unchecked personal items, as well as your entry documentation, and carry them on your person where they are readily available for inspection. Duty Free, casual dining, and the Slot Slot will remain open until thirty minutes before final approach, for your last minute shopping, snacking and gaming convenience."

The blister's other inhabitants swam aft. Polian remained, untempted by Trueborn cheeseburgers and their rigged games of chance.

He stared forward again. The Ring was close, now.

It was the only continuous orbital habitat conceived, much less completed, by mankind. The largest manmade structure in the known universe at a half mile across, thirty-six thousand miles in circumference, even the Trueborns ranked the Ring of Yavet first among the Union's manmade wonders. Nature herself had produced nothing remotely comparable. The natural rings of other planets were optical frauds, loose assemblages of orbiting dust and rock.

The Trueborns themselves had expanded into near orbital space in much the same way, at first. A clutter of communications satellites, surveillance facilities. Then a sprinkle of facilities to capture solar energy and to manufacture specialty products in perfect vacuum.

But now the Ring marked the divergent history of the Union's superpowers. The Pseudocephalopod War had depopulated Earth, and spared her the challenges and opportunities of population growth and exponentially accelerated industrialization. Historians said that if one wanted to see Earth as it would have been, but for the Slug War, one should look at Yavet.

Perhaps. The difference, Polian thought, was how one appreciated what one saw. Polian saw greatness, fettered only by the Trueborns and the accident of their starships.

To Polian, the story of the Ring was the story of pragmatic progress. Yavet had avoided nuclear war by melding its nations under a central government. As a unified people, more Yavi needed more, and produced more, and by their industry warmed their planet.

The resultant rising seas shrank the land upon which Yavi lived. This allowed Yavet to raise great cities, and to select among the citizens who inhabited them those who contributed and those who were mere burdens.

The Trueborns complained that the Ring was built by slaves, as an overflow prison for slaves. Easy for them to say, gifted a planet kept pristine by the accident of war, and then further gifted with the means to expand from that planet to other worlds. Yavet had been denied those gifts, but had fashioned greatness from adversity. Yavet and the Ring would prosper for a thousand years.

The Trueborn cruiser drifted stationary above the rotating Ring, so the great edifice sped past below. Linear miles of factories gave way to the agricultural quadrant, its solar arrays drinking in sunlight.

The House, dark and foreboding as befit a penal facility, next flashed past, then the military quadrant crawled by as the cruiser slowed.

At last the cruiser's speed matched with the Ring's, and Ring Station came into view, now only a mile beneath the Trueborn ship. Red-winking visible light beacons outlined the sole starship mooring tower. Even the empty, waiting tower dwarfed the Yavi intrasystem ships nearby. They drifted in their berths like flimsy white insects, their anti-matter bottles joined by spindly frames.

Yavet had developed antimatter drive decades before the Trueborns had, years before the Trueborns stumbled into the gravity manipulation of cavorite drive courtesy of their war against the Pseudocephalopod Hegemony. A Yavi antimatter drive ship needed months just to reach the other cold rocks that orbited her sun. In a similar time a Trueborn cruiser could travel between, and jump across, temporal fabric insertion points. The Trueborns' accidental gift let them reach five hundred verdant and diverse planets spread across entire galaxies. The Trueborns exploited their gift to dominate the rest of mankind, and to suffocate it with their self-referential and self-indulgent culture.

An electronic whistle trilled, then the purser spoke again. "Ladies and gentlemen, we've begun our final drift approach into Ring Station. If you aren't already in line, please move to disembarkation immediately. From your Earth-based flight crew, it's been our pleasure to show you a little bit of our universe."

Polian snorted.

The Trueborns claimed that today their cruisers carried only defensive weapons, not nukes. Nobody believed it, and even if it were true, the Trueborns could take nukes aboard as easily as Polian could change his shirt. Enormous as they were, gravity-manipulating cruisers could nonetheless outspeed and outmaneuver any antimatter ship. The Trueborn's smaller Scorpions were big enough to carry a nuke, too, and were shiftier and stealthier than their cruisers. The power projected by the Trueborn fleet hung above Yavet and the rest of the Union like a sword. When the Trueborns called it "our universe," they were right.

Polian looked back as he paddled aft. The mooring tower was now just five hundred feet away. He smiled. If things went according to plan, it wouldn't be the Trueborns' universe much longer.

The moment he disembarked the cruiser, Polian noticed a bounce in his step. Not entirely due to his pleasure at being home. Unlike starship rotational gravity, the Ring's rotational gravity was less, and less consistent, than planetary.

As Polian waited in the immigration line like an ordinary tourist, an arrivals steward moved down the line handing out arrivals robes. Unlike the Trueborn's cruisers, most of the Ring's interior volume was minimally shielded against the destructive cosmic radiation that a planet's atmosphere filtered out. The lead-foil-lined robes were more security blanket than protection, given the minimal exposure time transfer passengers experienced.

Polian slipped on a robe like everyone else, anyway, to deflect attention more than to deflect radiation, but also because the lead ballasted him.

At baggage claim, Polian pointed out his bags to a porter. "Bay fourteen."

The porter eyed the civilian one-piece visible beneath Polian's arrivals robe, then wrinkled his pale forehead. "There's an official shuttle in fourteen just now, sir. You want seventeen, maybe."

"Fourteen."

The porter's shoulders slumped. "Fourteen. Right away, sir." He had probably hoped Polian was bringing in contraband, which might have garnered him a few extra coins in his tip, but no one risked smuggling aboard an official shuttle when it was so easy to do it on a civilian vessel.

The Ring, for all its wonder, presented its share of Cold War contradictions. Yavet's borders were policed by the External Operations Directorate, not by Polian's Internal Operations Directorate. Therefore, immigration and customs procedures were ruthlessly and efficiently airtight when it came to blocking Trueborn spies and saboteurs. But Trueborn heroin got smuggled down, and the payments for it up, with a wink and a nod.

Not that Polian minded. The junk palliated the little people. And the human rot and violence that the drugs fueled thinned population without government expense. And best of all, illicit drugs could be blamed on the Trueborns and cited as an example of their system's decadence and moral bankruptcy.

The skeletal, stooped porter, scarcely taller than Polian's waist, struggled even with the two modest bags. The fellow was the first second-generation Ringer Polian had seen.

The odds of a child gestated and born in the Ring surviving radiation exposure, muscle atrophy, bone-density depletion, and workload to adulthood were tiny. But the downlevels little people waited years to get up-emigration permits because, regardless of laws and incentives and biologic controls, they wanted to make babies. Tiny odds were still better than the odds of dodging the sterilization codes, then getting a permit for a downlevels birth. And the odds of an Illegal and its parents surviving down below, given the efficiency of Polian's Directorate, were virtually nil. The porter would be dead inside a year. But there were plenty who longed to take his place.

Polian trailed along at the back of the small knot of returning up-levels Yavi until he reached a door marked "Internal Security. Access Restricted." He leaned forward, tripped the retinal, slipped through the doorway.

Back at last to the friendly confines of cubic volume he controlled, rather than volume controlled by the External Operations Directorate, Max unbelted his lead robe. Polian's aide waited in an interrogation room off the corridor beyond the door, and snapped to attention when he saw Polian, so abruptly that the boy's salute nearly knocked his provi cap off.

"Ease, Varden."

Provisional Lieutenant Varden relaxed as he straightened his cap.

They said that the only thing more awkward than a provi was the long-billed cap provis wore for their first commissioned year.

Varden flashed a thick-lipped smile. “Pleasant trip, sir?”

“Three months among the Trueborns? Successful, perhaps. Pleasant, no. Anyone inquire about my ‘medical leave?’”

Varden removed a uniform bag from a wall hook and held it out to Polian. “No, sir. Everyone knows the best medical’s offworld if you’re—”

“Old?” Polian smiled.

Geriatric medicine wasn’t a priority on an overpopulated planet. The privileged, like Polian, went elsewhere, and went elsewhere quietly. Polian smiled and peeled the bag off a freshly pressed uniform.

A half hour later Max Polian sat beside Varden, the two of them alone in the twenty-four-seat passenger compartment of the downshuttle as it bucked through the leaden clouds of Yavet’s stratosphere.

Polian gripped his seat’s rails until the shuttle’s gyrations smoothed. He opened his briefcase, walked his fingers through the papers and chips in its compartments.

Varden said, “It’s good to have you back, sir.” The boy’s face glowed as he said it. Varden wasn’t a boy, of course. He had worked two tours as a noncommissioned vice inspector, as Polian himself had once, down among the little people in the constriction and grime of the downlevels.

When Polian had needed a new aide, he had chosen Varden not so much because he had worked vice, but because Varden reminded him a bit of Ruberd. Except that Polian’s son had chosen the romance of external service rather than follow his father’s path up through the internal security ranks. And Ruberd’s choice had let the Trueborns kill him.

Polian kept digging through his case until he found what he wanted, a napkin bearing a handwritten scrawl that Cutler had made during one of their meetings on Rand. “As soon as you drop me off, run this.”

Varden unfolded the flimsy cloth, read, then pursed thick lips. “What is it, Director?”

“A surname. A few details.”

Varden frowned. “It’s not much to work with, sir. Priority?”

"Highest."

"I'll go straight to the office and get started after I drop you at home, sir."

Polian shook his head. "Not at home."

"If I may, sir, you look beat."

Polian waved his hand as though a fly buzzed between them. "At External Operations."

The younger man squirmed.

As an inspector, Varden had been accustomed to asking questions and getting answers. As an aide to a cabinet-level official, he knew better.

"Yes, sir. They say not much's getting done over there these days. Shall I wait?"

Polian shook his head again. "I may be awhile."

NINE

Three months after Kit and I renewed our acquaintance at her father's boathouse, Howard Hibble invited us to join him for a picnic lunch, which invitation was an event as frequent as a total eclipse of the Sun.

We met in a field in the middle of the Okeefenokee Chemical Weapons Test Range, a hundred yards from a rusty corrugated steel Quonset known as "The Barn." The Barn was the only above-ground structure within the perimeter fence. The Quonset had a sliding door at one end that looked to be made of weathered wooden planks, and was big enough to admit a taxiing tilt-wing, an eighteen-wheeler, or an ambling alien the size of a bus. Between the Quonset and the main gate wound eleven miles of roads that, if one thought about it, were better paved and maintained than they needed to be to provide access to a rusty tool shed.

Eighty feet beneath the Quonset, at the base of an elevator shaft, a subterranean tunnel complex radiated out like an octopus. The octopus was home to one hundred fifty troglodyte xenobiology nerds, who rotated in and out by bus in monthly shifts of seventy-five nerds per, and all the equipment they thought they needed to understand Mort. The nerds were kept happy and quiet by the opportunity to study the sole other intelligent species in the known universe, which species communicated telepathically in real time across distances that light traversed only over years. Also by a cafeteria with a passable wine list.

The whole operation was overdesigned, secret to the point of paranoia, and the work it did had the potential to change history. In other words, it was pure Howard Hibble.

Howard, Kit and I ate at a folding table covered with a red-checked cloth, beneath a four-posted canopy that shaded us from a warm sun. We dined on cold chicken, bone-in, served with a drinkable Chablis.

Howard's third lunch guest lounged sixty feet from us, curled in the grass and mercifully downwind. Mort dined on a half-ton, three-week-old woog haunch, also bone-in, served with a wading pool of pH-optimized water. The afternoon's calm was broken only by the drone of flies that roiled around Mort's lunch like an impending thunderstorm.

Howard set his napkin on the tablecloth as he waved fingers at the three of us. "You all finish your meals. I'll just get started."

Mort twisted a tibia as long as a fence post in his forepaws. The bone creaked, then split lengthwise with a crack like a discharged rifle, and rotted marrow blebs exploded in my direction like a claymore had detonated. Mort cocked his head and scraped the bone's exposed interior with one tusk.

I set down my drumstick. "S'okay. I'm done."

Howard said, "I wanted to tell you three about this before I address the staff. You deserve to hear the truth in person."

At the word "truth," Kit looked across the table at me, eyes wide above her wine glass. Hair rose on my neck.

They say that on the first day of kindergarten, Howard Hibble's teacher asked him "How are you today, Howard?" and he answered, "Wouldn't you like to know?"

Maybe Howard was born a secretive paranoid. Maybe the War made him one. Regardless, Howard Hibble gave up the truth like Leonidas gave up Thermopylae.

Howard said, "We're shutting The Barn down."

Kit coughed Chablis back into her glass. "What?"

"Without proximity to Mort, the program can be conducted cheaper in a conventional setting."

I looked over at Mort, who was washing down marrow with fifty gallons of water, and pointed. "Proximity? He's right over there."

"It will soon be my time, Jazen." The first time a grezzen speaks into your head while his mouth is full, he seems like an eleven-ton ventriloquist. But you get used to it.

"Ah." I nodded.

Mort's "time" was the onset of puberty.

Grezzen were apex predators so perfectly adapted that they dominated their world with no need for tools or cooperation, no need to exercise the breadth and depth of intelligence with which nature had blessed them. They communicated across vast distances, joined only mentally, as an anarchy comprised of mother-and-child absolute matriarchies. If the grezzen's place in its own ecosystem resembled the place of any animal on Earth in ours, grezzen resembled killer whales. But the two species were hardly identical.

Once weaned, grezzen lived physically isolated from one another, but socially connected by telepathy, and a mother parented her offspring from a distance throughout her life.

Physical contact occurred only once in an adult's lifetime, during each male's sole period of rut. The female who chose to be impregnated by him mated again only in the rare instance that her single offspring failed to survive to adulthood.

In most ecosystems, zero-sum procreation is a ticket to extinction. Babies get sick or get eaten, so a successful species is *ipso facto* a prolific species. But the grezz were so physically and mentally advantaged that their species dominated Dead End for thirty million years without the need to bear spares in addition to heirs.

Grezzen society, if you could call it that, was perhaps as purely libertarian as any society that had ever been tried, much less any that had flourished for thirty million years. If grezz drove cars, grezz would not only let grezz drive drunk, they would defend to the death their cousins' right to do so.

But as the only grezzen who had ever crossed the interplanetary road to see what was on the other side, Mort had to be feeling some telepathic heat from his cousins to come home and get busy.

As a fellow bachelor, I could imagine how bad Mort needed a date when he was only going to have one. Ever. But to maintain the ecological balance point, his race needed him to get laid even more than he did.

Kit cocked her head at Howard. "So you're sending Mort home? Releasing a high-value asset? Howard, that's uncharacteristically compassionate of you."

It was. We were in the middle of a Cold War. If this were the first

Cold War, Americans versus Russians, a ruthless spymaster like Howard would have ignored ecological balance. He would simply have ordered his most voluptuous female agent to seduce the horny high-value asset and then satisfy the asset's most twisted and lustful fantasies for as long as necessary.

Mort thought, "You are correct, Kit. The true reasons the nerds are repatriating me are that I have become too costly to support here, and they no longer find me useful."

Howard tried to look hurt and failed. "Mort could've gone home any time he chose. He finds us as interesting as we find him."

Mort thought, "That is true, Howard."

It *was* true. Mort fancied himself a three-eyed Jane Goodall, enduring privation to study the cultural interactions of a lesser species on its home turf.

Howard shrugged. "But the decision *was* multifaceted." Meaning Mort was right. Not even Howard bothered trying to lie to a mind reader.

Kit nodded like a politician's daughter. "New administration. New priorities." Then she shook her head, like a cold warrior. "But Howard, you can't let Mort go. He reads minds! In real time. From light years away. He can eavesdrop on anybody."

Howard shook his own head. "No. He can eavesdrop on *everybody*. That's the problem. TMI. It's been the problem."

Now it was my turn to nod.

TMI—too much information—had been the American intelligence community's problem ever since the early years of the last century. In those days, computing power was increasing exponentially year over year, and virtually all human information not locked in someone's head was adrift somewhere in the electronic ether. Every shared secret was available somewhere.

True, the spooks in those days might have had to sift a thousand billion grocery lists and decrypt a thousand million love poems to find it. But eventually the Trueborn spooks built enough computers to know all the shared secrets they wanted to know.

Of course, being spooks, they still wanted to know everybody's *un*shared secrets, too. That was where Mort was supposed to come in. He could read any human mind, anywhere in this universe, in real time. He could zero in on a mind to which he was physically close, as he had on John Buford's when John was reading about Cutler's pardon.

Even from a distance—a serious distance—Mort could also recognize minds with which he became familiar. For example, Mort and I had survived dangers together, in a boy-and-his-monster sort of way. So Mort could pick me out of a crowd from light years away, given time.

But the Jazen-Mort bond was nothing compared to the Kit-Mort love-in. Since the day Mort's mother had died, Mort had been able to converse with Kit across a galaxy as though the pair of them had their heads together across a two-top bar table. The nerds ascribed their relationship to "transuniversal transparency optimized by maternal bond transference."

Maybe I was vaguely jealous that my brawny pal liked my girlfriend best. At least I didn't have to worry that he would wind up between the sheets with her.

Mort's coziness with Kit and with me aside, there were fifty billion other human minds spread across five hundred planets. Each of those fifty billion minds thought, dreamed, fantasized, truthed, and lied throughout every single day. But there was just one of Mort. Mort, or even a thousand Morts, could never distill that much information into usable intelligence.

This biologic bottleneck had always been apparent to Howard and his nerds. OCWTR was never intended to enslave, or to enlist, or to breed grezzen as full-time mind readers, like some gargantuan K-9 Corps. Howard's spooks planned to study Mort, then duplicate artificially what nature had created in him.

The spooks' humanitarian goal was to allow mankind to communicate across space in real time, rather than by the current best alternative method. That alternative method was sending messages physically, aboard starships, like mechanical carrier pigeons. Starships jumped across narrow places where the fabric of folded space bent back upon itself. The mile-long carrier pigeons traveled distances in weeks or months that took light, or anything else that traveled as fast as light, notably radio waves, which traveled the long way round, years or centuries.

But Mort could read a mind light years away as fast as if it were across the room. Of course, since nothing in this universe could travel faster than light, the nerds assumed grezzen had a way to communicate by accessing a universe next door to this one. But no matter how Mort did it, he did it. So the nerds wanted to do it, too.

Of course, the nerds' objective wasn't just faster birthday cards and junk mail. They had a less benign goal, too. Eventually, whatever made Mort tick would allow them to build a vast bank of mind-reading computers. The mind-readers would feed all the information they discovered into an equally vast bank of computers that would analyze it.

The good guys would finally know everything. The bad guys would finally be cooked. And nobody would ever abuse the system. Of course.

Howard frowned. "We do think we've learned about all we can from Mort. But we're years away from any sort of practical application. We can't read anybody's mind."

That was a relief, considering the fantasy I was just having, with me in the role of the lustful high-value asset and Kit in the role of the voluptuous and compliant female agent.

Kit's eyes lit. "So Jazen and I can go back to field work?"

No, that wasn't my fantasy.

For the last eight months, Case Officer Team Seventy-one, which was Colonel Catherine Trentin-Born and her junior case officer, which was me, had been detached from field work. "Field Work" was a euphemism for nasty things done unattributably in places where we weren't supposed to be. In lieu of field work, we were attached for organizational and pay purposes to the OCWTR task force, which in turn was funded within black-ops line item 776312 of the American Defense Budget, most of which budget was these days expended in support of the activities of the Human Union.

What that meant to anyone who lodged a Freedom of Information Act request was absolutely nothing, which was the idea.

What that meant to OCWTR's nerds was that Mort had the only two humans who he trusted nearby. With Kit and me figuratively holding his paw, he would allow the nerds to poke and prod him until they unlocked the physiologic secrets of grezzen telepathy.

What that meant to Kit was an annoying delay in prosecuting Cold War II, which she believed she was obliged to do single-handed if the chain of command would just stand aside.

What that meant to me was a vacation from sleeping on the ground in places where I wasn't supposed to be that were too hot, too cold, too wet or too malarial, and from getting shot, or at least shot at, regularly. And I still got to wake up alongside the loveliest woman in the universe.

Howard answered Kit's question with a frown. "Field work? Kit, the numbers haven't improved."

"The numbers" referred to case-officer pair survivability. For any given field operation, any given pair's survivability averaged thirty-two percent. The odds were marginally improved for mixed-gender pairs like Kit and me. One theory that explained the improved odds was that het couples fit more plausible cover legends, so they got caught less. Another was that mixed-gender teams made sounder decisions, because they melded contrasting temperaments and viewpoints. For example, the spook shrinks judged Kit a risk taker, and me risk averse.

Kit raised her chin and crossed her arms. "Howard, the numbers don't take into account the quality of the pair. We'll be fine."

Fine? I disagreed. American Trueborns like Kit believed that the future would always work out, because for them it always had. The rest of us believed the future would fuck us, because it always had. And the future usually met expectations.

As for the quality of the pair? Even if a case officer pair was Batgirl and Robin, the Joker was bound to turn up if you played the cards too long.

Kit wanted us to return to field work. I wanted us to live happily ever after, playing the high-value asset and the voluptuous agent often. What the hell, maybe even raise some little assets.

I squirmed in my chair, and at the motion Kit burned me with a look.

If a man and a woman have been together long enough, neither needs a grezzen to read the other's mind.

I dunno. Some days I wondered how many teams among the missing sixty-eight percent went dark not due to enemy action but because the idiot's contrasting temperament and viewpoint annoyed her so much that she shot him.

Howard removed his glasses, then polished the lenses with his napkin. "Regardless of the numbers, Kit, you were right in recognizing that this new administration has new priorities. We're pulling the teams out of the field."

"You're taking us out of the war?" Kit's eyes bugged.

I suppose mine did, too.

TEN

Kit and I sat open-mouthed, staring at one another for what seemed like minutes. Then the two of us turned on Howard, with what I suppose looked like mutinous blood in our eyes.

Howard raised his palms. "The President was a history professor before he entered politics. He refuses to preside over Cold War II deteriorating into the second phase of Cold War I."

I cocked my head. Over the last months of babysitting Mort, I had time to burn, and had burned it reading lots of Trueborn history myself.

At the middle of the last century the American Trueborns won a massive war started by some of the other Trueborns. That war was so long and so devastating that it was divided into chapters, World War I and World War II, separated by a halftime show called a depression.

The Americans won that war so thoroughly that when the second chapter ended they were the only ones with the capacity to nuke the crap out of everybody else, who had all pretty much stuffed one another down the economic toilet during chapters I and II.

The Americans thought their preeminence was earned, because they were the demonstrated good guys. The people in the toilets thought the Americans were naïve opportunists who had simply come late to the brawl, were insufferably full of themselves, and would fuck them, just like the future always had.

Surprisingly, the Americans thereafter lived up to their own fine self-image. They helped the rest of the Trueborns climb out of their toilets, and then prevented them, in the main, from restarting the stuffing-one-another process. After World War II ended, nobody else got nuked. Almost everybody was getting rich, although the Americans made sure that they were getting richest of all. It was the time that Howard had just described as the first phase of Cold War I.

Then the Soviet Union, the part of everybody that was managing to *not* get rich, stole the capacity to nuke the crap out of people from the Americans. The Soviets had been both big stuffers and big stuffees during the World Wars, and remained comfortable stuffing people, including their own, down the toilet.

This changed everything. Phase two of Cold War I became an ever-escalating pissing contest between two superpowers. Nuclear missiles by the tens of thousands were planted in the ground like seeds, were floated beneath Earth's oceans, and were loaded into the bellies of airplanes, that circled the skies like nervous hawks. Neither the Soviets nor America wanted to be second on the draw. Inevitably, an itchy trigger finger somewhere was going to blow Earth to hell. Pundits drew up an imaginary clock that counted down the day before Doomsday. The hands were always set just minutes before midnight.

Kit said, "But Howard, the Soviet Union imploded. Not a single nuke out of all those thousands was ever detonated. The good guys' strategy won."

"True." Howard shook his head. "But luck and a belief in the folly of collectivist economics is hardly a strategy to bet the farm on."

I turned to Kit. "Howard actually could be right. One fuck-up from Armageddon's no way to run a universe, Kit."

Kit's lip curled. "Jazen, that's not the way we're running it. The Yavi can't nuke anybody but themselves. So we'll never have to nuke them or anybody else."

Howard nodded. "This administration wants to keep it that way."

Kit said, "That's what the teams have been doing for the whole Cold War! Keeping it that way. Containing the Yavi with a poke in the ass here, a slap on the wrist there. Hell, it was your idea, Howard."

Howard shrugged. "This administration thinks the teams and the rest of the strategy are too expensive. The nonaligned worlds hate our meddling, and even our allies aren't crazy about it."

I raised my palm. "Howard, during Cold War I, in the first phase before the Russians got nukes, plenty of American planners wanted to nuke the Russians first. If you pull the teams down, that'll be the only strategy that's left."

Howard raised his palm back at me. "There's no reason to think it will come to that. The Yavi don't have starship technology."

"But if they *get* starship technology, this administration will nuke them?" I rolled my eyes. "To save money? And suck up to a bunch of outworlders who take that money? But still they hate our guts." I heard my voice quaver.

The quaver, I realized, resulted less from righteous political indignation than from fear. Fear that Howard's announcement might change my crummy life, or more accurately, change my relationship with Kit, which was the only thing that made my life uncrummy.

Kit turned to me, eyebrows raised. "Since when does Mr. 'Trueborns are pricks' take the side of us against the outworlds?"

"Us? Kit, I grew up on Yavet. So did thirteen billion other people who don't give a shit about Cold War politics. Killing them and claiming premature self-defense is fucked up." I pointed first at Kit, then at Howard, and snorted. "I shouldn't be surprised. After all, you people exterminated an entire intelligent species and call yourselves heroes for doing it."

Howard leaned forward, eyes hard behind his glasses, "Jazen!" Howard stabbed a bony finger at me so hard that it quivered. "Jazen, your own parents fought that war right alongside me. Don't judge people and events about which you know practically nothing!"

I pointed back at Howard, and my finger shook, too. "And why do I know practically nothing? Because you won't *tell* me, you mendacious old paranoid!"

I knew Howard didn't know where my parents were in the universe at any given time, or at least he claimed he didn't.

I knew, because they had both been enlistment age when the War started, that their straight-line chronological age now could be pushing one hundred. But I knew from what Orion told me about the way they had looked, and my mother's condition when she gave birth to me, that their subjective physical age was now more like fifties. That partly reflected Trueborn medical care, and partly reflected a lifetime of war spent traveling time-slowed near light speed.

I knew my father had been a hero, a dumb grunt like me, who had risen through the ranks. And my mother had been a kick-ass pilot all her professional life. Then they had both been involved in something that happened at the war's end, something so bad that the two of them disappeared from the history books, and now wandered the universe as clandestine exiles. Profiteering, atrocity, who knew? If you can do something terrible even in the context of something as terrible as war, it had to have been unspeakable. And it was unspeakable. Only people at Howard's clearance and above knew the details.

My parents' disappearance from history meant I'd never even seen so much as a paper photograph of either one. Hell, I might have passed them on the street and never have known it.

And so I was a downlevels mutt with no speakable pedigree, born illegally and raised in poverty in a culture that the Trueborns despised. So I clung to my relationship with a woman out of my league the only way I knew how, which was by risking my life for her.

With uncharacteristic restraint I shut my big mouth for once. Partly because I had just backtalked a general officer who outranked me by seven grades. Mostly because I'd never, ever seen Howard angry before.

All three of us sat back and took deep breaths. Sixty feet away, Mort dozed after his meal, the rasp of his snore mingling with the drone of flies that swarmed his leftovers.

Finally, Howard drew another breath, laid his palms on the checked tablecloth, and stared at Kit, then at me, as he spoke. "Jazen. Kit. Neither you nor I can predict American policy. Nor as members of the military can we set it the way we prefer. You may think I'm some goofball professor, but I'm soldier enough to know my place."

On the rare occasions when I saw Howard in uniform, I noted that he wore the Silver Star, the Purple Heart, and the Combat Infantryman's Badge. Just because I didn't care for medals, they proved to me that Howard Hibble was soldier enough, alright.

Howard sat back, folded his arms across his scrawny chest. "If either of you have trouble knowing your place, file your discharge forms."

Kit and I shared a glance. Discharge? Yikes.

The two of us had most recently been party to one of those poke-and-slap outworld actions that Kit had just mentioned. A spaceport had been destroyed, a neutral shuttle had nearly been shot down, a

Yavi major and hundreds of Yavi troops had been killed, and the Yavi had gotten away with enough cavorite to fuel a fleet of starships. To say nothing of torturing Kit and nearly killing us both. But cavorite's useless without C-drive technology.

Since that dustup, the Yavi had bungled a high-risk attempt to salvage a power plant from a Scorpion that had crashed on Dead End last year.

The Trueborn intelligence community had failed to sustain reliable human sources on Yavet for years, and so relied by necessity on electronic eavesdropping to produce predictive intelligence product. Howard's tea-leaf readers, wherever they were hiding, believed that the Yavi External Operations Directorate, his and Kit's and my blood enemy in this Cold War, was currently in disfavor and disarray, and harmless for the forseeable future.

My rant, however righteous, seemed mismatched to real-world probabilities. Especially if it required me to resign in protest.

I hazarded a question. "Uh. Howard?"

"Yes, Jazen?"

"If this place is shutting down, and the teams are standing down, is this an exit interview? Do the two of us still have jobs?"

He smiled. "I thought you'd never ask."

ELEVEN

The orderly behind the desk in the outer office of the Director General of External Operations sprang up and saluted when he saw Polian's shoulder boards. "Sir!"

"Keep your seat, sergeant. I need to see the director."

Polian glanced around the vastness of the outer office. Unopened shipping plasteks were stacked along one wall, and the other walls were bare of the usual tiling of unit citations, statements of general orders, notices of promotion boards, and chain of command portraits common to such places. What Varden had told him about EOD's upset looked to be true.

The orderly stared into his screen and poked at it. "Ah—sir, Director Gill's so new here—we all are—your appointment must have gotten—"

"I don't have an appointment." Polian pointed at a door set in the opposite wall of the directorial suite, which was a twin to his own eight miles away. "I'll meet him in the bubble."

Four minutes later Polian stood alone, hands clasped behind his back, and stared out through the single, multilayered window set in the curved wall of the suite's secure conference room. It had been three hours since he had left the Trueborn cruiser, ten minutes since he had shown up here unannounced. Cops were used to waiting, and he still thought of himself as a cop.

Polian stretched again as he stared across Yaven. Vented smoke from Yavet's capital hung like a delicate veil between him and the brass toned pyramids of the other directorates that studded the main pinnacle. The directorate offices were all at level Eighty Upper and above, and the executive levels sparkled with optical windows, like the snow he had seen on the peaks of the High Rand. Through the shimmer of vented heat, he made out the pyramid that housed the Internal Operations Directorate, with his own suite at its apex.

It was a grand sight, but one to which he had become accustomed. He yawned, turned away from the window. His only prior contact with Ulys Gill had been the condolence letter Gill had sent after Ruberd's death, as Ruberd's commanding officer. Max didn't know the man personally. But cops were used to knowing a person of interest by what they didn't say. What the room, bare, silent, businesslike and anonymous, said about Ulys Gill was consistent with the man's story.

Ulys Gill had a flawless up-through-the-ranks external military record. On merit, Gill should have risen higher than he had before now. But Gill had been held back by the suspicion that he was born and raised illegal in the downlevels, skipped offworld by joining the Legion, and returned with a phony—albeit perfect—identity bought at Mousetrap or one of the other cesspool hubs where Trueborn starship routes intersected.

Polian's Directorate tolerated Legion skips, because little people gone were as good as little people dead. And Yavi lucky enough to survive the Legion and buy a hub scrub usually began a life elsewhere, rather than risk exposure and execution by returning here.

"Director Polian." Max turned and saw Ulys Gill enter the bubble, closing the door behind him.

No wonder the promotion boards had been suspicious. Gill was slight and stooped by age, but even if he had been young he would have stood a head shorter than Polian. His uniform was impeccable, as was his bearing.

He took the hand of his co-equal ranker, laid his other across it, and smiled beneath a gray moustache that had been out of fashion even among field-grade officers since the Insurrection. "Sir—"

"Call me Max."

"Max, it's good to meet a man about whom I've heard so much good. I'm only sorry about the reason I heard it. Ruberd was proud to be your son. And I was proud of what he did for Yavet."

Polian nodded wordlessly.

Gill had been a passed-over two-leaf, on the cusp of retirement. Then the death on Tressel of that mission's commander had thrust Gill into command there. Gill's massive success in the Tressel action had catapulted him past his betters into this post. Yet, if Gill was some sort of late-blooming political kiss-ass, Gill's humility and his affection for Ruberd seemed genuine.

Gill motioned Polian to a chair at the table, and they sat across from one another. Gill leaned forward, cocked his head. "Max, you're only two hours back on dirt. What brings you to External Operations?"

Polian smiled.

Gill might be new to this job, but he knew how to pull its strings. External Operations didn't monitor citizens with the precision that Polian's own directorate did, but in his new job Gill controlled planetary arrivals and departures, not only of persons but of communications, overt as well as crooked. That control was what made Gill indispensable to Polian's scheme.

"Director—"

"Call me Ulys."

Polian nodded, laid his palms on the tabletop. "Ulys, you and I both know that we've got cavorite now, thanks to you and to Ruberd. But like the little people say about whisky, unless we can open the bottle, it's useless."

Gill steepled his fingers, frowned. "You know the operation to recover the C-drive unit failed, then?"

Polian nodded. "I do."

Hell, even Cutler knew. At considerable political risk, Gill's predecessor as Director General of External Operations had inserted a covert team, covered as a nature-film crew, on a remote Trueborn-colonized planet. The team's objective had been to locate a Trueborn Scorpion fighter that had crashed in dangerous country, extract the fighter's C-drive power unit, and smuggle it off the planet. The team had perished in the attempt, and the Central Committee had sacked Gill's predecessor.

"Ulys, have you developed another option?"

The new Director General of External Operations shook his head. "As you see, we haven't even unpacked."

Polian leaned forward on his elbows. "I have a suggestion."

It took Polian ten minutes to summarize Cutler's overture, and another ten to summarize the plan that had grown from it.

Polian paused, leaned back. "Well?"

Gill sat back in his chair, too. "Max, the little people say that it's better to stab a shiv artist before he can stab you."

Polian nodded at the proverb.

Cold War II stayed cold only because the Trueborns were smugly certain that their strategic advantage allowed them to merely contain Yavet, rather than destroy it. But if the Trueborns ever became aware that they might lose their advantage, no thoughtful Yavi believed the Trueborns would hesitate to strike Yavet first, and with nuclear weapons. "You're afraid that this proposed operation could give the Trueborns an excuse to strike preemptively? To destroy us?"

"I'm sure I wouldn't be the only one. Max, I got this job because the fellow who sat in this chair before me ordered that attempt to steal that C-drive. He was dismissed because the Central Committee thought he ordered a reckless, provocative plan."

"They didn't think what you and Ruberd did on Tressel was too provocative. They promoted you!"

Gill shrugged. "Success silences critical tongues. Besides, Tressel's Yavet's ally. We were on Tressel with the local government's blessing. The Scorpion recovery team made a covert armed incursion onto a Trueborn colony."

Polian smiled. "Ulys, that's the beauty of this plan! The actual activity all takes place right here on Yavet. The Trueborns can't call that provocative."

Gill leaned back, steepled his fingers beneath his chin. "But not all the table setting takes place here. Don't forget, the Trueborns have been manufacturing provocations to justify wars against one another for centuries. If they wanted to nuke us they could have done it yesterday and made up some story to justify it. This Cutler could be planted for just that reason."

Polian shook his head. "I've not only met Cutler, I've researched him. He's no plant. He's a venal, unprincipled Trueborn. His government jailed him and took away his empire. He wants to get even."

"Assuming for the sake of argument that you're right about Cutler, what you're suggesting *is* a provocation. After the Scorpion fiasco, the

Central Committee's even more gun-shy. They'll never approve it." Gill sat stiff and silent.

Gill was right, of course. Central Committee members achieved their rank by growing ever older and ever more timid.

As a young up-and-comer, Polian had appeared before the Central Committee once, and presented a plan to smuggle nukes onto the outworlds to blackmail the Trueborns. It was a superb plan. The Trueborns tolerated smuggling even more readily than they tolerated weakness and sloth. But the Central Committee's old men had stared at him as though a turd had materialized in their witness chair. That moment, Polian still believed, had forever and unjustly disqualified him from consideration for an External Operations post. Not that he wanted one, really.

"Ulys, I'm not suggesting the Central Committee be consulted. The entire scheme can be handled within our two directorates with minimal resources. It's well within our respective discretions. In fact, the resources are so minimal that the plan can fail with no one the wiser. And nobody gets the sack."

Gill's jaw dropped. "It may be espionage on the cheap, Max. And technically within our respective discretions. But go around the Central Committee with a plan that could destroy Yavet? Max, what you're suggesting is closer to mutiny than it is to exercise of discretion."

Polian had expected reticence. He could, of course, now simply threaten to air his own suspicions about Gill's birth status. Gill had dealt with suspicions that he was a scrubbed Illegal throughout his career, but never when they were aired by someone of Polian's rank and reputation. The threat would provide all the coercive leverage Polian needed to force Gill's cooperation.

But Polian needed a willing ally, not a foot-dragging conscript. So he dangled just a hint of the threat.

"Hell, Ulys, I've devoted more manpower to tracking down one Illegal than this whole operation would take."

Gill remained silent, fingertips noiselessly drumming the tabletop. If he had taken the hint, he gave no visible sign.

Finally, Gill sighed. "Max, I don't want Ruberd to have died for nothing any more than you do. I'm not saying I'm with you all the way." The small man paused, then cocked his head. "But what do you need from me, for starters?"

TWELVE

Three months after Howard Hibble had announced to Kit, Mort and me that Mort was going home and that Kit and I were going into non-combat mothballs, Kit and I floated weightless in the eighty-foot fishbowl that was the cruiser *Gateway*'s forward centerline observation bubble as the great ship sped away from Earth bound for connections to the outworlds.

We drifted there along with one hundred forty-eight other wedding guests while a live string quartet, which was drawn form *Gateway*'s resident orchestra, played the processional.

Ahead of us, guests, the bride, groom and one of the starship's tri-captains in dress whites drifted like fighters in formation, while flower bouquets formed into globes orbited them like rainbow planets, all against the slowly revolving backdrop of star-salted black space.

One of the recording holo 'bot pair hovered just out of its counterpart's frame, beneath the bride's feet, lenses-up.

I leaned toward Kit and whispered, "Now I see what you meant about the pants."

She frowned with ice in her gaze. "This may be boring for you, but it's special for this couple. Try to appreciate that."

To say that Howard's lunch announcement had changed Kit Born understated matters. Howard had forced Kit to contemplate a sedate rest of her life, and she hadn't adjusted seamlessly.

For the first week after we got the word from Howard, she had spent every morning kicking all comers' butts, including mine, as often as I kicked hers, in the hand-to-hand combat pits, until she lay in the sand, victorious but exhausted. Afternoons she spent at the ranges, until she was barred from the close-quarters battle house after she insisted on mowing down every target with a full magazine hosed out on full auto. An adrenaline junkie gone cold turkey is painful to watch, but I gave her her space. Eventually, denial and acting out gave way to acceptance of a more restrained future. Maybe too restrained.

When we were dressing for this event in our stateroom, Kit had mentioned that women at bubble weddings wore some species of trousers, to avoid unladylike displays caused by drifting weightless.

Kit, accordingly, wore a blue silk jumpsuit. I had told her it looked "demure yet flattering." She had smiled, said that I had matured, that in the past I would have said something puerile, like that it would look more interesting if she wore it without panties.

I now know that the mature response to that is not "*Would* you?"

The music stopped and the captain cleared his throat. He was officiating in his capacity as a vessel master, to join said bride and groom in holy matrimony.

Trueborns, Kit apparently included, loved their weddings, and rich Trueborns loved their exotic destination weddings most of all. Today's happy couple was proceeding onward for a ski honeymoon on Rand. Connected Trueborns like Kit's father got invited to so many bubble weddings that, although they could easily afford the ticket, they couldn't afford the round-trip attendance time. So our little party of two were standing in for Edwin Trentin-Born and guest at Edwin's request, in order to bulk up the crowd and to earn him a cashable political chit.

Actually, our party could have bulked up the crowd a lot more. Four hundred yards aft of us, behind the shoot-on-sight marine guards who guarded the engineering spaces against espionage and sabotage, Mort was enjoying the voyage in solitude. With Kit and me assigned as escorts at government expense, Howard was sending Mort back home to Dead End so he could get lucky at his first and last homecoming dance.

So, for Kit and me, the wedding invitation via her father had come as a coincidental antidote to boredom.

Mort's VIP suite far behind us had been created by adiosing the bulkheads separating no fewer than six cargo bays, then reinforcing the cruiser's structure and outfitting the resultant vastness to suit an eleven-ton homecoming king. Among other expensive peculiarities that resulted from *Gateway*'s reconfiguration was that Mort, Kit and I had to stay aboard this one particular starship from Earth to Mort's homeworld, Dead End. That meant that the voyage between Earth and the major hub at Mousetrap, normally relatively direct and short, would now be circuitous and long, because unlike most passengers and cargo, we couldn't change vessels at intermediate hubs. The cost was prodigious.

If the other passengers had known they were sharing space with a monster who called six hundred pounds of live meat a continental breakfast, and who had inadvertently destroyed the last starship he rode on, they would have jumped ship like rats down a hawser. If the tax-paying public had known what Mort's first date was costing them, they would have thrown tea into a harbor somewhere.

But they didn't know. Such is the latitude an intelligence community enjoys during a time of Cold War. *Glomar Explorer*. Look it up.

I glanced sideways as the couple exchanged rings. Kit's eyes were leaking.

I passed her a handkerchief from my tuxedo pocket. "You okay?"

She dabbed her eyes then honked into the wadded cloth. "I always cry at weddings. You?"

It was a strangely vulnerable reaction for a woman who never cried at assassinations. Had her acceptance of life without adrenaline rushes gone too far?

I shrugged. "My first. You know what'll make an outworlder cry? Hanging this fishbowl on a starship so Trueborns can take home prettier wedding albums."

The string quartet struck up the recessional, and the couple drifted aft past us.

As we swam in behind them, to the reception in Ballroom F, Kit's eyes were dry. "Actually, the fishbowl's a vestigial design element. Like a human appendix. The old chemical-fuel transports had a clear nose blister. For astral navigation and piloting if the computers failed."

She caught me rolling my eyes.

The history chips said the first bubble wedding took place when the captain of the first Trueborn ship got married to an enlisted assault soldier in the bubble enroute to the First Battle of Ganymede. Then the captain sacrificed his life, piloting the ship from the bubble, and saved the human race. It was a nice story. But the history chips were written by the Trueborns. The same folks who flooded the universe with those overacted holos about Trueborn cops and robbers.

Normally my eye roll would have lit the fuse toward an argument about the nature of patriotism, courage and virtue versus snarky cynicism.

But instead she touched my cheek, and her eyes were soft. "If I'd grown up like you, hunted and hungry every day, I'd be cynical, too. But you've never been cynical about us."

I *had* grown up dodging cops by crawling through the utilities where the cops were too big to fit, and stealing food for Orion and me when her business was slow or the heat was on. And only when I grew too big to fit in the smaller-diameter utilities had Orion been forced to let me join the Legion. But to a kid, it was all just life. A two-bean-bar day was a good day, nothing more, nothing less. I considered myself a realist, and lucky to be alive, not a cynic.

But if peace and a wedding made the hard-ass love of my life wax this sentimental, I would gladly be whoever or whatever she wanted me to be.

The right response in this tender moment was to tell her how she had never been cynical about us, either. How I knew she never would be cynical about us. Take her fingers in mine, kiss them. Talk far into the night and grow our relationship, bonding at an interpersonal emotional level. Lament that the stress of mortal combat had heretofore denied us this introspection.

Instead, I said, "I don't suppose this means you've reconsidered about the panties?"

Kit may have matured, and she may have wished I had matured faster, but she hadn't traded in all of her sense of humor, or any of her libido. What happened the rest of the night is none of your business. Suffice to say that escorting an unmarried woman to a wedding can reward her date on undreamed-of levels. But, yeah, there was some interpersonal bonding, too.

The next day we cleared the beltline marine security detachment and went aft to visit Mort face to three-eyed face.

When we ducked in through the last human-sized hatch into his domain, Mort was standing up on his two hind legs, his back to us. With his mid- and forelimbs he pummeled a plastex-wrapped tilt-wing fuselage that hung suspended from cables, as though he were a four-armed boxer at the heavy bag. The metal screeched and groaned with each blow, as though it were alive.

He kept punching but spoke in our heads. "You have stopped coitus at last."

Kit flushed. "Didn't you have anything better to do?"

Mort dropped onto all six, ambled from the swaying fuselage to a water trough fabricated from another fuselage split lengthwise, and drank. "I might ask the same of you. Such vigorous exercise with the expectation of neither improved muscle tone nor the production of offspring seems a waste of food energy."

I said, "Trust me, my friend. When your time comes, you won't stop 'til she's screwed your brains out."

Kit punched my arm so hard I staggered.

Mort ignored the post-coital byplay, and said, "Why have you come to me?"

I shrugged while I rubbed my bicep. "Thought you might want company."

"Your physical presence is unnecessary."

Mort wasn't blowing us off, and he wasn't lonely. He was perpetually in the mental company of all the other individuals in his species, who were all his cousins, even though they were ten jumps away. He could eavesdrop on literally billions of other non-grezzen intellects across the universe. Especially he could eavesdrop on those close to him aboard *Gateway*.

Grezzen generally found physical proximity to other living beings distasteful, unless the grezzen was about to eat the proximate being. The only exceptions were grezzen's mothers, and a mother's offspring during early childhood, and a grezzen's mate during heat and rut.

Kit asked, "Need anything else right now?"

"Solitude?"

"You're getting the hang of sarcasm, Mort."

"I did not intend it. The cooks bring me food and water and remove waste. I enjoy conversing with each of you, but we can continue that at any time or distance. Please do not interrupt your relentless coitus on my account."

I turned to Kit, shrugged again. "You heard the man."

Kit's and my next few days, weeks and months were, therefore, our own. It was the first time Kit and I had ever travelled together without knowing that at our destination waited folks determined either to debrief us or to kill us. It turns out that a starship's a movable feast if you aren't spending your time preparing to get shot at or recuperating.

Howard had booked us first class, and first class aboard Trueborn starships was designed to please the likes of, well, Trueborn royalty like the Trentin-Borns. Kit signed us up for ballroom dancing lessons; wine tasting class, where she learned that a bartender knew as much as a rich girl did about cabernet sauvignon, Trueborn bowling, where I learned that sparing the seven-ten split is as hard for a rich girl as for a bartender, and yoga.

I expected to hate it all, but enjoyed myself immensely. Maybe it was the company.

One afternoon Kit and I were stretched out side by side on chaises beside the deck twenty-four pool. Except for a few other passengers reading and sleeping, and a steward who periodically delivered cocktails and little silver bowls filled with nuts, we had the place to ourselves.

Kit said, "What if the war really is over for us?"

"Sorry. I dozed off."

"What are you going to do if it is?"

I woke so completely that I sat up and spilled my nuts. "Me? Singular?"

She smiled. "I was hoping you'd react like that."

I propped myself on one elbow and faced her. Without the stress, she looked more like a girl in a bikini and less like a soldier every day. "I suppose we could try mercenary work. With five hundred twelve planets, there'll always be a war on someplace."

Kit shook her head. "Killing for peace is enough of a moral contradiction. Killing for money's worse."

To say nothing of getting killed for money, a result that my beautiful amazon rarely considered.

I said, "I guess robbing banks is off the short list, too, then."

She reached across the table that held our drinks and took my hand. "We don't have to do anything, you know. At least not anything that could get us killed. The family owns a wildlife holography company. It's a nonprofit. Conservation, species protection. We could still travel, do rewarding work."

I frowned. Kit the marksman as my commanding officer was one thing. Kit the heiress as my sugar mama was another.

She shook her head. "I know. You're always going to be hung up because we each chose the wrong parents."

She swung her legs off the chaise, sat up across from me, and slapped her palms on her bare thighs. "Hell, Jazen. If you want to buy another bar somewhere, you pour and I'll mop the floor. All I want is that we do it together."

I bent forward, kissed her, and one thing began to lead to another.

She pushed a hand against my chest, laughed. "Somebody's gonna tell us to get a room."

"We have one, remember?"

She stood up, took my hand, led me toward our stateroom and grinned over her shoulder. "Don't you ever get tired of checking on Daisy?"

"Would that be a problem on a going-forward basis?"

Kit fixed me with a look that was the last thing many people ever saw, then she smiled. "Not as long as it's my daisy."

I said, "If this is the first day of the rest of our life, I'll take it."

THIRTEEN

"Sir, we've got it!" Varden stood in the open doorway to Polian's office, his fool provi cap ajar as he grinned and held a reader out in front of himself. Polian had once owned a cat that displayed rat carcasses that way.

Polian dimmed the file flickering before his eyes. Then he rested his elbows on his desktop and rubbed his face. "Got what?"

"The woman. The surname you gave me when you got back from your trip. When General Gill's aide and I compared notes, we figured it out."

Polian dropped his hands and straightened. He had almost forgotten it himself. He glanced at the calendar in his display. It had been, what? Three weeks?

He waved Varden forward, and his aide stepped across the office and propped the portable on the desk at an angle so they could both read the display.

"Sir, it was a homophone error. Trueborns commonly mistranscribe Standard when it's spoken with a Yavi accen—" Varden caught himself.

Theoretically, Varden didn't know that the name that Polian had provided had been supplied to Polian by a Trueborn. Varden's principal military virtue was loyalty, not cleverness. But the boy was bright enough that he had realized that anything his boss held this close had to involve the Trueborns.

Varden ran a finger across the display. "Someone with a Yavi accent said 'Orion.' To a Trueborn, it sounds like 'O'Ryan.' That's a common Trueborn surname. But it turns out it was actually what you or I would instantly recognize as the common first name for a downlevels Yavi woman."

Polian ran a hand through his thinning hair.

This should have taken three hours to figure out, not three weeks. But internal security people like Varden had different expertise than Gill's external security people. Over the course of history, compartmentalized, unshared intelligence had probably lost more battles than a thousand incompetent generals. It could have lost *this* battle before it even started.

"Sir, the note on that scrap you gave me said this woman was a midwife, actively delivering illegal children about thirty years ago."

Polian raised his eyebrows. "And?"

"Once we came up empty on every other inquiry line, we just ran the first name, 'Orion,' against convicted, suspected, or fugitive midwives named Orion who fit the age window. We got nine matches."

Polian frowned. "Nine?"

Varden nodded. "Five of the nine were incarcerated during the period in question. One was theoretically still working, but she had lost one hand during an attempted robbery. I gather that makes her line of work difficult."

Polian sighed.

"That leaves—"

"Three, Varden."

Varden nodded. "But two of those were KRA last year."

Polian sighed again. "Killed Resisting Arrest" was a leading cause of death downevels. It was common banter in vice locker rooms that peeps could resist arrest in their sleep. Then Polian frowned. "So there's only a one-in-three chance that the person we're looking for is the one who remains alive?"

Varden shifted his weight. "Well, actually, sir, I kind of figured it's for sure that the survivor is the one you're looking for. I mean, what are the odds?"

"The odds of what?"

"You don't remember her? According to her record, Orion Parker was an informant of yours when you were a downlevels patrol officer."

Polian sat back, stared into space.

He hadn't worked vice hands-on for thirty years. He had utilized tens, maybe hundreds, of snitches. They ran together in his mind now, no more distinct than potatoes in a bin. "Image?"

The mug shot Varden pulled up was flat and grainy, but, yes, now Polian recognized the little she-gnome. Large blue eyes, the spiky black hair they all wore then. And, by the background grid behind her, short even amongst her peers. She had been feisty and clever. No wonder she had stayed alive.

Polian stroked his chin. "She was damn good at disappearing from us. How can you be sure she's alive down there still?"

Varden smiled, pulled up a second mug, this one sharp and recent. The same face, now worn and gray. Even thinner, skeletal. And wearing detention fatigues.

Varden pointed at the image sidebar. "She went down for the long one eight years ago. Third strike. Her sentence was commuted from termination to life because of the work she did for you."

Polian nodded. This was better than he could have hoped for. "Draw release documentation for this inmate. Compassionate release for health reasons."

Varden's eyes widened. "Sir? Lifers aren't eligible for—"

"They are if I say so."

Varden seemed to have trouble keeping his jaw from dropping, but managed, "Yes, sir.

"I'll go down and handle her exit interview myself."

If a Director General had ever visited a detention facility before, Polian himself had never heard of it. But Varden was either learning to keep his reservations to himself, or simply numb by now.

The younger man just nodded.

Polian took out a paper orders form and a physical pen, wrote for three minutes, then folded the paper and sealed it in a tamperproof. He slid it across the desk. "And drop this off with Master Sergeant Creter in Graphics. His instructions are inside."

Varden cocked his head. "I thought Sergeant Creter retired, sir."

"Some skills are too valuable to be retired, Varden."

Varden picked up the envelope like it was a grenade and stood, brow wrinkled.

"Varden? Off you go. Dismissed."

The boy saluted, spun on his heel and was gone.

Three days later Polian's bed woke him a half hour before virtual sunrise. He dressed in the sort of cheap civilian one-piece a downlevels advocate might wear to an inquest, stepped onto the pedway outside his residential on Eightieth and Park, Seventy Upper. Traffic was so light that early-rising joggers wove around him without a touch, panting. Three minutes later he transferred to the express downtube for Ninety-six Lower.

The car was half empty, mostly engineers bound for early-shift supervisory jobs in the heavys on Ninety-six Lower. He let them exit before he stepped out.

Max Polian hadn't been this deep, indeed hadn't been into the lower levels at all, in ten years. And never to Ninety-six Lower. Vice cops went where the weak and the dishonest went to indulge their vices, and that wasn't on a manufacturing level.

The dim, cheap light, low ceilings and narrow warren of the traffic grid were nonetheless all too familiar.

The ceaseless, floor-shaking mechanical rumble, the hot stink of machine lubricant, and the empty, pedway-less passages were unfamiliar. Not that Ninety-six Lower, or its counterparts in Yavet's other stack cities, was deserted. Behind the sliding doors that lined the passages the little people toiled and sweated in their burgeoning billions.

It took Polian ten minutes to cross the industrial zone of Ninety-six Lower to the entry gate of City of Yaven Detention Block South.

The bored gate guard didn't recognize Polian in the one piece he wore, but when Max leaned in to the retinal, and his ID flashed up, the man sprang to attention.

Polian had been sweating from the heat in the corridor, but moments after he entered the block he was blinking away a torrent. Detention blocks were always sandwiched between the basic industry fabrication facilities where the inmates worked. The blocks functioned as heat sinks because even the vast exhaust stacks couldn't vent every byproduct of the furnaces, fabricators and forges to the atmosphere.

The guard who guided Polian along the cell-lined corridor to the interview cubicle wore a head lamp, because the block's minimal lighting came from the red-hot glow of the ancient, riveted iron common wall panels, where they were left exposed to provide illumination.

As the guard walked he turned his head, and his murky beam shone through the bars into each of the gang cells as he and Polian passed them. Every other cell stood empty and silent, its shift of inmates laboring a half day, every day, in the furnace spaces, the even less hospitable world of molten metal, din and danger adjacent to each block.

The occupied cells were floored with a cobbled pavement of sleeping inmates, curled like a squirming, snoring, farting mass of root vegetables dumped into an iron bin. The stench of too many humans permeated the walls and floors and ceilings and bars of the place deeply. But not so deeply as did the absence of hope.

He snorted to himself even as he breathed through his mouth. The Trueborns made up myths about hell in another life to encourage good behavior in this one. All that the Trueborns had encouraged by doing so, so far as Polian could tell, was libertine chaos. The Yavi made palpable, actual hell in *this* life to encourage good behavior. And the resultant society was the most efficient mankind had yet created.

Ten minutes later, Max sat alone, wiping his brow, at the center table of a windowless, steel-gray interview Kube. The door through which he had entered was closed, as was the other to Max's front. In his pocket rested the Kube's sensor link chip, which Max had removed when he entered. The block's commander probably wouldn't dare eavesdrop, but Max Polian hadn't risen from downlevels vice cop to Director General by being careless.

Polian started at the metallic thump when the door he faced opened, and the guard thrust a spindly, limping figure through into the Kube. As the guard shut the door and left Polian and the inmate alone he said to Polian, "There you are, sir. Four triple zero two two."

Before Max Polian stood not so much a person in detention fatigues as a bundle of sticks jumbled in a dirty sack that had once been orange. The person shielded its eyes against the Kube's dim lighting with a skeletal hand.

The note of her cough rather than her face or figure identified her as a woman.

She stood motionless, hairless head down.

"Parker?"

The woman looked up, and for a moment Polian thought she recognized his voice. Then he realized she was simply surprised to be called by a name and not by her number.

She squinted at him through eyes sunken deep in dark sockets. "Who're you?"

"Long time no see, Parker."

"You know me?" The small woman cocked her head.

He motioned her to the chair opposite him. "Have a seat."

She shuffled to the chair opposite him, dragged herself up onto it.

He poured water from the thermal carafe on the table into a clear tumbler, and the cold liquid sweated the glass in seconds. He pushed the tumbler toward her.

She seized the glass in trembling hands, sipped, then coughed. Finally, she looked up at him. "You know me. Should I know you?"

He nodded. "Parker, I'm Max Polian."

She gulped the water this time, then shivered.

It was probably the coolest she had felt in eight years.

She turned the glass in her hand and shook her head. "If you were Polian, you would've brought bourbon I could chase with this."

"You're lucky the guards let me give you water."

Her drawn face twisted into a diminutive smirk. "So it is you, Polian. Lying your ass off as usual. I heard you got made Director fucking General. The goons here would let you give me anything you wanted to." She snorted, spat water out. "Asshole."

He smiled. "Appreciative as always, Orion. To tell you the truth, I assumed you had been dead for years." Polian had figured it right. Not one in a thousand lifers lasted as long as she had, and by the look of her she wouldn't last much longer.

Orion Parker had always been a hard case. So hard that, in her current failing condition, even enlightened interrogation methods would have killed her before she told him the single, critical fact that Max needed to learn, assuming she even knew it.

If she knew what he thought she knew, and if she acted on that knowledge in the way he expected her to, that would be perfect.

If she *didn't* behave as he expected she would, he would pull her back in and take the risk of getting the information that he needed to know in the conventional way.

It was a humane strategy. Either way, she would live slightly longer and far more pleasantly than she would down here.

She stiffened and her eyes widened. "You found out I got commuted to life?"

"I did." He nearly smiled as he understood her reaction.

Orion now thought that her original commutation from termination to detention had been an undiscovered error. She thought he had discovered it, and had come here at this moment to have her executed. Well, good. Fear of imminent death always increased a subject's malleability.

He poured water for himself, drank, while he let the fear build in her.

He said, "You delivered thousands of Illegals. That's a lot of capital crime, Parker."

"Not as many as you killed. That's a lot of murder, Polian."

"The difference is you were breaking the law. I was enforcing it. And if I were you I wouldn't be so quick to condemn my job. You helped me do it."

She sat silent, eyes glaring out from deep sockets.

Some snitches informed for money, for drugs or to avoid pain. She had given him information only because it kept her free. Free to commit the crime of delivering and hiding illegally born infants. Polian estimated she had saved a thousand illegals for every hundred she gave up. Hell, by Trueborn moral standards, she was a heroine.

He sat back in his chair. "We both did what we did, Parker. But we've both gotten old."

"Me maybe a little faster down here, you prick."

"And I'm maybe getting soft in my old age." He laid his hands, palms down, on the tabletop. "Parker—Orion—I'm here to tell you that I've ordered you released."

At first she just sat there. Finally, her eyes widened and her mouth opened. "What?

"Released. Freed."

"Why?"

Because once she was free, she would have access to the sub rosa network of offworld smuggling and communication that criminals like her knew so well.

But Polian said, "I think someone like you has suffered enough."

"Bullshit. God, how did such a lousy liar get to be Director General? Polian, making someone like me suffer is what you live for."

He shrugged. "Maybe I *did* just get soft when I got old." He slid his chair back. "If you'd rather stay here . . ."

She raised a tiny palm. "Okay! Fuck yes, okay. Where do I sign?"

He nodded, pressed the call button beneath his side of the table, and the guard reappeared, with an armful of civilian clothes, release papers, and Parker's personal effects box.

Ten minutes later, Orion Parker emerged from the Sanex adjoining the Kube looking almost human again in cheap civvies, cradling her release documentation chip and the effects box like it was a newborn. The guard tightened leg cuffs on her for the trip uplevels to resume a very ordinary life. It wouldn't be a long or pleasant life by the standards of Polian's class, but for someone from the detention blocks it was an ascent to heaven from hell.

As the guard led her past Polian, she paused, looked up at him. Her hard, old eyes were moist. "I don't know why you're *really* doing this, Polian. But," she swallowed a sob, "may you be in heaven for an hour before the Devil knows you're dead."

Polian stood still and unblinking until she and the guard left and he was alone in the Kube. Then he wiped the tears that had welled in his own eyes.

FOURTEEN

A half hour after Polian had left Orion Parker in the detention block interrogation Kube, he sat shivering in the blessed coolness of the first-class car that bore him back uplevels. Before he opened the reader in his lap he looked round the car. He was the only passenger. Downbound workers were long since at their jobs. So were the few domestics who could afford to commute to their uplevels jobs first class.

Polian reviewed the copies of Orion Parker's transfer documentation. His action in releasing her was unusual, but hardly unprecedented. Not a few persons of station had wangled releases for personal domestics of whom they were fond, who had committed crimes. But usually some family cook's release was granted in lieu of detention, not after incarceration. Few who actually entered detention stayed alive long enough to come out at all.

So Parker had grit in plenty. But after the stresses of her life, she also had scant months to live, according to the results of her detention-block exit scan. That abbreviated timetable had forced Polian's decision to proceed with the plan and proceed quickly, while his bait still wriggled. Now he hoped it would also force the bait herself to wriggle sooner rather than later.

He flipped to the contents screen of the "Outprocessing Personal Effects box."

In order for his plan to work, Polian was betting that Parker remained in old age as frank and as gritty as she had been when Polian, in his uniform days, ran her as an informant.

But the old woman also had to have remained sentimental and gullible. There were no such things as Outprocessing Personal Effects boxes in the detention blocks because nobody ever processed out. At inprocessing, any personal effects of value were repurposed, and the rest were incinerated as fuel.

However, Parker scarcely would be able to compare notes with others released from a detention block and learn that. Because there were no such others. Parker knew returning personal effects was normal after casual interrogations. She had certainly survived casuals often enough. And because the evidence that she would find in her box would conform to what she wanted desperately to believe anyway, she would believe it. People generally believed "facts" that confirmed their hopes or relieved their fears.

Polian skipped to the document, shook his head in wonder. Two centuries ago Yavet had become a digital universe, in which government monitored every digitized communication. It had been only a bit later that spies, criminals, anyone with a secret, had responded by reviving the art of couriered paper messaging.

It mildly surprised Polian that it occurred to few that the revival of paper messaging would revive the art of forgery. The writing sample Cutler had provided from the Trueborn covert operator's personnel file, along with the background dossier, even fingerprints lifted from the writer's personnel jacket, were melded perfectly into the document. If forgery was an art, Sergeant Creter was an artist without peer.

Polian blinked, then read the letter again.

Dear Orion,

I figure you think I'm dead, and you almost think right. But I got through my Legion hitch, and even through a couple years as an officer in the Trueborn Army. I own my own business, now. Jazen's. It's a bar in Shipyard on Mousetrap. You'd like it. Well, you'd like the imported single-malt. Orion, I found out that my parents were Trueborns. That makes me legal under law! Their names are Jason Wander and Mimi Ozawa and they were officers in the Trueborn forces during the Slug War. Apparently they screwed up, which I suppose is where I get it.

Sorry this is so short after all this time. But you wouldn't believe what I paid (we say here that in the Free City of Shipyard nothing's free, but everything's available if you've got cash) to have this delivered to you.

If this reaches you know that I think of you often, miss you terribly and owe you everything. I would love to hear from you, and to find my birth parents. I've prepaid for a reply, just send it to the P-mail return address.

Your loving son, Jazen

The letter was dated eight months after Orion was remanded to detention. Polian closed his reader, sat back as the car slowed, and smiled.

If Polian knew Orion Parker well enough to predict her behavior, and he did, and if Bartram Cutler knew this Jazen Parker equally well, and he apparently did, this portion of the plan was only a matter of time, now.

FIFTEEN

Orion Parker awoke in her windowless Kube in the mid-range downlevels. It was no bigger than any of the plain, worn Kubes she had occupied over the decades of her life on the run in the downlevels. As long and tall as her height, as wide as her wingspan, and accessing a shared Sanex, it still stunk of the previous tenant, who had died in the place the day before her release.

The previous tenant had been another poor released nobody, like herself, although he had only suffered a casual interrogation, not detention.

Just by surviving one day, she had already made more of her new lease on life than this Kube's previous tenant had made of his. But Orion's was still a short-term lease. Her exit scan showed she had a year or less. What the hell. Most little people never got to play with house money. There was no point bitching that she hadn't won enough of it.

Orion sanexed, stepped out, and the threshold plate announced that, since she had arrived, she had already gained one pound. Not much more than a big dinner for a Trueborn, or for an upper class Yavi like Polian, but she felt fat.

She popped a therm cup of coffee—coffee!—and a bun, and as she ate her breakfast in luxuriant solitude and blessed coolness she took out the letter from Jazen that she had found in the effects returned to her by Polian's dungeon masters. Orion turned it in one shaky hand while she held her thermcup in the other. By the pay marks, it had apparently been left a month after she entered the detention blocks, at one of the dead drops she used to receive payments, both from customers and from vice.

Polian's weasels would have monitored her drops for a month or two, hoping some preg would be dumb enough to contact a midwife that way. Vice were a tunnel-vision bunch. Any document they recovered that didn't point toward an impending illegal birth they would have ignored.

She ran her fingers over the blue marks on paper, the penmanship she had taught the boy unmistakable, and she cried.

Polian had no reason to suspect that his least appreciative snitch had raised a Trueborn Illegal to adulthood. He had even less reason to suspect that the anxious parents had entrusted Orion with an avenue by which to contact them.

But then, Max Polian didn't have much reason to care, either. Sure, if he found out about the boy, he would killed one more Illegal. And for that reason alone, if not just to stick it to Polian one more time, Orion would have taken that secret to the ovens with her.

But Polian had no reason to suspect. And even less reason to care, now that Jazen's confirmed lineage had lifted the death sentence on him.

Orion finished her meal, then she sat down and wrote two paper letters that she would send via P-mail. The first was a brief reply to Jazen. The second shared the glad news with the two people in the known universe who would be as happy as Orion herself to know that Jazen Parker was alive.

SIXTEEN

Carl Otto stroked his red beard with his right hand as he peered at the couple seated inside the Bank of Rand's depositor hospitality suite. The two were displayed on the surveillance screen alongside the suite's outer door.

The woman looked barely older than she had on the couple's last annual visit. Otto guessed her physical age at middle fifties, and she remained slim and handsome, with the exotic eyes common to Trueborns of Asiatic lineage.

The man was taller, with close cropped gray hair and traditionally Trueborn complexion and features. He sat erect in the way that, say, a soldier typically did. The scanner showed that the man wore a blocky gunpowder pistol in a shoulder holster beneath his jacket, and the woman a slender shiv sheathed to her inner thigh beneath her skirt.

Neither weapon troubled him. These two were hardly the first of the Bank of Rand's depositors who armed themselves. And the only thing of value he would carry into the suite was the couple's safe deposit box, cradled in his left arm. They would hardly rob him of what was already theirs.

Besides, he liked them. The stipend they picked up each year was a comfortable sum, but far less than the bloated withdrawals made by most of the bank's customers. Also, when he had taken them hunting that first visit, each had proved a better marksman than himself, but had declined the opportunity to kill game in favor of paper targets.

Mostly, he supposed, he liked them because they were spies like him. Meaning spies on the side of right in this wretched Cold War.

Not that anyone had told Otto that the couple were spies. But the same agent handler who had recruited him had introduced them to Otto as "very special depositors."

Otto clicked off the screen, straightened his tie by the reflection in its shiny black surface, then entered the suite wearing the Class One Account smile that matched his tie. The three of them sat after greetings.

The couple declined kaffee, and the woman leaned forward, now unsmiling. "Your message at the hotel moved our meeting up two hours, Mr. Otto."

He nodded, pulled the sealed paper envelope from his pocket. Class One accounts like this couple's included the unofficial perquisite of a P-mail box. This couple received their stipend funds by secure, anonymous electronic transfer. Perhaps not coincidentally, Otto's compensation for information he passed on via his handler arrived the very same way.

But many depositors' funds arrived by physical "black bag" transfer. The P-mail system facilitated this, bypassing customs and declaration protocols. Why a depositor might prefer to avoid such entanglements the Bank of Rand considered none of its business.

Otto slid the envelope across the ironwood tabletop. The address was, of course, only the account number at the bank. He pointed at the layers upon layers of pay marks. "The sender paid for special handling. Therefore I assumed you would want to see it sooner rather than later, and took the liberty of accelerating your appointment." Otto stood to leave, but the man waved him to stay.

Otto knew of only one special handling service that cost the ransom that this letter had cost. And that service was to get anything off Yavet.

The woman frowned as she tore the letter open, then as she read the single sheet inside her eyes widened and her hand trembled. "Jason, he's alive!"

The man squeezed his eyes shut, and when he opened them, they glistened. He said to Otto, "Maybe you should give us a minute, after all."

Otto reached the door, switched off a red key in a wall socket, and laid it on the table. "Surveillance is off. Take as long as you wish. Reinsert the key and turn it when you wish me to return."

Thirty minutes later, Otto sat at his desk when the hospitality suite's call chime sounded on his console.

When he returned to the suite, the woman's eyes sparkled, while the man paced the room, unsmiling.

She said, "Mr. Otto, we'll be needing extra funds this time."

He smiled. "A loan?"

Such more familiar banker's business was a refreshing diversion for Otto.

She said, "We'd like to liquidate a physical asset."

"Of course. We do it all the time." And we realize a fair but substantial fee for doing so. The Bank of Rand was no fence outfit. But extraordinary customer service took many forms. "We maintain appraisers on premises for everything from Trueborn impressionist canvases to precious metal cargoes. What sort of asset?"

The man turned up the lid of their box on the table and lifted out a diamond as large as a breakfast egg, turning it between forefinger and thumb.

Otto's jaw dropped. "Weichselan?"

Otto's clients knew jewels. And therefore, as a matter of extraordinary customer service, so did Otto. The thing had, in aggregate, to weigh over two hundred carats. A stone so massive could only be Weichselan.

On frigid Weichsel, legend had it, such jewels could be picked up off the ground like pebbles. But nobody really knew, because the Trueborns had declared the distant outpost a "strategic reserve" during the War, after a clandestine military operation there.

The man called Jason nodded. "Blue-white, with a one-hundred-six-carat perfect core if it's cut right, I've been told."

"It's so large that the market may limit what we can appraise it for as-is, where-is." Otto frowned. "We would pay fairly, of course, if that's your preference. But I'd advise that for now you let us determine the value of the salvageable stones that would be cut away from the core, and pay you that today. Then we'll have the core stone prepared. We know several cutters here on Rand who apprenticed in Amsterdam, are most discreet and charge reasonable fees. We will insure the stone against loss or damage in the process, of course. Then we'll have the resulting major piece auctioned on your behalf. Otherwise, you might not break even."

"We need to settle this today, so let's go your way, Mr. Otto." Jason nodded, smiled. "And let's just say I picked it up. Cheap. So breaking even won't be a problem." He swiveled his shoulder, winced, then smiled again.

"Of course." Otto should have seen it before. Jason had a scar on his neck that his collar scarcely covered. The woman, a smaller one, at the throat. War wounds. A modern shoulder-down regrow was indistinguishable from natural. But limbs regrown back during the War, when the process was new, often ached. If Jason, here, had brought back a war souvenir from Weichsel, these two were veterans of the Pseudocephalopod War.

Simple mathematics suggested that these two apparent middle-agers could be pushing a hundred years old, chronologically. Otto had heard that time dilation from near-light-speed travel extended some Trueborns' lives as much as their medicines. Now here was the proof.

The woman said, "We're also going to need travel documentation and passage."

"Certainly. I'll ring the travel department and—"

"We're going to Yavet."

Otto sat back in his chair, smiled. "No. Seriously."

From what he knew of the place, no one of right mind would go *to* Yavet. Though there was a tourist industry of sorts. If one's homeworld exchange rate put Rand or Funhouse beyond reach, Yavet offered a cheap, if bleak, alternate holiday.

"Seriously," said the woman.

"That would require, ah, extraordinary documentation."

Yavet wasn't merely drab and industrial. It was a police state. These clients were Trueborn spies who intended to go where Trueborns were unwelcome. Each of them would need a scrub-quality identity change, including retinals.

Before he could catch himself, Otto blurted to the two spies, "Your employer is in a far better position to provide it than the bank would be."

The woman didn't bat an eye. "This isn't a business trip. We're visiting a relative." Then she fixed him with a stare. "In fact, Mr. Otto, we would be quite disappointed if our employer learned that we were making the trip."

Otto glanced at the bulge in the man's jacket. "This is the Bank of Rand. You may rely on our complete discretion." Otto cleared his throat. "The Bank doesn't provide travel documentation directly, but we do have a list of preferred vendors."

The woman smiled as though she were dress shopping. "Perfect. Can we have the list and the settlement by the end of the day?"

The two rose to leave, and the man took the woman's arm in his.

Otto called after them, "And may I offer a recommendation about how you take the funds?"

They turned to him, and both nodded.

Otto said, "Twenty percent in your usual assortment of currency, but this time the balance in brilliant cut blue-white diamonds, VS1 or better, one to three carats each. Diamonds are so much easier to carry when traveling."

The woman smiled and nodded. "And *so* much easier to fence than most stones. Very thoughtful of you, as always, Mr. Otto."

These two were thirty years older than Otto's own parents, who Otto thought remained pretty lively. He could only wonder what this pair's kids thought of them.

SEVENTEEN

Months of meandering travel after Kit and I had actually talked about what to do with the rest of our life together, the two of us floated once again in *Gateway*'s forward observation blister.

My pulse quickened as *Gateway* finally drifted toward her layover point, Mousetrap.

Mousetrap is a football-shaped nickel-iron meteor twenty miles long in its greatest dimension, an unimaginably tiny mote that drifted lifeless and cold for a billion years across the equally unimaginable nothing of the universe. The drifting mote was finally captured by the gravity of the gas-giant planet Leonidas, and there the mote spun for another billion years. And it probably would have spun on, unchanged, for another billion years.

Except that Mousetrap happened to spin along within just one month's nearlight travel from twenty-six Temporal Fabric Insertion Points. So when mankind clung on the edge of extinction while it fought the Pseudocephalopod War, the only speck of solid ground at the crossroads of the inhabited universe became valuable real estate. If you counted the price paid for it in blood and treasure, it was the most valuable real estate in human history.

I heard Kit swallow a sob. Soldiers do that. Even—maybe mostly—the ones who've had to kill other people.

No one who's been under arms sees a battlefield the way others do. First Battle of Mousetrap. Second Mousetrap. The shipyards that birthed the armada of cruisers, like the *Gateway*, that had finally won the War. Even hovertanks had been built in Mousetrap. Some of the rattletrap Kodiaks I bet my life on during my time in the Legion had originally been fabricated on the Mousetrap Lockheed plant's line.

I swallowed, myself. "But it's beautiful, too."

The moonlet spun slowly in vast, empty space, silhouetted as black and as tiny as a peppercorn against Leonidas' boiling orange disc.

She cocked her head at me. "Especially for you, I guess."

I nodded.

Born to Trueborn parents on Yavet, and raised there by the midwife who delivered me, I grew up inside a layer cake, where a park chamber fifty yards long with a twelve-foot ceiling was the wide open spaces. I was a wandering orphan in reality, if not in technical fact. But if I felt anyplace else had become my second home, it was Mousetrap.

My view of home shifted as *Gateway* shifted her mile-long mass toward the main entry portal at Mousetrap's North Pole. Through the plasteel grab bar I felt the old girl quiver. Maybe she was excited.

Mousetrap was my second home but it was *Gateway*'s first. Her skin and bones were mined and refined from the moonlet's own body, and *Gateway* was fabricated on the ways and in the vast shops of Mousetrap's north end.

After the War was won, the north end where *Gateway* was born was abandoned to the unemployed miners and shipwrights who built her and so many like her, and became the Free City of Shipyard, where, they said, nothing was free but everything was available if you paid cash.

Gateway yawed nose-on toward the north portal, matched rotation, and shuddered again beneath my hand, almost in the way Kit had sobbed. In that instant it struck me that, like me, *Gateway* was a sort of orphan.

In the way of history's great capital ships, whether they traveled wet oceans or black vacuum, *Gateway*'s first captain had lived with her every day for the three years between her keel-laying and commissioning, like an expectant father. He had memorized her every system and rivet the way a father memorized his daughter's eyelashes and laughter.

Few of those original keel-up starship captains had survived the war-winning battle for which *Gateway* was named. Fewer still had survived the mundane physical ravages of the decades since. And so, like most daughters, *Gateway* survived her father.

Starships nowadays were remade, not born. Too expensive to build without the goad of imminent human extinction, cruisers were now repeatedly repainted, refurbished, rebooted, and repurposed. Hardly a new idea, though. During the Cold War I era, Trueborn pilots sometimes flew aircraft older than their fathers, and sailed in wet-bottom warships older than their grandmothers.

Today, starships, repurposed as interstellar buses, were driven by teams of prodigiously skilled and trained officers who were in a way little more than bus drivers. No one driver knew exactly how the whole bus worked. Partly, team command was used to fly starships today because starships were the most complex buses in history. Mostly, team command was used to fly starships today because compartmentalization of information assured that no one person could spill all the C-drive technology beans to the Yavi during a time of Cold War.

As we floated there, my 'puter pinged. We were close to Mousetrap, so it was likely spam, so I ignored it.

Once a starship emerged from a jump, the port for which the ship was bound and the ship could "see" one another line-of-sight. Once that sight line got short enough that message traffic traveling at light speed could pass between the starship and the port in minutes, the ship's directional antennae began downshipping everything from hotel reservation requests to holo wedding albums. Simultaneously the port began spewing uptraffic to the starship, mostly advertising.

Ting-ting. Kit's 'puter double pinged.

I cocked my head at her. "Howard?"

Before he packed us off with Mort, Howard had told us he would be at Mousetrap on other business when we arrived. Not, I suppose, because he was anxious to share his itinerary but because he knew we were traveling with a mind reader who could blow his cover anyway.

Kit nodded, rolled her eyes when the message didn't come in immediately. "Who else?"

The double ping that Kit and I had just heard her receive announced that her 'puter was receiving an encrypted message. The delay in that message actually coming up on her 'puter's screen meant that the receiving 'puter was reformatting Military Spec Encryption, the only kind of encryption that really worked. MSE was absurdly expensive. MSE was usually unnecessary. Naturally, Howard Hibble used MSE for everything.

Kit finally read her message, then frowned. "Something new in Mousetrap."

I frowned back. "Howard's inviting you to tour the Gateway wing?"

She shook her head. "If he did, I'd plead a headache."

Kit and I had both visited the Pseudocephalopod War Museum, but the Gateway wing was new. The Museum's extremely well done, and admission's free, even if you use an audio 'bot. But if you're a soldier you cry more than you listen.

Gateway was overdue for its own wing at the museum. Not *Gateway*, the ship aboard which we were traveling, but the place for which she was named. Gateway, the place where mankind finally won the War. Although "place" is not a term that really applies to fifty million cubic miles of vacuum at the end of the explored universe. People called the battle that won the War "Gateway" because the official name, "Strategic Engagement of the Massed Fleets of the Human Union and the Forces of the Pseudocephalopod Hegemony, Contested in Interstellar Space Earthside of Temporal Fabric Insertion Point Situated at Grid Reference Golf Alpha Tango Echo Whisky Alpha Yankee," was too long to fit on a cruiser's nose, much less into the chorus of that crappy country-and-western song that cheapens the battle's memory.

I answered her comment. "I'd fake a headache too."

Neither of us wanted to be reminded about Gateway. The Slugs had attacked Earth, killed sixty million people, and tried to extinguish mankind as a species. But the best solution mankind had been able to come up with was extinguihing the Slugs first.

Kit, even more than I, was unapologetic but ambivalent. Neither of us wanted mankind's eventual tombstone to read "Their greatest talent was exterminating other species."

I asked, "Then how has Howard decided to ruin our layover?"

She shook her head. "Not ours. Mine. Coordination conference on suspension of covert field ops. Field Grade officers and above."

I smiled. Captains are company grade, Colonels are field grade. "Rank hath its privileges."

"Bite me, Parker." Kit slapped my arm, smiled. "How will you amuse yourself wihout me?"

I shrugged. "Go north, maybe."

Shipyard was in Mousetrap's north end. Kit's smile disappeared like an unplugged holo.

"Just to check my P-mail."

P-mail was illegal, but compared to what Kit and I did for a living, hardly immoral. P-mail wasn't what was bothering her. We both knew what was.

She stared ahead as Mousetrap's mile-wide North Portal irised open to admit *Gateway*.

I winced. "Problem?"

"No. No problem." She kept staring.

Oboy.

An hour after Kit and I disembarked and went our separate ways, I stepped off the tuber at Lockheed Station, in Shipyard.

Shipyard was, basically, the north half of the football that was Mousetrap.

Mousetrap was originally mankind's interstellar Gibraltar, our bulwark against the Pseudocephalopod Hegemony. Since we won the War, the South End had remained the crossroads of the Human Union, the gateway (little "g") to the temporal fabric insertion points that led, directly or indirectly, to the five hundred twelve planets that comprised the Human Union. As such, the South End of Mousetrap was insufferably bright and clean and boring.

After the war, the abandoned North End, where the great ships that won the War for us had been built and berthed, had been abandoned by the Human Union. Eventually Mousetrap's unemployed shipwrights had squatted there, then declared themselves an independent and, uh, socially liberated community. Today the Free City of Shipyard was the graffiti-tagged nest of addicts, villains and libertines that I had called home during the two years after Kit and I split and before Howard Hibble weaseled me into reenlisting.

The basic look and smell of Lockheed Station hadn't changed much since my first visit, when I was a laid-over Legion Basic skinhead bound for his first duty station.

Lockheed was a fifty-foot-ceilinged neon and steel cave hollowed out of the nickel-iron captive meteor that was Mousetrap. Music and voices still echoed out of a half dozen bars, and four establishments with active picture windows still offered other distractions for hire if you didn't care to drink. The crowd that clattered across the deck plates was as raucous and as drunk as ever.

Directly across from the platform, Lockheeds' pink-and-green sign had faded, but still blinked. There had been a time when the joint, which had once been the tank plant's cafeteria, was a friendly place that offered two-for-one well drinks with a Legion Tanker ID. Later, refurbished, the place had attracted Trueborn tourists who sought a homogenized taste of North Mousetrap.

Somebody told me, in those days after the Trueborn tourists began arriving, that the urine on the deckplates in front of Lockheed's still smelled the same, but the customers who staggered out and deposited it had become much better dressed. At the time, I thought the comment clever.

Maybe I had spent too many years on neat and tidy Earth, with Kit and her neat and tidy rich friends. Because today my nostalgia for home had evaporated like the urine on the deckplates, and nothing was left but an unpleasant smell.

I ignored the crowds, and most especially ignored one passage I knew too well, and walked seven minutes to Shipyard's P-mail office.

I glanced once over my shoulder to assure I wasn't followed, but my motive was to be sure I wasn't mugged, not because I was worried to be visiting the P-mail office.

P-mail was a creature of the fourth generation of the digital information age. That generation began when encryption technology at any level below military or diplomatic spec, which only the military and diplomats could devise, maintain and afford, became so hackable that it was more speedbump than firewall.

Would generally available encryption technology hide porn downloads from mom, or fart jokes about the boss? Sure. Secure your paycheck from hackers? Mostly. Keep client lists safe from your competitors? With luck, maybe.

But any digital information about subversive or criminal activity that passed across government-monitored digital media or hung in the government-monitored Cloud and its successors was an open book to The Big Eye. And what the government didn't monitor automatically it monitored whenever it chose to.

So, in the field of secure communication among the shady, or even among the merely shy or private, everything old became new again. And thus P-mail was born.

If your life has been more sheltered than mine, you may never have heard of P-mail. Most people who *have* heard of it think the term "physical mail" derives from the definition in the statute that first outlawed it: "unlicensed physical carriage for hire of (1) regulated substances, and/or (2) uninspectable intellectual property."

Like much of what most of us "know," that's a crock. The term "P-mail" actually originated last century, for "paradise mail." The Americans were hunting the Islamic terror cabals of the day to extinction, tracking the terrorists by their use of digital media. So the terrorists shifted to courier-delivered physical messages. "Paradise" was where the couriers wound up when they got caught, which they usually did.

P-mail's come a long way since then.

Once you arrived at the P-mail office, its interior physically resembled the "post office" you might see in some Trueborn cop-and-robber holo set fifty years before the War. Behind a counter stretched along one wall, a clerk collected dropped-off parcels and handed out incoming ones, and opposite that was a wall of locked, numbered boxes of various sizes. But a central retinal scanner console substituted for physical key slots on each box.

However, getting to Shipyard's P-mail office resembled getting to no post office Holowood had ever depicted. The facility was built originally as a ready room for interceptor pilots, just a bored-out cave, barely a hundred feet below Mousetrap's cratered suface. Deep enough to survive a tactical-sized Slug kinetic projectile, or an above-surface nuke, shallow enough to allow an interceptor crew to race from easy chairs to launch in three minutes.

That ready room could be accessed from inside the moonlet only by a twenty-minute trip up from Mousetrap's inhabited core levels through eleven miles of solid nickel-iron, via a series of high-speed elevators, staggered to slow any attack down the elevator shafts. The elevator series began from an unnumbered suite, behind an unmarked armored door, on a back passage in Shipyard. The suite and each way point were guarded by armed goons who would turn you back or crack your skull if your box rental wasn't paid up or you scanned wrong on the retinal.

As the three-hundred-pound goon at the first waypoint packed me in to the shoulder-wide next-stage elevator then slammed its wire gate closed across my face, I smiled out at him through the mesh. He stared back like a stone with hairy nostrils.

I managed a narrow shrug.

Most P-mail customers considered a visit to the Mousetrap P-mail office a claustrophobic nightmare. I, having been raised downlevels on Yavet, found it nostalgic.

From the office's ready-room-become-lobby, man-sized crawl tunnels radiated out like a starburst to the interceptor sally ports, long empty of defending fighters. Today the sally ports remained tight and secure enough to recover and launch a hodge-podge fleet of small, stealthy and unregistered craft. Those craft shuttled contraband and P-mail onto and off of slowly approaching cruisers via the lifeboat ports, now empty, that had once served the cruisers' vast troop-carrying spaces.

Politicians, and so the cruiser drivers who served at the politicians' pleasure, didn't crack down on P-mail for the same reasons that the politicians didn't crack down on numbered account banking havens like Rand and Funhouse. First, some politicians were *paid* not to crack down. Second, if one's enemies seized control of the ship of state, it was wise to have lifeboats available.

In the P-mail office the clerk behind the counter looked up, then ignored me, even though I'd been coming there for years. The system thrived on anonymity.

I thumbed the contents of my box, chucked the physical spam into the inst-cinerator and began reading the rest. First I opened the dupe sheets for Jazen's, and found a check so big that I whooped, which caused the clerk to frown at me.

When I reenlisted, I had sold my bar to the proprietress of the business next door to Jazen's. It was a long-term installment sale, with payment amounts tied to profits, and the duplicate ledger sheets that accompanied the check showed profits had soared.

Jazens' official ledger showed Jazen's was losing its ass, but so did the official ledgers of every bar, whorehouse, poko parlor and janga den in Shipyard. That was because Mousetrap was a Trueborn Territory, and the taxes that the Free City of Shipyard kicked up to the territorial government were calculated from the official ledgers.

The Free City of Shipyard was also supposed to collect and kick up to the territorial government confiscatorily high point-of-sale taxes on imports like Trueborn single-malt whisky and slow-burn janga from Bren. The Trueborn politicians like Kit's father, who thought these taxes up, believed they shielded the citizens of developing economies from societal burdens like alcoholism and drug addiction. Us shielded citizens believed the Trueborns were simply annoyed that someone, somewhere, who was not them, was having a good time.

Shipyard ignored the taxes, and so, having done their moral duty, did the distant Trueborns. Don't believe me? On any day when a cruiser from Earth is laid over you'll find Trueborn politician passengers passing their layovers guzzling untaxed single-malt and blowing untaxed janga at Shipyard's finest whorehouses.

I eyed the whopping check payable to cash from Jazen's, LLC one more time, shook my head, then tucked it into my jacket pocket along with my remaining wad of P-mail, still unopened. Payments like this one wouldn't make me as rich as a Trueborn. But they would make me self-sufficient enough that I would no longer feel like a charity case every time I rubbed shoulders with Edwin Trentin-Born.

I exited the down elevator and passed Lockheed's again. But this time I didn't return to the station. I dodged through drunks toward the passage that led to Jazen's.

Since I reenlisted I normally kept my distance from Jazen's when I passed through Mousetrap. Orion had taught me that pain and temptation are best dealt with by avoidance. That's why I got my statements and payments through third parties. But a businesslike drop-in to offer congratulations on a job well done surely couldn't hurt.

EIGHTEEN

Two minutes later, I turned down the side passage opposite Lockheeds for the first time since I had reenlisted. The ambient light was dimmer down all the side passages in Shipyards, and I ducked by long-conditioned reflex as the ceiling and walls squeezed down to a Yavi-friendly seven feet by seven feet.

I stopped at the sign glowing above the first door on the left. It still read JAZEN'S, and the sign next door to Jazen's still read MAISON DESSELE. The two businesses were now commonly owned, but operated better as complimentary providers than competitors.

Jazen's was known for reliable scotch, quality blow and a tolerance for GI dustups. Maison Dessele was Shipyard's only companionship salon staffed exclusively by courtesan-class Marini hostesses. And a few hosts, if that floated one's boat.

Jazen's and Maison Dessele were considered tame by Shipyard standards. After all, at a place around the corner you could buy oral sex with a six-eyed catfish.

Jazen's was open but empty most mornings, even when a cruiser was in, and this morning was the same. When I stepped through the door, though, I cocked my head. Something was not the same.

Jazen's occupied an asymmetrical, vaulted cavern that had originally been filled by a blob of pure copper. The copper had been scraped out and sent to war as starship wiring. By the time I took the joint over, the humid exhalations of thousands of drunks had oxidized the copper residue on the walls and ceiling to verdigris, the gray-green color of those statues in those open-air parks that the Trueborns have so many of.

My eyes widened as I craned my neck.

Today the walls and ceiling gleamed like a cathedral dome paved with museum-quality Trueborn pennies. Maybe it was true what they said about a woman's touch.

In the bar's center a lone figure bent on hands and knees with her back to me, scrubbing the floor tile. Based on my two years doing the same, she was cleaning up spilled beer and vomit. Which tells you all you need to know about the glamour of bar ownership.

A successful bar, even when empty of customers, still needed an owner there working his, or her, ass off. And in this case, the ass was as lovely as I remembered it.

I dropped my chin and lowered my voice to deep bass. "Y'all serve infantry, Ma'am?"

She kept scrubbing, but waved a hand. "Only the ones with charming accents! Always two for one for GIs at Jazen's."

Syrene Dessele stood, hands on her waist, stretched and moaned.

She turned, scrub cloth in one hand, and combed ebony hair back from her eyes with the long fingers of the other.

"So, soldier, what'll it—" Her enormous brown eyes widened and she stiffened as she recognized me. "Be?" It came out a squeak, and she cleared her throat.

A courtesan-class Marini dressed to scrub floors outglitters any ten New York runway models on an opening night. And that was when the courtesan was vertical and not even trying. Syrene's outfit was glistening black, jeweled at the throat and wrists, and covered her neck to toes. It looked painted on because it *was* painted on, then peeled off and sewn to fit. Marini courtesans had been dressing that way since some unsung genius had discovered a way to thicken Bren tree sap six hundred years before. Fashionable Trueborn women at the time were wearing layered pantaloons. Look it up.

I said, "Got Trueborn single malt?"

Her voice quavered. "All out, I'm afraid."

I drew a breath, scared my voice might crack, too. "Small batch bourbon?"

She pointed at an empty spot on the top shelf and her finger trembled. “Run on bourbon last night.” She thrust one foot forward while she swung her arm at the bottles glistening behind the bar. “Have a look. Maybe the gentleman will see something he wants that we *do* have.”

I stepped toward her, smiled. “Maybe the gentleman already did.”

Before I reached her she blinked, and her eyes narrowed. “God damn you, Jazen!” She pegged the wet scrub cloth and it slapped across my nose and mouth and stuck.

I mumbled through beer and vomit, “Great to see you, too.”

“What?”

“Nothing.” I peeled the cloth off, dropped it, and scrubbed my face and hands with a Sani.

Hands on hips, chin out, her eyes burned me. “Three years! Not a word. Not a note.”

“There was the contract from the solicitors.” I glanced round at the new decor. “You’ve done well here.”

“Up three hundred ten percent. I assume you got the check.” She paused, crossed her arms. “Why? Why like that, Jazen?”

“Long story.”

She stepped to the taps, drew two lagers, then motioned me to sit with her at a two-top. “Bore me.”

I stared into my beer before I answered. “I went back to my old job. I can’t talk about my job any more now than I could before.”

“You went back to the blonde.”

I sighed. “It wasn’t that simple.”

“She’s very rich. And Trueborn royalty. I call that simple.”

“We worked together before. We work together now.”

Her lip curled, and she turned her head away. “You lie worse than you make love.”

“I never told you it was only work. Not before. Not now.”

Syrene stood and walked to the bar, her back to me, and leaned, arms out and head bowed for a long time. “I should have known it would happen sooner or later. Most girls like me don’t even get two years.” She sobbed.

I went to her, laid my hands on her shoulders, and rubbed them. “Don’t give me the ‘girls like me’ crap, Syrene. On Bren it’s ‘girls like you’ who’re the royalty.”

She reached her hand up, took my fingers and kissed them. "I know. There's no shame in being a courtesan. But the Trueborns don't see it that way, and you grow more Trueborn every time I see you." I felt her warm against me, closed my eyes.

"The sign says open. Guess it depends on open for what."

At the sound, I spun away from Syrene toward the door as my heart sank toward my navel.

Kit stood silhouetted in the open doorway, hands on hips and feet planted.

I said, "What are you—?"

"Howard bumped the meeting. I figured I'd find you up here, drunk and lonely." She shook her head, snorted at the beer glasses on the table. "I see I was half right."

I held up my hand, palm out. "Kit, this isn't—"

She looked sleek, brunette Syrene up and down. "I'm blonde, Jazen. Not blind. And I was stupid enough to think—" Kit pivoted back into the corridor.

"Kit! I—"

She was gone.

I started for the door but Syrene caught my arm. "Let her go."

I pulled away, but by the time I reached the corridor, Kit was nowhere to be seen.

I ran out to the square, stood on tip-toe, and peered across the crowds swirling in front of Lockheeds. Not a blonde head anywhere.

"She's more beautiful than I imagined." Syrene stood beside me, arms crossed.

"Jesus. Could I screw this up more?"

"Yes. That's why I tried to stop you. Apologizing too soon to a woman who's in no mood to take crap just makes you both say even more that you can't take back."

I looked down into those enormous eyes. Then I smiled and nodded. "How many times did I forget that in two years?"

"Too many."

She threaded her arm through mine and turned me back toward Jazen's. "Buy you a drink, soldier?"

"You wouldn't take advantage of a sensitive guy when he's vulnerable, would you?" I smiled as I said it, but I pushed her hand away harder than I had to.

She spun me to face her. "No, Jazen. I wouldn't. And at the moment I think you're wise enough to be neither. But we should talk."

"About?"

"Your future with the blonde princess."

It turned out Syrene had a single malt in the back. She tabbed the sign to closed, locked the door, and we sat again with the bottle between us, no glasses. Like the old days.

She swigged, passed the bottle across. "Did you tell her about us?"

I took a pull, let the liquor burn all the way down. "Yes." I felt my face flush. "Well. Not, you know, about the thing with the thing."

She smiled. "That's not what I meant. Technique is trivial. I mean did you tell her it was more than that?"

I raised my eyebrows. Technique hadn't seemed trivial at the time. Speculating on the technique of Kit's old boyfriend, Brad Weason, he of the perfect hair and teeth, didn't seem trivial when I thought about *that*. "Well. Yes. I mean, I told her the truth. Why?"

Syrene tilted her head back, swallowed, pushed the bottle across to me. "It may take longer for the princess to forgive you."

I paused, blinked, shook my head. I'd forgotten. Canned atmosphere like Mousetrap's caused the human body to assimilate alcohol faster. "Huh?"

"A woman can accept a man following his prick in the wrong direction better than she can accept him following his heart there."

"But you and I didn't even—"

"It's not whether we did. It's whether you still wanted to. And *why* you wanted to."

"Men always want to! If we didn't, you and your grandmothers and cousins would have been sewing quilts for the last six hundred years."

"True." Syrene smiled.

Marini courtesans have perfect teeth, by dint of six hundred years of breeding. So did Kit, by dint of Trueborn orthodonture. So did Brad Weason. I was lucky I had all of mine.

We drank in silence for ten minutes.

Finally, I swigged, then tilted my head against my hand as I felt the scotch. "You know what else is true? Kit's father hates me. I have ordinary teeth."

Syrene's head wagged like one of those dolls the Trueborns give away at baseball games. Six hundred years of breeding hadn't enabled Marini courtesans to hold their liquor any better than I could. When Syrene and I drank together, the experience was frank, but brief.

Syrene said, "An' you're a crinimul. They hate me, too."

"I'm not an Illegal anymore. And they don't even know you. So how can they hate you?"

"They know what I do. They define a person by what they do. 'S a fact."

I tilted the bottle and peered at the golden contents. Not enough left to rinse a glass.

"I make people happy and the Trueborns call me a whore. Your blonde kills people she's never met and they call her a hero. That's fucked, you know?" Syrene laid her head on the table.

It *was* fucked. I lay my own head on the table and stared across at Syrene's porcelain cheek as she breathed soft and even there.

What "they" should know about her was that she was an innocent child who couldn't hold her liquor, even though she knew how to do the thing with the thing. That she was smart and hardworking enough to grow a new business three hundred ten percent annually even while she made payroll running another business that kept fifty employees and their dependents fed. And that she was tough and honest and funny and didn't take crap.

She reached across the table, touched my hand and mumbled, "People like you and me, we're alike, Jazen. We'll never be like the Princess and her kind. Not ever."

My eyelids weighed five pounds each. I saw my hand beneath Syrene's, turned my palm up, and closed my fingers around hers. She cooed in her sleep.

She was right. We were alike. In a way that Kit and I would never be alike. I meant to tell Syrene so, but I slept instead.

I woke still seated and slumped across the two-top table with my cheek in a drool puddle. The evening shift bartender stared at me as he wiped a glass. He was new. To him, I wasn't Jazen, himself. I was just another drunk left over from the early shift. Syrene was gone, but the bottle we had emptied remained.

I stared at the bottle without moving so my head wouldn't fall off.

In single malt *veritas*.

With a lurch I stood, stiff and aching, begged a headache cap from the barkeep, and visited the restroom before I returned to the ship. Whether I felt like it or not, and whether Kit felt like it or not, we were going to talk this out. In the past, my failure to confront my issues with Kit had bought both of us nothing but trouble.

And she had probably cooled off by now.

When I stepped off the elevator at our stateroom's deck, the passage lights were dimmed to evening level. When I got to our door, the "Do Not Disturb" light glowed blue.

I thought about knocking, then quietly punched into the code pad D-a-1-s-y. The DND light still glowed. I tried again. No dice. I got a bad feeling, turned and walked down the passageway to the deck steward's desk.

The evening duty steward looked up, smiled. "Ah! Captain Parker!" He reached under his desk, drew out a note-sized, sealed ship's stationary envelope, and slid it across the desk to me. "Colonel Born left this for you."

I wrinkled my forehead. "Did she go somewhere?"

"I don't believe so, Captain. But I just came on at the hour. I understand from the turn-down steward that the Colonel took the evening meal in your stateroom with an excellent Bordeaux, then left the note and turned in."

I slid the notecard out of the envelope.

> Dear Shithead,
>
> Changed the door password. Try to break in and I will have you thrown in the brig. Go fuck yourself. Or whoever.
>
> Me

Maybe it would be best to postpone our talk after all.

"Everything alright, Captain?"

"Perfect." I pointed at the note. "She just had a little headache so she turned in early. Actually, I'm not feeling tired, myself." I pumped my arms as though I was running in place. "Think I'll take a stroll," I pointed down the corridor at our stateroom, "Before I, you know, turn in, myself."

"Of course, sir." The steward started to turn away, turned back. "By the way, Captain, the poolside chaises on deck twenty-four are made up with sheets, blankets and pillows every night."

The purser turned his back discreetly and resumed his business, his screens flickering in the dim light like colored gauze as he whispered them on and off until he found what he needed.

What *I* needed to find tonight was a fellow bachelor with a sympathetic ear and time to spare.

Fortunately, I knew where to find one.

NINETEEN

Clang.

The physical sound of metal scraping metal awoke Mort as he lay curled on the deckplates in his nest within the nest of HUS Gateway. *He sprang up, four down, claws out, as he probed the space beyond the opening hatch in the bulkhead that separated him from* Gateway's *forward decks.*

Humans were creatures of habit, and on his previous starship voyage, visits from humans at nonhabitual times had proved threatening.

Mort knew this was a nonhabitual visit partly because the level of artificial lighting in his space was lowered, but more because most of the five thousand intelligences that drifted just ahead of him within Gateway *normally emitted a vast drone, but were now dormant.*

The few immediately ahead, the staff who attended to his personal needs, rarely conveyed much beyond dissatisfaction and fatigue. Of the remaining thousands further forward, the few awake were either engaged in coitus or fantasizing about engaging in coitus.

In his waning prepubescence, Mort still found coitus distasteful and disinteresting, human coitus all the more. So distasteful and disinteresting, in fact, that he had reversed his sleep patterns from a predator's normal largely nocturnal habits.

He shook his head to clear it of sleep, and saw his visitor before he felt him. The human male carried, in one forepaw, a tidbit of frozen woog, perhaps as large as the man's torso. From the other foreclaw, six connected metallic cylinders dangled like a plucked bunch of berries.

"On the way back here, I wheedled the cooks for a six-pack for me and a snack for you."

"Jazen!" Mort cocked his head to convey curiosity. "You are sad."

Jazen dropped the woog portion onto the deckplates, then folded himself onto one of the little metal frames with which the humans had furnished Mort's space.

"No, I'm bewildered, unjustly accused, flummoxed, insensitive and monumentally stupid."

"I do not understand fully. Your mood resembles your mood the time when you informed me that you were totally fucked."

Jazen cocked his own head, in his case to convey contemplation. "Actually, this is more the opposite."

"Now I understand even less."

Jazen picked one of the cylinders off the bunch, then drank from it. "Kit and I were close until we split for a couple years. Remember?"

Mort nodded his head to prompt continuation.

Jazen audibilized, "The split was Kit's idea, mostly, and it hurt. I came here to Mousetrap to start over. Then I met this other woman, Syrene. And Syrene was wonderful. Is wonderful. Then when Kit was in trouble, Howard finagled me back to the service. And I saved Kit's life, which pretty much squared things with Kit. But I sort of didn't tell Syrene I was leaving. Which was stupid. And so today I just went back to Syrene to try and square things with her. But I didn't tell Kit. Which was also stupid. Not that I was gonna square things, you know, that way. But Kit thinks it was that way. Now they both hate me. Hell, I hate me." Jazen lowered his head, shook it slowly.

The dizzying deluge that marked streaming human consciousness during times of agitation and stress often defeated Mort. He plucked the emotional essence from Jazen's thoughts as he plucked the zesty pituitary from a brain.

Then Mort carefully patted his human's diminutive shoulder with a claw tip. "Ah. You fear you will now be unchosen as a mate. But do not worry. Even at this moment Miss Jan Wofford of Blackpool, England, in cabin two four two zero, is thinking that she is so randy she would shag a goat. Jazen, I believe many women would consider you a more viable mate than a goat. Many."

"You're not just saying that?"

Mort sat back, waved his forepaw, palm out. "No. I am quite serious."

"Mort. I know."

"Ah. Sarcasm is so complex."

Jazen sighed. "So is human mating. I don't want many women. I just want the right one."

"Ah. Your situation resembles mine in the moment when I have cut the two fattest undiseased woog from a herd. Each flees, and I must choose the more desirable."

Jazen dropped his empty cylinder, and it tinkled atop the full ones he had placed on the deck plates. "It's not like picking steak or lobster, Mort! Well, it is. I mean, Kit's blonde and athletic and incredibly alluring, and Syrene's brunette and seductive and incredibly alluring. And they're both so far out of my league that I pinched myself every morning I woke up beside either of them."

"Sometimes I bring down both woog."

"Huh?"

"I have noticed in Kit's thoughts that she believes you are an insatiable horndog. That means—"

Jazen raised a foreclaw. "I know what that means."

"Clearly, then, you have the physical capacity to service each of them in turn."

Jazen's tiny eyes widened. "Polygamy? You've never even gotten to first base. But for me you recommend ménage a trois? Mort, one of these women is a trained killer. I'd be dead before the proposal left my mouth."

Mort sat back. "Oh."

Perhaps he understood humans less well than he thought.

"Grezzen mate to make life, Mort. Humans, at least when we're true to our better natures, mate for life."

Mort nodded. "An emotional bond."

Jazen nodded. "Kit and I have been through wars. I've saved her life. She's saved mine. She laughs at my good jokes and tolerates my bad ones."

"Then you have made your choice."

Jazen shook his head. "But Kit and I inhabit different worlds. Even though both our parents were Trueborns. Syrene and I come from the same side of the tracks. And she laughs at my jokes too."

"Can't humans track from either side?"

"Idiom. Doesn't matter." Jazen bent to reach another cylinder from his bunch, then grunted and touched his torso with a foreclaw. "Forgot to open all my mail."

He withdrew tiny leaves from a pouch in the ventral side of his integument. "Let's see what—"

Mort felt Jazen's shock as he stared at one leaf, tapped its outer surface with a foreclaw tip. "Look at all these pay marks. This has to be from Yavet."

Jazen tore at the leaf, plucked an even smaller one from it.

Mort felt emotion swell within Jazen. "The news is happy?"

The skin above Jazen's eyes wrinkled. "It's from Orion."

"Your life mother?"

"She says she's alive . . ." Jazen's respiration became ragged and for a moment he stopped audibilizing his thoughts. ". . . Very excited I'm doing so well—how the hell did she hear? How the hell did she get my P-mail address?"

"You have said she was resourceful."

"Yeah. Keeping me alive can't have been . . . oh God."

Pain spiked through Jazen's consciousness as he reached a point further into the message. His whispered words sank until they were barely audible, although they screamed in his mind. "A year or less. From now, six months."

"Orion is dying?"

Jazen nodded without sound. "Mort, it's not fair."

Mort's own head sagged.

Every grezzen was a part of a single, anarchic family. He knew all his cousins, their thoughts, their whereabouts. Yet he, like every grezzen ever born, bonded and felt love only for the mother who bore him and suckled and trained him throughout his growth to independent size.

Mort's mother had been old when Bartram Cutler's henchmen had abbreviated her life. Yet Mort had felt her loss as though she had been taken from him while he was a cub.

"Jazen, whether death is fair or is not fair, it is inevitable. It is part of life."

"That's not what I meant, Mort. It's not fair that life's making me break my promise to her. When I left Yavet, I told her I would see her again. She said no, that would get me killed. So I promised."

"When Orion dies, you will have said that which is not?"

Jazen tilted his head forward and back. "Yeah. It won't be a prediction like saying Cutler wouldn't get pardoned. It will be a lie."

"But Orion is your life mother. She did not ask you at this time to keep the promise. A mother will not love her son less if a promise is unkept."

"Exactly." Jazen's small eyes began to leak. "That makes it worse. Mort, did you see your mother before she died?"

Mort dropped his head. "I did not."

"But you don't feel bad about that, do you? I mean, you're a grezzen. You were in her mind."

"Yes, that is true. If I had not been in her mind my grief would have been unbearable. Even so, failing to reach her before she died haunts me even now."

Jazen remained folded and silent for a long period. His thoughts were a scrambled and conflicted mass. Finally, he stood, and walked toward the hatch as his thoughts became clear.

"You'll still have Kit to keep you company all the way to Dead End. You don't need me."

"That is true. But Jazen, what about Kit and Syrene? And what is in your mind will break many rules."

"Taking leave from a cush job like this is bending rules, not breaking them. If everything goes according to plan, I'll square all that later. If the plan goes wrong, I won't need to."

"But you have no plan."

"True. I also have no time. A minute late in this is late forever. So I also have no choice." Jazen resumed his walk toward the hatch.

Mort considered bounding past Jazen, and blocking his exit. What Jazen was planning could result in Jazen's own death. And would certainly create sorrow and anxiety for Kit.

But Mort stood motionless and watched Jazen disappear through the hatch.

Perhaps if he, Mort, had said that which is not, had refrained from sharing his remorse that he had not reached his own mother, Mort's human would not be attempting this foolish and dangerous thing. But, as a mother's son himself, he knew he would do exactly the same. It would not matter what others said or did not say.

TWENTY

I disembarked *Gateway* after I left Dr. Mort's Mojo Restoration Clinic, then rode the tuber north again, to Shipyard, then walked straight to Jazen's.

As I entered Jazen's I bumped shoulders with a departing het couple. They had to hold one another up, and giggled while whispering unprivately about what came next. Given their condition, they would be disappointed when they found that what came next was catatonic sleep followed by the mother of all hangovers. The night had slipped away to that time in bars when it was no longer young, and the pair turned out to be Jazen's last remaining customers. But Syrene wasn't alone.

She stood behind the bar, side by side and heads together with a very slightly younger and very slightly thinner version of herself. The other courtesan wore the scarlet of a senior apprentice, and propped a handheld on the bar top with one hand so Syrene could read its screen.

The two looked up, saw me.

Syrene whispered a single word to the young lady in red, who closed down her handheld, and carried it as she passed me on her way out. As far as she knew, I was a potential customer, and the look she gave me almost made me one.

I turned and watched until she disappeared out the door, as she returned to Salon Dessele next door, where the night was young all day.

Syrene said, "That one'll have her own salon inside three years. She's got a head for business."

"Not just a head."

On Bren, a senior Marini courtesan isn't regarded so differently from the way the Trueborns regard, say, a matron of registered nurses. The therapies differed, but each society respected the practitioners for their professional detachment as well as their ability to improve the human condition. A big part of Syrene's job now was mentoring up-and-coming talent, and managing the business. Although she still kept her hand in.

"You're back because of what I said. Forget what I said, Jazen. You know the whisky talks for me."

And for me. If I didn't get to the point of this visit, I'd be thinking too much about Syrene keeping her hand in, and that way lay trouble. "No. I didn't come back because of that."

She raised her eyebrows. "Oh? I don't know whether I'm relieved or disappointed." Tonight she had her professional detachment armor strapped on tight, which made the conversation easier for both of us.

I said, "I need to disappear."

"What?"

I leaned on the bar, keeping it between us, and told her about the P-mail from Orion.

When I finished, Syrene's eyes were wide. "You can't go back to Yavet."

"I'm not an Illegal now."

"No. Now you're a spy for Yavet's blood enemy."

"No. I'm just a relative visiting family."

"Don't be delusional. Jazen, even scrubbed, you'll still be a spy." Syrene laid her hand over mine. "Jazen, trust me, I know men. Stupidity is part of the equipment. But of all the men I've ever known, you're the best stupid. I know you'll take any risk for Orion, without a blink of consideration. Just like—"

Syrene looked down, scrubbed with her fingertip at a nonexistent drop on the bar, as her armor slipped for an instant. She was about to say just like I had gone to Tressel to save Kit, without settling up with another woman who I had come to love.

Syrene looked up. "Just like you did for those other soldiers so many times."

"Alright. Then we agree there's a profession where *I'm* the expert. Do I tell you how to smile at men?"

She smiled at me. Once I got her to smile, things were always okay.

Syrene shook her head. "But can you even do this? You *are* a soldier. You can't just leave. And a scrub costs the moons."

"Compassionate leave in case of immediate family illness? Routinely granted when you're on admin assignment. Especially leave from spook central. Kit always says Howard runs the teams like one of her graduate-school seminars. Cut class now, tell me later. And I've got leave accumulated clear out *past* the moons."

"But the money?"

I grinned. "I've got a check from a business that's up three hundred ten percent. Remember?"

She smiled, nodded. Then the smile faded. "The princess is going with you?"

Why hadn't I seen that one coming? "Uh, no."

"But you've made peace with her? And she approves this thing you intend to do? She's a bigger soldier even than you. If she thinks it's too risky, I won't help you."

Orion was dying. There wasn't time, even if Kit and I were on speaking terms. And "go fuck yourself" wasn't precisely an invitation to make peace. Well, Orion told me once, after she had spoofed a vice cop she snitched for, that if the truth won't set you free, lie your ass off.

"Of course."

Syrene frowned.

And if lying your ass off still doesn't get you where you need to be, just play off two women you love one against the other, like a total jerk. An overriding noble cause earns one get-out-of-jerk-free card. Doesn't it?

"Kit thinks it's risky, too, but she says she supports me in my decision because she loves me. Do you disagree with her?"

Syrene looked away for a minute, looked back at me. "Okay."

I don't think she believed one word I said. But maybe she told herself it was all for a noble cause, too. Or maybe she had also finally decided I could go fuck myself.

I said, "I haven't kept up. Who do I need to see these days?"

"To get to Yavet clean? That hasn't changed, Jazen. Cohon controls all the contraband that moves between Mousetrap and half the outworlds, especially Yavet. Girls, guns, opiates, janga, alcohol, OB and drug paraphernalia, even the silly stuff like porn . . . everything but P-mail."

Everybody knew Ya Ya Cohon by reputation. Nobody admitted to ever having seen him.

I asked, "You know how to reach him?"

Syrene blinked.

It was only a blink, but it didn't need to be more than that between us. It only stood to reason that Shipyard's most notorious gangster would know its most professional professional, uh, personally. If you can't deal with a courtesan's work, don't fall in love with one. Or with an assassin, for that matter.

She said, "I can arrange for you to get to Ya Ya. Jazen, he'll drive a hard bargain. Don't cross him. And don't lie to him. He'll test you, even at times when you don't know he's still testing. And if you ever fail one of his tests, he'll have you killed in a heartbeat."

"A sweetheart. Anything else?"

She touched my cheek. "Remember me." She turned away, straightened bottles behind the bar. "I'll text you in clear with contact information as soon as I get it." She shooed me with one hand. "Get out of here."

In that moment, I realized that Syrene had done the thinking for the both of us.

Syrene knew, even though I hadn't until that moment, that, despite the gulf in backgrounds that separated Kit from me, that would *always* separate Kit from me, I loved Kit. I had loved Kit from the first moment I saw her, and I always would love her, even if I never saw her again.

Syrene had the foresight not only to perceive that truth, but the courage to decide that it was a truth neither Syrene nor I would be able to live with in any future we might share.

I wanted to hug her. I wanted to thank her. I wanted to praise her wisdom and her nobility and her strength. But for once I had the wisdom and nobility and strength to know that would just make this ending worse for both of us. The best thing I could do now for both of us was to remember her.

When I got to the door I looked back. She still hadn't turned around, but I saw her raise that hand she had shooed me with to her face, as though she were wiping her eyes.

Emotional armor's hell to keep in place.

I wiped my eyes, too.

TWENTY-ONE

An hour after I left Syrene at Jazen's, I finally got pinged with a meet setup for Ya Ya Cohon.

I had used my hour productively. Orion had always told me there was nothing you could do at three in the morning that you couldn't do just as well during the day. In Shipyard the reverse was true.

I cashed Syrene's check at only a modest discount for the transaction to go unreported, then cleaned out my other accounts. I could've raked off a boatload from Kit's and my petty cash field account here on Mousetrap—ops maintained several at various locations around the union—and rationalized it to myself as "a loan." You'd be surprised what qualifies as petty for a team that kills people. But I never stole from any employer, or from anybody, except to keep Orion and me from starving, and I wasn't about to change now.

I also pulled up the compassionate leave form I had to file. I clicked the duration box marked "Indefinite," typed into the contact information space "To be provided when determined."

I left the optional "Explanation" block blank. If I entered the true explanation, I would be confessing intent to violate about a dozen regs and four statutes. If I filled in the "Explanation" block, but lied, I would only be violating one statute. But fraudulent procurement of leave constituted constructive desertion. For constructive desertion, they hung you.

Finally, I backdated the "Effective Date" box for yesterday, but set the "Submit" timer for tomorrow.

Next, I checked on the next outbound from Mousetrap inbound to Yavet.

Iwo Jima upshipped in the Trueborn morning. In Shipyard we defined "Trueborn morning" as the dead space between seven a.m. and noon when only mad dogs and Trueborns went out.

I didn't check further into the schedules after I thought about it. Cohon was the smuggler, not me, and there were plenty of zig-zag routes to Yavet. How best to get a scrubbed package like me onto Yavet was what I was paying Cohon for. I hoped.

The contact info that came to me via Syrene was innocuous for her profession. Some things hide best in plain sight.

I did what I was told, which was to show up at 4 a.m. and wait in front of the Nasty Nurse.

The Nasty was a Jazen's competitor, and its reputation for dirty needles and dirtier glassware was beneath reproach. I did have to concede that its waitress uniforms were supremely slutty.

At 4:21 a.m., two large gentlemen escorted me into the utility passage alongside the Nasty. They bagged, gagged, detagged, then zagged me.

Bagged and gagged are self explanatory. Detagging was an unpleasant procedure that removed or blocked tracking devices on or within the person. Zagging was what was done in Shipyard to a bagged, gagged, and detagged visitor who the visitee wanted to insure was so disoriented that the visitor would be unable to return uninvited.

So after being run around and up and down for thirty minutes, I couldn't tell you where Ya Ya Cohon's place was if I wanted to.

I can tell you it was luxuriously appointed and spacious for Shipyard. The large gentlemen unbagged and ungagged me, then chucked me into an office two stories tall, and left me there.

The deck plates were covered wall-to-wall with imitation grass. That would have impressed me in the years before I first saw the real thing, which on Earth even grows wild. Behind a desk in the room's center hung a spot-lit, gilt-framed painting of dogs playing poker. If you've spent time on the Motherworld, you know that's a schlocky, mass-produced Trueborn picture that Edwin Trentin-Born's lawn boys might have hung in their shed, if Edwin would have allowed them to defile the place in that way.

A cart, the kind that could hold cleaning supplies, was parked near the office's door, and a dwarf with his back to me stood tiptoe on a stool, lovingly dusting the painting's frame with a puffball on a long handle.

I sat down in a faux-leather wing chair and waited.

A gold-encrusted analog wall clock clack-clacked toward six a.m. as the dwarf kept dusting.

Finally, I asked him, "When does Mr. Cohon usually get up?"

The small man waddled down off the stool, turned, and I saw that he wore an eyepatch that matched his black brocade vest and trousers.

"Ya Ya up earlier even than this time most day."

I raised my eyebrows.

Cohon's butler was peep. "Peep" were Yavi little people, in the sort of pejorative slang that the Trueborns condemned as "politically incorrect." A little person could call another little person or himself "peep." But if a mid-levels Yavi addressed a cook or utilities sweep as "peep," that was rude. Orion was peep. This guy was peep. But he wasn't like Orion, who was short, but not a dwarf.

Another difference between Orion and this guy was that Orion and I lived in Yaven, Yavet's two-hundred-level, three-billion-population stack-city capital. This guy, by his accent, was from Yot, a one-hundred-level, hundred-million-population hick stack in the Eastern Hemisphere.

Yot was known today for its odd-talking little people, who tended toward dwarfism. Yot was also known for having once been Yavet's opium capital, when Yavet's cities weren't stacked and her poppies grew as wild as grass.

I said, "I grew up downlevels, too. In Yaven."

He turned and looked me up and down with his eye. Then he scratched a three-day-old beard and shook his head. "You see Ya Ya, you better no lie to him."

I smiled. "So I've been warned. Don't worry. My mother raised me to tell the truth."

When you thought about it, Cohon was a damn shrewd crook. When the nerds devised our cover legends they always tried to bring in planetary locals so we got the details right. This little guy had offworlded on his own somehow, or Cohon had upsmuggled him. Either way, this dwarf's perspective made him worth his weight in gold to a businessman whose cash cow was Yavet and its billions of junked-up little people.

A guru in the Cold War I Soviet Union said that religion was the opiate of the masses. On Cold War II Yavet, opiates were the opiate of the masses.

And this guy was worth his weight in gold when sniffing out competing opium smugglers trying to milk his boss' cash cow.

Hair rose on my neck.

This guy didn't just *happen* to be dusting. Cohon had assigned his resident Yavi to interrogate me, because Syrene would have let Cohon know where I wanted to go.

I pointed at the painting. "That's superb. It hardly looks like a copy."

"No copy. When comes gambling Ya Ya go first class, always." He narrowed his eye. "You know Trueborn old masters. You Trueborn big. No peep. How you growing up downlevels?"

"My parents were Trueborns, passing through, so no permit, and I arrived early. My midwife raised me."

"Is possible. Many midwife soft spot in head." The little butler nodded his own great head. "Good boy go home visit little mother?"

I nodded back. "She," I took a breath. "She's dying."

"Oh. What her name?"

"Huh?"

The dwarf squinted his eye. "Good boy not know little mother's name?"

The *Iwo Jima*, if that turned out to be the ride I needed, upshipped in three hours. Between then and now I still had to get scrubbed. But if Rumplestiltskin here hadn't even finished playing his name game, price negotiations with Cohon remained a distant hope.

I rolled my eyes. "Orion Parker. The midwife who raised me was named Orion Parker."

My little interrogator stepped to the desk, waved his stubby fingers above the universal while he kept his eye on me.

"Accounting. This is Bobbi." The voice was disembodied, female, and yawned.

"Bobbi, we do business ever with Orion Parker, midwife of Yaven?"

Syrene always said that a successful businesswoman knew her customer base. But Cohon's organization served more little people on Yavet than McDonalds of Earth served hamburgers. At any given moment the practicing midwives in Yaven alone may have numbered in the tens of thousands.

Pause.

I slumped into the faux leather and stared at the clacking clock while the dubiously original dogs played poker.

Bobbi the yawner said, "Well . . . I don't *see*—"

I came up out of my wing chair. "Seriously? This is the stupidest—"

"Here we go! She just hasn't ordered in awhile. Last: Mid-cavity forceps, two boxes of sponges. Frequency: Customer twenty-seven years. Pays: Never late."

The dwarf smiled. "You in very early, Bobbi. Or stay very late night?"

"Both. End of quarter closing."

The dwarf grunted. "Give yourself raise three percent."

"Why, thank you, Mr. Cohon."

I plopped back into the faux leather so hard that it made a human noise that sounded embarrassingly un-faux.

Ya Ya Cohon waved his stubby fingers over his universal and hung up, then flicked his hand at the door. "This one no lie, Peter. You go now. Take cart, too, and pack up."

I leaned out of the chair and looked back toward the office's door. One of the two goons who had delivered me here to Ya Ya pointed at the cleaning cart that had been alongside the door, nodded.

I hadn't even realized he was standing there, which now appeared to have been the idea.

Before he departed, he used his left hand to unscrew the suppressor from the barrel of the gunpowder pistol that he held in his right.

I suppressed my own shiver.

Syrene had warned me about Ya Ya Cohon's testing program. Apparently he really was a tough grader.

"You owe life to little mother. But you think little person just fit come in early, clean office."

I shook my head. "Orion always said good things come in small packages. I'm a big but my heart's peep."

Ya Ya Cohon smiled, nodded. "Okay. I make for boy of Orion most first class passage to Yavet."

I bowed my head, not just for show. "Thank you, Mr. Cohon."

"How long she kick?"

"Uh. She may have less than six months, sir." I swallowed.

He stroked the whiskers on his cheek, narrowed one eye. "My people get you quick scrub, then we go *Iwo Jima* today together."

I stiffened.

A couple introspective, luxurious months of most first-class passage aboard a starship? Great. Road trip with a sociopathic, one-eyed dwarf? Less great.

I waved my hand, palm out. "You've already been so kind, Mr. Cohon. That's hardly necessary."

Ya Ya waved his hand over the universal again, and Peter poked his head through the door.

My heart thumped.

Maybe Ya Ya had made me an offer I shouldn't have refused.

Ya Ya waved Peter in, and it turned out that he was the mob equivalent of a utility infielder. Behind himself Peter now towed the formerly-empty cart I mistook for a cleaning cart. The cart now squealed beneath the weight of more matched luggage than a Trueborn trophy wife needed for a roundtrip to Pluto.

Ya Ya smiled, patted my arm as he rocked past me toward the door. "Ya Ya already booked on *Iwo* today anyway."

"Oh."

Ya Ya smiled up at me while he circled his arms horizontally and swayed side to side. "Downlevels peeps bust it together. Will rock?"

I was not a little person, but I may well have been the first downlevels-raised person Ya Ya Cohon had made the acquaintance of off Yavet since he had left home. And it was probably tough to upgrade acquaintances to pals when you kept blowing their brains out. And I really, really needed this ride.

I nodded. "Will rock."

Peter delivered perfectly-scrubbed me, Ya Ya, and the trophy wife luggage into *Iwo*'s inprocess lounge with ten minutes to spare.

I cleared the retinal as smoothly as I ever had with a scrub job from

Howard's finest nerds. In the time it took to walk twenty feet, Captain Jazen Parker disappeared from the official universe. That alone justified Ya Ya's price to me, which had turned out to be less peep-to-peep friendly than his dwarf boogie had implied. In fact, if it had been any less friendly, I would have been broke.

"Most first-class passage" also implied better than steerage, which was what my berthing turned out to be. Not that I'm complaining. Quad-bunk compartments and shared lavatory facilities beat the Legion's platoon bays and gang showers. Steerage passage also included meals, but not alcohol. Ya Ya, who berthed in a suite up in *actual* first class, got all of both of those that he cared to stuff himself with.

One thing that was included with steerage class but *not* with first class was a full body cavity search at boarding. Again, I've endured far worse indignities in my life, but it was a stuffing I didn't care for.

Ya Ya and I agreed to meet after *Iwo Jima* got underway, in her electronic gaming facility, a repurposed elongate bay that in the days when cruisers transported infantry had served as a pistol practice range. On all cruisers it was called the "Slot Slot," a phrase the Trueborns liked so well that they trademarked it.

We agreed on the Slot Slot because it was a common facility open to all classes. Also because it turned out that when Ya Ya vacationed from running dope and guns, and bankrupting suckers desperate for identity scrubs, he recycled his obscene profits by gambling.

Ya Ya actually wound up spending most of our underway time in the casino forward, which was first class only. I didn't feel deprived, either of his company, or of the experience.

When Kit and I traveled, we visited starship casinos when our "Mr. & Mrs." legend of the moment was posh, and when you've seen one gilded pleasure drome, you've seen 'em all. First-class casinos offered high-stakes games with names like *chemin de fer, roulette*, and *trente et quarante*. Kit translated all of them for me from the original Trueborn French as "lose your entire ass here." When Kit tried them, she usually won. When I did, they lived up to their names.

I squirmed through the Slot Slot's crowds, and between rows of honking, ringing machines, until I found Ya Ya.

It wasn't hard. He had changed into a shiny green silk suit with matching eyepatch. His legs dangled from the high stool atop which he sat, and he played an entire row of machines like it was a pipe organ, while a waitress pair shuttled him drinks.

He was playing holo poker machines, which were a way for us regular folks to gamble while losing less than our entire asses, and to do so in English. Holo poker is like poko, but the physical version of poker, from which holo poker is adapted, uses just fifty-two flat cards.

Ya Ya waved me over, grinning as if he had just been elected king of the leprechauns. "How room?" He shouted to be heard over the bells and sirens.

"Terrific. You winning?"

He shrugged. "Stakes here too low. But odds not so bad." He scooted over so I could squeeze one cheek onto his stool. "You try."

I shook my head. "I prefer higher stakes, too." And pigs flew.

He leaned toward me, winked his eye. "You wait then. You gonna *love* this trip."

TWENTY-TWO

When Mort felt the two humans approach, he was reclining on his side on the deck plates of his space within the Gateway *nest, plucking with a foreclaw at the clean-picked ribcage of a once-frozen yearling woog. Most of the rest of the woog he hadn't even skinned. Mort's appetite lagged, and his principal purpose in plucking the ribs was to amuse himself by producing sounds of varied pitch.*

Gateway *remained at rest within the larger nest Mousetrap, even as other nests like* Gateway *came and went, and Mort's eagerness to continue toward home grew with each departure and dull meal. He understood that the delay was in part an accommodation to him, because the modifications made to the* Gateway *forced changes in the travel patterns of the many moving nests. Regardless of the cause of his impatience, the prospect of physical visitors uncharacteristically stimulated him.*

The pair entered through the bulkhead hatch, and he recognized Kit and felt her excited demeanor well before he saw the visual cue of her distinctive pale forelock.

The other human moved forward upon a half shell that floated like a leaf upon pond water.

Such constructions preserved mobility for lame or old humans, and this human's forelock had grayed with age.

"Kit! Howard?"

"Mort," In the presence of another human, Kit spoke to Mort aloud,

but her tone in his mind at this moment reminded him of his mother's tone when she had caught him playing with his food. Worse, Kit's forelimbs were crossed over her mammaries, and her eyes had closed down to slits, gestures which in combination indicated disapproval. He glanced at the bare, bloody ribs. How had Kit known?

Kit spoke again. "Do you know where Jazen is?"

"I do not."

"Don't you dare lie to me!"

He sat back to display affront. "I do not lie! You did not ask whether Jazen had recently visited with me here. Or whether he received word while we were together that his life mother lies ill and near death on Yavet. Or whether he asked my advice whether he should go to her. Or whether I advised that he should go, which I did. Or whether he then left this place, agitated, which he did. However, if you do ask, those will be my responses."

Kit raised both foreclaws to her head, then turned away, shaking it. "Sonuvabitch! Damn, damn, damn, damn!" She faced him again. "You call yourselves an intelligent species. But you were stupid enough to let him go, just like that?"

"I considered intervention. But Jazen is determined once he has reached a decision. And a loving son should *go to his mother when she is in need. Jazen is a very loyal and loving human.*

Kit paused, inhaled. "Yeah. I've never met a more stubborn dickhead. I've also never met a more loyal and loving human being." Kit nodded. "Okay. Can you find him?"

"Will you reconsider mating with Jazen again if I do? The initial purpose of his visit was for consolation. He was emotionally devastated that he had lost you forever. Kit, the love Jazen feels for you is beyond even that which he feels for his mother."

"Oh." Kit straightened, then she shook her head. "This isn't about . . . that."

Howard's leaf glided forward. "Mort, you know that Jazen's and Kit's and my job goes beyond our relationship with you."

"Of course. Both the Trueborn Earthmen and the Yavi expend a disproportionate percentage of their respective Gross Planetary Products on what you euphemistically call defense. Of many unendearing human behaviors, I find killing one another not for food least endearing."

Kit stepped forward. "Mort, you're smart enough to understand

Gross Planetary Product. So you're smart enough to know that Trueborns make mistakes, but we're different from the Yavi."

He knew that Kit's job had included killing other humans not for food. So did Jazen's. Mort also knew that each of them did that job because each believed more humans would live than would die because it was done.

He swept the woog carcass aside, to remove any barrier between himself and the two humans. The gesture was designed to signal impending frank communication. "Kit, never worry about that. I do understand the difference."

Howard slid into the vacated space.

He had always been puny, even among humans. But now his downcast posture reflected an inner weakening palpable to Mort. In her last months, his mother had displayed similar weakening.

"Mort, I may have recently made one of those mistakes Kit mentioned."

"Humans make frequent mistakes, Howard."

Howard shook his head. "No, I may have really screwed the pooch this time."

Kit raised her foreclaw. "Ignore the metaphor. Howard's saying he's afraid that he made an error in judgment in his job that could lose the Cold War. And he needs your help to unscrew the pooch."

Mort eyed Howard. "I have helped humans assure that Bartram Cutler was foiled and punished. I have helped humans learn about me. I will not help humans kill one another not for food." Mort turned to the woog carcass, licked a bone.

Kit spoke not aloud, but he heard, "Mort, principle's a great soapbox to stand on. But Howard's backed into a corner here. Don't make him turn this car around."

The human habit of punctuating vital thoughts with obscure metaphors exasperated him. But he felt both in Kit's and Howard's minds the warning she meant to give him.

Mort turned toward the two humans and planted all six limbs firmly on the deck plates. Then he lowered his head so that all three of his eyes stared into theirs. He bared his teeth, then snarled.

It was a posture he assumed at home only on those rare occasions when a lesser predator, or a scavenging scrounger, challenged him over a kill, and it always got results.

Howard did not disappoint him. Mort's roar shook the frail old human's leaf, and Howard retreated, small eyes wide. Kit stepped back a pace, but then held her ground.

Mort thought, "Howard, you can prevent me from returning home in time to fulfill my life obligation. Even if you do, we will survive and flourish, as we have for thirty million years. Your own species' flawed tribalism has barely survived for thirty thousand years. So I will not entangle us in your mistakes. Is that clear?"

Kit stepped forward again. "Mort, Jazen's blundering into a trap that could get him killed. Whether you help or you don't, and whether Howard likes it or not, I'm going to do something about that or die trying. I understand you don't care about human politics. Hell, most humans *don't. But I thought you cared about Jazen and me. We care about you."*

Mort looked away, as though he would find an answer to his dilemma in the blank alien walls that confined him. Despite his bold threat display to Howard and Kit, he didn't know what he should do, really.

Unlike Mort and his cousins, humans were opaque to one another. But because humans were individually puny, they depended on one another to survive. So humans were forced to trust or mistrust one another blindly, at worst, or based on imperfect knowledge, at best. Human relations therefore were largely a painful series of mistakes, misunderstandings, lies, and sometimes treachery. Humans trusted and cared for each other not because they were perfect, but because they had no other choice.

Now that he had become part of Jazen's and Kit's lives, and they of his, he had no choice either.

"Very well. How may I help?"

Kit paused, then stepped forward.

Mort grimaced in anticipation of what the humans referred to as a hug, but when Kit's forelimbs wrapped round his paw and he felt her face in his fur, the tactile sensation of contact with another individual not food seemed almost pleasant. Perhaps physical maturity was nearer than he had thought.

Kit stepped back. "Mort, if you don't know where he is, can you find him?"

"I will try."

Howard said, "How did he find out about this?"

"He read a leaf."

Kit and Howard looked at one another, and she said aloud, "He said he was gonna check his P-mail."

Kit looked back at Mort. "You're sure the ill person was his life mother?"

"He spoke 'Orion.'"

Kit turned to Howard, tilted her head to convey puzzlement. "But you said the problem was his birth mother and father. Not the midwife who raised him."

Howard puckered his lips. "The source reported receipt by the subjects of a secure communication at a drop point maintained—"

Kit rolled her small eyes, which indicated exasperation. "Source? Drop point? Howard, Jazen and I have taken bullets for you more than once, remember? Cut the need-to-know crap. Speak English. And speak fast. Time's not slowing down while we're sitting here on our asses."

Howard shifted himself on his leaf, expelled breath. "Jason Wander and Mimi Ozawa, Jazen's birth parents, have been working for us casually, off and on, since they retired from the service after the War."

"Jazen's mother was a starship captain, Howard! You let her run around the universe as a spy emeritus?"

"There was no Cold War when I made that decision, Kit. Jason Wander and Mimi Ozawa made sacrifices beyond telling during their service lifetimes. It's fair to say that the human race may owe its continued existence to Jason and to Mimi, even if no one knows it. They earned the freedom I gave them."

Howard paused to breathe, then he spoke again. "Anyway, months ago we received a report from the source I just mentioned. He reported a meeting between a rich Trueborn and a high-up Yavi. It should have been a red flag."

Howard shook his head, in the way that signaled frustration, rather than a simple negative. "But we didn't connect the dots. I said I may have screwed the pooch. Two days ago, word arrived from the same source that Mimi and Jason visited their numbered account box to pick up pay and allowances, turn in expense reports. You know how that works. But a P-mail, not from us, was also waiting for them. The P-mail apparently persuaded them that Jazen was alive, and either was on Yavet, or someone on Yavet knew where he was. They asked our source for help in arranging travel to Yavet."

"And they didn't ask your permission, obviously."

"Obviously. We afford personnel in the field wide latitude and encourage initiative. But some smart asses," Howard focused his eyes on Kit, "have taken initiative to extremes."

The corners of Kit's mouth turned up. "I'm sure you mean that in the best possible way." She frowned. "But Howard, I know how well you don't pay. Two top-quality scrubs for Yavet on retired military pensions?"

"Jason and Mimi aren't holo stars. But I imagine they have enough socked away, and they'd sell their blood to see their son."

"Assuming they left Rand—it had to be Rand, you're too cheap to do your banking on Funhouse—at the same time your mole at the bank sent the message that ratted them out to you, they're probably a third of the way to Yavet already."

"I estimate halfway. The plan that I fear's targeted them seems redundant and inelegant, but some of the best espionage has been. The Yavi learned, my hunch is from Orion Parker by guile or by torture, how to get a message to Mimi. They could've simply fabricated a story that would lure Mimi in. She obviously jumped at the mere possibility that she could find Jazen on Yavet. That's no surprise if you know Mimi. She can be as headstrong as, well, as you can."

Howard removed the transparent cover with which he protected his eyes, exhaled upon it, then rubbed it against his integument before replacing it and continuing. "I say 'mere possibility' because we know Jazen hasn't yet told Orion he's coming to Yavet. We also don't know whether 'Orion' is really still alive, or just a Yavi spoof. But if the Yavi actually could lure Jazen into the net, they would have a real, live bait to dangle before Mimi if it came to that."

"Howard, do you think maybe Jazen's not just bait? That he could be an independent prize? He's done his share of damage to the Yavi."

Howard shrugged. "So have you. Either way, we need to head him off before he leaves here." He turned to Mort. "You find him yet?"

"For an instant only. He left Mousetrap two hours ago in the nest called Iwo Jima*."*

"Crap." Kit spun back and faced Howard. "But we can still stop him!"

Howard was peering into one of the small leaves humans called handhelds. "No."

"Whaddya mean, no? Radio Iwo *and turn her around!"*

"Kit, I said I can't."

"You're King of the Spooks! You rerouted this *starship. You can—"*

*Howard raised one foreclaw. "*Iwo Jima *entered her first jump four minutes ago. When she pops out on the other side, a line-of-sight radio message would take sixteen years to reach her. The real space distance between the* Iwo Jima *and Mousetrap will just increase exponentially with each succeeding jump she makes. Mort, can you try to reestablish contact with him?"*

"Now that I have lost him, it will be difficult."

"I have faith in you, Mort."

Kit said, "Howard, you told me a few months ago that luck and faith were crap strategies. And you just told me that good espionage is redundant."

Howard canted his head. "What is your point, Colonel?"

"Let me chase Jazen. Yorktown*'s outbound via the same jumps and arrives at Yavet two days after* Iwo. *If* Iwo *runs late, I might head him off. If I can't head him off before he gets to Yavet, I can link up with him there. And you know the two of us improvise like freakin' bandits when we're together."*

"Kit, I've recently been ordered by my commander in chief, who is also yours, in case you forgot, to cease covert aggressive operations. I call infiltrating my most headstrong case officer onto Yavet with orders to improvise like a freakin' bandit covert and aggressive."

"You've already got one case officer inbound to Yavet. So is the biggest intelligence failure since the Russians stole the A-bomb. If you had time to consult our commander in chief, he'd tell you to do something. *Howard, take some damn initiative* yourself."

Mort watched as Howard sat and thought.

Mort touched Howard's mind and found an impenetrable jumble of conflicted considerations, and then a curious sadness.

Howard said to Kit, "Alright." He raised one digit. "However, I see your options this way."

At that moment, as Mort searched for Jazen, he touched a speeding nest of five thousand intellects. Mort grasped and dropped threads of consciousness within the nest until he found one that showed promise. She was one of the ship's masters.

He felt her fatigue, heard her yawn. "Log entry, HUS Yorktown*—" Mort recognized that he had found the nest of which Kit had just spoken, which was coming toward them, not the nest within which Jazen was now traveling away from them.*

Mort discarded the thread. He would encounter countless threads and pockets of intellect in his search for Jazen, great ones and small, bright ones and dull. The only pocket he would pause at to search in detail was named Iwo Jima.

He returned his attention to Howard and Kit.

They stood facing one another, but were no longer speaking.

Whatever they had said while he was distracted they had already relegated to their respective memories, as disciplined humans did. The residue that remained was emotion, and in both Howard and Kit that residue was hope and energy, but also apprehension and sadness. And in Kit, bitter anger.

Howard turned, then floated out through the bulkhead hatch.

Kit turned to Mort. "Okay. Here's the deal. You're going home in this ship to mate. I'm going to Yavet in Yorktown. *Both trips will take months. If the xenobiology nerds' estimates are right, you should be through mating before* Yorktown *pops out into line-of-sight space inbound to Yavet. Can you keep searching for Jazen in the meantime, and still keep a line open to me?*

"I think so."

"Think's not enough. Mort, we can't afford a dropped call on this one."

"I have never mated. I don't know what effect it will have on my ability to keep the line open to you."

"Fair enough." Kit turned away, then turned back. "Mort? When you meet her, if you can't be good, be careful."

"Ha-ha?"

Kit nodded. "Yeah. Ha-ha." She turned and walked toward the bulkhead hatch.

Mort thought, "Kit? What did you and Howard discuss just before he departed?"

She waved her foreclaw, but did not turn to face him. "Details. Not important." She vanished from his sight.

The human nerds who knew of his gift were fond of saying there was no lying to a telepath. He realized now that they were wrong. Unimportant details did not make a human feel as sad and as angry as Kit was.

TWENTY-THREE

In the course of *Iwo Jima*'s journey to Yavet, and my journey to find Orion, *Iwo* made her scheduled layover at her halfway port, which was Foundationally Earthlike 117. At FE 117 cruisers drifted all the way down to surface.

They did this because they sometimes offloaded cargo vital to the economy of FE 117, which cargo was too large and too fragile to downshuttle. So the instant Ya Ya and I stepped out through *Gateway*'s main hatch, we stepped from canned atmosphere into sea-level local.

FE 117 was as far as Ya Ya was going, his vacation destination, and he was accordingly decked out in a tiny Trueborn tuxedo and matching eye patch. He had made me rent a tux too, because he insisted I go with him wherever he was going during our layover. I suppose the pair of us resembled one of those carnivale organ grinders with his monkey.

As Ya Ya waddled down the gangway alongside me, he breathed deep. Then he turned his face up at me, grinned, and beat his barrel chest with both fists. "Feel that? Today Ya Ya win many bets, pork many women. This I promise on my mother's grave."

I did feel that, "that" being something in the air. And it made me grin just like it had on my one prior stopover at FE 117 when I was a Legion skinhead.

FE 117 was relegated to "foundationally" Earthlike status because it differed from Earth in one seemingly inconsequential way. FE 117's Planetary Oxygen Concentration at sea level measured plus-six above

Earth normal. Not enough to make humans go blind, which too much oxygen can do, just enough to make them giggle. The locals acclimated to the elevated POC, but it turned offworlders into party animals at breath one.

And FE 117's locals stood ready to feed the animals. Ya Ya and I stepped off the gangway onto the boardwalk that led to the ground transportation roundabout. A smiling redhead, wearing a chauffeur's cap, sparkly high heels, and nothing in between but what looked like a yard of dental floss, stepped alongside us and held up a printed card. The card offered prospective fares assistance with the other thing that Orion had warned me would make a human go blind.

I stopped and gawked at the girl, until Ya Ya grabbed my arm and pulled me forward. "No need quick chick. Sporting Club car meet us."

At the roundabout's closest approach to the boardwalk, a gasoline powered limo as blacked out, sleek, and almost as long as a Scorpion fighter rumbled past a double line of cabs and electrovans. The chartered limo cut them all off and muscled up to the curb.

Its driver, a knockout brunette wearing disappointingly complete chauffeur's livery, sprang out, dashed around to the passenger door, held it open and smiled at Ya Ya. "Welcome back, Mr. Cohon."

Ya Ya tucked a bill roll as big as a baby cabbage into the back pocket of her uniform trousers and copped a feel. "You been working out, sweet Juju. What you lose, four pounds?"

"Three." She smiled again as she closed the two of us into the limo's rear compartment. Through the one-way window glass I tracked her baby cabbage until it swayed around the limo's front fender and vanished.

Pop.

As I swiveled myself into the compartment's rear-facing jump seat, Ya Ya, stretched out across the red velvet rear banquette, pressed his mouth over the champagne bottle he had just uncorked, and contained most of its overflow foam.

The compartment was lined floor to ceiling in red velvet, even the headliner, which looked and smelled brand new.

"Let me help you with that, Mr. C." One of the two rear-compartment hostesses tugged the bottle out of Ya Ya's hand and sucked off the remaining foam while she stared into his eyes.

These two young ladies obviously worked out as productively as Juju did. Probably more often, too. Because they had apparently just showered down and hadn't had time to get dressed.

The other hostess crawled forward toward me, and blinked. Her eyelids were made up in silver and black, like snakeskin. It was a terrific grabber, not that she needed more grabbers than nature had already provided her. "Been here before, Mr.—?"

"Parker. Jazen Parker." Not my scrub name, but what the hell. Girls like this were paid to forget. I swallowed. "Once." But Legion liberty hadn't been like this.

She curled alongside me on the adjacent jump seat, traced my ear with her fingertip and whispered, "Well, Mr. Jazen Parker, welcome back to Funhouse."

Funhouse. The day I fell in love with Kit Born, which was the first day I ever saw her, she was a mud-smudged tomboy in khakis who gave me a lift from the spaceport on Mort's home world, DE 476, into Dead End's human "capital city." The "city" was a mud hut cluster that the colonists had misnamed "Eden."

Kit had smirked and asked me whether I had ever seen an outworld planetary capital with a name that fit. I had told her "Funhouse." I think she had agreed with me.

Nobody who saw the capital of FE 117 disagreed that the name "Funhouse" fit this planet. In the years since that day, my tomboy and I had disagreed as often as we had agreed. But there had never been a day when I had loved her any less.

"Hel-*lo*! Jazen whatever-your-name-is." My hostess had her hand inside my tuxedo shirt, and she smelled of cut lemons and jasmine. "Am I boring you?"

Syrene had counseled me that a woman forgave a man who followed his prick easier than one who followed his heart, but I was in no position to press my luck.

"No. Not at all." I shrugged. "It's been a long flight."

"No problem. But just so you know, I'm included in high-roller service for the duration of your stay. And Mr. Cohon is a *very* high roller."

She uncoiled from her jump seat and pythoned aft to assist her work-out partner, who was helping Ya Ya keep the back half of the promise he had just sworn on his mother's grave.

My voyeuristic cup of tea isn't *troll a trois*, so I stared out the window watching Funhouse roll past while the limo rocked side-to-side down Lucky U Parkway.

The world that rolled past looked a lot like the lushest parts of Earth, the roadside riot with outsized trees that perpetually blazed pink, purple and cantaloupe orange. The trees rose from flower carpets studded with turquoise and lemon-yellow blossoms the diameter of dinner plates.

Funhouse's vegetation swayed in breezes that never seemed too brisk or too still, too cool or too warm. The few buildings visible from the road were resorts and casinos that curved and soared up above the treetops like alabaster yacht sails. The Funhouse tourism bureau even claimed it rained on Funhouse only after the last floorshow and before the breakfast buffets opened.

The planetologists say all those trees and flowering plants are bigger mostly because they get more carbon dioxide. They get more carbon dioxide because the animals breathe more of it out. The animals breathe more carbon dioxide out because they're bigger. A lot bigger. The animals are a lot bigger because the Planetary Oxygen Concentration lets them breathe so much more oxygen in.

"Titanopods ahead on the right." Juju's voice dripped like honey through the speaker set in the forward partition.

Three heartbeats later the limo slowed momentarily as it passed by a half dozen fawn-colored, droop-snooted quadrupeds as they pruned treetops like living maintenance 'bots. Except titanopods stand twenty-six feet tall at the shoulder. If Mort's biochemistry had allowed him to digest Funhouse animal protein, I expect he would have given his left tusk to retire here.

That's why I described Funhouse's elevated POC as *seemingly* inconsequential. Funhouse's megafauna tentpoled Funhouse's core business.

That business was gambling. Not poko or traditional Trueborn casino gaming, though Funhouse offered bags of both. So did Shipyard, and most nations on Earth. And of course, so did every cruiser.

Gambling was fun for plenty of people. Funhouse gambling was fun for all those people and plenty more people besides. Betting on contests of power and speed between and among monsters combined spectacle with gambling.

"Funhouse Trust, Mr. Cohon." Sweet Juju announced our first stop as she swung the limo off the Parkway and down an underground ramp into a gated drive-through monitored by a mini-gun-equipped security 'bot.

As the gate rolled up into the ceiling to admit us, Ya Ya disentangled himself, tugged his tux pants back on. Then he buzzed down the side window and leaned out. From the drive-through window a big-eyed girl in a low-cut gold lamé jumpsuit leaned out and pipped Ya Ya with a handheld retinal.

Ya Ya's withdrawal came back in seconds. It arrived as crisp bills tightly wrapped by a gold lamé band that matched the teller's jumpsuit. I thought that was good customer service. It was such a large packet that it required her to lean *way* out of the window in order to hand it to Ya Ya. From where I was sitting, I thought that was extraordinary customer service.

So far this trip, every customer-service job on Funhouse was held down by a seductress. It made me wonder who shoveled up behind the titanopods.

Ya Ya tore the gold band from his bills, peeled off a handful for each of the hostesses, then folded the rest and stuffed the wad down his pants.

Three minutes later, we stopped briefly beneath the portico of the Funhouse Grand Luxoriana, waited while our hostesses slithered into gowns, then we dropped the pair of them off at the hotel.

The one who had stuck her hand down my shirt spun a disc-shaped, pink business card into my lap. Then she said, "Remember. For the duration," blew me a kiss, and disappeared.

I held the card under my nose. It smelled of cut lemons and jasmine. As the limo pulled back out onto the Parkway, I turned the card round between my fingers while I looked out the window. Then I folded the card and stuffed it as far down into the limo's side door pocket as Ya Ya had stuffed his tip money down his pants.

I muttered, "I'm either the smartest man in the universe or the dumbest."

Ya Ya frowned across the compartment. "What you said?"

"Nothing."

The discarded gold cash wrapper at my feet read "Funhouse Trust." FT was the biggest numbered-account bank on Funhouse, but far from the only one. Big gamblers needed big money, needed it fast and needed it quietly. In fact, only Rand hosted more, and more discreet, numbered-account banks.

In addition to petty cash accounts in various locations, Spook Central maintained a numbered account that Kit and I utilized in the field to collect pay and allowances. However, our main account was on Rand, rather than on Funhouse. Not because Rand's banks were more numerous and more discreet, but because Funhouse banks charged higher administrative fees to their high-rolling depositors than the pucker-butt yodelers on Rand charged to theirs. And when it came to admin costs, Howard Hibble threw coins around like hatch covers.

Ya Ya waddled forward, hitching up his pants while easily standing straight in the rear compartment, until he stood alongside me. Then he tapped the sliding panel that separated us from Juju.

She slid the panel open, and spoke back over her shoulder. "Another stop, Mr. Cohon?"

"Usual. Drive good, Juju."

Ya Ya waddled back to his seat, screwed his butt down into the cushions like he was a human lag bolt, then cinched his seat belt tight and pointed at my dangling seat belt.

The shrinks said that risk-averse personalities, like they said that I was, compensate by developing faux-risky fetishes. One of mine was that I forgot my seat belt most of the time.

A heartbeat after I tightened my belt, the limo broke right like a Scorpion dodging a heat seeker and roared down an unpaved trail that led away from the Parkway at a pace that no run-of-the-planet electric could match.

Ten minutes of road ping pong later, the limo rolled to a stop in the middle of forested nowhere.

Juju spoke back through the still-open bulkhead slider. "Clean, Mr. C."

Ya Ya nodded, then undid his seatbelt and stuck his hand farther down his pants than he had when he stashed his tip money. A lot farther. When his hand came out, it clutched a white, non-metallic capsule the size of a Trueborn dill pickle, sheathed in an old-fashioned birth control latex.

No wonder Ya Ya had paid to travel first class, where body cavities weren't searched.

Ya Ya opened the car door, peered up and down the road, then listened to silence broken only by the limo's gasoline engine and brakes, crackling as they cooled.

Finally, he hopped out and walked to a tree that had a lower limb snapped, but still hanging. He held his nose, searched around until he found a stick on the ground, then used the stick to pry up and lift something that at first resembled a discarded toupee, but turned out to be a dead local rodent. Very dead.

Ya Ya poked the cylinder into the ground like a tent stake, stomped it flush with the surface, then dropped the carcass back on top of it. He broke the hanging limb completely off the tree, then backed away, hands to the ground like a lazy Tassini praying half-ass, and stirred fallen leaves across his tracks until he reached the car.

As soon as he closed the door behind himself and plopped into his seat, Juju accelerated away without a word.

Dead drops had been staple ways to pass tangible objects probably as long as there had been spies and smugglers. They were still used because, when done right, they worked.

The literal "dead" drop variant that Ya Ya had just employed, using a rotten carcass both as an identifying lid and to discourage random discovery by passersby, had been popular with the old Soviet Union's agents during the first Cold War. If the passed objects were small, like microfilm canisters, they were sometimes actually sewn into the carcasses.

As with most techniques, how well it worked depended on local conditions and timing, and actually it was a pretty lousy variant. In tidy urban neighborhoods, the technique stunk, not only literally but figuratively, because of conscientious concierges and diligent street cleaners. In ghetto neighborhoods, dead rats were viewed as windfalls, too often hauled home and boiled down for dinner. Ditto in natural areas like this one, where a carcass left too long would be dragged away or consumed by scavengers.

So I figured that Ya Ya, who had signaled that this drop needed to be serviced by breaking the hanging tree limb off, expected it would be serviced soon. "Serviced" meant Ya Ya's dropped package would be picked up, probably within minutes or hours.

The limo meandered along, working us back to increasingly trafficked roads.

But a hundred yards before we reached the intersection that would put us back on Lucky U Parkway, the limo pulled over again down a dirt track walled by thick woods.

Ya Ya stared at me as I faced him from the jump seat, then narrowed his eye. "What you just see back there?"

I returned his stare without blinking. "Back where?"

He eyed me, craned his neck, frowned. Then he smiled. "You this Orion's boy, okay."

"Just like that, you trust me?"

"I watch your eyes. Gamblers watch eyes. Eyes tell Ya Ya whole story. Syrene trust you, too. Syrene don't lie to Ya Ya."

"But what if my eyes had told you the wrong story?'

Ya Ya pointed forward at the open slider. "Sweet Juju blow your brains onto headliner with suppressed nine millimeter."

"Oh." Hair rose on the back of my neck and I swallowed. "That would make a mess."

Ya Ya shrugged. "Headliner replacement cheap."

Juju's voice drifted back through the open slider. "Very cheap. Mr. C's bought me four new interiors in the last two years."

Ya Ya stretched, yawned, and swung his feet up onto the back seat. Then he crossed his arms, closed his eyes, and within three minutes was snoring.

The limo rolled on down the Parkway toward our final destination, and I stared out at the pretty landscape.

What object that was small enough to fit up a dwarf's butt was so valuable that Ya Ya Cohon, who employed half the smugglers in the universe, muled it himself? And was so critical that the only witness to its passing had been subjected to one last pass-or-die test?

I swallowed.

And, most important, had what I just experienced really been the last test?

Through the still-open slider, I heard Juju humming as she drove, her fingers tapping the steering wheel in time.

It sounded like a lullaby, but it didn't put me to sleep.

TWENTY-FOUR

Funhouse's suns had sunk into twilight when Juju's limo bore Ya Ya and me onto the grounds of the Funhouse Sporting Club. FSC's high-rise hotel, spa, villas and casino consistently earned five stars, but the complex's signature attraction, indeed, all of Funhouse's signature attraction, was the Coliseum at the complex's center.

FSC Coliseum's light banks glowed against the darkening sky, already shining down from the Coliseum's roof to light its interior, as we pulled in. Juju dodged traffic and dropped us just feet in front of the light-studded, transparent express elevator that carried high rollers like Ya Ya up the Coliseum's outer wall to the sports book and lounge that necklaced the Coliseum's top level.

When Ya Ya stepped out of the limo, nap or not, he looked the worse for wear. Juju, standing smiling and perky alongside the limo's rear door, held out to us a little silver tray, waist-high on her, at eye level for Ya Ya. It was the kind of tray limo drivers often extend both to offer good-bye breath mints and to supply a landing pad for tips.

Juju's tray, however, was sprinkled not with breath mints, but with red rockets that probably had a street value equal to the last expense reimbursement report Howard had signed for me. Industrial-strength uppers seemed like overkill on a world where people got stoked just by breathing.

I had no intention of ingesting anything from a tray held by Juju, in case her hidden talents extended beyond hit chauffeurette to poisoner with a great ass.

Ya Ya, however, raked off half of her rockets, gulped them, then left Juju a tip that moved her to bend forward and kiss the top of his scruffy head.

Three minutes later, when we stepped off the glass elevator into the sports book, Ya Ya's red rockets had kicked in, and he was bouncing off the walls again. The book was a smoky, chandeliered, two-story crescent, with floor-to-ceiling windows that looked down into the Coliseum on one side while the opposite curve was a wall of massive, blue-glowing flat screens.

With the evening's undercard barely started, the book was already awash in high rollers, walk-into-a-pole-gorgeous escorts, and cocktail waiters and waitresses wearing neat black vests.

The book was also thick with Funhouse Gaming Authority regents wearing gray suits and frowns. People who played Funhouse's games understood that the house always won. But Funhouse's government cracked heads to insure that the house didn't win too big, and neither did any individual cheater. Not because fair gaming was the right thing to do, but because if gamblers thought Funhouse was rigged, the whole place could shrivel back into just another backwater planet with pretty flowers.

Ya Ya squinted his eye at the great blue screens, where the pari-mutuel totalisator numbers fluttered and winked as bettors within the Coliseum and at locations all across Funhouse placed bets and thereby shifted the odds. "Big night. Very big."

I'm neither a gambler nor a xenoeconomist, but if I was reading the numbers right, the planetary handle, the total value wagered across Funhouse, on tonight's main event already exceeded the Gross Planetary Product of some of the less populous outworlds. And the night was young.

"Mr. Cohon!" A guy in a chestnut-brown tux and string tie, a silver cup on a chain dangling from his neck, waggled up to Ya Ya, cradling a flat leather book in the crook of his arm. He waved his free arm at a seating area of five stepped tiers of tables that faced the windows, indicating the third tier down from the top. "Usual table?"

Ya Ya shook his head, pointed to the top tier, which was set with only a single table in front of a gilded burgundy velvet banquette. "That one, tonight, Harry."

Harry's mouth fell into a small "O," the size and shape of a persimmon. Then he grinned down at Ya Ya. "So *you're* the one!" Harry rolled his eyes to the ceiling. "An honor for *moi* to serve you."

Ya Ya looked down at the floor, smiling like the gnome who swallowed the canary, and nodded.

Once Harry seated us at the pinnacle table, Ya Ya looked over Harry's leather book, pointed at a line on a page, and Harry bustled away. I glanced around the room from our perch and was surprised to see how many people, who looked like they were rarely impressed by anyone not them, gawked at us. I said to Ya Ya, "Wow!"

"Big wow."

Knowing I would be laying over on Funhouse, I had read up on high-end gaming during *Iwo Jima*'s line-of-sight run up to her first jump, while I was down in steerage nursing my dignity after being body-cavity searched.

Most high-roller gamblers prefer to win and lose in anonymity. But some (to choose a purely hypothetical example, gangster trolls with serious adequacy issues) glory in the limelight. The exhibitionist high rollers show up at casinos and sports books to visibly gamble big money on the turn of a card or a hoof. They love to display daring and nerves of steel that make strong men gasp and weak women swoon.

The most envied, highest-rolling sports book in the known universe was this one atop Funhouse Sporting Club Coliseum. And within this book the highest of the rollers did their showing off pursuant to highly structured etiquette.

If your idea of a big night at the tables or the races was to risk a few thousand, you'd get better gawk mileage from the crowd in some pissant casino. But a bettor who had wagered, either on premises or in advance online, a five-figure total could claim a table to see the evening's contests here at FSC's book on tier one. Six figures, tier two, and so on.

They say a hundred million's not the pile it used to be, but if you wagered one hundred million or more on a single night's events, you could plant your butt publicly in the seat at the pinnacle, if you chose. Of course, that exposed you to losing your butt publicly, too.

I stared at Ya Ya, my mouth open. "You spread a hundred million around on a single night's events?"

"No."

"Then why are we—?"

"Whole bazoomba on main event."

Before I could close my mouth, Harry the sommelier returned with a bottle, displayed it to Ya Ya, uncorked, tasted with his little silver cup, and decanted the wine without drifting a grain of sediment up the neck. Say what you will, Harry knew how to handle wine. Take it from *moi.*

At that moment a party of four got seated two tiers down, in the six-figure cheap seats. They initiated a worshipful discussion with Ya Ya, tonight's king of high rolling. The attention swelled him up like a balloon that needed a shave. But the level of detail concerning the merits of the upcoming bout and the odds soon underwhelmed me.

I slipped away cradling a glass of Harry's finest, which proved in fact to be a Trueborn first-growth Bordeaux, with a texture and nose that knocked my saloon-keeper socks off. They say a wine's first duty is to be red, and its second is to be a Bordeaux, and over the years and the planets, I'd come to agree.

I doubted that I could ever be comfortable with high rolling, but I wished that Kit could have been here with me to share this moment of gawking at how the other half lived. Until I realized that she *was* the other half. She had probably spent spring breaks in places like this on Edwin's coin, with her poison-ivy-league friends, who, if they were here now, would be sniggering at the uncultured rube what brung her. Regardless of how much he had taught himself about Bordeaux and about life.

I stepped out past the glass windows into the open, now dark, night air, and looked down into the Coliseum.

Funhouse Sporting Club Coliseum seated fifty thousand spectators in a single-purpose, circular amphitheater with steep sides that gave it the proportions of a bucket, rather than a bowl like a Trueborn football stadium. The seats that tiled the bucket's sides were upholstered in arterial blood red. The bucket's bottom was not solid, but the one-hundred-yard-diameter circular surface of a tank of gin-clear salt water that continued down to a depth of four hundred feet, and glistened beneath the Coliseum lights in a turquoise shade like a Trueborn's backyard pool.

Already, only a spatter of red marked empty seats, and crowd buzz echoed up off the still and empty water.

Although the water was still and empty, the crowd was hardly unentertained.

In the open air above the tank the biggest and brightest jumbholo in the Human Union projected other contests live from venues across Funhouse.

The current feed was full-contact titanopod racing from an affiliated track I had glimpsed from the limo, thirty miles from this Coliseum. The image and sound were first-class. It was as though the race was really going on below me.

Full-C T'pods don't resemble the docile grazers I had glimpsed from the limo earlier. As I watched, two titan stallions, one black with crimson armor, one palomino with blue, broke ahead of a pack of six and thundered down the home stretch. Two jockeys rocked side by side atop the rolling shoulders of each titan, clutching its reins. All four of the forward jocks fought to keep their respective mounts focused on the finish line as the neck-and-neck beasts crashed shoulders, staggered apart then crashed again. Each titan dipped his great head as he galloped, fighting to gore the other with the spikes studding his headpiece and shoulder plates. Each animal already bled down its flanks and legs, and blood spray spattered all the jocks in crimson, from boots to helmets. White saliva foamed from each titan's bridled muzzle.

Crowd roar welled up loud now, and thousands of spectators in the Coliseum stood and shrieked. They were the ones who had suddenly realized that a mount on which they held a ticket was coming home to win, or at the very least to place.

The third jock on each titan was called the croup, because he or she rode atop the titan's upper butt, which on Earth horses was called the croup. For most of the race the croup's job was to apply the whip as necessary to motivate his titan.

At the moment, however, each titan's croup was applying the whip with homicidal vigor not to his mount, but to his opposite number.

Violence was part of the sport, and acrobatic croups good with whip and spiked boots were crowd favorites. The added animal-on-animal and jock-on-jock contact dimensions made conventional horse racing seem flat, according to the Funhouse Gaming Authority.

As I watched, the palomino's croup snatched the tip of his opponent's whip in both hands, and heaved backward like he was in a tug of war.

The black's croup was jerked from his saddle, tumbled twenty-six feet to the track, and, just as he got to his knees, was pummeled into bloody paste as the closely following pack thundered over him.

The crowd fell silent. Well, half of it did. Not because they had witnessed a fellow human's quick and violent death. Mayhem was part of the draw here. But because a titan that came home with fewer than three jocks up was disqualified. The silent fans' sure win or place tickets had become worthless.

The palomino crossed the line, his jocks pumping their fists in triumph, and thousands cheered. The black limped home, bleeding barrels from a shoulder gore. He would be put down. It was, apparently, very exciting. It was also insane.

Thum-thum-thum.

The titanopod race image winked off.

The crowd buzz rose in pitch and volume at the sound of sky crane impellers approaching in the distance. The Coliseum's now-open retractable roof existed not so much to let nice weather enter but to let competitors enter with aerial flair.

The two sky cranes, one carrying the main event's champion and the other the challenger, drew close, then began orbiting the Coliseum just beyond the glow of the lights.

Each contestant dangled beneath one of the sky cranes in a sling, wrapped in a protective hydration jacket studded with flashing colored lights. Gold for the champion, crimson for the challenger. Simultaneously, the crowd clapped and stomped to ancient Trueborn tribal chants about who would rock whom, so loudly that the Coliseum shook.

The look was like what fans saw when advertising aerostats orbited Trueborn football stadiums during games. The objective here, however, was not to peddle beer, but to whip up the crowd and increase the handle, and it was working so well that I was getting a headache.

I went back inside and sat beside Ya Ya.

"Which one did you bet the farm on, Ya Ya?"

"Underdog."

I turned and eyed the tote board. At the moment, the challenger's odds were one hundred twelve to one against. "Yikes! Is it smart to bet the 'dog?"

Ya Ya shrugged. "No money made playing favorites. I was you, I bet everything you got in world on the 'dog."

I shook my head. The only things I had left in the world were my hope of seeing Orion again and my hope of patching it up with Kit, and the odds of either were too slim to buy me a ticket. Besides, I had already tried betting everything on the 'dog on Funhouse once.

During my previous, long-ago layover on Funhouse, four of us skinheads went to The Bugs, because they were Funhouse's cheapest pari-mutuel alternative. We bet everything we had on the underdog, because we were advised that there was no money to be made playing favorites. We adopted this strategy because we needed to win big, so we could afford to get properly laid. A handjob didn't last long.

Fun facts from the stand-up card for beginners that was on our table that day: Bugs breathe through openings like portholes down the sides of their exoskeletons, which is inefficient, so air with a higher oxygen content benefits bugs even more than it benefits higher animals. Earth's fossil dragonflies breathed air with nearly double the oxygen concentration of today's Earth air, and grew bigger than carrier pigeons. What does that have to do with going to The Bugs?

Funhouse's scorpions and spiders didn't just grow bigger than Earth scorpions and spiders, they grew as big as Earth crocodiles and grizzly bears. The Bugs were also lightning fast, and tactically more sophisticated than one expected when they faced off against one another in a cage and fought to the death.

Here's a tip, though: It says on the how-to-bet-for-beginners card that tiger-stripe scorpions *can* go to their left. But if you bet on that you will never get laid.

"Ladeeez and gentlemen!"

The lights in the sports book dimmed, the Coliseum lights shrank to a pencil spot that shone down onto the center of the circular tank's surface.

The crowd roared, and a tuxedoed announcer slid into the spotlight, standing on a doughnut skimmer platform that wobbled ten feet above the water. He clutched the skimmer's grab yoke with one hand and grasped a microphone in the other.

Quiet.

"Tonight, for the unlimited fighting championship of the universe, an unrestricted battle to the death with a sixty-minute time limit." The announcer paused until the echoes of his voice died.

The crowd roared, but in reality the announcer was promising more entertainment than one of these actually delivered. Funhouse death matches were spectacular, but seldom lasted longer than a hand job.

He pointed up and out, at the circling red lights. "In the scarlet livery, from Bren, weighing in at one hundred ninety-eight thousand Trueborn pounds, and measuring ninety-seven feet nose to tail, the challenger—"

Another roar.

The sky crane thrummed in above the Coliseum's far parapet as the lights came back up.

"Cronus the rhind!"

Bren's fauna paralleled Earth's, but retarded back to the Cretaceous period. Except for Bren's human population, including Syrene's Marini, which was introduced there thirty thousand years ago by the Slugs.

Rhinds essentially paralleled Earth's extinct short-necked pliosaurs. Pliosaurs were air-breathing reptiles that resembled whale-sized crocodiles but with flippers replacing their legs. Pliosaurs were so agile, powerful and quick that they literally ate Cretaceous great white sharks for breakfast. Bren's rhinds grew to more than twice the size of Earth pliosaurs.

Cronus the rhind had been captured on Bren and shipped to Funhouse as a fellow passenger with Ya Ya and me aboard *Iwo Jima*. Cruisers actually landed on Funhouse precisely so captured monsters from all over the universe, like Cronus, could be delivered to Funhouse in fighting trim. On Funhouse, they would eventually kill or be killed by other monsters, so that humans could have less boring vacations. If full contact titanopod racing was insane, kidnapping and killing other species for sport seemed criminally insane.

Many humans found a starship trip relaxing, but Cronus' voyage had not mellowed him. As he dangled above the Coliseum's lip in his sling, like a hundred-foot-long, black stadium hot dog writhing in a crimson bun, a flagpole on the Coliseum's canopy came within range of his jaws.

The pole was plasteel as thick as a man's waist, but Cronus snapped it like a chopstick, then spit it back onto the canopy. Spectators cringed and retreated from seats below the severed pole.

I turned and glanced at the tote board to see what the late money did. Cronus' bad-ass display had narrowed the odds against him to ninety-two to one.

As Cronus' sky crane settled him toward the vast water tank's surface, his thrashing caused him to rock like a pendulum in his sling, so that the rear third of his length swung above the lowest fifteen rows.

Cronus chose that instant to relieve himself, a deluge that would have filled the average Trueborn backyard pool, and it inundated the spectators in the lowest fifteen rows.

These incidents taught me two things.

First, the lowest fifteen rows were the cheapest seats in the house for good reason.

Second, differences of opinion between bettors are what make gaming fascinating. Cronus' latest behavior caused even more late bets to, uh, flood in. But the odds scarcely changed. That was because as many bettors thought Cronus would fight better lighter as thought he was so scared to fight that he had peed himself.

As soon as Cronus had been released into the tank, he undulated around it in confident circles like the supreme predator he was.

Meanwhile, the introduction ritual was repeated for Cronus' opponent, who drew even bigger roars because she was so heavily favored.

"—undefeated champion of the universe, weighing in at four hundred six thousand Trueborn pounds, and measuring one hundred forty-six feet nose to tail, She of the Thousand Arms, Funhouse's own favorite daughter, Leeeviaa-athan!"

Leviathan had done this before, eleven times, in fact, according to her official bio. So she dangled aloof as her sky crane lowered her. Her given name was also her species' common name. Leviathans were aquatic air breathers native to Funhouse. They resembled the translucent gray love children of needle-toothed, gelatinous anacondas bred with four-eyed millipedes.

As Leviathan dangled with her thousand wormy prehensile arms twitching scant feet above the tank, the jumbholo flickered back to life. The feed showed Cronus' belly and flippers from below, as he paddled slowly back and forth, thumping his tail against the tank wall every few seconds.

No fewer than twelve 'bots, both submarine and flying, would feed every detail of the fight not only to the crowd here but to a pay-per-view audience.

I glanced at Ya Ya, who sat smiling and seemingly unconcerned, though his rookie was outweighed two-to-one, out-reached by fifty feet, and out-armed by one thousand.

When the gong sounded, and Leviathan belly-flopped into the tank like a launched cruise ship, I checked the tote. The alien animal on which Ya Ya Cohon appeared to have risked everything he had went off as a one-hundred-four-to-one underdog.

They say you have to have skin in a game to care, but even though I personally didn't stand to lose or win so much as a cup of coffee, my heart hammered. It had just occurred to me that if Ya Ya lost his whole bazoomba in the next few minutes, and couldn't make any remaining payoffs he might owe on my behalf, my path to Yavet and to Orion could be blocked.

TWENTY-FIVE

Leviathan circled the tank along the wall at the surface, pushing white water ahead of her as though she had a bone between her teeth. Out in the tank's center, Cronus jumped completely clear of the surface, arcing through the air like a black rainbow and sucking a collective gasp out of the crowd. When he plunged back, his momentum torpedoed him to the tank floor.

The bottom-mounted 'bot cam showed Cronus' quick reversal. Then he rocketed up through four hundred feet, toward the target silhouetted against the water's surface. Cronus' snout struck Leviathan's lower midsection with a force that, if one did the math, probably equaled that generated by an old-fashioned runaway railroad locomotive.

Again the crowd gasped.

Ya Ya glanced at me, pumped his fist, and grinned.

But Leviathan just kept swimming, her arms churning the tank water to foam. The bottom cam showed she was leaking the yellow circulating fluid that functioned like a leviathan's blood, but in unsubstantial quantity. More a razor nick than a fatal gore.

Cronus repeated his maneuver three more times, with similarly ineffectual results. Then he meandered at the surface, seemingly either exhausted, bewildered or both.

The crowd's small pro-Cronus faction had cheered his furious beginning, but now fizzled. Leviathan had given her fans nothing to cheer about so they fizzled, too.

As the two competitors circled, some in the crowd stamped feet, whistled for action. Leviathan seemed to swim slower, the foam churned by her arms less frothy, as if her puny challenger bored her.

Even apart from my self-interest stoked by Ya Ya's wager, I found myself pulling for sleek, acrobatic Cronus against butt-ugly do-nothing Leviathan. No style points were on offer, but if there had been, Cronus would have been running away with the bout.

Suddenly, Cronus spun and drove at Leviathan. He had no room to build speed, and his resultant head butt into Leviathan's flank seemed like a mere tap.

But Leviathan thrashed once, floated inanimate for an instant, then sank like four hundred six thousand pounds of mush in a one-hundred-forty-six-foot-long sock.

The crowd outside in the arena and up here in the book went still.

After thirty seconds, Leviathan settled onto the tank's floor in a loose, lifeless coil, her condition flashed on the jumbholo from four angles. She of The One Thousand Arms didn't claw for the ropes with even one of them.

Leviathan was down for the count. Cronus seemed to sense it, tail-walked across the surface, then dove down four hundred feet. He clamped down, shook his great head and tore a limousine-sized chunk from the former champion's flank. The wound in Leviathan's carcass bled clouds of yellow slime into the crystalline tank water.

Ya Ya was the first inside the book to find his voice. He sprang to his feet alongside me, hopping foot to foot in a jig, fists punching the air in counterpoint. "Oh yeah! Oh yeah!"

Down in the arena bucket, one in one hundred bettors joined Ya Ya's celebration. Others grumbled, booed or headed for the exits.

Up here in the book, bettors mobbed my table mate, pounding his back. Ya Ya Cohon had arguably broken the promise I had heard him make earlier today to "win many bets," because he had won just one. However, that was mere semantics. One hundred million may not have been the number it used to be, but one hundred million times one hundred four was an uncountably large number on any day.

The celebration flowed and ebbed for perhaps three minutes before I heard the first shout.

"Fix!"

I shook my head, smirked. There were sore losers in any crowd.

Then I looked round the book from our perch on top of the gambling world and noticed a knot of gray-suited Gaming Authority regents huddled together beneath the blue totalisator wall. Moment to moment, one of the regents, then another, would glance our way.

I muttered to myself, "Crap."

Not all Howard's flag-waving nerds spent their time trying to weaponize telepathic, pyrophobic, eleven-ton grizzly bears. Oh no. Some of them fabricated weapons almost as odd but far more attainable. Like micro-bore, neurotoxin-packed sniping bullets, fabricated from an organic ceramic, that hit no harder than bee stings, then dissolved slowly and left scant trace of bullet or poison in the target's body. The shooter could be miles away before the target abruptly dropped dead. Kit and I had never actually popped anybody with one, but we had trained with them for some jobs.

The universe was full of nerds who, unlike Howard's nerds, would fabricate anything, not for a flag, but for a price. The discreet way to have such a suspiciously single-purpose round fabricated, that was right-sized and right-juiced to kill an alien monster, would be to commission the work far from where the round would be used, then smuggle it in.

A monster-stopper round would have to be bigger than the bee stinger that could kill a person, perhaps as big as a dill pickle. And so it would have to be fired from some kind of elephant gun. But there would be no need to smuggle an elephant gun in. They had to be easily obtained on a planet where the scorpions grew as big as crocodiles.

As for hitting a hundred-forty-six foot-long target in her ass while she swung spotlit up in the dark, a few hundred feet above a million secure hides, for twenty minutes? That would be a piece of cake for some anonymous journeyman sniper, who would never even see, much less be able to identify, the one-eyed gnome who hired him. Which one-eyed gnome wouldn't have trusted just any normal mule to smuggle in the disappearing poison bullet.

Four gray-suited Gaming Authority regents muscled through Ya Ya's well-wishers.

The lead gray suit said to Ya Ya, "Mr. Cohon? Could we have a private word with you," the regent nodded at me, "and your partner?"

Partner? *Moi*?

Two hours later I paced from one end to the other of the main room in a lavishly appointed suite in the Funhouse Sporting Club's hotel tower. Ya Ya and I weren't technically under arrest. The Gaming Authority just wouldn't let us leave the room. And so, by extension, the planet.

On Yavet, if you were a peep with a starving mother, caught in the upper levels and suspected of stealing a bean bar, cops in body armor kicked the shit out of you with chain-mail boots. On Funhouse, if you were a high roller suspected of stealing ten billion and killing the universe's most valuable broodmare as collateral damage, cops in gray suits gave you a fruit basket.

Ya Ya sat on the sofa, feet up and the basket in his lap, and peeled an apple with a gold knife. "Sit. You make Ya Ya nervous."

"I can't sit. Ya Ya make *me* nervous."

Ya Ya waved up the suite's music 'bot, crooked a finger so that I came close, then he whispered, "Is perfect plan. Today regents mad at Ya Ya suspected fixer. Tomorrow is no evidence. So big hypocrite regents say, look! Poor one-eye dwarf win big in Funhouse on up and up, so why not you? Book trip now!" Ya Ya balled his fingers into fists, then pantomimed scrubbing tears from his eye and eye patch with them. "Warm heart story make you cry from happy." He dropped his fists into his lap, shrugged. "Couple days, you and me walk."

I spread my hands, palms out and pleading. "Ya Ya, *Iwo Jima* upships tomorrow. A couple days is too late for me. Why did you get me into this?"

"Ya Ya no get you into this, you do. Plan is plan before you come. Little mother dying. Very sad. I make you most first-class price."

"Yeah, okay. That's fair. Thanks. But you didn't have to drag me along into *this* mess."

He tongued an apple slice off his knife blade, shrugged. "No mess. I do boy of little mother big favor. Bet the 'dog, Ya Ya say. Boy not listen."

I ran my fingers through my hair, sighed. "I'm sorry. That was very thoughtful. But I didn't come on this trip to get rich. I came to get to Yavet. Quietly."

He set his knife and apple down. "Okay. Tell you what is. I call local mouthpiece. You upship with no skin on teeth, maybe. But you upship. Not cheap for Ya Ya, but I make you most first-class price."

At "mouthpiece," my heart had leapt. Then it sank. "Ya Ya, I don't have that kind of money left to pay you."

"I say most first-class price, not money." He smiled. "You kiss little mother for Ya Ya. Promise?"

I nodded, and my eyes got moist. "Promise."

In fact, after considerable negotiation with the gray suits, which negotiation on my behalf may have haircut Ya Ya's eventual payday by a hundred million, Ya Ya's local mouthpiece himself dropped me off at *Iwo Jima*'s gangway ten minutes before it was pulled in.

So I upped ship aboard *Iwo Jima* an hour later with plenty of skin on my teeth.

Maybe it's true that great lying, scheming minds think alike. It was actually a favorite expression of Howard Hibble's that his people sometimes made it by the skins of their teeth, but he believed they would always make it.

Whatever else Ya Ya Cohon had done in his life, he had done the right thing by me. I hoped he would always make it, too.

As things turned out, *Yorktown* was running just two days behind *Iwo Jima*. So if I *had* missed *Iwo* I simply would have transferred my ticket and used it to board *Yorktown* when Ya Ya and I walked, the promised couple days later. There's really not much aboard one starship that isn't aboard another. It probably wouldn't have changed a thing.

TWENTY-SIX

The moment when Mort remembered that he needed to reconnect with Kit Born's consciousness was shortly after he had left behind the remarkable and all-consuming distraction of mating. So obsessed had he become that he had scarcely eaten, an error he now sought to remedy.

Mort was ambling along a riverbank that had frequently come within his territory during his youth. The skies were, as always, reassuringly cloudy, he felt his cousins everywhere, and the scents and intellects of prey drifted nearby in abundance. The river was a safe day's travel removed from the nest of humans with whom grezzenkind deigned to share their world, and from the fields of homing mines, deadly even to grezzen, behind which the humans hid.

When he found Kit, he realized from what he saw through her eyes that Kit rode within the belly of a moving nest like the Gateway, *which had borne him home. In fact, she rode within the nest called* Yorktown, *the nest he had stumbled upon when searching for Jazen at that time that now seemed so long ago. At the moment, Kit appeared to be within a pyramidal space within the* Yorktown *smaller than, but otherwise similar to, the quarters he had inhabited aboard the* Gateway, *called a "bay."*

"Mort? Izzat you?" Mort felt Kit's thoughts, and heard her elation as she spoke them aloud when she felt him return to her mind. Her audibilized words were slurred by a salty liquid she was drinking.

*As he saw through her eyes, she unconsciously read markings on a hatch in front of her, “*HUS Yorktown, *Bay 6, No civilian access.”*

“Kit! Yes, it is me.” He pronked, springing vertically from all six legs simultaneously.

He repeated the behavior three times, then thought, “I apologize for my delay in reestablishing contact. I was distracted.”

“No problem. Your mating’s over, then?”

“Yes. As Jazen predicted, I did not quit until she screwed my brains out.”

He felt Kit panic, like a drowning woog, then heard a snort and a splashing noise. “What is wrong?”

“S’okay. You just made me honk a quart of hydration fluid out my nose.”

“Oh.”

Kit spoke. “Well? How did it go? Was she hot? I want details.”

“The female was—is—in excellent health. Strong, with a wide pelvis.”

“Did you knock her up?”

Mort paused and drew himself up onto his back two, to denote affront. Then he realized that the learned physical gesture was meaningless, when performed out of the sight of humans. “It was vigorous contact, but non-violent.”

“What I mean is, is there a little Mort in the oven?”

“Ah.” He nodded, despite her absence. “Yes. My potency is incomparable.”

She paused, then thought, “Mort? If you try to date again? Don’t use that for your pickup line.”

“I do not understand.”

“Men never do.” Kit paused again. “Seriously, what a stud! Congratulations.”

As she walked toward a glistening black object in the chamber’s center, Kit sipped liquid from a pouch. The object resembled a melon seed with an upturned stem curving from its tapered rear end. The seed hovered above the deck plates, quivering, like a sapsucker at a blossom, but the melon seed was longer than he was. Three humans covered in red integument bustled around the object with apparent but incomprehensible urgency.

“Kit, what is that?”

She reached the seed, then crouched and crawled beneath it, eyes on the thing's underside. As she crawled, she touched and prodded the thing's belly, which was warm, vibrant, and metallic. "Scorpion-T. Four-place special operations variant of a Scorpion fighter."

"A shell in which humans fly? It does not look like a tilt-wing."

"A Scorpion's no tilt-wing, Mort."

One of the red-clad humans held out a leaf to her.

She examined the leaf's surface, nodded, then pressed one of her foreclaw digits to one of the leaf's corners. "If you saw the number I just thumbed for, you'd know that. If I bend it, I'll be working for free 'til I die. This thing doesn't just fly. It flies in space. Like a starship, but more maneuverable."

"You are about to fly it? Where?"

*"*Yorktown*'s just come out of her last jump. She's inbound through line-of-sight normal space toward an on-time arrival at Ring Station above Yavet. So you got back to me just in time."*

"Yavet? I advised you and Howard that Jazen was attempting to reach Yavet."

Another of the red-clad humans laid a metallic lattice against the Scorpion's flank, and the seed split, its dorsal side opening like a jaw.

"And a good thing you did. Jazen's a stealthy little rascal when he tries. You'd think he grew up an urchin sneaking around through sewers on his belly just to eat. I can't be sure it was him, but somebody left a mess behind on Funhouse. My guess is Jazen's inbound right now on the cruiser just ahead of this one." Kit clambered up the lattice, and slid inside the seed's mouth.

Mort paused where the river shallowed as it roiled among flat rocks. Tasty reptilians abounded beneath the stones, but so did venomous snakes too stupid for him to easily detect. After his long absence from home, the prospect made him vaguely apprehensive. "I sense from you that you are apprehensive for Jazen's safety. And for your own."

He probed, unsuccessfully. "And something else troubles you greatly."

The black seed closed its mouth and sealed Kit inside where she squirmed in darkness. Then a sparkle of lights illuminated the small space that surrounded her. Some flickered red, some yellow, then all winked and shone steadily green.

*She spoke aloud as she fastened flat vines around her torso. "*Yorktown *offload control, this is bay six occupant. Do you copy?"*

After a pause a voice reached her ears. "Uh. Bay six, this is Yorktown *offload control. We copy. Colonel Born? Ma'am, I hear you've had the ship prepped? And you're aboard?"*

"Locked and loaded, Eddie. Wall to wall green in here. She's good to go."

There was another pause, during which Mort heard through Kit's ears her command, "Forward canopy to max visual."

A whir like a skim bug's mating call filled Kit's ears as a wide slit opened, splitting the green lights above and below, so that Kit saw out into the ship's bay. The three red-clad humans were now visible behind a transparent screen, peering out at her. "Bay is clear, offload control. Depressurize and open outer doors."

"Colonel Born, you're not the first spook we've been asked to insert. And I'm sure you're very good at what you do. But we were told your bird would drop four days out."

"I hate getting stuck in traffic, Eddie."

"Colonel, even at a Scorpion-T's best economic speed you're seven standard days out from Yavet now. That ship's life support's max rated for four days."

"That's with two crew. I'll take shallow breaths."

"Ma'am—"

"The Yavi know a Scorpion's published range as well as you do. By the time Yorktown*'s four days out, you'll have a Yavi fighter escort the size of the Spanish Armada keeping you within visual range. And they'll know the difference between a Scorpion and those smuggler's barges this cruiser will be crapping like turds."*

The voice chuckled. "Colonel, the Captains would be shocked—shocked!—to learn smuggling was going on aboard this ship."

"Exactly. If you don't open bay six's doors within two minutes, the captains and I will be having a conversation that will be more uncomfortable for them than for me. Especially when I get back to Washington. Call 'em. I'll wait."

There was silence, broken by Kit whistling softly. Then Mort heard a great roaring hiss somewhere beyond the seed, like a gale through treetops.

The disembodied voice called Eddie muttered, "Fucking spooks."

Moments later the view before Kit changed. The bay's doors yawned like a vast mouth, and revealed blackness punctuated by tiny lights.

Mort felt a metal bit, cool against Kit's foreclaw as she rotated it forward. She said, "Yee-ha."

Then the bay was gone and blackness surrounded the seed. There was no sensation of motion, except as betrayed by Kit's elevated heart rate and respiration, which indicated to him that the seed was now traveling very fast indeed.

Mort resumed his amble along the riverbank. "Now what, Kit?"

"Now I set the autopilot to keep hauling ass 'til I'm a hundred thousand miles wide left of Yorktown's *inbound track. Then this ship will turn itself to Yavet, and make an ecliptic approach to the planetary vicinity, just like a million boring little rocks do every day to a million other boring planets."*

"What happens when you reach the vicinity?"

"Plenty, if you do your job between now and then."

"My job?"

"Mort, I still need you to find Jazen for me. Precisely."

Mort paused with one foreclaw fishing beneath a likely stone. "I cannot."

"You can. Your potency is incomparable, remember?"

Mort flipped a reptilian out onto the bank, where it thrashed until he severed its spine with a claw slash. "The cosmos are too vast."

"Cut down the odds. Like when you hunt. First find Yavet. It shouldn't be hard to cut it out of the herd. It's the most populous planet in the Human Union. There are thirteen billion human intellects in one lump."

"Perhaps that is possible, if I concentrate. But it is one task to search within three thousand migrating woog for the weakest. Quite another to search for a particular intellect within thirteen billion."

"You know Jazen. You said that makes it easier."

"It does. Nonetheless—"

"Attaboy. Get crackin'. Keep this line open and we'll talk again in six days."

"Six days? And what will you *be doing while I am cracking?"*

"As little as possible. Once I dial back the life support, and the sedative I just shot up kicks in, this thing's gonna be one very hot, very stuffy coffin. In six days I will be dehydrated, punchy, and

sweaty as a locker room." She spoke aloud, not to him. "Canopy to max protect."

The eye ahead winked shut, the lights faded, and Kit rested in absolute darkness.

"Kit! A coffin is a shell for dead humans."

"Figure of speech. Nighty-night."

"Kit?"

He felt her heart rate and respiration slow to hibernative levels as her consciousness faded.

Mort located the crook of a boulder in the river, from which point he could both drink from upstream and urinate downstream, and within which he could curl and remain undisturbed for days. Then he harvested a half-dozen of the reptiles, skinned and hung them from a branch a paw swipe away. Then he settled in and began sifting through the vast number of intellects that populated the even vaster emptiness of the universe. The task seemed hopeless. He wondered whether Jazen was even in *this Yavet nest he was looking for.*

TWENTY-SEVEN

I first saw him just after I exited the downshuttle terminal in the midlevels. I was weaving through the midday crowds that thronged Sixty-first and Sylvan, Thirty-two Upper. Until then, I had been enjoying my first moments back within the unfriendly confines of Yavet in general, and my homestack of Yaven in particular, in spite of myself.

I turned in to a kaffee stand that I remembered, bought an extra large, and the bald proprietor smiled and thanked me for the tip.

The last time he saw me, although he didn't realize it, he had been a busboy with greasy hair, I had been thin enough to crawl through a class three utility, and he had run me off for stealing spilled sugar from the floor beneath his tables.

Today I sat at one of his tables, sipped my kaffee with a spoonful of sugar, and thought about Orion, how she had looked then, how I imagined she might look today. And about my parents, who I had never seen with eyes capable of focusing, and how I imagined *they* might look today.

The neighborhood wasn't one I had visited often. It was middle-class, medium-lit, with menial and domestic peeps packing the passages shoulder-to-hip with bigs who lived, or owned retail shops, mixed with the Kubeowners in the neighborhood who they served.

The docs Ya Ya had provided hadn't merely freed me to walk the passages of Yaven as a big for the first time, and to pour sugar into kaffee until it mounded up and overflowed, if I chose, like I had once imagined rich men could.

The bribes Ya Ya had caused to be pre-placed where needed had gotten me from Trueborn cruiser disembarkation to the Ring to the down-shuttle terminal in four hours. The same steps typically took Kit and me six hours when arriving under business or tourist cover on planets with half the security of Yavet. In that area, at least, Ya Ya had delivered most first-class passage.

Immigration and Customs had even waved me through a VIP line that I had all to myself. There, a friendly but incompetent hostess exchanged my jacket for one of those lead-lined anti-radiation robes while she took my jacket and pressed it for me as I cleared customs. I say she was incompetent because she had my coat longer than it usually took to plant the tracking bug every offworlder wasn't supposed to know they were going to be carrying.

Despite my hostess' extra effort, I felt the bug out easily during the ride down from the ring, then at the down-shuttle station I cut it out of my coat pocket's lining and flushed it down a Sanex.

I finished my kaffee, wiped the table clean, then walked on down the passage. I would now begin a whirlwind, unguided search of what had been Orion's favorite hangouts. Surely someone there would remember, and could send me to her. Midwives, like drug dealers and other criminals, moved around a lot to stay a jump ahead of vice, so there would have been no point in her giving me an address even if she thought I was coming.

As I wove through familiar congestion, I frowned.

The big, the one I had seen that had motivated me to stop for kaffee, was still there, which was unpromising. There was no question it was still him. He was my height, so he stood out above the peeps. He wore a medical technician's snug blue cowl headcover. And eyeshades, which were just a bit out of place in medium lighting.

Spies in Indian country learn to notice things that are a bit out of place, or they aren't spies for long. Bug or no bug, I had expected to be tailed, right from the down-shuttle station. That came with being an offworlder, no matter how tight the legend.

My legend was that I was a lighting technology sales representative from Freyen. Freyen was a pre-nuclear seeded world known for making really good incandescent lamp bulbs. Freyen was non-aligned, so the Trueborns permitted nonmilitary commerce between Freyen and Yavet. Freyens were considered as harmless, as utilitarian and as behind the times as their principal export.

As a low-risk, low-interest subject, I had expected my tail would be just a snitch, a little person who "volunteered" to assist Internal Security in order to avoid the living hell of detention.

Orion had been a snitch for years, for a rat bastard vice cop (but I repeat myself) named Polian.

A snitch tail was no worry. First, conscripts in any society rarely did their jobs zealously. Orion, for example, had fed her rat bastard vice cop control officer crap intel whenever she could get away with it. Second, snitches transferred their info only by meeting their control officer, an event so choreographed and infrequent that the tailed subject could be long gone by the time vice learned that they were up to something.

I slowed and window-shopped a store along the corridor.

One of the first urban surveillance and evasion skills a spy is taught is using windows as mirrors for indirect observation.

In the reflection, I saw Headcover bobbing behind me above the crowds like a blue balloon on a long string.

Crap. My heart rate climbed.

Unlike a snitch, a plainclothes regular tail looked like just another civilian big, but was wired. Where little people or offworlders were concerned, a plainclothes tail had the same summary enforcement power as his uniform counterparts, although the tail would never reveal himself by arresting a subject personally.

If something that the tail's subject did appeared suspicious to the tail, the tail just called it in. Then, suddenly, a couple armored uniforms would appear. The something that converted a subject to a suspect usually involved peep-on-big crime, or less often big-on-big. The crimes ran mostly to pocket picking, or less often armed robbery. Peep-on-peep crime was pretty much considered by vice as a benefit to society, because it reduced the peep population at little government expense.

If the plainclothes tail's suspect was lucky, the uniforms would just kick the shit out of him or her. If the suspect was unlucky, he or she was shot to death on the spot. Or, perhaps unluckiest of all, the suspect was hauled downlevels to detention.

I turned to walk on, and looked up the corridor.

Crap again. A two-man uniform foot patrol walked toward me, fifty yards ahead.

Their needlers were reverse slung, their helmet faceplates were up, and they seemed to be paying more attention to their own conversation, and to the little people and the bigs who parted immediately before them, than to anyone ahead of them. But their indifference could be for show.

My heart chattered now, more than beat.

What if Headcover was just driving me toward them like a herded cat?

The gap between me and the two uniforms shrank to twenty yards, then the cop on the right swung his needler up and aimed it my way.

My heart rate whirred, but I just kept walking toward him as though I didn't notice. The bigs around me did the same.

If the cop intended to shoot me, I was dead. If he didn't, I was fine. Rule one of peep street survival on Yavet. Let the other peep take the needles.

Yavi cops carried needle carbines, rather than the gunpowder pistols Trueborn cops carried. All things and all available technologies considered, Yavet's cops had the best equipment for their job, which was killing peeps without breaking the furniture or injuring persons of value, who were by definition bigs.

Quick-draw, Trueborn pistols seem like the ticket for use in urban close quarters, compared to a cumbersome long gun.

But in a genuinely bang-bang, stressed, moving-target tactical environment, a Trueborn cop, or even a Trueborn case officer unless she was Kit Born, couldn't *guarantee* a shot group the size of a fist, or more to the point, the size of a human heart, every time at the distances to targets that Yavi cops dealt with inside a stack city. And no matter how tight or how reproduceable the shot group, gunpowder bullets passed through human tissue and damaged bystanders, or heaven forbid, property, more often than needle rounds. Needle rounds exhausted their kinetic energy and violence within a body, ruining soft tissue and bone with an efficiency Trueborn dum-dum bullets could only dream of, if bullets dreamed.

And repeatable shot group size is less relevant anyway, because even a half-blind Yavi cop rarely needs more than one shot with a needle carbine. A needle carbine's length allows for effective aiming, as well as space to install its active barrel stabilization system, so a needler's basically as point-and-shoot as your 'puter's camera. A single squeeze of a needle carbine's trigger delivered, without recoil, a whirling hornet swarm of tiny razor darts, that expanded to the diameter of a fist at a range of twenty yards. A center-mass chest shot at that range was unsurvivable, period. Just about anywhere else in the torso, the victim bled out in minutes. Beyond fifty yards, however, a needler had the accuracy and stopping power of a water pistol.

Bottom line? Never hunt bear with a needler. Never bother to hunt peep with anything else.

I blinked as the cop's needler flashed blinding blue.

Hsss.

The needle carbine's report echoed simultaneously with a scream, and the touch of a hand on my left sleeve, and I looked down.

The bulging eyes of the gangsta peep who the cop had spotted trying to pick my pocket stared up at me, and the peep's mouth was wide and already bubbled blood as he screamed. The cop's shot had opened a hole the diameter and color of a raw Trueborn hamburger center mass in the peep's chest, and the little Yavi's heart would pump him dry long before the Cleaners arrived.

What had just happened was an everyday occurrence in any stack, and pedestrians, whatever may have been their inner horror, simply rerouted themselves around the thrashing little peep, and hoped they weren't going to have to remove bloodstains from their clothes.

I had seen this feature often enough, too. My peep self-preservation reflexes overrode any sensitivity that years among the Trueborns might have rebuilt in me.

There was nothing I could do for the peep who was dying for attempting to rob me. But there was something he could still do for me.

While one of the cops was calling for the Cleaners, the other was snapping helmet-cam photos of the suspect.

Whether or not Headcover had yet called the pair of them to pick me up as a suspicious offworlder, I didn't want to be found and questioned, even as an innocent offworld victim big, either.

During the precious window of seconds that the cops were distracted, I walked five yards, then stepped to my right, into the next vertical, and dropped two levels unbuffered by the updraft.

Then for three blocks left, one ahead, and one up I sprinted and dodged like I had just stolen something. Nobody gave me a glance.

Except on the uppermost levels, people ignored street crime that didn't happen to them. So did the system, except when the crime could be dealt with on the spot with a needler, a fist or a boot.

Still, every moment I expected to hear a needler hiss, then feel the round tear my lung out.

Finally, puffing like a steam engine escaped from a pre-industrial, I snuck a direct glance over my shoulder. No uniforms. Headcover's blue balloon had disappeared, too. I slowed, straightened up. Lost 'em.

Then I spotted him, fifty yards back, and my heart skipped. My tail had shed his headcover and eyewear, revealing steel-colored hair that framed a square-jawed face. But it was still him, alright.

My shoulders slumped.

Another lesson spies learn quickly about urban surveillance and evasion is to change appearance on the fly. A headgear change was the school solution, because it yielded the quickest and most dramatic results and was readily reversible if you could pocket the hat.

Headgear's quick change squashed any hope of coincidence. He was a pro, and now my evasion antics had confirmed to him that I wasn't here on Yavet to sell light bulbs.

I swore again.

Busted an hour after hitting dirt. If Kit were here she would laugh her ass off.

No, Kit would never laugh about a Trueborn case officer taken alive by the Yavi. She had survived interrogation once. She talked hard-ass about the experience when we were among those cleared to hear it. But each time the dreams woke her, screaming, beside me, I had to rock her in my arms, like she was a little girl, until she sobbed herself back to sleep.

The prospect of capture nearly made me run again. Instead I dodged ahead through the crowd, merely like a salesman late for an appointment, and let my mind do the sprinting. The longer I walked along with my tail dragging behind me, the more certain it was that a goon squad would pounce on me. Anything I did would be a bad option, but doing nothing would be worse.

A peep wearing gangsta leathers, not so different from the one who had died alongside me minutes earlier, passed by me. I jostled him and picked his pocket for the shiv protruding from his shoulder scabbard. He turned and snarled up at me. I flashed the shiv and snarled back, twice his size, and suddenly better armed.

The gangsta did the math, then moved on, cursing.

Somewhere ahead of him, somebody was about to lose *their* shiv.

I pocketed my new weapon and kept walking. Ahead, the corridor intersected with a smaller tributary transverse, low-ceilinged, sparsely trafficked, and dim, that branched left. On the far side of the transverse, however, a display window of the shop that fronted the main drag wrapped around.

I sauntered around the corner into the transverse, then pressed my back against the wall on the shadowed near side. To my front, the display window now showed me a mirror image of oncoming traffic that had been following me up the main drag, while from the main drag my own reflection was invisible in the shadows.

Four heartbeats later, I glimpsed steel-gray hair as the reflected image of my tail flashed into my view. His stride was smooth, and his jacket lapel bulged. He moved left, across pedestrian traffic, so he could turn down the transverse.

My heart raced. I drew the shiv, and held my breath.

He was close, now.

There was something about his face. Lean. Familiar. Maybe he was a uniform cop who I had seen when I was a kid, who had in later years graduated to plainclothes duty?

He turned in to the transverse passage. I stepped and slashed at his jugular with the shiv as I wrapped my empty hand behind his head, grasped his jaw, and twisted.

Then in that instant I knew. People rarely see themselves except in mirror image. They say it's one reason nobody thinks they look like their driver's license photo. When I saw Headcover's full face for the first time, I had seen him straight on and direct, as though I was looking at his driver's license photo. He was a stranger.

But when I saw his reflection in the shop window, from the same reversed perspective I saw myself every time I shaved . . .

My blade was already flashing across the shadows, its momentum uncontrollable.

I hissed, "You're my father!"

TWENTY-EIGHT

Varden stood at attention in front of Polian's desk, the boy's hands trembling in spite of himself.

Polian waved him to at ease and continued reading the morning reports. But the way the boy fidgeted, it had to be something about the Cutler thing, at last. He had ordered loyal, close-mouthed Varden, and only Varden, to coordinate the operation, but to report only concrete developments.

Not because the boy was clever, but because he wasn't. It kept Polian at arm's length from a plot that offered low success probability, and high jeopardy if it went wrong. And it kept older, wiser heads among Polian's subordinates from questioning a plot that edged Yavet closer to a Trueborn preemptive nuclear attack. It was a dangerous game, but one Polian thought worth playing.

"Out with it, boy."

"The assassin's arrived, sir."

"You're sure?

"Positive. He came in under a damn sophisticated scrub. If I hadn't alerted General Gill's people in Immigration and Customs what to look for, he'd be out peddling light bulbs now."

"And by that I take it you know what he *is* out doing?"

"Well, we know exactly where he's doing it."

"Not by tailing him, I hope. A Trueborn case officer's not some gangsta. He'd scrape off a tail like garbage off his shoe."

"No, sir! I and C diverted him to a special customs line, distracted him, and planted a tracker on him."

Polian rolled his eyes. "The first thing he'll do is find the bug and kill it."

Varden raised a finger, smiled. "Yes, sir. The decoy tracker they sewed into his coat pocket lining died before he left the down shuttle station. But the worm transponder they wove into the jacket's shoulder fabric's new tech. The Trueborns probably don't even look for it yet. It's indistinguishable from sewing thread without a lab-quality microscope or a scanner."

Polian raised his eyebrows. Worm transponder? He *really* had to spend more time with the tech bulletins. "Good boy, Varden."

"It's transmitting five bars." Varden's chest puffed visibly inside his tunic.

Polian stood, walked to the window and gazed down through the bronze fog of early evening at the city that sloped away below, a mountain slope of burnished metal. Then Polian turned back to his aide. "I don't suppose we were lucky enough to pick up an arrival of the other Trueborn? The woman?"

Varden shook his head. "Sir, we had no idea who we were looking for, where she was inbound from, when she might arrive or under what cover. Gill's people shared a rumor they picked up that Hibble himself chooses not to know where some of his people are. But I had a P-mail cover put on the midwife's outbound. She wrote roughly what you said to expect, so I had it resealed and sent on."

"If she'd written something different, I would have had you substitute a forgery that said what we wanted. All we needed from Orion was the contact information for the assassin's mother."

Varden's uplifted eyebrows said that hadn't occurred to him.

"Where did she send it, son?"

"The address was a numbered box at the Bank of Rand."

Polian sighed. "Cold trail from there."

"It was. I'm sorry, sir. But we can still pick up the assassin. Still a coup. Don't the Trueborns say half a loaf is better than none?"

Polian rocked back on his heels. He had thought Varden was quicker on the uptake. "Sorry? Pick him up? Nothing of the kind, Varden! We don't need to find the woman now. She'll come to us. Or rather, she'll come to the assassin."

Varden wrinkled his forehead. "Sir? How sure are you?"

Polian turned back to the window and peered down into the deepening darkness, as the workday ended and lights began to twinkle in the residential Kubes of the up levels. Ruberd's assassin, or one of them, was down there now, in Polian's grasp as soon as he chose to squeeze. And the prize that would win Cold War II was, or soon would be, also.

Polian drew a breath before he answered the younger man's question. "Sure, Varden? As sure as a parent's unconditional and enduring love for a child."

TWENTY-NINE

The gray-haired man had blocked my shiv thrust with his forearm as easily as any close-combat instructor ever had.

I had staggered back, mouth agape, and stared. At myself, but with wrinkles. His eyes glistened, and he shook his head slowly as he stared at me. "My God." He paused, swallowed. "So long. I never thought . . ."

"Long is right, old man."

I couldn't get my head around the idea that somehow he was my father, though his reaction confirmed what my eyes showed me.

He stood silhouetted against the bright bustle of the main drag. A passerby paused, peered into the gloom, presumed a robbery in progress, and hurried on.

If the old man wasn't my tail, one would be along shortly.

"We better get out of here, Pop."

"Yes, yes, I suppose . . . Jazen. Did I pronounce it right?"

"Perfect. For not having much practice." I started off down the transverse with him following. It narrowed, the ceiling stepped lower again, and the smell got worse. A utility I had used in the past was clogged. I tried another wide enough for bigs without armor, and we dropped six vertical. Our height made us stand out downlevels, but now I knew where I was going. The little people who passed us hurried by, heads bowed. Bigs could have been plainclothes vice.

"I guess you know your way?"

"Too well, old man. I spent a lifetime down these shitholes, thanks to you."

He opened his mouth, then closed it.

Then we headed even farther down into Yaven.

THIRTY

"Mort?" Kit's audible voice came to him via her ears, as faint and as raw as the thought came to him indistinct and confused.

He turned within the shallow shelter he had occupied and eyed the now-bare limb where six meals had hung. "You are punctual. Are you well?"

She coughed. "I will be, once the wake-up shot circulates." He sensed her foreclaw digits prod her head above her eyes. "Christ, who crapped a boulder into my skull while I was sleeping?"

"I do not—Oh. Ha-ha."

"Ha-ha? You try it, hairball."

Mort stood, stretched, raised his left back two and urinated. "I am sorry. I sense your discomfort is acute."

"You find him?"

"I believe I have found Yavet. It is by far the largest human hive I have encountered. But it is unpleasantly crowded even by human standards, and most of its humans live in misery."

"That's the place, alright." Kit unfolded herself within the Scorpion seed's darkness. "Canopy to max visual."

The seed's forward eyelid opened again, and the lights above and below it winked on. Ahead, the light-studded blackness Kit saw looked no different than it had when the great eye had closed.

Kit's heart skipped. "Where the hell is—?"

One of the lights ahead winked out, and Kit commanded, "Forward magnification to max."

A disc grew in the center of the Scorpion's great eye, the way that ripples grew on still water, and the blackness within the disc appeared larger. Now Mort realized that the light ahead had winked because a dark object had passed between it and the Scorpion.

"Enhance."

The dark object grew, continued growing, until it seemed to hang so near that Kit could have reached out a foreclaw and touched it. It was a pockmarked rock, dull gray and slowly tumbling.

"Gotcha! Come to Mama." Again Kit rotated the metal bit with her foreclaw and the Scorpion sped toward the object.

"Kit!"

"Relax. Objects in windscreen are smaller than they appear."

"Oh."

"So, how's that for spot-on astrogation?"

"That is Yavet? It appears tinier even than Mousetrap. It could never hold thirteen billion humans."

"It isn't Yavet, Mort. It isn't even a moonlet of Yavet. It's a big rock in eccentric orbit around Yavet. It's a half mile in longest dimension. It circles the planet once every three years, in an egg-shaped orbit that takes it no closer to Yavet than one hundred thousand miles and no farther away than six hundred thousand miles. When it's at apogee, you couldn't see it from the surface of Yavet without a telescope the size of a silo. But astronomically speaking, it's in Yavet's backyard."

"It excites you because it proves you are near Yavet?"

"It excites me because it proves the Yavi aren't as smart as they think they are."

"I don't understand."

Kit spoke aloud. "Transmit recognition codes."

A row of the green lights winked red, then back to green. Two heartbeats later, the lights winked red again, twice.

"What does it mean?"

"That I'm invited for dinner with a bunch of nerds in Utility 5. Mort, Earth hasn't been able to keep an effectively placed human source,—a spy—native or imported, alive on Yavet since before I graduated from college. The best intelligence we get from Yavet we get by reading their electronic mail."

Kit maneuvered the Scorpion closer to the elongate rock, matching the seed's speed and direction to the rock's tumbling pattern, so that the seed's forward end pointed down into one of the hoofprint-shaped depressions that pocked the rock's surface. The particular depression spanned perhaps four times the width that the Scorpion was long. The floor of the depression shifted, then opened like the iris of a frightened animal's eye.

Then Kit edged the Scorpion down, through the opening, into the lit cavern concealed beneath.

Mort sat back on his rump, middle two forward.

Humans never ceased to amaze him. The ingenuity and peculiarity of their nests was a marvel.

In the time it took him to locate, bring down and dismember a mid-sized mite sucker, Kit had climbed out of the Scorpion and floated within the tiny rock, which had been hollowed in the way mites hollowed a fallen tree trunk.

Mort growled.

He had experienced weightlessness once, and the sensation had caused him to regurgitate repeatedly.

Along one wall of the space in which Kit now floated, two rows of humans hunched with their backs to her, peering into bright lit windows that seemed to look out to nowhere.

One of them, a blue-clad female smaller than Kit, swam toward her. The female had a topknot darker than Kit's, and tiny dabs of silver shone atop the joints where her forelimbs joined her torso.

As she drew close to Kit, she touched a foreclaw above her own eye. "Colonel, my pleasure to welcome you aboard. We don't get many visitors between shift changes. Especially not with engraved invitations like yours."

Kit touched her own forehead. "Trust me, lieutenant. Six days alone in a Scorpion? The pleasure's mine. How's the eavesdropping business?"

"Booming, ma'am. Thirteen billion Yavi put out lots of traffic."

Kit and the other female drifted behind the others, each of whom kept his head turned toward the window in front of him.

The one called lieutenant said to Kit, "May I ask how we can assist you, ma'am? We have all the comforts. Galley. Infirmary with state-of-the-art 'bots. Gym."

"For starters, a quart of the coldest water you can spare, then some information about Yavet."

"Perhaps a bunk, Ma'am?'

Kit shook her head. “Just had six days of rack. But I’d kill for a Sanex. I have got *to get out of these clothes.”*

The two humans nearest Kit and the lieutenant turned their heads rapidly and stared.

Kit leaned toward the female. “What’s their *problem?”*

“Shifts last six standard months, and we’re four months in. Crew complement is twelve and—”

“You’re the only female?”

The lieutenant nodded. “References to disrobing are best avoided.”

“Got it.”

Mort returned to the search for Jazen within the mass of humans around which Kit now circled, then briefly pounced upon lunch.

When he next heard Kit speak, she was again with the lieutenant, the two now drifting within a smaller space, in front of a glowing, translucent gray ball, surrounded by a silver ring no thicker than a hair, which seemed to revolve around the ball, even as the ball itself turned slowly.

The lieutenant touched her foreclaw to the ball. “The red dots on the holo mark the locations, beneath the cloud cover, of stack cities with populations of one hundred million or more. As you see, they’re located in two clusters, one in the eastern hemisphere, one in the western. There’s not much sub-aerial solid surface left on Yavet since the polar caps melted.”

Kit stroked her chin with her foreclaw. “If you had to guess where an offworlder might be?”

The lieutenant tapped with her own foreclaw at a yellow dot larger than the rest. “Yaven. It’s the Capital. The two martial directorates, Internal Operations and External Operations, headquarter there. All the down shuttles from Ring Station land there. Yaven’s our high-value traffic hotspot by a factor of ten. Population at least three billion. Probably more. If the Yavi can find an excuse to ignore a little person, they do.”

“Could you isolate a particular individual down there?”

“We track each member of the Central Committee 25/7.”

“Seriously?”

“The product we get’s not as valuable as you’d think. Their average chronological age is eighty-one. They mostly text message each other about what foods give them gas and whose proctologist is gay.”

"I was thinking more about tracking an offworlder. 'Puter locator chip? Hotel registration?"

"Directly locate?" The lieutenant shook her head. "There are three billion people down there, and most of them have 'puters or phones. Yavi Internal Security tracks them, but it's beyond our capacity. The hotel registrations are actually done point-of-sale on physical cards, so you wouldn't pick up a registrant 'til the stay's compiled digitally. By that time, the subject of interest would probably have checked out. Actually, some smugglers sell out of mid-levels hotel Kubes for that very reason, or so we hear. The Yavi don't pay much attention to smugglers. And we don't pay much attention to smugglers up here, either."

"Nobody does, apparently." Kit pressed her foreclaws together, and her eyelids narrowed her field of vision. "What can you tell me about the near-planet defense network?"

The lieutenant's small mouth turned up at its corners. "Now you're talking, Colonel! That's the kind of traffic Teufelsberg Station's used to monitoring and interpreting."

"I thought this listening post was called 'Utility 5.'"

The lieutenant nodded. "Officially. But you may have noticed Utility 5 has a, uh, unique aroma?"

"I've lived with worse."

"Yavi sensor technology's so far ahead of Earth's that Utility 5 emits as little radiation of any type or frequency as possible. And emits absolutely nothing besides radiation, to avoid detection. Raw intelligence, and any intelligence product we're able to develop here, ships out only once every six months, along with the relieved crew, aboard a stretch Scorpion shuttle. So does our solid waste."

Kit nodded, then raised both shoulders toward her ears. "The name?"

"During Cold War I, the good guys emplaced a listening post called Teufelsberg Station on the border of the Soviet Bloc. To improve line-of-sight reception, they piled up three hundred feet of garbage first, then built the listening post on top. We feel a historical bond."

The lieutenant waved a foreclaw and a translucent green bubble made up of a lacing of flickering vines surrounded the gray ball and the silver ring. "Okay. Near space defenses. We call this bubble the "Iron Helmet," after the two-dimensional Iron Curtain from the Teufelsberg days. It's basically an extraordinarily dense hunter-killer satellite network orbiting at geosynchronous speed and altitude."

Kit pointed at the flickering green ball. "The Yavi being the Yavi, I assume some of the warheads are nukes?"

The lieutenant nodded her head. "One in twenty, shuffled randomly. The other nineteen are homing mines with conventional warheads."

Kit whistled. "That's—"

"Six thousand nukes in orbit, Ma'am. The Yavi have a boatload of 'em that they can't deliver onto anybody else, so they use them to keep us out."

"They do *know that thing wouldn't keep us out? Stand-off cruiser weapons and Scorpions would penetrate that like gnats through a tennis net."*

"That's why we call it the Iron Helmet. You could hit those codgers on the Central Committee upside the head with a bat and they wouldn't learn. It's also why we've stopped the drone probes."

Kit swam closer to the ball. "Tell me about that."

"The cruisers used to drop off autonomous chemical drive drones that would make spoof runs at the Helmet, to try and draw responses and map the nuke versus conventional pattern. We quit partly because it pissed the Yavi off. But mostly because we were afraid the Yavi would detonate a nuke to stop some crappy drone, and accidentally take down the Ring."

"Hey. It's their *Wonder of the Universe."*

"Colonel, a hundred million people live in the Ring."

"I know. Poor joke. I am *right? A Scorpion-T could get through that bubble easily?"*

"Hypothetically? Definitely. The fighter patrols in the layer between the helmet and the Ring might be tougher to defeat without detection. A scorpion's faster and more maneuverable, but the Yavi have more fighters up at a given moment than the Teufelsberg garbage mountain had flies."

"How about not hypothetically?"

The lieutenant's small eyes bulged. "Ma'am? I figured you were here to maybe make a tease flyby? Maybe swing in within fifty thousand miles. See if the bad guys lit you up, gauge their radars."

"Actually, the reason to use a Scorpion-T is so the bad guys can't light you up."

The lieutenant straightened and crossed her arms. "Colonel Born, are you seriously proposing that I allow you to fly a Scorpion through the Helmet? Where it could trigger an interplanetary incident? And maybe hand the Yavi a C-drive power plant if your ship's lost?"

"No."

The lieutenant slumped and smiled. "Oh."

"I am seriously assuring *you that I am going to fly a Scorpion through the Helmet. Then I am going to parallel park it smack in the middle of downtown Yaven. Nobody asked you to allow it or not. Read your orders, lieutenant." Kit raised her eyes to the chamber's ceiling. "Why does nobody get this? What part of 'render all assistance requested without question' is hard to understand?"*

The lieutenant floated motionless, her eyes wide, her tiny mouth open in a ring shape.

THIRTY-ONE

My father and I walked without speaking, the only sound our footsteps in the slop and the thrum of the machines, closer now beneath our feet as we got into the lower seventies.

From time to time, we cut through utilities barely wide enough for a full-sized human to crawl through, and far too narrow for a cop in armor, until we emerged into some other pedestrian passage. Then we did it again, and again. Finally, I felt sure we were so deep in the stink that even vice cops couldn't or wouldn't follow.

I stopped, turned and faced him. "What the hell are you doing here?"

"I came back for you. I've been meeting every down shuttle for the last week."

"What made you think I—?"

"Orion sent word. She's always had an address where P-mail could reach us. Just in case."

"Orion sent you word? Bullshit. I never told Orion I was coming here. I never told Orion anything. She just sent me a P-mail."

"You didn't have to. Mothers know what their children will do. Or they think they know. And she said you did send her a P-mail."

"You came all the way to this crappy place because Orion thought her good boy would visit when she was sick?"

"No. I came because your mother also thought her good boy would show up. And I go where your mother goes."

I stood there with my mouth open. Finally, I whispered in the dripping, vibrating silence, "My birth mother's here? Are you two staying with Orion, then?"

My father shook his head. "Orion's—"

My heart sank. "God. I'm too late."

"No. She's alive. She was in detention but got released because—because she was ill. So at the moment, she's bunking with us at our hotel."

"Hotel?"

"We're 'tourists.' This time our docs say we're from Rand. Just like we were 'tourists' when we came here while your mother was carrying you."

A knot puckered in my gut.

Nobody in detention got released because they were sick. Or even because they were dying, which is when I realized that my father couldn't bring himself to tell me. The only fragments of humanity that left the detention blocks were corpses bound for incineration.

I narrowed my eyes.

Orion may have been old and feeble. But she was so confused that she thought I sent her a P-mail that I never had? She hadn't mentioned in her P-mail that she had been in detention, just that she was terminally ill. I had been so moved by the news that it had only fleetingly bothered me that I had never sent her my address. After all, she could have tracked it down. I knew better than most that almost any information was available for a price.

But now I wondered. Orion would pay to P-mail her son, sure. But would she have blown the price of a lifetime supply of whisky searching for the address of an illegal who was very probably dead?

I didn't know my mother, of course. But what had Howard Hibble told me once about her? That she had been not just a pilot, but a starship captain, one of the original ones, during the War. So much for the "fact" that the keel-up starship captains, the ones that knew not just how to fly one, but how to build one, were all dead.

"You let my mother come back to Yavet?"

My father snorted as he shook his head. "She's my wife, not my property! And remember, we got in and out of here once before."

I sighed. Sure they did. But when I was born, the Cold War was more like the Cold Disagreement.

All of this didn't answer all of my lifetime of questions, not by half. One remaining whopper was, what had my parents done that had been terrible enough to get them expunged from the history of the end of the War?

But all my other questions were suddenly pushed back by one new question of considerable immediacy. Orion improbably gets out of jail free. Orion improbably finds out I'm alive, and where to find me. From a P-mail I never wrote. But given those two improbabilities, any average student of human nature could bet I would probably come to Orion, and in turn my mother would probably come to me, if Orion knew how to contact her.

I cocked my head at the old man. "Could the Yavi have set this all up to get at my mother?"

My father stared. Then he said, "Oh, crap. By the way, I say that a lot."

I nodded. "Actually, so do I."

"Odd."

"Not really, when you think about it."

He grasped my elbow. "Orion said she told you why we left you with her?"

I nodded. "You told her you were tourists. But Orion always figured spies. Mom was eight months pregnant, but I came early. And I was coming messy, so you hired a midwife. And a dozen vice goons found the three of you. They were breaking down the door."

On Yavet, parents caught with an undocumented child were summarily executed after watching their newborn suffocated on the spot. The evidence proved *prima facie* that both parents had managed to willfully violate the sterilization code, and the only "intent" an illegal newborn had to demonstrate in order to be guilty was attempting to breathe. Niceties like non-resident status were resolved after the corpses were incinerated. Oops.

Orion, literally red-handed after delivering me, escaped with me out the back door. From then on, my best chance of surviving to adulthood lay in all concerned pretending I didn't exist. There was a bounty on illegals, and few of us grew up, as it was.

My father said, "I didn't stay and protect you. I've remembered that every night of my life since. And the best I can do today is tell you that I'm sorry."

I wasn't. One versus twelve gunfights end badly for the one. If my father and my mother and Orion hadn't in that moment done exactly what they did, all four of us would have died that day. I should have told him all of that. I owed it to him to tell him all of that.

But I had preplayed this moment for decades, even though I never expected it to happen. Now here it was, and nothing was the way I had imagined it might be. So I just stood there.

"We never heard from Orion. So we had to assume the worst." My father wiped his eyes. "We always hoped. But after awhile we didn't really think . . ."

I stared, tight-lipped, as he spoke.

A lifetime's resentment didn't dissipate with one speech. But hearing the story from his mouth at last was like hearing it from my own.

"Jazen, we let you go once, and we lived with that mistake every day of our lives. The moment your mother and I knew where you were, the only way to keep us away would've been to kill us both. Please believe that you mean that much to us. Anyone who knows us knows that's the truth."

Howard Hibble knew my parents, so he knew that.

It almost explained why Howard Hibble played fast and loose with what had become the sole walking, breathing repository of the greatest strategic secret in human history. Why he let my parents roam around the universe in some kind of self-directed combination retirement cruise and witness protection program. And why he let them think I was dead, even after he learned differently, because my job took me places crawling with Yavi, places from which two spooks in three didn't return. Howard couldn't take a chance that my parents might follow.

Because in Howard's paranoid but sentimental mind, his options in order to keep my mother secure from a Yavi interrogation were to have my parents imprisoned for life in some velvet retirement bunker. Or have them killed. Up until now, Howard's plan had been pretty effective. Plenty of riskier longshots had come home for Howard Hibble over the decades.

I reached out and laid a hand on my father's shoulder. "Dad, would you mind taking me home and introducing me to my mother?"

"Sure." He reached out with his own hand, and laid it on *my* shoulder.

Then, for the first time in my life, I saw my father smile at me.

THIRTY-TWO

Mort looked out through Kit's eyes, and out through the open eye of the Scorpion she flew, at the shining, gray ball that swelled in the distance. Now seen in reality, rather than in the incorporeal replica that had provoked conflict between Kit and the female lieutenant, the silver ring around the ball glistened as fine and as reflective as a web spinner's silk adrift on the breeze.

Mort thought, "This is unexpected. The Yavi are as evil as Cutler, yet their nest is beautiful."

Kit thought, "Maybe from this far away. But those clouds? Excess greenhouse gases. Fossil fuel and chemical particulates. Atmospheric nuclear test fallout. And that pretty ring? It's a combination slave-labor colony and prison. But the slaves clamor to go there because stack-city living down below is worse."

"Oh. Jazen is within such a city."

Kit's heart took an irregular beat. "You found him?"

"He is deep within the great nest of which you and the female lieutenant spoke, called Yaven."

"He told you?"

"No. I have been unable to penetrate his consciousness. But those around him know the place where I have located him as Yaven. It is vast."

Kit's heart skipped again. "Who's around him?"

"Too many to begin to know. I am sorry. I have accomplished nothing."

"You've accomplished plenty. You've corroborated the listening post lieutenant's hypothesis. In another hour or so, can you narrow Jazen's location down more?"

"Perhaps."

"Okay. Then I'm playing out this hand while we see if you can draw aces." She spoke aloud to the Scorpion seed. "Maintain course. Maintain speed. Alarm at five thousand miles to first contact."

"You intend to enter the nest of Yaven itself?"

"Relax. I'm still seventeen minutes away from first contact with the Helmet perimeter.

"The female lieutenant thought that even penetrating the Helmet would be unwise, although she grudgingly conceded your authority."

"Grudging. I knew *she didn't like me. It's the blonde thing. Wait. Mort, you know what she was actually thinking?"*

"Yes."

"Well?"

"I did not understand her thoughts, but they seemed uncomplimentary. I would prefer not to share them." Humans, females in particular, expended extraordinary energy attempting to decipher or discover hidden meanings in the words and actions of other humans. Mort, particularly in this time of stress on himself, found this a waste of energy.

"Come on! Share! Buddy to buddy. Spill and I'll tell you *anything you wanna know. Deal? It's a fair trade."*

No grezzen individually possessed a skill, knowledge or an object that another grezzen needed, so grezzen didn't trade.

However, the community by which humans survived in a universe that was stronger than they were depended on division of labor, and division of objects, and so on trading. Mort had learned that human bargaining involved rapid, familiar banter, temptation and interpersonal goading. And Kit possessed something he wanted to know very much.

"Very well. You are on, lady." He paused for effect. Humans did that. "The lieutenant thought you were stubborn, overbearing, hot for a granny with a fat ass, reckless and a complete prick when she was just trying to help. And you obviously hadn't gotten laid in a long time."

"Granny? Fat ass?"

"Do not kill the messenger. Ha-ha. Kit, a deal is a deal. My turn."

A metallic voice said, "Multiple contacts. Range five thousand."

"Talk fast, Shylock. Gettin' busy here."

"When Howard spoke with you at Mousetrap, I was unable to perceive what he told you. Only that it made you angry and confused. Since then you have trapped the memory in the part of your mind that I cannot reach, in the way I have trapped snakes beneath rocks in hopes that they might weaken and die before I must return and risk their venom. What did Howard say?"

The voice said, "Range four thousand."

He felt the tension in Kit's muscles, which had increased sharply when the voice first spoke, increase further.

"Mort, I can't look under that rock right now. The present's trying to bite me."

"But when you must look? What lies beneath?"

He felt anger and sadness well up in her.

Kit did not speak aloud, but thought, "Mort, not now! Shop talk I can deal with. Not the other."

"Range three thousand."

Kit said, "Resume manual."

Then Mort felt the metal against her foreclaw, and in that moment her anxiety fell away, as it fell away within him when he finally confronted a striper or other competing predator that he had felt from a distance. It was when Kit was hunting that she felt to him most like his mother.

Kit spoke, her voice free from expression. "Heads up: display targets."

An angular pattern glowed before her eyes.

He modulated his inquiry so that she felt only a whisper. "There are machines ahead that will seek you? Like the crawling mines that have killed my cousins?"

"Exactly like that, actually. Except this minefield is three-dimensional, and the distances are longer. And so far it's asleep."

"That is good."

"That is expected. A Scorpion-T's got the radar cross section of the bluebird of happiness and the heat signature of day-old pizza."

Ahead of Kit points of bright light showed, now diverging visibly because the Scorpion seed sped toward them so rapidly.

"I'm gonna punch through equidistant from those six HKs in front

of me at center display. Probably none of them will wake up. If one does, I'll be through so fast it'll think I was a system fault. If one chases and detonates, I'll outrun the shrapnel, but the doorbell will ring down below."

"But detonation would pose no physical danger to you?"

"If the chaser's the one in twenty that's nuclear, I'm not in danger, I'm dead."

Ahead, the light points were gone.

"Huh. Non-event."

"What?"

"I'm inside the chicken coop already, and the Yavi don't know it. If we ever go postal on these people, they are so screwed." Kit expelled breath through her nostrils, indicating derision. "Iron Helmet, my ass. Which, by the way, is not fat."

Now the area ahead of Kit was soft gray, not black. She was now so close to Yavet that the ball consumed her view.

"Heads up: reset target display."

The space before Kit's eyes swarmed with lights that spread all across her field of vision.

"Hello! That is a lot *of fighters."*

"Fighters. Shells like yours, directed by humans?"

The roiling lights both grew and diverged as Kit closed the distance to them.

"Not like mine. They aren't C-drive. Slow. Sluggish. Visible to radar, which lets their controllers direct them onto targets easier. And their controllers are all in one fat-ass room in the Ring, looking at fat-ass radar displays."

"Your task is harder, then."

"No, my task is easier." Kit spoke aloud. "Evasive action."

Kit's view again shifted to black, then gray, then back, faster than a nectar sucker's wings beat. "A scorpion's not as straight-line fast as a cruiser, or durable enough to jump reliably. But it's got the same gravity cocoon, so it can juke right angles at Mach 6 without squishing its payload."

Mort stared at the landscape ahead of him to relieve the disorientation he felt from the flickering view through Kit's eyes.

"Even if a radar in a brilliant moment sees me, the radar's brain doesn't register what its eye sees. An object moving nonconformably to

Newtonian physics doesn't exist to it. The Yavi can't remodel their computer algorithms to match C-drive fighters, because they're just guessing what C-drive fighters can really do. An unalerted centrally directed fighter is no fighter at all."

Mort shook his head to clear it. Too many concepts. He referred to a simpler hunting technique that grezzen and humans shared. "But the pilots might see you. You can see them."

"They won't see me if I go where they don't want to go. Cancel evasive action. Resume manual."

Mort peered again through Kit's eyes. Her view ahead was again gray, and the wispy silver thread now floated so close that he saw it was an angular human shell, immensely vaster even than the cruisers like the Gateway. *Within the great shell, he felt too many human intellects to count. "There are many humans inside the great thread. If you continue, you will butt it."*

"I won't butt it. Not exactly. You see that brown haze floating beneath the Greatest Manmade Wonder of the Universe?"

"What is it?"

"Mort, what do one hundred million humans make more of than noise?"

"You mean—"

"The Yavi don't mention that *in the tourism holos. The Ring vents its solid waste to vacuum, into a designated lower orbit. It freezes, then its orbit decays, and it burns up on atmospheric entry. Except for maybe a few million tons."*

"Ingenious. Eventually it fertilizes the surface."

"Makes you want to go sing in the rain, doesn't it?"

Already Kit had slowed the Scorpion so that it drifted below the great shell's belly scarcely faster than a gliding gort.

Whump. Whump.

Through Kit's ears, Mort heard objects strike the Scorpion's skin. Kit's view was of dark and irregular objects ranging from smaller than a human head to larger than the Scorpion itself, tumbling as the Scorpion itself now tumbled.

"Your shell has been damaged!"

"At this speed, all that's damaged is her dignity. The pilots are up in the umbrella patrol at orbital speed because they have to cover a whole planet from equator to poles. Their hard deck's miles above the Ring

because jettisoned debris smaller than a lug nut could *hole their ships. Besides, what fighter jock wants to fly his shiny baby through a shitstorm? That's the beauty. A Scorpion can't just go fast, it can go slow. It can yaw and roll like a hunk of frozen shit, unnoticed among a billion other hunks. I'm working my way down gradually. Once I'm through this, it's clear sailing to the surface for a ship as stealthy as she is."*

As the Scorpion drifted, Kit asked, "Find him yet?"

Mort paused, sought a better response, found none. "It is hopeless."

He felt anger flash in her. "It can't be hopeless! Mort, I've come too far. And the hardest part's still ahead. A stack city like Yaven's a hundred-level-tall pyramid, twenty miles wide where the base meets the surface. And another hundred downlevels beneath the surface. And the whole hive's crawling with armored-up Yavi cops who shoot on sight. I've got to know where I'm going."

"Please! I am looking for one needle in a hay storm."

He felt Kit's body sag along with her spirit. "I know. There's three billion of them, and only one of him."

The Scorpion continued drifting, the silence broken only by the thump of frozen excrement against its flanks.

He felt adrenaline surge through Kit, saw her view shift as she came upright.

"Mort, I said there was only one of him. Would it help if there were more than one? I mean, not multiple Jazens. Somebody near him genetically similar?"

"Oh, immeasurably. Of course, the signature of a woog herd is vastly stronger than a lone woog. But within the herd a cow with her calf is distinct. If the sire bull remains nearby the calf, the signature is strongest of all."

Mort felt Kit strike the Scorpion's inner skin so hard that her palm registered pain. "Sure! Your ancestors that could spot a cow and calf ate better, survived better. If they also knew how to avoid calves protected by bulls, better still. Natural selection."

Too many concepts. "Perhaps."

"Mort, stop looking just for Jazen. Look for two Jazens in relative proximity."

"I will if you ask. But as you have said, there are not multiple Jazens."

"Yes and no."

"How will I recognize this other Jazen?"

"Find a stubborn dickhead with a heart of gold. Just like his son."

The view before Kit cleared to gray clouds, across the bulbous, churning tops of which night began to fall.

Kit again touched the metal that accelerated the Scorpion. "Work fast, Mort. It's about to get real warm for me down there."

THIRTY-THREE

Mort scooped larvae from the heart of a fallen tree, swallowed them, wood fiber and all, without even savoring the taste, and returned to his work.

He sifted human intellects he encountered within the distant hive called Yaven as rapidly and dispassionately as if they had been larvae. He discarded each when it did not resemble Jazen, then probed the next. The great mass within which he felt Jazen, and the other who was like Jazen nearby, shrank with each discard, but Jazen remained too distant and indistinct.

As he worked, he watched through Kit's eyes as the Scorpion overflew a rolling and seemingly endless nightscape, rendered oddly luminous by peculiar eyelids that Kit called "Snoops." The Scorpion flew so close to the barren soil that had he been beneath it he could have risen on two and swatted the Scorpion's belly. The sensation of velocity was profound, but Kit's actual progress toward the hive called Yaven seemed nonexistent.

Ahead, a round hill loomed. The Scorpion, without a touch by Kit, rose abruptly, passed barely above the obstacle, then dropped back with scant change in velocity.

Aloud Kit said, "Hooah!"

"Kit, I recognize that hill! You are traveling in circles!"

"Not exactly circles, but good point." She spoke aloud, not to him. "Reset random loiter. Reset speed four nine zero."

"When you evaded the killing machines and the fighter jocks you flew much faster."

Kit said, "In vacuum no one can hear you speed. I've gotten this far unseen. Staying subsonic keeps me unheard." Then she thought, "Besides, the autopilot's governed. It only flies nap-of-the-planet below five hundred miles an hour."

"You urge me to work faster. But you meander like a blind woog."

"It's early. The best time to sneak past humans is when most of them are asleep and the ones who aren't wish they were. And I'm waiting on weather."

"The weather there seems clear."

"Exactly."

Mort peered again across the bleakness, animated only by wind-beaten scrub. Hunting there without cover would be difficult. Since he began the search for Jazen, food, or the lack thereof, was constantly on his mind. "This is prairie. Where are the herds?"

"Bad air, bad water, bad agricultural and wildlife management . . . Yavet's non-cultured megafaunal population became unmeasurable a long time ago. No cows. No cow-feed farms. But no cowboys or farmers outdoors to look up and see me fly past out here, either. Mort, you're ninety years late for the last round-up."

With his forepaw Mort slapped a glider that passed near enough, swallowed it whole, but still felt weakness in the forelimb with which he had swatted the morsel.

No grezzen had the means or the vanity to count calories, but grezzen knew that, as in humans, the organs that consumed the greatest proportion, fully twenty percent, of the energy they produced were their disproportionately large brains. Thirty million years of grezzen evolution had sharpened the balance point between metabolism and a predator's measured violence to a knife edge unrivalled in the universe.

Grezzen, above all other species, had to hunt constantly to live. By his disproportionate mental activity in his search for Jazen, Mort was slowly starving himself to death.

"Why have the Yavi not starved, then, Kit?"

"Spoken like a carnivore. The upper classes get their meat from tank-raised livestock. The rest buy shaped vegetable protein grown in tray farms. Jazen said it tastes like crap."

"How did the Yavi come to such a dreadful system?"

"Hard to say. My poli-sci profs got in a fist fight once over whether Yavi society was analogous to democratic capitalism run amok or totalitarian socialism run amok."

"Human politics seem to be a waste of perfectly good violence."

"Fair point. The Unified Republics of Yavet is a worldwide totalitarian police state. So they haven't wasted any violence on nation-to-nation politics in two hundred years. The Yavi think nothing's *amok. At least the upper classes think so."*

"What do you think?"

"I dunno. When the few make every decision for the many, the many eat mung-bean bars, the few eat steak, and a society can rain shit on itself from outer space and think nothing's amok."

"Understanding humans is painfully difficult."

"We're really not that bad. But overthinking us'll kill you."

Two crawlers scurried through the moss alongside Mort. He stabbed sluggishly with his left midlimb and impaled one. Normally he would have gotten both. He returned to sifting intellects, aware that Jazen's and probably Kit's lives depended on it. But overthinking was, indeed, killing him.

"Ping. *Weather advisory."*

Mort's head snapped up.

Time had passed. His mental acuity had deteriorated to the point that he could no longer discern precisely how much time had passed. But he knew that he had made many failed probings since his last conversation with Kit, before the metallic tone and voice broke Kit's concentration.

Her eyes scanned a moving pattern of multicolored light on one of the leaves in front of her, then she said aloud. "Control to manual. RWR to max."

Mort felt her increase the Scorpion's velocity as she turned it sharply.

"Kit, what are you doing?"

"Relax. Nothing bad. The weatherman's getting friendly, the sentries are getting sleepy, and I've turned to a heading into Yaven."

"Now the Yavi will hunt you?"

"Not yet. The Radar Emissions Warning Receiver's just a good habit. Yaven's got radar to watch weather and airliners, but not air-defense radar to detect hostile bombers. The Unified Republics haven't bombed their own capital in two hundred years."

Kit's consciousness focused on flying. Mort resumed his work, made steady progress.

"Wow." Kit whispered aloud. "That is some big pyramid."

In the Scorpion's eye a mountain grew out of the darkness ahead of Kit. As the Scorpion's eye grew clearer, Mort saw the mountain's flanks were smooth and angular, and shimmered, in the way of most human constructs. The reason that the mountain's flanks were visible through the darkness was that they were studded with great jets of dull flame. The jets tapered into curls of smoke as black as the roiling clouds that scudded so low above the mountain's peak that they seemed to scrape it.

Kit was counting aloud, softly. "Thirteen . . . fourteen. Fourteen stacks a side. That's Yaven, alright."

Kit slowed the Scorpion, inching it forward, narrowing the distance between it and the great fiery mountain.

Jagged lightning ripped the sky between the clouds and the peak.

Boom!

Mort felt Kit stiffen. "Shit!"

He drew back from Kit's consciousness, blinked all three eyes. Around him daylight dappled the familiar forest with light and shadow. Insects buzzed and the breeze blew gently.

Nonetheless, his heart pounded. Fire. Why did there have to be fire?

Unbidden, Kit whispered, "Crap, that was close," and her voice drew him back in to her consciousness.

Mort heard in her ears a steady rumble, looked through her eyes and saw black rain sheet across the Scorpion's eye, smearing the great mountain's image into smudges of bronze and gold and shimmering, flaming orange.

"That cannot be Yaven. If Jazen were within that place he would have perished."

"Easy, Mort! I'm not crazy about fire myself. But I'm the one who's here, and I'm a big girl. I need your help now more than ever."

He drew a deep breath. "You may rely on me."

"The pyramid's not an enclosed bonfire. It just looks that way at night. They don't call these places stack cities just because the people live on top of each other. Those stacks exhaust airborne waste from the industrial levels underground."

Again lightning flashed, then boomed. The rain beat harder against the Scorpion's skin, as it now hovered close enough to the flaming pyramid that he could have run to the thing in three bounds. Though he would not have.

"Mort, time to get specific. You know where I am. How close is Jazen to me? A cruiser's a mile long. How many cruisers?"

Mort concentrated on Kit's location, then on the larger spherical volume to which he had reduced Jazen's location, then felt his heart sink. "He is nine cruisers distant. But he is deep within the mountain. As many Yavi surround him as prey animals surround me here. Many of those Yavi are without doubt hostile to Jazen and to you. They may already be restraining him."

"I know."

"You and Howard told me you were going to pursue Jazen and assist him. Neither you nor Howard revealed to me that you would have to dig away a mountain filled with evil humans to do so. You deceived me."

"No. Humans don't know what the other guy doesn't know, like you do. Ask a question, get an answer. That's how we roll. If you'd asked, I would have told you I had a plan."

"What? Ask at the front door for the Yavi to deliver Jazen like a gift?"

"Wow. Sex usually makes humans less grumpy."

"Sarcasm remains new to me."

"No, you're right. I never planned to go in the front door. And I never planned to dig my way in. But I think I can drop down the chimney."

"Through fire?"

"It's not fire. Waste stack upflow is mostly toxic gas, superheated steam, cinders, metallic sparks and flaming debris. Most points on the inner walls of those stacks, you could barely fry eggs."

"Oh. Piece of pie."

"Cake. Piece of cake. But you nailed the sarcasm."

The rumble of rain against the Scorpion's skin diminished.

"Mort, I gotta go before I lose the storm's cover. When I get inside, you have a precise location waiting for me, okay?"

His head sagged with fatigue and he paused.

Kit believed that she had concealed from him the manner of her initial phrasing, which had been "If I get inside alive." And he felt that, beneath her banter, she was as coldly terrified as any limping woog was when it heard him approach.

"I will do my best."

"You sound tired. Go get a bite while I'm busy."

Humans often attempted a joke to ease stress in others.

He thought, "Kit? If you cannot be good, be careful. Ha-ha."

He felt her inner terror turn for an instant, but not to amusement. It turned to sorrow. "Mort, assassins can't usually choose to be either."

Then her thoughts became cold, precise and impenetrable, as his own did, and his mother's had, when tracking dangerous prey in dangerous terrain.

Through her eyes, he saw Yaven's broad, bronze skin, only a paw's reach away as the Scorpion crept up the pyramid's flank. Slick with rain that coursed down its slope, the metal sparkled in bright white flashes less and less frequently as the storm weakened and the lightning strikes ebbed.

Red glow flooded Kit's vision as the Scorpion rose above the edge of one of the great stacks.

The Scorpion's nose jerked toward the clouds, struck by the gale roaring up from deep within the great nest. Caught and buffeted, the Scorpion tumbled as insubstantially as a leaf.

Kit forced the Scorpion's nose back down. The stack's opposite wall was so distant that had the circular opening been a plain, a hundred woog could have grazed comfortably within its area. The wall's texture was distorted by the shimmer of rising heat and interrupted by an inverted storm of sparks, translucent steam, and twisting, unidentifiable, flaming bits.

The entire mass roared upward twice as fast as one of the humans' wheeled shells traveled across level ground.

Kit tipped the Scorpion so that it floated, like the melon seed it resembled, blunt end down, its belly nearly grazing the stack's vertical inner wall.

Then the shell that protected one of the two humans who Mort most valued began to crawl down into smoky darkness and flame.

For a time that seemed interminable, the Scorpion crept deeper inside the great pyramid, as he heard in Kit's ears the roar of the scorching maelstrom that buffeted her. He saw through her eyes fire and sparks that rushed up and past her.

It suddenly seemed to Mort that the Scorpion was more fragile than an eggshell.

"Kit, can the Scorpion protect you within that fire?"

"Piece of pie, Mort. Outside air temperature's two twenty, in here a cozy seventy-two. A Scorpion fuselage gets twice that hot just poking along in atmosphere at two thousand miles an hour. The headwind I'm bucking from the updraft is only one hundred ten."

"How far are you descending?"

"The map that rude lady at Teufelsberg Station uploaded shows an emergency maintenance hatch at level Thirty Lower. It exits into an inspection-'bot storage chamber, then out to a quiet neighborhood. I'll park alongside the hatch, pop the canopy, lean out and paste a couple thermite strips on the latch. Burn my way in. By then you'll have Jazen pinpointed for me, right?"

Mort touched the lining of his mouth with the tip of his index foreclaw.

Already, the membrane was stiff and dry. Next, his vision would deteriorate. Since his cousins all across his world had realized that he had undertaken this task, he had felt first their mild consternation, then bewilderment. The death of a cousin was inevitable, but an untimely death rare. However, he had mated successfully, so his life had served its purpose. His demise, if he chose a behavior that hastened it, would be merely sad. But the choice was his to make.

"Right?"

"Right. Kit, you will go out into the fire?"

"This flight suit's fireproof and insulated, and I've got a rebreather. I could work outside in that crap for ten minutes before I was toast."

He felt her rock forward as the Scorpion paused. "Level Thirty Lower. All passengers transfer here for hell. Thank you for flying Air Born."

As his mind touched human minds with increasing urgency and decreasing efficiency, he scraped the soil, recovered a few grubs, and smeared them inside his mouth. He tried to pound the soil in frustration, but could no longer curl his foreclaw into a fist.

He could no longer save himself. Worse, he feared that, despite his sacrifice, he could not save his friends.

THIRTY-FOUR

"Sonuvabitch!"

The voice in his head startled Mort out of his weakness. The faint afternoon shadows before him had scarcely shifted since he had last communicated with Kit. "Kit?"

"There's no hatch at Thirty Lower! Or anywhere else down to Ninety-two Lower, 'cause that's where I am now. And that's as low as the Scorpion can go. There are structural transverse braces across the stack at Ninety-three Lower that the ship can't fit between."

"How can all that be?"

"Spying's an inexact science. Teufelsberg Station hacks into these maps from a half million miles away."

"The plan has failed?"

"The plan is every battle's first casualty, Mort."

Despite her confident words, he felt her anxiety and fear swell, then heard through bone conduction in her skull the sound of her grinding her teeth across one another. The sound now seemed amplified in the Scorpion's confined space. The sound was replaced in Kit's ears by metal jingling against metal, and he saw in her hands bundles of multicolored vines around which dangled irregular wire bits.

"What are those?"

"Rappel ropes. I can extend the ramp tow hook and anchor one of these to it. The Scorpion will hover here on auto indefinitely, solid as houses. Basically, I can make a controlled fall down this rope to Ninety-Six Lower. There's a grating across the stack at that level that catches

crap that fizzles and falls back down the stack. I'll crawl through one of the grate's clean-out ports, then I'll be through clean and safe into the industrial levels. Simple backup plan."

"You said you would be toast in the stack if you were outside the Scorpion."

"I said I'd be toast in ten minutes. I can be out one of those ports in five, tops."

"Are you sure these clean-out ports exist? The hatch did not. And when you return, will you be able to ascend your rope in the same way that you descended?"

Kit sighed again as she plucked at the multicolored vines. "I said it was a simple backup plan, not a complete one."

When she had finished with the vines she grunted, then manipulated a round, red stone that protruded from the Scorpion's forward interior space until it chirped rhythmically, in time with a similar chirp from a tiny vine that she fastened round her foreclaw.

"What is that sound?"

"Countdown timer."

"So you will know when ten minutes have elapsed?"

"I won't need a timer to know I'm toast. Howard almost handed one Scorpion to the Yavi already. He wouldn't let this one get within a half million miles of Yavet without booby trapping it. If I'm not back here in three hours, this ship will burn itself to ashes. All the Yavi will have to analyze will be cinders. So when I get out the bottom of this stack, I'm gonna need a rock-solid location for Jazen and company. And I'm gonna need it fast. Deal?"

Deal? He blinked to clear his head, because he could no longer shake it. Had he not made a deal with Kit before, to resolve a question that had troubled him greatly? She still owed him, and the matter seemed vital, but he was too weak to insist, and closed all his eyes as he said, "Deal."

Through Kit's ears, he heard a hiss, then a great roar as the Scorpion opened like a shelled nut, and she climbed out into the blast and heat of the stack.

Chee-chee-chee.

He opened his left eye slightly without turning his head.

Scroungers? A trio of the vile beasts scuttled toward him, bellies down and each propelled by six muscular legs. Smaller, black-furred, and stupid grotesques of his own race, they were the size of creatures Trueborn humans visualized as lions. But unlike lions, the scroungers' mottled red-and-blue snouts were hairless, the better to poke into the carrion they scavenged to survive.

If he had been healthy and undistracted, they would never have been able to approach so near undetected. More to the point, they would not have dared.

The largest of the pack rose onto all six, trotted forward, sniffing.

The scrounger's bravado startled Mort. Did he really appear to them to be that near to death?

Mort steeled himself against the revulsion he felt when the pack leader nudged Mort's flank with his snout, and Mort stifled even his shallowed breathing.

When the leader's exploration yielded no response, his two minions capered forward, black eyes aglitter, chittering and careless.

It was over in a violent instant.

The leader lay sprawled beneath Mort's left midlimb, his skull crushed by a single punch. The smallest still whimpered as it lay immobilized alongside the leader, licking obscenely at its own intestines, which had spilled from an underbelly ripped by a slash from the claws of Mort's left rear leg. The third scrounger's head rested within Mort's mouth, severed cleanly by one bite.

Mort dropped his jaw slightly, then used his tongue to position the head between his upper and lower right molars, bit, then felt the skull crackle deliciously as the sweet taste of brain flooded his mouth.

He lay still a moment after swallowing, devoid of joy or remorse at the simple act of being what he was. He felt strength and mental energy begin to return even as he tidied the rest of his windfall meal into piles with his forelimbs.

"Kit?" As his confidence swelled, he reached out to her mind.

"Sonuvabitch!"

It was the same expletive she had employed when she had discovered the nonexistence of the hatch, and his heart sank. "There are no clean-out ports?"

He saw by the light of a tiny artificial beam, which humans affixed to their foreheads at the place where their third eye should have been, that Kit was struggling to move irregular slabs and branches piled around her that rose as high as the hinge joint of her rear limbs.

"You'd think when somebody installs clean-out ports, they'd come and clean out once in a while."

Her breathing was labored, and her limb muscles burned with lactic acid. He saw her pause, straighten, then direct the beam at the small vine that encircled her forelimb.

"How long do you have remaining?"

"Two minutes. But I feel like toast already. Mort, I can see the goddam way out!" She growled, kicked a battered, cubiform object as large as her torso, and pain shot up from the tip of her hind limb. She screeched aloud, limped in circles on the heel of the injured claw, and again he heard the sound of her grinding her teeth.

She said, "But I can't budge this big hunk of Yavi junk. And now I broke my fucking toe."

Mort paused.

To his knowledge, the injured appendage and coitus were unrelated, but now hardly seemed the moment to address his question.

He thought, "When I need to move a rock to access food beneath, I prise it up with a tree trunk."

The tiny light jerked across jumbled debris that flapped in the scalding gale thundering up through the openings beneath Kit's feet.

"A lever? Mort, where in hell would I find a—oh." Kit dug an elongate, tubular metal root from beneath rubble, wedged its tip beneath the object she had kicked, then shifted all her tiny body weight onto the root's far end. "Ahhh!"

The object atop the lever's short end remained stationary.

Kit stepped back, folded forward, foreclaws on her upper hind limbs and panted. "'S no use."

"Kit, reascend your vine and recover inside the Scorpion seed."

"Nope."

"You must! Or you will die there. And so perhaps will Jazen. If you will not try for yourself, try for Jazen."

"My suit's sleeve patch is already in the yellow, Mort. I'd never finish the up rappel." She gasped, then whispered aloud, "I'm cooked."

But despite her words, this time she stepped back four paces, sprang forward toward the root, then leapt up and twisted her body so her hindquarters landed on the root.

The root bent beneath her weight, then snapped, so that Kit landed on her hindquarters amid the debris. But when her light swung back, the object had shifted, exposing a long passage tall enough for a human to crawl through.

Kit yelped, then scrambled through the opening.

Mort had picked the carcass of the first scrounger clean to the major bones by the time Kit had recovered sufficiently from her ordeal to direct a thought to him.

He saw that she sat with her bare hind limbs sprawled ahead of her, visible by the beam of her forehead light. The cubic space in which she rested was vast, but dull gray, calm, and no longer scaldingly hot.

As she thought, she pulled a replacement integument from the bag she had worn on her shoulders. It was the shade of tree bark, and she pulled it up over her hind limbs and torso. "Yavi civvies. Not my color, but now I blend."

"Your final effort was most impressive."

"It had nothing to do with the size of my ass."

"I said nothing. Kit, if you are prepared to continue, I am prepared to assist."

Kit stood, slipped one of the small stingers that humans carried into a pouch in the Yavi civvies that she now wore, then stepped to the closed hatch that separated the chamber from the rest of the Yaven hive. "How far do I have to go, Mort?"

"Forward one half of the Gateway*. Upward one fourth of the* Gateway*. Forward again one half."*

"A mile and a quarter? Piece of pie."

"Ha-ha."

Kit touched one foreclaw to the chirping vine that wrapped the other, silenced it then tugged the civvie down so that the vine was concealed. "Two hours, twenty minutes and counting. Have you been able to contact Jazen, let him know I'm here?"

"No. It is unlikely that I will. It is easier to maintain contact as I have with you than to reestablish it, even with Jazen."

"When I get to Jazen, where will he be?"

"In a chamber much smaller than the one you occupy now. Some around him that I have touched think of it as a crummy hotel room. Others think it represents good value for money."

"Is he alone?"

"Three humans share the space with him."

"Three?" She grasped the hatch latch with a foreclaw, then pulled

the hatch toward herself, opening a slit perhaps as wide as the diameter of a human forelimb. Then she pressed her cheek against the hatch edge, in the way that a coot peered round a tree trunk to avoid detection.

Through Kit's eyes Mort saw a dimly lit, featureless passage that stretched ahead perhaps one-tenth of the length of the Gateway, *then ended where it intersected another.*

Kit opened the hatch and looked in one direction, then the opposite direction, down the passage that crossed immediately to her front.

When she saw it was also empty, she sprang out into the long passageway, then ran as though pursued until she reached the far intersection.

Breathing heavily, she rounded the first corner, and he felt her elation. Even the pain in her coital toe appeared to have diminished.

"Kit, you appear rejuvenated."

"Damn right! I've still got two hours and fifteen minutes to get to Jazen, get everybody out, get them back aboard the Scorpion. Then it's adios freakin' Yavet. The foot traffic ahead will slow me down, so I blend, but the Yavi have no clue I'm here. Mort, I hit a little speed bump back there, before. Maybe even got a little down. But from here on out, this job is a piece of pie."

THIRTY-FIVE

Max Polian woke in the middle of the night and felt pressure in his bladder.

He was, regardless of how he felt otherwise, an old man, and he woke for that reason every night. Then his bed quivered, and he swore. It had not been an old man's need to pee, but the damn bed that had awakened him. He could have sworn he had set it to do-not-disturb. But he must have forgotten. Another curse of aging. In body, if not in spirit, Max fit the profile of a Central Committee member already.

And who the hell was calling in the middle of the night?

When the notification buzz came again, this time accompanied by a chime, Max realized that the notification was not of a message, but a warning of movement in the passage outside his doorway. At least that meant he hadn't forgotten to set the do-not-disturb.

Max swung his legs onto the floor as he squinted at his 'puter, and the fringe of hair remaining at the back of his neck rose.

Three hours past midnight. Someone or something was moving in the passage outside his front door in the middle of the night.

Foraging little people, who wormed into even the better uplevels neighborhoods like this one through the utilities, were more nuisance than danger. But he was paying for peace and quiet up here.

Max shrugged into his robe. Then he lifted the hand needler he kept on his nightstand, thumbed off the safety and padded out of his bedroom and across his main living space. As the foyer felt him, its flat screen alongside the passage door flicked live and displayed the outside passage's monitor feed.

A lone figure stood in the dimness, shifting weight, foot to foot. Polian recognized the provi cap, then exhaled a breath he hadn't realized he was holding and spoke into the microphone beneath the screen. "Varden!"

Polian safed his needler, then rubbed his wrinkled forehead. Had he somehow forgotten something? It was hell to age. "Varden, by some chance did I tell you to bring the slider?"

"Uh, I pick you up on the odd days, sir, and today's even. And it's actually much earlier than pick-up time."

Polian closed his eyes, shook his head. "Why, thank you, Varden. I hadn't noticed the hour."

"Yes, sir. I mean, sorry, sir."

"You should've called. I could have mistaken you for a forager and shot you through the door." Not really. A needler couldn't penetrate a Yavi door like a gunpowder pistol could. But if he could frighten Varden a little, the boy might think more clearly next time.

"Sir, I couldn't have called. Your bed was on do not disturb. Sir, may I—?"

Polian squeezed his eyes shut again for a beat, then opened the door.

Varden stepped in.

"I take it you didn't come over to tell me to turn on my bed?"

"Uh. Not exactly, sir."

Polian shuffled back in to the living space, waved on the lights, then sat on his divan, bent forward, elbows on knees.

"Then what, exactly?"

Varden stood there, fumbling a folded handheld. "Sir, an hour ago air flow out of Stack Fourteen Eastern dropped two percent."

Polian flattened both palms across his eyes, rubbed his face, exhaled. It was an unconscious movement he had made a thousand times. Now he realized why. He hoped that when he removed his hands from his eyes Varden would be gone.

He said to the boy, "Next time you get a call that should have gone to the Directorate of Industry, just transfer it."

"Uh. I didn't get that call. Industry *did* get it. So they sent an inspection crew with a wall crawler 'bot to check."

"That sounds appropriate. And still nothing that concerns Internal Operations Directorate."

"The 'bot found an aircraft in the stack just above Ninety-six Lower."

That surprised Polian. But then he nodded.

Smugglers used aircraft more often out in the hick stacks, where over-water travel made flying the practical way to transfer inventory. But crickets full of junk had crashed and burned inside the stacks of Yaven before. Once maintenance dragged out the wreck, he'd send an investigator to have a look. "Varden, next time tell them to just call you the following morning.

"Actually, Industry didn't call me, sir. They called External Operations."

"Gill's people?" Polian dropped his hands into his lap.

Varden nodded.

Polian stiffened. "What the hell for? Inter-city smuggling's *our* jurisdiction." He hadn't expected Gill to be a turf poacher.

Varden opened his handheld, clicked a flat image then rotated the device so Polian could see its screen. The image was a still frame from a 'bot feed.

Polian leaned close, squinted at the grainy frame. "This is the best image you can bring me, Varden?"

"It's the only image, sir. The 'bot's insulation failed. Apparently it's over two hundred degrees inside a stack." The boy shrugged. "I never thought about how a city works. I suspect most of us never do."

"But why External Operations?"

Varden said, "Somebody thought it looked like something."

"Well. There's a reason."

"External applied some of their software to the image." Varden reached and keyed the display.

A green, teardrop-shaped, three-dimensional, skeletal outline faded in, then rotated itself and settled over the grainy image. A red label flashed on screen. "Identification Positive. Probability ninety-nine percent."

Polian's jaw dropped and he gripped the handheld and stared. "That's impossible."

"External Operations claim they used the same image-matching software for after-action reconnaissance of that wreck on Dead End last year. The mass and the shape are laydowns. The 'bot did get a mass and motion reading before it failed. There's nothing alive inside the aircraft."

Polian stared at the grainy black teardrop that hung in thin air while smoke and flame roared up past it, his mouth still agape. Then he turned to Varden. "A Trueborn Scorpion falls in my lap and that son of a bitch Gill doesn't even call me?"

"He tried, sir. When he couldn't get you, that's why he called me. Remember? Your bed was on do-not—"

"I remember. What did he tell you, precisely?"

"Precisely?" Varden shuffled again.

"I'm old, Varden. Best make your points before I die."

"Director Gill told me I had ten minutes to get my provi ass over here and bring you up to speed. Or he would put a field boot up it. I think he meant figuratively."

Polian coughed into his fist.

So Gill realized the importance of this development to their plan, and wasn't withholding information. Good.

Polian looked up at Varden. "So what's Gill doing now?"

"Trueborn hardware's External Operations' exclusive jurisdiction. The Director's scrambled a wreck-recovery team with a mobile inspection unit to Stack Fourteen Eastern. They're shutting the stack down."

Polian sat a moment, narrowed his eyes. "Wreck? No, Varden. Trueborn case officers sometimes insert themselves into hostile environments in Scorpions. A C-drive craft, whether it's a Scorpion or a starship, can simply hover indefinitely. That ship's not wrecked, it's parked."

Varden shook his head. "No, sir, the Trueborn case officer didn't park it. Remember? The way we got the transponder on him was when he went through customs."

Polian cut Varden off with a raised palm. "Parker. The lightbulb salesman's real name is Jazen Parker. He's a Trueborn *junior* case officer."

Max Polian's normal business had always been maintaining order within Yavet. Securing her against external threats had been the business of others. Until the Trueborns killed Ruberd. Max now knew

Trueborn covert operational methods as well as any counterespionage instructor knew them.

"Parker didn't park that Scorpion, his partner did. Trueborn case officers work in two-officer teams, a junior and a senior. The book on this Parker was that his personal emotional compass overrode his professional compass once too often. He resigned his commission after his senior case officer downchecked him. He was too sentimental. Protected her to the detriment of accomplishing their missions. He reentered service only to rescue her when she was stranded on Tressel. Our plan assumed he would follow his heart again if the bait was strong enough, and come here alone."

"But he didn't?"

Polian nodded. "Present evidence suddenly suggests we underestimated the Trueborns' ability to keep Parker on their leash. He didn't come here on his own. He came here as a decoy."

"Then what do we—?"

"Lock down a cubic three vertical levels and four horizontal blocks centered on that hotel room you said his transponder's stationary in. If either he or she tries to get in or out, pick 'em up."

"She? Sir, about the woman, I also need to tell you—"

"That Parker's senior case officer partner's a woman? Oh, I know that, Varden. I also know that, among other things, she's a pilot. I'll bet my pension she's the one who flew that Scorpion in here." Polian shook his head. The Trueborns were a devious lot. "We think we've got their presence under control because we've got Parker tagged. And all the while, he's a decoy, so his partner runs free, doing God knows what."

"What would she do, sir?"

"Nothing good. She's already confessed to more war crimes than a Trueborn Nazi. We know that because Director Gill's staff intelligence officer—" Polian paused, swallowed. The officer was Polian's son. "—interrogated her on Tressel. But the Tressens let her get away."

"Oh. I didn't know about any of that, sir." He shifted, foot to foot, again. "When I mentioned the woman, I meant the *other* woman. The older one. The one we couldn't find, who you've been so concerned about."

Polian's breath hitched, and he reached out and grasped his aide's forearm. "What about her?"

"Well, the detail just came in from the surveillance team that dogged Parker's worm transponder. He was down and up and all over the place. Slippery as a peep. He knows the utilities like he was born here."

"He was. That's beside the point right now."

"Frankly, he embarrassed his surveillance team a little. By the time they finally got a visual on him, he was in the vicinity of this hotel, and in the company of a middle-aged male big. The two of them entered the hotel room when a middle-aged female big opened the door. If the team hadn't been looking for something out of the ordinary, nothing would have seemed unusual. But all of the subjects' movements were executed tactically. Not the way a lightbulb salesman and a middle-aged tourist couple would behave."

"Tourist couple?"

"The room was taken by a medical technician and a bank vice president from Rand. They arrived on a cruiser a week ago. We'd never have looked at them twice. They just got fifty-hour bugs implanted in their clothing, like normal arrivals. Their bugs have already died. Even knowing what to look for, their legend's impeccable, right down to the retinals."

"I told you it would be. That's why we needed to get Parker the lightbulb salesman here in the flesh. To bring us together with them. Did the surveillance team check with the hotel?"

"Yes, sir. The couple prepaid their stay in cash. Smugglers sell out of that hotel, so the management saw nothing unusual in that. All the desk personnel remember is that these two carried in all their meals. And the man went jogging every morning."

"But the only tail he had was a snitch tail, who lost him. So we have no idea what he was up to."

"Why, yes, sir. Also, the couple called down for a foldaway, but the desk clerk says a lot of their guests rent foldaways to display goods that they sell out of the room."

Polian raised a hand, smiled. "Don't tell me. The day they rented the foldaway is the day Orion Parker slipped her tails and dumped her bug."

"Why, yes, sir. Exactly."

Polian shook his head. "We lost a dying she-gnome older than I am. Varden, tomorrow get me the files of the officers who lost her. No. The *former* officers.

Varden swallowed. "Yes, sir."

As Polian sat on the divan and thought, he realized that he still hadn't urinated.

Varden sat patiently, finally said, "Sir, it looks like we've got the high-value old woman, and Parker the case officer, and maybe even Parker's partner the war criminal, and the old midwife all in the bag right now. Shouldn't we mobilize a horizontal tac squad, and a punch-down team to blow the roof, and a punch-up team to blow the floor, and go pick 'em all up? Before something changes?"

Polian smiled.

Maybe he had underestimated Varden. From most perspectives, the provi's plan had things just about right. But the only perspective that counted right now was Max Polian's own.

He stood and shuffled toward the bedroom.

"Sir?"

"Varden, what I want you to do is to go liase with Gill's team that's pulling that Scorpion out of the stack. But keep your distance. They won't know a Scorpion from a bathtub, and the thing's undoubtedly booby-trapped to blow itself to hell and take them with it."

Varden's mouth hung open. "Alright, sir. But what are *you* going to do?"

Polian looked back over his shoulder. "Me, Varden? I'm going to go take a leak."

The boy stood like a statue once again, until Polian shooed him, with a hand that Max thought suddenly looked less old and less bony. "Off you go, Varden!"

THIRTY-SIX

Mort felt Kit peek around another corner, again, with the technique employed by a nervous coot.

"Sonuvabitch!" She whispered it aloud.

Two humans, backs to her, stood thirty human paces from Kit. They were wrapped in hard shells, similar to the type John Buford, who brought his meals, wore. These two also carried the long black stingers that frequently went together with such shells. Small humans surged around them, but the two blocked the way such that Kit could not pass them without being seen. And the hard-shelled pair intercepted all larger humans who attempted to pass them.

"What has happened, Kit?"

"Dunno. This is the fourth passage I've tried. The Yavi have locked down the area above and below and around Jazen's location. They're pulling over all the regular-size pedestrians. That either means they know where Jazen is, or they know I'm here in Yaven, or probably both. I'm good at disguises, but I can't shrink. That was Jazen's problem once he got grown up here."

"It is no longer a piece of pie?"

"Now it's a piece of something else. I'm two hundred yards from Jazen, and I still have twenty minutes to get to him and get him out and headed back to the Scorpion. But I might as well be two hundred light years away. Goddamn it, I'd kill for a phone that worked in this goddamn hive. And Jazen's number."

"You do not seriously mean you are going to kill not for food?"

"Correct. A gunfight would just announce me. A couple hundred thousand Yavi wearing body armor against one Trueborn wearing clothes that aren't even her color are bad odds. You're sure you can't phone Jazen for me?"

"As you say, one among hundreds of thousands are bad odds. It is certain that I cannot contact him soon enough. But if I could contact him, what would you have me ask?"

"He knows his way around. Ask him where I can get a piece of pie."

"Ha-ha?"

"Yeah." Mort felt in Kit a surge of hope, an idea that came, and was stored, before he could understand it. But then, emotionally, she plunged again.

"Mort, I could never have gotten this far without you. But I think we'll both be happier if you stay out of my head from here on out."

"But I may be able to assist! And I wish to know how this matter resolves. Have I not earned that?"

"You've earned the right not *to know. Just leave me alone!" Kit turned and followed the throngs of small humans who were moving away from the Yavi with the stingers, rather than toward Jazen. It was as though Kit had given up trying to reach Jazen.*

Her anxiety pressed against him now. He knew few jokes to lighten a human's mood, so he thought, "Kit, if you cannot be good, be careful."

She continued her progress with a huntress' singlemindedness that kept him from reading her intentions clearly. Rather than lightening her mood, the restated joke had turned her sullen and angry.

Exactly as it had the last time he had made the same joke to her.

He felt a woog nearby, and began to stalk it. He remained weak, and hunting was that which he did best. Kit, also, knew that which she did best. So had Mort's mother known. He had always done as his mother had bidden him, because she knew best. He remained puzzled and disappointed at Kit's secrecy and remorse. But he decided to do as Kit had bidden him.

So, despite reservations, he left Kit alone, as she had demanded, and resumed his pursuit of the woog.

THIRTY-SEVEN

Once Varden had left and Max Polian had relieved himself, Max walked to the utility closet off the study, opened the double doors wide, and unloaded cartons until his back ached. When he at last uncovered the wheeled, sealed plastek he sought, he dragged it into the center of the room, unlocked the lid, then stood, stretched and rested.

He hadn't worn his tactical armor since he had been promoted to his first desk job twenty years earlier. But the container had preserved even the seals and the batteries, which winked green on the tester, as though the suit had been hanging in his closet overnight, waiting for him to slip it on like an old friend, and begin pounding his beat.

As soon as he lifted his helmet out and turned it in his hands, memories, both muscle memory and the other ones, washed over him like the sea had the day he first took Ruberd to stand waist-deep and feel the water's chill through his resistant waders.

Baryl hadn't been there to see it, of course. She had never seen their son at all. She had never regained consciousness after Ruberd's birth, leaving Max to raise the boy alone. Sometimes it seemed almost wrong that a man whose wife had died giving birth to a legal child spent his own life hunting down women because they gave birth to an Illegal.

He lifted the first-aid pouch, checked its contents. Even in so menial an object Polian saw the contradictions in his life. The Expansion Compress was intended to stop the bleeding that a needler was built to maximize. But it was more commonly called a smother pack because it worked so well when repurposed to smother newborns. And so Max Polian had learned to keep his personal life and his professional life sealed in mental boxes as perfectly insulated as the one he had just opened.

Until now. Now was a time to serve Yavet, to do his duty. But it was also a time to avenge his son's murder.

Max lifted out his old needler, charged the cylinders, cleared, locked and loaded. Then he raised the weapon until its receiver rested cool against his cheek, then sighted down the barrel. He flicked the selector to "Test," then squeezed the trigger.

The familiar hiss and accompanying blue flash lit the dim room, then faded. The single zeroing dart quivered in the scarcely damaged far wall, an inch left of his point of aim.

Max dialed the windage knob right one click, then set about shrugging into the rest of his uniform.

Unlike the brutal gunpowder bludgeons the Trueborns still wielded, needlers were the elegant weapons of disciplined warriors. That was what he had been, what Ruberd had been, what the Trueborns could never be.

Max lifted out his webbed harness, shortened it round the shoulders where he had lost muscle, let it out round the middle where he had gained girth.

His 'puter chimed; he read the display, then answered.

"Max? Ulys Gill. Did your provi tell you what's afoot?"

"It's all falling into place, Ulys. The Scorpion's a bonus."

"If we can keep it from blowing up. I don't want to send any of my kids on a suicide mission. But Max, this changes the poko game. This is no longer just some kid we've quietly lured in to use as bait to catch his mother, then call her a spy. If the Trueborns have risked a Scorpion, they know the stakes. If we take this agent's mother alive, we may force the Trueborns' hand. If we hand her over dead, they'll think we pumped her dry first. What's in her head isn't worth the risk."

"Risk?" Max found himself shaking his head at the invisible hand-wringer on the phone.

"Max, a one-sided nuclear war that could start within months and be over in a day."

No. If this worked, and it couldn't *not* work now, Max Polian would be Chairman of the Central Committee within weeks. Then the plan the old men had scorned when he had presented it years before could be reality in just weeks more. Yavet could easily smuggle suitcase nukes onto outworlds that the Trueborns valued highly, like Rand and Funhouse. Trueborn smuggling "security" was a sieve. Once the Trueborns could no longer strike Yavet without killing a few hundred million of their bankers and their valued customers, they would be stalemated. Yavet would build her starships. This was no time for hand-wringing.

Early in the Trueborns' own Cold War, Russia possessed scant ability to deliver *her* nuclear weapons onto America, but America possessed the means to annihilate Russia. Russia tried to draw to a poko hand as weak, and as strong, as the one Max and Yavet now held in this moment. Russia secretly began emplacing nukes on an island near America. But when America called Russia's bluff, her leaders lost their nerve, folded, and removed their nukes from Cuba. Thereafter, as the Trueborn historians overdramatically put everything, Russia sank onto history's ash heap.

The Trueborn historians were also fond of saying that those who did not learn from the past were condemned to repeat it. Max Polian had not given his life and his only son to arrive at this moment, then lose his nerve and fold like the Russians had folded.

"Max? Are you still there?"

Polian blinked. "Yes, Ulys."

Gill would fold. If the little old moustache were allowed to play the game, he would fold.

Max said, "I agree. Ulys, I'm going to order the cordon around the Trueborn spies to stand fast until further notice. That will give us time to work out a plan. Some accommodation with the Trueborns. They're not bad sorts, really."

Now the silence came from Gill's end of the conversation.

"Ulys?"

"Yes, Max. I think that's wise of you. Very wise. You'll let me know if you have additional thoughts?"

"Of course. Immediately." Max cut the call, then punched up the major in charge of the cordon. With each unanswered trill of the ring signal, Max fidgeted. Gill sounded uncertain, perhaps even suspicious. If Gill followed up, Max wanted to be sure that Gill found the situation precisely as Max had described it to his weak-kneed coconspirator.

Polian squeezed his 'puter, as though he could wring an answer from it.

The major's voice came to Max, at last. "Director! How may I be of service, sir?"

"Major, I want all of your men to hold their positions. No matter what, no one approaches that hotel room. Freeze the punch-down and punch-up teams. I don't want so much as a sound or sight of our presence to spook the Trueborns. Best shut down the surveillance video and audio feeds, too. Can't be too careful."

"Uh. Yes, sir. What if the Trueborns come to us?"

"Excellent point, Major." Max buckled on the last of his armor, tucked his extra magazines into the pockets on his web belt, along with the first aid pack. "Do as I say. Hold your positions. I'm on my way. We'll discuss it when I arrive."

"*You're* coming *here*, sir? Very good, sir."

Polian cut the connection, turned in front of the reflective glass on the closet door. Neither he nor his armor were as sleek as the current models of cops or armor. But both would do.

He rummaged once more in his old chest for a breaching charge, tucked it away then locked on his helmet and walked out to win the Cold War.

Even without his slider, it took Polian only ten minutes to drop and jink to the major's command post on foot. The nearer Max got to the cordoned cubic volume, the emptier the passages and verticals grew.

Even, or perhaps especially, empty of little people. They had realized this wasn't about them when only bigs were being stopped and questioned. But they knew something was afoot, and if a needler round did go wrong, the peeps knew a cop wouldn't waste his smother pack to stop *their* bleeding. So they had taken to the utilities, as they always did, where Polian's police could not, or now, by long habit, did not follow even where they could.

The old mail was heavier than he remembered, and by the time he arrived at the Command Post, he was puffing.

The CP consisted of four sliders arrayed to block a major intersection, manned communications consoles, and a twelve-man tactical ready-response team who milled about, but at a hand wave would do the major's bidding.

"Sir!" The major's salute was crisp, and he smiled out through his open visor. He eyed Polian's aged armor, his needler, and the Director General's insignia Polian had affixed over the suit's original badges. "I didn't expect to see you tactical, Director."

"I'm going in for a look round."

"Oh." The major's forehead wrinkled, but he motioned for a sergeant to assemble the Tactical team.

"Alone."

At this point nothing good could come of the application of excessive force by Polian's men. The astropolitical crux of this moment was to take the Trueborn starship captain alive. A nervous trigger finger, a miscalculated top- or bottom-breaching charge, misdosed gas, the slightest error could render the woman worthless meat. And, of course, if Max's plan failed because she died uninterrogated, he at least retained the chance to spin his version of the story if there were no witnesses to contradict his version.

The personal crux of the moment was that Max Polian intended to confront one, or in a perfect world, both of Ruberd's killers, look into their eyes, then end their lives by his own hand. As cold-bloodedly as they had ended Ruberd's. And if Parker's own mother watched him die screaming, so much the better.

Perhaps Max could send a team to take them alive, then interrogate them at leisure. But the risk that too many cooks would spoil the taste of his revenge was too great.

The major waved the tacticals to stand down. "Yes, sir. If they did try to make a run and you happened across them, the surveillance people estimate they're four individuals total, possibly one peep, too. Armed with two gunpowder pistols at most, and maybe a couple shivs among them. And no personal armor." He eyed Polian again. "No match for even . . ."

Polian clapped the major's shoulder like the gentle uncle he always was to the men, and smiled. "For even an old man like me? Don't worry, son, I can still take care of myself. But I may need some target practice. So even if you hear shooting, don't come running."

THIRTY-EIGHT

My father shook his head at me, smiled. "It's not a crock! I was Commodore Metzger's best man at the first starship bubble wedding. His bride was my gunner, and the two of them were the best friends I ever had," He reached across the square, gray table in my parents' hotel Kube at which he sat with Orion, my mother and me, and patted my mother's hand. "Until I met your mother." My father's voice cracked and he blinked. "Neither of them lived to see the War end."

Obviously, my mother hadn't been dad's date at that wedding. So I studied her face as he told the story. She seemed to look not at him but through him, as though there were a part of him missing, a part she had never seen and would never see. Although he didn't mention it, not in his words, not in his eyes, whoever *had* been Dad's date had been more than a one-night stand. A lot more.

The ten thousand humans aboard that cobbled-together ship on that long-ago wedding day went on to fight and win the Battle of Ganymede. My father wound up commanding the seven hundred who came home. Evidently that person had not been among the seven hundred.

I cocked my head.

My father was turning out to be far less jerk, and far more intelligent, funny, noble and astonishingly experienced than he had been in my mind all my life.

Orion, who sat beside me nodding, smiling as my father told the story, dozed off and slumped against my shoulder. She felt no more substantial than a windblown scarf. I caught her with my opposite hand, then lifted her like a gray-tufted bundle of sticks, carried her to the foldout set along the room's far wall and laid her on her side.

Before I tucked the sheet around her shoulders, I lifted the chicken bone that had been her arm and read her dosimeter patch. It had slipped to yellow, and stress had begun to stretch Orion's face, though the pain hadn't awakened her yet.

I frowned, spoke over my shoulder to my mother and father, "Mom? Can you bring me more junk? One blue vial."

Just because Orion never let me get within spitting distance of anyone who used or purveyed Ya Ya Cohon's most first-class opiates didn't mean I hadn't learned how they worked. Junk was as much a part of peep life as stealing bean bars and dodging cops. If you grew up peep you saw the junk. You smelled it. You saw it kill good people. You saw bad people kill to get it. And now, perversely, what I had learned about the junk was a blessing and not a curse for Orion.

My mother pressed a blue into my palm. "There are two more of these. Then three greens. Then nothing."

I looked around the Kube.

Luxuriant to a downlevels Yavi's eyes, it was just a cheap hotel room to a Trueborn. I was a feeling like a little of both these days.

Like me, this room could pass for Trueborn, but worn down by too much hard use.

The floor tiles were the gray of the walls, which were the gray of the ceiling, when it didn't glow, and the gray of the furniture, when it wasn't retracted. Compared to a cheap hotel room on Earth, the square footage here was lower, the cubic less due to the lower ceiling, and if you didn't pay extra, and my parents hadn't, you didn't get a window to the passage. So the flimsy door, set in the middle of the room's short front wall between two benches, was the only feature that relieved the smooth featurelessness of the box. There was the usual Sanex and temp cube at the rear.

I rolled the blue between my fingers, nodded. "We've got the morphine straws. She can suck on those to tide her over even if I can't make the same connection tomorrow."

My mother sat down opposite me on the foldout. There was plenty of room. Curled up asleep, Orion occupied no more space than a rolled throw rug.

Admiral Mimi Ozawa, star ship captain emeritus, semi-pro spy and my bonus mom, shook her head as she frowned down at sleeping Orion. Mom laid her palm on Orion's forehead, nodded. "Cool. Good."

Mom turned out to be a woman of few words. She also turned out to be a couple inches shorter than Kit, but just as physically trim and mentally and reflexively quick. She had hair as ebony as Syrene's, streaked with gray and pulled back, and brown eyes with the exotic shape common both to Marini courtesans like Syrene and to Asian-descended Trueborns. She also looked just young enough to be trouble, if she hadn't been my mother. I wasn't surprised that my father never seemed to tire of looking at her.

I plugged the blue into the cat I had installed on Orion's forearm, when a vein had been less difficult to find than it would become. The cancer was literally eating her alive hour to hour now, and plumbing's as easy to buy as the junk itself.

A team's junior case officer's the medical specialist. My medical training was here and now as much a blessing for me as the junk was for Orion.

Not just because my training eased Orion's pain here at the end, but because ministering to Orion gave me something to do that helped her. If I just had to sit by and watch her suffer, I might have lost my sanity. Not that pumping junk into a woman whose only previous drug of choice had been bourbon filled me with joy. I don't think even the kick-ass Trueborn doctors Edwin Trentin-Born counted in his circle of friends could have done anything better for her. Even the Trueborns shot their patients with junk to palliate someone in the advanced stage of deterioration Orion had reached.

My little peep's chest barely raised the sheet as she breathed, but she would get a few hours of what passed for quality time now.

I stepped back to the table and sat opposite my father.

He had field stripped a gunpowder pistol he had bought, and was wiping the parts with a towelette for the third time since he and I had arrived back here. It had been a cheap local street buy, and probably had an effective range of ten yards.

Orion had always told me he had carried a nice antique Trueborn piece, a real hand cannon, but smuggling it in this time would have been a stupid risk.

My father turned periodically and peered at a wireless micro-cam receiver that he had also bought. The thing was the size of an old Trueborn paper book, and it showed the feed from the tack cam out in the corridor that had been pinned above this room's door.

It wasn't high-tech stuff. Trueborn children had been throwing away better electronics than that, as soon as the batteries died, since before the War. But what was taken for granted off Yavet was dear on Yavet if the government didn't want you to have it. Children being the most obvious example.

While my parents had learned some lessons about surviving on Yavet since their last visit, there was one lesson they had not learned. They had bought a local phone on the street, even though they had no particular need to call anyone. I took it back to the street, set it down and turned away. It was gone in ninety seconds, making it somebody else's problem and maybe confusing the vice lice who spent their days and nights monitoring phones.

Not that phones on Yavet were useless or inexpensive. That's why the one I set down had become gone so fast. The trouble with phones on Yavet was the trouble that spawned P-mail in the rest of the known universe. Little people who were engaged in something illegal, which was pretty much all of them as well as the rest of us, called phones peep traps, because not only did the phone's internal chip track you as though you had swallowed a vice bug, but anything you said, as the cops in the trueborn gangster holos said, "could and would be used against you." Of course, the part about "in a court of law" was, on Yavet, replaced by "to kick the shit out of you anytime your government feels like it."

No phone meant that changing my plans to meet my abruptly changed circumstances was not as near as every Trueborn's wrist 'puter.

Kit and I had learned to live with the maxim that the first casualty of any battle was the plan. We had learned to live even longer by improvising like bandits when the plan went up in flames during the first fifteen seconds of the battle.

So I improvised.

My original plan had involved spending some quality time with Orion, then using the contact Ya Ya's people had provided me to book return passage, upship, return to Mousetrap and get on with sorting the mess that the rest of my life had become.

My plan now had to be to make the time I could spend with Orion even higher quality, and to get my parents and myself the hell off this rock pronto. Tomorrow was the soonest I could leave word of my slight intended plan change for Ya Ya's person at a dead drop at Green and sixteenth, Twenty-seven Lower. And while I was out I would buy junk for Orion.

My dad worked the slide on his very clean pistol, reinserted the magazine in the butt, and laid it on the table.

We had time to kill. I had questions. He and Mom had answers, and a son who shoots his own life mother up with the junk isn't going to be offended if those answers revealed ignoble conduct. So I was blunt. "Dad, what the hell happened at the end of the War?"

My mother, who had been fixing tea paks at the temp box, gathered three cups as deftly as any Shipyard waitress, came and sat with us. Then she raised her eyebrows at Dad. "What do you think?"

Dad looked into my eyes, pursed his lips. "You've had a fine career already. You're a highly decorated officer. A successful businessman. Does it mean that much to know ancient history about two old folks you never met until yesterday?"

My mother touched my arm. "You're even better looking than your father. With a wonderful smile. And Kit seems like the most wonderful woman. The past doesn't really matter, does it?"

I canted my head. "Is this another Hibble blow-off?"

They both laughed.

Apparently they knew the same Howard I knew.

I said, "I don't care if you ran guns or dope or sold us out to the Slugs. I don't care if you killed all the Slug babies like you were vice cops, then peed on the bodies. I just need to know."

My mother stiffened. "My God. You think it was something like that?" She turned to Dad. "All they can do is hang us. Tell him."

"Why me?"

"You did it. I'm just the only living witness."

"They'll hang you too."

"They'll have to catch us first."

Did normal children have this much trouble getting a straight answer from their parents?

I steepled my fingers. "Please? Just the nutshell. I deserve to know."

I was starting to think that whether I deserved to know or not, I didn't want to know. But the Trueborns didn't hang the child for the sins of the parents. The Yavi owned the patent on doing that.

My father sipped his tea, like GIs do before they tell a war story, then cleared his throat. "You want the nutshell? Gateway wasn't a great battle. It was a clusterfuck."

So far, to me as a GI, my father sounded one hundred percent credible.

"It was a ship-to-ship engagement, not infantry. I stowed away to be there. When the cluster unfucked, I, the dumb grunt stowaway infantryman, wound up the only survivor on the only ship that made it through the last jump into the Slug rear. I could have killed him."

"Them."

"Him. It's just one entity. We talked. It's a telepath. Talks to the rest of itself in real time all across the universe."

I shook my head. "Three intelligent species and *we're* the slow kids who can't read minds. No wonder we don't advertise this."

My mother wrinkled her forehead. "What, Dear?"

"Nothing." I leaned forward. "Then you killed them? It."

My father shook his head. "I could've. It said it just wanted to leave this universe."

I stared at my mother, pointed at my father. "He let the Pseudocephalopod Hegemony go?" I shook my head at my father. "Your duty—"

"My duty was to try to do the right thing. I decided the right thing was to trust and not to kill anymore."

"It didn't kill you."

"It trusted me. It spit me back across the jump."

My mother said, "My cruiser just picked your father up. He was half dead."

I sat back in my chair.

Holy crap. History was a lie. Well, of course it was. I knew the liar who wrote it. "And who knows about this?"

Mom said, "The intelligence officer who took your father's after-action report in the infirmary knew a hot potato when he heard it. He brought it straight to me. I ordered him to shut his pie hole. I reported it straight to Howard Hibble when his ship rendezvoused with us. The intelligence officer died in Encino fourteen years ago. So, who knows the truth? Us. Howard. Now you. And I think Howard has told each incoming President since."

I shook my head slowly.

Double holy crap. "Sixty million dead and you let him go? And the Slugs are still out there? If people knew, they'd hang you both. And they'd go nuts."

"Howard knew that. But Jazen, will you sleep worse now that you know it's a lie?"

After the war we had passed the Intelligent Species Protection Act because we never wanted to commit species genocide again. How could it be wrong that we hadn't done it in the first place, after all? "No. I suppose I won't."

My parents weren't baby killers or profiteers or deserters after all. Therefore, I slept damn well while my father, the good, if arguably criminally naïve, Samaritan took the next watch.

I had just wanted to know, for better or for worse. Knowing it was for better was icing on the cake.

Orion laughed. "He was on the *crapper*?"

I was awakened two hours later by Orion's and my parents' collective laughter as my father told yet another war story.

I levered myself up on one elbow, threw off the blanket and sat up on the floor tiles where I had slept. The tale my father was wrapping up sounded slightly less improbable than the one about the giant telepathic Slug, but it made Orion laugh, which made it better than true.

I made Orion tea and carried it to her on the foldout. Her dosimeter was still in the green.

She wiped tears from her eyes before she sat up and sipped. "God, it doesn't get better than this."

She had laughed so hard she cried.

I blinked back tears, myself.

What had Ya Ya Cohon said on Funhouse about how he would beat the rap? "Make you cry from happy?"

Orion patted the foldout beside her, and I sat. She looked at my mother, pointed at me. "Isn't he the best-looking man you ever saw?"

My mother nodded. "He looks like his father."

"Poor bastard." My father was sitting at the table, watching the passage monitor while he polished that damn cheap pistol again. He slid it across the table to me. "Your watch."

As I picked his pistol up, Orion lay back, then pulled my head down to her lips and whispered, "It really can't get any better than this, baby. Now you got another mother, I can rest."

Then she pressed her thin lips to my cheek and closed her eyes.

I sat with her there, and held her hand while she breathed, shallower and shallower, and ten minutes later her tiny hand turned cold in mine.

I wept for my mother while my mother held my hand and rocked me. Maybe Orion was right. It couldn't get any better than that for a kid who had nobody for so long. It certainly couldn't get better for Orion, who chose to die on her own terms. Not many of us get that choice.

"Jazen!" My father whispered, as he stood beside the table, pointing at the monitor screen with one hand.

He held out his free hand, wiggled the fingers, whispered again, "The pistol!"

THIRTY-NINE

Adrenaline crackled through me like an electric shock, and I stood and stepped away from Orion and my mother, then peered at the monitor as I drew my father's pistol from my trouser waistband.

The lighting in the passage was crap. The cheap camera made it worse.

Mom and Dad had chosen the room because it was isolated, surrounded by the blank walls of machinery rooms. There would be no other guests in this passage but lost ones. This shadow moved deliberately, not lost.

I had thought that we were pretty safe here. I had dumped my bug, Orion had dumped hers before she came, and, after I went over their clothing, I figured my parents were clean. After all, their legends were dead solid perfect. That meant that they would have been assigned a snitch tail, which was, of course, about like no tail at all.

I had also gotten rid of their damn phone in time, I thought.

Dad whispered, "A little person foraging for food?"

I shook my head. "Too big for a peep."

"It's just one person, Jazen. Not a squad."

I adjusted my hold on the pistol grip. "Doesn't mean anything. You got a twelve-pack last time because they were busting an illegal birth. Vice overkills Illegals to set an example."

"But just one cop?"

"If they drop a twelve-pack on us, or punch up from below or down from above, or gas us, Mom could get hurt. She's the prize."

The figure had gotten within ten yards, now, but still was just a clump of animate pixels. I couldn't distinguish whether he carried a long gun, but that would be the worst case.

Plan for the worst, be pleasantly surprised if it's better.

If the guy had a long needler, and got through the door in tactical armor, my father's pistol wouldn't be worth jack. If I shot the cop through the door first, however, I might knock him off balance. Yavi cops use and are used to being shot at with needlers, which won't penetrate doors worth spit. The element of surprise isn't all that great unless it's the only element you've got.

I dropped into a tactical crouch, selected an aiming point, based on where a cop of average height's neck ring would join his helmet, then thumbed off the safety.

My father slapped my arm down, pointed at his button monitor and whispered. "Don't the cops here all wear body armor?"

The silhouette creeping toward the door wasn't peep short, but the profile didn't match the sleek new style of body armor I had seen since I had been here, either. I leveled the pistol at the door again.

A barely audible whisper rasped in the passage. "Parker?"

I whispered to my father, "It's not Cohon's contact. He doesn't know my name."

My father kept his hand on my forearm. "Orion's name is Parker, too."

I shook my head, shrugged off his hand, tightened my grip on the pistol butt and snaked my finger inside the trigger guard.

"Jazen! It's me."

I guess the voice you most want to hear in the world is unrecognizable if it's also the voice you least expect to hear in the world.

My jaw dropped. "Kit?"

"Open the freakin' door!"

She scooted inside, my father closed and locked it behind her, and we faced each other.

We generally limit kissy huggy during tactical situations anyway, and she was holding a big-ass nine millimeter. Not unusual, but it would be hell if your death certificate read "accidentally shot due to euphoric hug."

Her face looked like a tangerine. "Sleep in the tanning bed again?"

"You always know how to make a woman feel special, Parker. Long story."

The four of us stood staring at one another like delegates to a jaw-dropping convention.

Finally, I said, "How the hell—?"

Kit said, "I remembered how you said you could still dodge the cops and swipe food by moving through the utilities, even after you got big. I followed the little people and asked them directions as I went."

I eyed her Yavi civvies, shook my head.

She picked at her blouse with thumb and forefinger. "I know. Not my color."

I rolled my eyes. "I meant, you look mid-level Yavi enough. You didn't need to—"

It was her turn to head-shake. "The Yavi have the passages they *think* Trueborn spies would have to use cordoned off for at least two levels up and down, and two blocks all around this hotel."

I closed my eyes. "Crap."

"Not really. I made it in here through the utilities, and I'm a first time tourist. You're the last of the freakin' Mohicans in this place. All you have to do is lead the three of us to Stack Fourteen, Eastern, Ninety-six Lower."

I squinted. "Why would we—?"

"You think I walked here? There's a Scorpion double parked inside that stack waiting for us. Might be a warm climb, but—"

"Kit, that may be the reason this place is cordoned off. If the Yavi found your ship, it's not an escape vehicle, it's bait."

She rolled her eyes. We did that to each other a lot in these moments. It's that contrasting viewpoint thing.

"Jesus, Parker!" She threw up her hands. "Just once. Just *once*, would you cross bridges when you come to 'em? Then let 'em collapse underneath you?" She turned to my parents, who stood watching our back-and-forth like the two of us were chimps playing tennis. Kit held out her hands to them like she was pleading for a call from the line judge.

Then her mouth went round and she said, "Oh. Oh!"

Kit shifted her pistol to her left hand, used the fingers of her right to comb her hair, then stuck the hand out toward them.

I suppose there are more awkward circumstances for a girl to meet her boyfriend's parents than having to move your pistol to shake hands in the middle of a clandestine rescue attempt. Or maybe not, if your hair looks like you blow-dried it with a flame thrower.

I said, "Mom, Dad. This is Kit."

Kit said, "Jazen and I—"

My mother reached out and took Kit's hand in both of hers, smiling. "Oh, we know! Jazen never stops talking about you, dear."

Speaking as a boyfriend, this was all going surprisingly well. Speaking as a spy, though, we were all still up shit creek.

I said to Kit, "I assume that Scorpion's got a lit fuse?"

She nodded, slid up her blouse sleeve and displayed a locked on countdown timer on her wrist. Then she tucked the pistol away, bent and tightened her shoe laces. "Fifty-seven minutes and counting. Time to run like we stole something."

I glanced at my mother and father, and they nodded.

My father laid his hand on my mother's shoulder. "We'll keep up."

Then I remembered something I had almost forgotten. I stepped back into the room, knelt alongside the foldout and pulled back the sheet. Then I bent, kissed Orion's cold and slight cheek one last time, and whispered, "For Ya Ya."

Promises kept. All of them.

Kit knelt beside me and touched my arm. "Orion?" Kit's voice trembled.

I nodded, then stepped past the three of them to take the lead. As I inched sideways around Kit, I said, "I assume there's a pick-up point in the neighborhood?"

She nodded. "A listening post in a moonlet. It smells like garbage."

"Long, boring story. Later. Everybody stay close on me. This should be pretty straightforward." I drew the shiv I had stolen; Kit and my father each drew their pistols, then I stepped toward the room's door and reached out to open it.

Boom!

The door reached back at me like the fist of God, and slammed me backward and off my feet.

My back struck Kit, and she shot sideways like the seven pin on the way toward the ten of a seven-ten split.

In that slowed-down instant, I saw my father drop into a tactical crouch, and his pistol cracked, spit orange flame and kicked up from the recoil. I thought that he was quick for an old guy.

To his front, the blue flash of a needler spit back as I heard it hiss.

Then the room's rear wall introduced itself to the back of my head and I didn't see or hear anything at all.

FORTY

At first, when I got my bearings, lying on the hotel Kube's floor, I thought I didn't have my bearings at all and had reverted to childhood. A vice cop in armor stood in the blown, smoking doorway, his long gun needler trained on us.

The needler whined as its cylinders recharged. But I hadn't seen armor like he wore, the old mail stuff, since I was a kid. His visor was up, and I saw that he was an old man. Shallow in the cheeks, with thin, white hair, he looked older than my father looked, probably not older than my father actually was.

As the ringing in my ears subsided, I heard my mother sobbing to my left.

The room's door lay where it fell in the room's center, deformed by the breaching charge so that it rocked like a tray, and it still smoked and crackled.

Beyond the ruined door, my mother knelt in the room's far corner, cradling my father's head in her lap. The old cop's needler had caught Dad somewhere in the upper body. He was unconscious and bleeding buckets. I couldn't tell more specifically about the wound, because my mother had snatched the sheet off Orion's body and had wadded it to try and stop the bleeding.

I staggered to my knees, started toward my mother and father.

"No, Captain Parker."

I turned my head, then froze. The old man in armor was pointing his needler at me.

There were powder burns on the guy's armor. My dad had hit him at close range, but most of the guns the government allows to be sold on Yavet are specifically calculated to be good enough to kill peeps and other crooks but bad enough to be worthless against cop armor.

I said to the Yavi, "Can't you see he's wounded?"

The old man snorted. "I should hope so. I shot him. Didn't I, Colonel Born?"

I turned.

Kit stood in the corner of the room opposite my mother and father. She was apparently uninjured by either the blast or by getting pinballed into the corner, and she still grasped her pistol. But she appeared confused, because she didn't have the pistol trained on the bad guy, but sort of waved it listlessly, side to side.

"Kit!"

She looked at me, and I realized that tears streamed down her cheeks, and her head shook side to side, as slowly and listlessly as her pistol. She must have been injured in the fall after all, concussed.

"Kit!" I pointed at the guy's face.

His faceplate was wide open, and she could make that head shot at this range literally blindfolded. Even I could.

I pantomimed a pistol with thumb up and index finger extended. "*Shoot* the fucker!"

The old guy shifted his aim to Kit, needler trained center mass on her torso, but he spoke to me. "You don't get it, Parker, do you? Frankly, I didn't either until I saw your partner's face just now."

I got to my feet, stepped slowly between Kit and my mother, shaking my head at Kit. "No."

The Yavi said, "Yes, Parker. Yes. I thought you and Colonel Born were here working together, Mr. Inside and Ms. Outside. But that's not the case, is it, Colonel? Tell him. You were sent here with two priorities. Follow your deserter partner to Yavet, then assist him to get his mother the starship captain off Yavet without interrogation. But that was priority two. Parker, priority one for Colonel Born was and still is to kill Admiral Ozawa over there, so we can't interrogate her. And to kill you too, if you interfere."

I looked into Kit's eyes, and saw that the Yavi, whoever the hell he was and however he knew, was right. When I had said to myself that I had never seen Kit Born cry at asassinations, I had been amusing myself. Kit motioned me to step aside with a head jerk. Her tears kept flowing, and the tip of the nine-millimeter's barrel quivered like her lip did. But the muzzle remained aimed dead center mass at me, where I stood now, with my body shielding my mother.

Now I shook my own head. "No, Kit."

She didn't speak, just nodded yes. Then she waved me to stand aside with a tiny jerk of the pistol's muzzle.

The Yavi said, "It's so *interesting* to watch a cold-blooded assassin's mind work. Colonel Born is calculating, Parker. Not about whether to kill Admiral Ozawa. That's just duty and simple mathematics. The Colonel has her orders. And the trade is simple for a soldier. One life, or perhaps two, against her planet's future."

The Yavi was right. Kit had assumed it wouldn't come to this. She had been confident that when she came to the bridge, even if it collapsed under her, something good would happen. Because it always did for her. But this time nothing good had happened, and she didn't know how to deal with the awful reality.

From the corner of my eye, I saw the Yavi shift his weight.

Then he said, "No, the hard calculation for the Colonel in this moment is the *how* of it: If she shifts her aiming point to me, I'll squeeze my trigger. The Colonel will be lucky to get a shot off at all, much less an aimed one. So, can she hit her own partner fast enough and hard enough that he will fall away and give her the kill shot she needs? Before I blow a hole in her chest?" The Yavi said to Kit, "Well, Colonel Born, what do they say in those awful gangster holos you all pollute the universe with? Do you feel lucky, Colonel? Do you?"

Kit closed her eyes, then very slowly elevated her pistol's muzzle straight toward the ceiling. Then she tilted her head back and opened her mouth like a sword swallower.

I knew for that instant that she had made her decision, and that it was none of the above. She was going to turn her pistol's muzzle against the roof of her mouth and blow her own brains against the wall behind her, rather than make an impossible choice.

I leapt at her, hand outstretched. "No!"

My leap bought a millisecond's distraction from the Yavi.

Kit seized the opportunity. She dove to her left and snapped off a shot at him.

But my movement didn't buy her enough time.

The Yavi's needler hissed; its blue flash lit the room.

Kit spun to the floor, and her pistol skittered away, barrel smoking.

She lay on the tiles, eyes bulging, gasping, as her left arm flailed blindly and spastically.

I sprang to her, cradled her in my arms, and sucked in a breath so hard that I heard myself shriek.

I had dug bullets out of her before, sewn knife wounds, set broken bones. But this?

Kit's dive had kept the needler from tearing her heart out. But her right shoulder was gone. Not the bone and sinew. The shoulder's ball joint was visible, and bone white and slippery red with blood from the clavicle almost to her elbow. The muscle, the blood vessels, all nature's wondrous little intricacies, were shredded beyond recognition. Blood pulsed and spurted.

I forced myself to breathe.

She was gasping, swallowing air. Her airway was clear. Next.

Stop the bleeding. Where? Where was the bleeding? What was the mnemonic for the axillary artery? "Screw The Lawyers Save A Patient." The branch nearest the heart was "Screw." Superior thoracic. The biggest vessel. Calm. Start with that.

I probed bloody tissue with trembling fingers, over and over.

"Fuck!" There was no more superior thoracic, just its pulsing shreds.

The bleeding was everywhere. There was no hole in the dike to stick a finger in, no reason to follow the mnemonic toward "Save A Patient." The Yavi made needlers to kill human beings with a single shot, and needlers did that supremely well.

I looked up at the Yavi.

He had moved over to the bench near the door, and now sat with his helmet in his lap. He was dabbing blood from a graze wound on his cheek, where Kit's shot had almost found its mark. He dabbed with a steri that he had removed from his open first aid pack with one hand while he kept his needler trained on me with the other.

I cradled Kit with one arm while she teetered in shock on the edge of consciousness. Already her blood pooled slick on the floor beneath her.

I pointed at his first-aid pack with one hand. "Please. Your smother pack."

He made a thin smile while he dabbed his blood. He didn't answer.

I said, "I'll tell you anything. I'll do anything. The pack. She's bleeding to death."

"Tempting. Save her, then interrogate you both before we try you for war crimes."

I felt Kit's free hand claw my shirt, looked down. Her eyes were wide and she managed an infinitesimal head shake. "No interrogation. Never again . . . bleed out first."

I turned back to the Yavi, but he was glancing at my mother. She was focused on my father, pressing so hard on a pressure point, trying to contain *his* bleeding, that her forearms trembled.

I asked the Yavi, "Who the hell are you? Did we do something to you?"

"Not to me, directly. Remember Tressel? I'm Max Polian. You two murdered my son, Ruberd."

"Ruberd? Tressel? Hell, you're a soldier. If your son was a soldier you know how it works."

Polian. Hadn't there been a Major Polian on Tressel? Intel weenie. And this guy. His uniform markings were pin-ons, but they were a Director General's rank insignia. And Polian, Orion's control officer. No time to sort it now.

Director General Polian sighed an old man sigh. "I know how *this* works. I am going to sit here and watch you while you watch your assassin partner die. Then I will shoot you, too, and watch *you* bleed to death. Then your mother over there will tell us how to build starships. I suppose it would be more valuable, strictly from an intelligence standpoint, to keep you two alive for interrogation. And more humane to show you compassion and mercy. Just like you showed compassion and mercy to Ruberd."

I eyed Kit's gun.

It lay eight feet from me. I could go for it, and Ruberd's father would cut me down before I got within four feet of it. Or there was a one in a thousand chance that Polian would sneeze at that instant or something, and I could shoot him dead. I would rob his smother pack off his corpse, and maybe prolong Kit's life. Like Kit said, sometimes you just have to cross that bridge and let it collapse under you.

What would Ya Ya Cohon say? That one thousand to one against are still better odds than one thousand to zero against.

I measured distances, slid my hand out from under Kit. I didn't look at Polian, just listened until I heard him sigh, and hoped that in that instant he was also doing the old man stretch.

I sprang for the pistol.

As my fingertips brushed the pistol's barrel, I saw the blue flash, heard the needler hiss.

And waited to feel the spinning needles rip me open.

Didn't happen.

FORTY-ONE

Polian had shot Kit again!

Despite the gun now inches from my fingers, panic turned my head. No, Kit lay still and bleeding, but unchanged.

"Gaak."

I swiveled toward Polian.

The old man rocked back and forth as he sat, one gauntleted hand clawing at his neck ring, the other empty and his needler on the floor. His eyes bulged, and blood foamed and pulsed from an exit wound that gaped in his throat where his Adam's apple had been.

He managed to point his mailed index finger at Kit and at me, then blood exploded from his throat wound as he tried to scream through a shredded windpipe, and only whistled like a ghost. "You—"

He toppled forward, and before he hit the floor tiles I was on him, tearing at his first-aid pouch for its smother pack.

When Polian fell, I saw his killer standing behind him.

The small man wore modern armor, not old mail like Polian's, and the needler in his hand, whining as its small single cylinder cycled, was an officer's sidearm, a Yavi soldier's weapon, not a cop's long gun.

As I worked the smother pack free from beneath Polian's dead body, the other Yavi plucked his own smother pack out, tossed it to my mother and pointed at me as he said to her, "Watch what your son does with his. Do the same to your husband."

I sat back with the smother pack in hand, tore away the sterile wrap as I stared at our well-informed benefactor. His visor was up, and he was older than Polian, with a broad, gray moustache.

"Who the hell are you?"

I glanced at my mother, who still sat with bloody fingers pressed into my father's torso. Holding up my pack so she saw it, I grasped the red tape between thumb and forefinger, pulled.

She nodded, eyes wide, and mimicked.

"Gill. My name is Ulys Gill."

The small Yavi went to my mother, knelt and supported my father's body so she could work. The flashes on his armor were imprinted, not pinned on. Another Director General? There were only two uniformed service directorates, so the brass was thick in here.

As the pack swelled and heated, I molded it around the butcher's waste that had been Kit's beautiful shoulder. The pain stiffened her, her eyes flew open, and I pressed the side of my hand into her mouth when she opened it to scream.

"Bite! Ow." I nodded. "Good girl. Keep it up. It's a bitch 'til the air pockets are pressed out."

When she finally spit my hand out, she reached with her free hand and clawed weakly at the dressing.

I pulled her fingers away. "Tear that dressing and you *will* bleed to death."

Her eyes were closed, and she hissed through clenched teeth, "Deserve to."

I kissed her forehead while she slapped at my chest, her hand like a dishrag.

"It's the shock talking. We'll cross that bridge when it collapses underneath us."

Gill laid his hand on my shoulder. "Your father's stable, too. But I need to get you all out of here."

I stared at this small old man, shook my head. "Why the hell are you doing this?"

He had holstered his needler while he helped my mother. Kit's pistol lay a foot from my hand. This Gill was not just any Yavi, he was a high-value target. And I was a soldier whose duty was to whack high-value targets. But my father had been a soldier with a duty once, too. And instead of pulling one more trigger, he had trusted somebody he didn't even know.

I let Kit's pistol lay.

Gill said, "I want your mother off this planet alive, along with credible witnesses who can assure your leaders that Yavet hasn't used her to learn how to build starships."

"Because you think the Trueborns will preemptively nuke Yavet?"

"Will?" Gill shook his head. "I hope you won't. But you can. And you might. I'm a soldier. I prepare for what I know my adversary *can* do, then I have to guess what he *might* do." He nodded toward Polian's body. "I guessed right about Max. That he was prepared to sow the wind even if he reaped the whirlwind. He may not be the only one in our government who thinks that way. So I won't risk just turning you all in."

I nodded. "Your rank cut ice with the people out in the cordon. They won't come in here unless you or Polian tell them to. You each bluffed your way in here alone. But now, if you turn us in, there's explaining to do. If we 'escape,' less. Even a Director General can't get away with murder. Especially if the victim's another DG."

He smiled. "And one suspected of being a scrubbed peep, at that."

A Yavi officer who was a peep? I looked at his face again, pointed. "Tressel. You were the commanding Officer. You were five feet from me. I could have blown your face off."

"So I suppose this makes us even. Captain Parker, you and I are a pair of ex-Legion bastardized peeps with many stories to swap. But right now we hold in our hands the fate of the world that gave us life. And also the lives of Colonel Born and General Wander." He pointed at the countdown timer on Kit's wrist. "Shall we move our bastard asses before that spaceship of yours blows itself up?"

"I've aborted self-destructs before." I shook my head, "But I can't fly a Scorpion." I nodded toward Kit. "She's the pilot."

Gill tugged his lip. "We could get you all out however you got in. Criminals find government money spends as well as everyone else's. Medical attention in the meantime's a problem. The crooked physicians are incompetent. The competent physicians talk too much."

I looked at Kit again. She lay in a pool of her blood that was already drying up.

I said to Gill, "No time, anyway. And you say you can't control what the rest of the government may do with us if we wait."

I didn't ask to be in charge of this clusterfuck. It wasn't my fault. Well, not entirely. But now that I was in charge, nobody, not my mother, not my father, most certainly not Kit, was getting interrogated by the Yavi on my watch. Our way out was to fly to the moonlet Kit had mentioned. There, my mother would be safe from Yavi interrogation, and Kit and my father could get patched up. We had a ship. But we couldn't fly it.

Gill and I stared at one another.

Two clever scrubbed peeps who had come *that close* to pushing the doomsday clock hands back an hour. Instead, we sat and watched as Kit's timer winked down to twenty-one minutes. But we had not one decent idea between us.

My mother touched my arm. "Dear, if it would help, I've logged sixteen hundred left-seat hours in Scorpions."

"Mom?"

She raised her right hand. "Swear to God. If it's operable, I can burn the paint off that sucker."

Gill and I looked at the timer, which flicked to nineteen minutes as we watched, then at each other.

He said, "I'll get my car."

"Do it. My mother and I will get these two ready to move."

FORTY-TWO

It took Gill ten minutes to bring his car up.

While he did, I triaged Kit and my father, then shot them both up with syrettes from Gill's and Polian's first-aid packs. Both needed transfusions and more. But they were stable enough that if we could get them to Kit's listening-post moonlet, and if it had a decent infirmary, they each had a chance. Which was better than they had if they stayed here on Yavet.

Gill appeared in the room's doorway, still blissfully alone. Where does a Director General drive his car? Anywhere he wants to.

He frowned. "Can we move them twenty yards? My car's too big to get any closer."

Having now spent time on Earth, I smiled at that.

Actually, there were no "cars" in stack cities, where goods and garbage moved through the utilities and people moved horizontally on jammed sliding pedways, up and down in elevators or updraft tubes. Or just walked or climbed the old-fashioned way. Gill's "car," or "slider," was an underpowered four-place wheeled vehicle that Trueborns would derisively call a "golf cart."

"Golf," by the way, involved overlandscaping perfectly good countryside, then contesting upon it a game, played with flails and a small ball, that was so difficult that it was described as a good walk spoilt. The Trueborns fixed that not by taking away the spoilage, but by taking away the walk, replacing it with "golf carts." As if that wasn't fix enough, I hear there's now a full-contact version of golf you can bet on at Funhouse.

Three minutes later, we got my father and Kit into the back seats of Gill's vehicle. We discovered that, although it was designed for four, it held all of five people. As long as one of the five didn't feel weird riding with a woman on his lap who looked just young enough to be trouble, but was his mother.

Gill's car resembled a blacked-out egg on tiny wheels, was normally driven not by Gill but by his aide and bore Director General's tags.

That last proved critical. Few Yavi could afford sliders. Most wouldn't bother to afford one if they could. The passage crowds, in the passages wide enough for sliders at all, made sliders into egg-shaped black doorstops.

Unless the slider had Director General's tags. Then if pedestrians or other sliders failed to yield, the DG's driver shot the miscreant or had him or her questioned. "Getting questioned" involved the good old chain-mail boot kicking that I remembered so nostalgically. So shooting was usually unnecessary.

Ulys Gill was unaccustomed to driving himself, but he knew where the switches for the flashing lights and siren were.

The human seas parted everywhere we went.

With nine minutes to spare, we made a whooping, flashing, suitably theatrical entrance to the chamber at the base of Stack Fourteen, Eastern, Ninety-six Lower. The stack's main access door had been rolled open, and the chamber bustled with Gill's uniformed tech nerds.

Then an armored Yavi, needler in one hand, stepped into the path of Gill's car with his palm upraised. He was a cop, not one of Gill's nerds.

My heart pounded faster.

Gill may have been a DG, but his passengers were probably just a little too suspicious to pass muster if the cop peeked inside Gill's vehicle.

I looked over at Gill, then back at our unconscious cargo, and asked Gill, "Now what?"

Gill hopped out of the egg and slammed the door behind himself, and the guard snapped to and saluted. We sat invisible inside Gill's blacked-out staff car and I listened to my heart pound.

A fat-lipped kid in internal-security uniform peeled off the bustle, ran to Gill and the guard and joined their discussion.

My mother shifted on my lap. "That boy's hat looks ridiculous."

I reached round, took Kit's wrist and read the timer. "Four minutes."

Eventually, the kid in the ridiculous hat, which marked him as a provisional lieutenant, said something to the cop, whom he outranked. Then the provi formed up all the personnel, including the armed guard, then led them away, double time.

As soon as Gill's techs were all out of sight, Gill waved me forward.

I jumped out of his cart, ran toward him, then the two of us dashed ahead into the stack.

The stack had been shut down, but both the floor grate and wall plates remained too hot to touch with a bare hand.

Kit's Scorpion floated perhaps fifty feet above our heads in the stack's dimness.

The clock in my head said we had two minutes before our ride home blew itself to pieces.

A wheeled maintenance scaffold unit sat parked and still folded on the floor grate, directly beneath the Scorpion. A WMS was basically what Trueborns, for whom food still grew on trees, called a "cherry picker."

Gill and I clambered into the cherry picker's basket, Gill slammed down a lever on the basket's frame, and the whining machinery lifted the panting pair of us up toward the Scorpion's open canopy.

I said, "What lie did you tell the provi and the cop?"

"That she was gonna blow any second. Don't they say that in your holos?"

I raised my eyebrows. "Sometimes the truth *will* set you free."

The elevator platform lurched, stopped. I leaned into the Scorpion's interior, looked round the cabin.

Finding the countdown timer was easy. First, because it was a beer-can-sized bolt-on mounted in the middle of the center console above the monitors. Second, because its dinner-roll-sized slap button flashed red and read "ABORT?" in black letters, while the remaining seconds showed below, ticking down. Usually, an explosive timer started flashing only when time zero was less than one minute away.

Forty-four seconds.

I swung into the copilot's seat, and the seat harness buckles clanked as I landed atop them. Then I hammered the abort button with my fist.

The button kept flashing, but the display changed to five flashing green dashes across the red, and above them the words, "ENTER CODE."

Thirty-nine seconds.

What the hell had I been thinking? Of course it was password protected. And the Yavi had had no more clue what code Kit had set when she activated it than I did. And she wasn't talking.

Howard's cryptographic nerds taught me that the probability of randomly guessing a five-character letter-number password was less than one in fifty million.

"Fuck!" I pounded the button in frustration.

Thirty-six seconds and counting.

The display kept flashing red, but the message changed. "ENTER *CORRECT* CODE. ONE TRIAL REMAINING."

This time when I yelled "Fuck," I kept my fist off the button. I waved my hand at Gill, "Get away!"

I could run, too. Like a Yavi needler, the booby trap's violence was probably calculated to incinerate the Scorpion and its contents rather than to create collateral damage. If I ran this instant, thirty seconds might be enough to save my life.

But what life?

My experience with Ya Ya Cohon had taught me that there was no money in betting favorites. You had to bet the underdog to win big enough to make the game worth playing.

Kit had always wanted me to cross more bridges when I came to them, even if they collapsed. But that had been when the probability of Kit and me having a future together was less than one out of fifty million. I had ceased to be in Kit's plans for us months ago. Maybe.

I bet the fifty million to one 'dog that in Kit's mind there was still a chance for us together. I stabbed with my index finger at the keypad and entered D-a-1-s-y.

The timer flashed again.

Eleven seconds.

But the number didn't change.

Then the red light went dark, except for the words "CODE CORRECT. FIRING SEQUENCE ABORTED."

I released a breath I hadn't realized I had been holding, sucked in a fresh one.

After that, at our relative leisure Gill and I moved Kit, and then my dad, into the cherry picker's basket, then secured them like the invaluable cargo they were in the Scorpion's two side-by-side rear seats.

My mom slipped into the pilot's seat and began preflighting the Scorpion, humming as she fingered touchscreens, as though she were mixing cookie batter.

It occurred to me that a man of my age, and of sufficient life experience that he and his girlfriend shared what Mort would call a coital password, ought to be embarrassed that his mother had to drive him on a date. I wasn't.

Ulys Gill and I faced each other in the still-smoking and crackling stack beneath the flying black pumpkinseed that would, perhaps, carry my mother, my father, the love of my life and me safely away from this hell. Or at least carry us as far as a hollow rock that smelled like garbage, where we could wait for a ride home.

I said to Gill, "This may all be hard for you to explain."

Gill cocked his head, shrugged. "You think so? What we mistook for a booby-trap timer was an autopilot countdown timer. Trueborns are too cheap to blow up an expensive ship. The ship took off like a homing pigeon. The midwife shot Polian. The two of them have a history, you know. She isn't the first snitch who tried to shoot her case officer, although she may be the first one to get credit for succeeding. Pity all of you got away, and of course you took the weapon that killed Max with you. You're all still at large. Until some bodies turn up that will be unmatchable in the absence of DNA evidence."

I wrinkled my forehead. "Absence?"

"Don't Trueborns watch their own police holos? Bleach." Gill made a smile so small that it emerged a frown. "Captain Parker, Illegals like you and me learn to lie for our lives from the day we're born. It's risky business, but it's the only business we have."

"It's a business you're at ease with. My boss will be disappointed if I don't ask whether you'll do ongoing business with us."

"Me? A Trueborn mole?" Ulys Gill shook his head. "What I do here I do for Yavet. She's flawed, but she's my home."

"I understand being a soldier and a patriot. So am I."

"You and me? The same?" Gill wrinkled his nose as though something rotten had caught in his gray moustache. "Captain, I'm what we call an old moustache. A vestige of the day on Yavet when a soldier served civilians, rather than kicked them like Polian's people do now. In those days war was decided between combatants on a battlefield. I'm not fond of war at all. But this pretending? What you and Colonel Born call 'cold' war? I'm even less fond of that." He shook his head. "Treachery. Backstabbing conducted in the shadows."

"You don't like the way we do things."

"I don't like that you have to do them. Or that I do."

"It keeps mankind at a balance point. We both just saw how easily the balance can tip."

Gill stared up the stack, into the darkness. "Perhaps. Perhaps we can make it better."

I shook Gill's hand. "If Howard Hibble doesn't have a new mole here on Yavet, will you tell me whether he has a mole problem of his own back home?"

Gill looked down at the smoldering debris that dotted the stack floor, crossed his arms. "I told you I'm a patriot. So, no, I won't tell you anything like that. I should be insulted that you'd ask. But I will tell you this, only because it's in Yavet's self interest. This business was an aberration, not a military or intelligence operation conducted by Yavet. Please assure your boss, and his boss, of that. Max was a cop, not a soldier, and a cop whose sense of duty and of right and wrong was crippled by the loss of his son. He was taken advantage of by a man who was neither a soldier nor a spy of Yavet. In fact, Max got your personnel file, and the concept of this plot, from a Trueborn. An industrialist. The fellow wanted a free hand on DE 476, of all peculiar things, out of the deal."

My jaw dropped. "Rat bastard Cutler?"

"You know the man."

"I do. So does an eleven-ton monster who wants to meet him in a dark alley."

"I wish you both luck with that. And luck to us all for the future."

Ulys Gill saluted and spun an about-face, and I rode the cherry picker back up to the Scorpion one more time. My mother closed the canopy and rotated the Scorpion's nose up as easily as if she had backed out of the garage, then the Scorpion hovered motionless there, pointed up toward the pitch-black sky beyond the stack.

She tapped her fingernails on the universal joystick, looked around at the pretty green lights on the canopy.

Whooom!

The Scorpion shuddered as the stack restarted. Red flame and smoke began roaring around us, and the outside air temperature and windspeed indicators on the console changed from green to yellow to red.

A Scorpion's built to withstand vastly worse conditions, but even so . . .

Still my mother sat, oblivious. Sometimes I accompanied Kit when she stood in for Edwin and visited assisted living facilities, where elderly human shells sat vacant-eyed and oblivious.

My heart skipped. Then sank.

My mother looked and acted just young enough to be trouble. But in straight-line time, she may have been pushing one hundred years old. She had certainly known how to build a starship. Once. Maybe even fly a Scorpion. Once.

But now? Had we nearly gone to nuclear war, and spilled my father's and my lover's blood, to prevent an old lady from being asked questions to which the Yavi could force her to respond, but to which she had forgotten the answers?

The irony of it was bad. The reality of it made it worse.

Now the four of us were stuck hanging here in hell's basement. Sooner or later the Yavi would pick us up, and all our sacrifices would have been for naught.

But it wasn't her fault. And she was my mother.

I reached across the console, patted her hand gently, and whispered, "You've forgotten, haven't you?"

"Why, no, dear. I believe you have. And you've done this before, which makes it more disappointing."

I opened my mouth, shook my head in tiny strokes. "What?"

"I can wait as long as you can. Your father forgets, too. And I wait for him."

"Mom?"

"Big spy. Big general. That doesn't impress an Admiral, you know. There are old pilots and there are bold pilots." She reached to the canopy, touched a row of overhead keys with her index finger, her lips moving as she counted each one. "But this pilot doesn't cut corners. Dear, this ship doesn't budge until you fasten your seat harness."

I buckled up, and my mother blew the paint off that sucker.

FORTY-THREE

One year to the day after my mother flew my father, Kit and myself off Yavet, Kit and I "walked together on a lawn," which was another way of describing what golf was when unspoilt. The lawn was at a place located outside the Trueborn American puzzle factory called Washington, D.C. The place was called Walter Reed Military Convalescent Center.

Walter Reed was a Trueborn American army surgeon who noticed in 1896 that GIs who marched around in swamps caught yellow fever, while their officers, who sat on their asses back in camp, didn't. Reed theorized that this was because swamp mosquitoes carried the disease. Reed's insight eventually saved millions of GIs, and even more millions of civilians, from death by yellow fever. So, ever since, there has always been a military medical facility in the Washington area named after Walter Reed. If Dr. Reed had also invented a way to prevent officers from sitting on their asses, GIs would've named Washington after him, too.

As Kit and I walked on the soft grass, me in civvies, Kit still in convalescent whites, I gently squeezed the fingers of her new hand.

She smiled and squeezed back.

I said, "Stronger today."

She smiled again. "Stronger every day the therapy gorilla lets you sleep over."

The therapy gorilla said Kit's new arm would eventually be

indistinguishable from the one she lost. But it would be awhile before she would squeeze a trigger again. If I had my way, it would be forever.

The sleepovers were less about what Mort called coitus, though that was coming back nicely, and more about giving her an anchor when the dreams woke her, and about helping her through the other pathologies of Post Traumatic Stress Disorder, which the gorilla said in Kit's case were "exacerbated." Although from what I had learned by hanging out at Big Walt, unexacerbated PTSD was the kind that happened to somebody else.

The strip of lawn that Kit and I were crossing separated the rear of the hospital's eight-story main building from its parking lot. In front of the acres of spaces filled by the Chyotas of the people who did Big Walt's actual work were three VIP spaces, each occupied by a spook-black limo.

As we walked, the main building's rear glass doors hushed open and a squad-sized gaggle of briefcase-toting, gray-suited men and women bustled in front of us like ducks crossing a highway. The frowning ducks mounted their blacked-out limos, then sped away.

Kit raised her eyebrows. "Howard's legal eagles are flying the coop early today."

I nodded. "Then let's go upstairs and say hello."

Various legal eagles spoiled most of Howard's days lately, because while Kit, my parents and I were returning from Yavet, an anonymous source leaked to the Trueborn American media a report about how the Pseudocephalopod War had really ended. This report provoked outrage and widespread panic across the American Trueborn population.

It also provoked an alleged heart attack in the alleged anonymous source, who had since that time holed his allegedly lying ass up on Walter Reed's top floor like a reclusive billionaire. The best argument that the source was *not* Howard Hibble was that the report told the truth, a commodity unfamiliar to him.

Actually, what provoked the outrage and widespread panic wasn't so much the truth, but the Trueborn American media, which was as unfamiliar with the truth as Howard was. Outrage and widespread panic were the media's stock in trade, in the way that carrots and bananas are a grocer's stock in trade.

However, for Trueborn Americans, for whom the future always works out, outrage and widespread panic have the shelf life of grocery-store produce. After a couple of news cycles, the bananas turned brown. The outcome of a war that ended decades before, in a vacuum at the end of the universe, got replaced on media shelves by fresh and fragrant crises.

Not a few pundits reflected that the revealed truth reflected better on mankind as a species than the long-told lie did.

One suspects that the anonymous source knew all of that when he reportedly leaked his unconfirmed report.

More importantly, he also realized that the immediate relatives of the sixty million war dead, who would at the War's end have been rightly and egregiously offended for innocents and heroes unavenged, were now largely dead themselves, and so didn't care.

The dead themselves, who had the most skin in the game, had been dead a long time, would stay dead even longer, and so didn't care.

And mankind cared, and should care, more about preventing the likes of once and future yellow fevers than about dissipating its limited capacity for good by fearing and containing boogeymen who had long since left the closet.

So even though it turned out that mankind hadn't killed the Slugs after all, Trueborn America, and so the universe that followed its lead, went on about its business.

Well, almost all of it did.

When Kit and I disembarked the elevator on Walter Reed's top floor, a female nurse behind a desk that blocked access to the floor glanced up from her handheld. The printed sign on her desk read:

MATERIAL WITNESS SEQUESTRATION FACILITY
ACCESS LIMITED TO WITNESS' COUNSEL, JUDGE ADVOCATE GENERAL
AND COMMITTEE STAFF, JUSTICE DEPARTMENT COUNSEL,
AND AUTHORIZED GUESTS.

As a frequent authorized guest, I said to the nurse, "How's the material witness doing today?"

She shrugged. "Dying as usual." She pointed a stylus down the hall. "Go see for yourself."

Howard Hibble, the floor's sole patient, sat propped up in his bed, wearing a hospital gown. Tubes and wires sprouted from his shriveled body like those little rootlets that erupt on past-date carrots.

"Jazen! Kit!" Howard looked up from his handheld and smiled, looking surprisingly chipper for a man who had been dying regularly for the best part of a year.

I asked, "Did the lawyers leave because you're finally well enough to testify about the cover-up and the leak?"

Although the media's business was outrage and panic, and the general populace's business was business, Washington's business was, first, to be shocked—shocked!—about things that it had no ability to remedy, and, second, to find somebody besides itself to blame for them.

Therefore, for the best part of a year, Congress, the Justice Department, the Judge Advocate General's Corps, the Sierra Club, Amnesty Interplanetary, and, probably, the Chancellor of the Exchequer if America had one, wanted a piece of Howard Hibble. Of course, all those entities had wanted a piece of Howard for decades, and so far none of them had gotten one.

Howard coughed like the smoker he had once been, maybe one cough more than necessary to be convincing. "Regrettably, I'm not going to be able to testify yet. Actually, my cardiologists are talking replacement heart."

I rolled my eyes. The legal eagles had finally caught Howard Hibble in a lie. "That implies you had one in the first place, Howard."

Kit asked, "Do you buy your cardiologists the same place Bart Cutler buys his anonymity and his pardons?"

Actually, although Cutler had gone to ground as a fugitive somewhere among five hundred twelve planets, his anonymity was about to spoil like warm rutabagas.

Now that Mort had honed his ability to locate a single human being in the vastness of the cosmos by chasing me, he was spending his mental spare time hunting for the man who killed his mother. Cutler had been convicted and sentenced *in absentia* of treason. Cutler probably would still find a politician corrupt enough to sell him a pardon, as long as it became effective after Cutler was hanged.

But money could still buy anonymity for some.

Three months after Kit, my parents and I returned to Earth, news accounts of a Sotheby's auction reported that "the sole surviving authenticated original from the series of sixteen oils by C.M. Coolidge, circa 1903 A.D., frequently reproduced in schlock pop culture and collectively known as 'dogs playing poker,' sold for a record price to a well qualified buyer."

The accounts noted that "well qualified" meant an anonymous buyer with net worth in excess of ten billion. I'm no gambler, but I'd bet I knew the buyer, and knew how he became well qualified.

The same accounts also reported that at the same auction "a one-hundred-six-carat perfect blue-white Weichselan diamond, the largest such piece ever offered for sale, fetched a record price for undisclosed sellers."

By happy coincidence, my parents shortly thereafter purchased a retirement home on Florida's platinum coast, where my father is recuperating well from a procedure medically similar to Kit's.

My parents' little shack is just a yacht's throw down the beach from Edwin Trentin-Born's compound. I don't know whether Edwin's the kind of guy who loves his neighbors, but he seems to accept his neighbors' son better since my parents moved in. Or maybe I just accept being their son better now.

Howard grunted at his handheld as he got a report of something new from somewhere. He was still King of the Spooks, running his show from his hospital bed, despite dodging Washington flak. I suspect he kept his job, as he always had, because his hunches had so often wound up saving mankind's produce from the disposal.

Howard said, "We just got product back from Utility 5. Ulys Gill was elected to the Central Committee. Now that's a change that stabilizes the balance point."

I rolled my eyes again. "Change? Really? The Yavi still have nukes. So do we. The people in charge on Yavet are still repressive, genocidal environmental rapists. We're still over-privileged hedonists who waste our time and our money betting on bloodsports. While our politicians waste their time and our money arguing about nothing. Howard, do you really believe we're gonna make it?"

Howard looked from Kit to me, then he stared up at the ceiling, as though he could see through it all the way to the stars. "Make it? I believe mankind will always make it. We may make it by the skin of our teeth, but we will always make it. And that's the truth."

Then he lay back and closed his eyes.

AFTERWORD

Cliff's Notes for *Balance Point:*

My wife and I once sat my daughter down with us at our kitchen table to resolve some now-unremembered error that probably involved Kool-Aid and a Dustbuster. The Accused clutched her mother's forearm, wept, and pleaded, "I won't do it again! Just don't have Dad *explain* it to me!"

Like my daughter, fiction readers hate it when authors *explain* it to them. Fiction readers want to laugh a lot, cry a little, and learn something about life, and about the world, that they didn't know. But readers don't want a novel that turns into The Fourth Grader's Big Book of Story Problems.

Fiction editors know this. So, when fiction writers forget this, editors decorate our manuscripts with red marginal notations like "Cut! Readers will *get* this (or don't need to know it) anyway!" Or, in Hollywood screenplay-ese, "Cut!!! Too on-the-nose!!!"

What we authors cut, whether by editorial fiat or by self-inflicted wound, usually involves parallels from our life experience or from history that inspired some or all of our story.

This afterword adds back for curious readers a brief and "on-the-nose" guide to some of those anecdotes and historical parallels that would have slowed *Balance Point* as a story, or would have been "too on-the-nose."

I'm a child of the Cold War. So, therefore, is *Balance Point*. I hope it conveys, from the comfortable distance that conversational science fiction imparts, the mood of a time when every day that mankind didn't blow itself up was a gift, and much of the world presumed every foreigner was a spy.

But I know that generations who already see 9-11 as mere touchpad digits may already irretrievably see the Cold War only as a black-and-white non-war that was contested by dead people. But not *zombie* dead people, so who, like, *cares*?

Balance Point doesn't bid to retell the Cold War like a quasi-historic thriller. Maybe you got that from the three-eyed King Kong on the cover. Rather, *Balance Point* is more a memory quilt appliqued with interesting, telling and occasionally true anecdotes. Or at least the author hopes readers find them so.

So, in no particular order:

Starship technology is like the A-bomb, and the last half of the twentieth century would undoubtedly have been vastly different if the West had somehow kept the Soviet Union from getting the A-bomb.

The Trueborns are, overtly and on-the-nose, us Americans. With all our faults and contradictions, I challenge anyone to name a dominant power on the world stage over the course of recorded history that has been a greater net force for good.

The Trueborn's annihilation of the Slugs is like America's use of that A-bomb.

Bombing Hiroshima and Nagasaki horrifically and directly killed, immediately or eventually, between two hundred thousand and three hundred thousand people. But the A-bombings abruptly ended the thirty-one-year cycle of organized violence known as World Wars I and II, which killed over *one hundred million* people.

The so-called *Pax Americanum* that replaced that cycle of violence is blamed for less than *half* as many deaths from all wars and similar conflicts during more than *double* the time. That's still a numbing statistic, but *Pax Americanum* marks the first meaningful interval during human history during which war mortality as a percentage of world population meaningfully *de*creased, rather than sharply increased.

Yet as a people, America's strength is that we remain vigorously but peaceably of two minds whether that decision to use the bomb on Japan, and the ongoing World Police role it thrust upon us, was motivated by, or was for, the good.

Statistical asterisk to the two foregoing paragraphs: The "facts" cited about war dead vary among creditable sources over a range of more than forty million human souls. That's roughly twice the population of the continent of Australia, give or take the Holocaust. Some of those varied sources are neutral. Some have skin in the game, like Robert McNamara and Zbigniew Brezinski.

My middle name is "Douglas," after General Douglas MacArthur. MacArthur was an American general who became the effective military governor of Japan after the A-bombs. He introduced Japan to surrender, representative democracy and baseball. He later would have introduced Red China and North Korea to the A-bomb, if America hadn't restrained him.

My father served under MacArthur, as a tanker scheduled to invade mainland Japan, which never happened because of the A-bombings. The invasion would likely have killed my dad, along with perhaps a million other GIs and five to ten million Japanese. In which case you would not be reading this. So I admit to that skin in this game. Choose your own facts and conclusions if you disagree.

The monolithic, gray, repressive, paranoid, insular and nuke-rich Yavi stand in for, well, you pick 'em. The Soviet Union, Red China, and for a host of wannabes (North Korea, East Germany) come to mind.

Ulys Gill reminds me of Oleg Penkovsky, the Soviet Union GRU Colonel who in 1962 supposedly (In espionage every "fact" should be prefaced with "supposedly." I've said "supposedly" this time. Imply "supposedly" hereafter) feared that his countrymen, who were sneaking nukes targeted on America into Cuba, were crazy enough to use them.

Nuking America would have gotten Penkovsky's Mother Russia blown up far worse than America, to say nothing of ending the world as we know it. So Penkovsky revealed the nukes to America.

By that single sane, but treasonous, act Penkovsky gifted mankind with one get-out-of-blowing-ourselves-up-free card that we have to date used wisely.

But if Penkovsky was a sane traitor, he wasn't a profligate traitor. Like Gill, he refused to rat out other Soviet spies he knew about to his adversary. Unlike Gill, Penkovsky's sanity earned him a Soviet bullet in the back of his head.

In *Balance Point,* Max Polian, who was crazy enough to blow up his world, got the bullet to the back of the head. Because if reality were just, we wouldn't need fiction to teach us what justice should be.

Historical allusions to dead-rat dead drops, eavesdropping from purpose-built garbage mountains, bugging the car phones of hypochondriac Politburo octogenarians, and most of the tradecraft portrayed in *Balance Point*, sound too nutty to be made up. They are in fact presented as accurately as a short-term Cold War era spy knows how.

Another area where *Balance Point*'s fiction is more-or-less true is that although it may be hard and dangerous to smuggle spies and secrets across borders, it's much less hard to smuggle drugs, booze, bulldozers, luxury sedans and people willing to work for less than minimum wage.

Any and all references suggesting familiarity with alcohol, sex for hire, drugs and gambling are in no way autobiographical. And I'm stickin' to it.

All that said, the lives of children of the Cold War have been about other balance points, too. And the book touches on those, too. Like the balance point between risk-taking, and risk-averse, people in love; and the balance point between the green but prosperous planet that Earth, by the skin of her teeth, still is. Compared to the gray, dirty Yavet we might make her into. And maybe the balance point between who children want their parents to be, and who the world lets them be.

Finally, if you know classic science fiction, not well but too well, you recognize that Howard Hibble's last optimistic words about mankind "making it by the skin of our teeth" echo Robert Heinlein's words in a nationally broadcast radio interview with Edward R. Morrow in 1952.

If you don't even know that "nationally broadcast radio" was YouTube without skateboarding cats, Robert Heinlein was a quintessentially American bundle of the conservative, liberal, and libertarian contradictions that characterized the Cold War. In the century following Heinlein's, he remains in any conversation about history's greatest writer of classic science fiction.

But a little homage to science fiction classics goes a long way. Sometimes as long as eight books. So I'll just say so long, and thanks for the fish.

—Robert Buettner

ACKNOWLEDGMENTS

Thanks, first, to my publisher, Toni Weisskopf, for the opportunity, encouragement and insights that helped not only make the Orphan's Legacy books, but made them better. Most of all thanks for her extraordinary patience and encouragement with *Balance Point*, which came as easily to me as pulling grezzen teeth.

Thanks also to my editor Tony Daniel for wisdom, to my copy editor Miranda Guy, for perfection, and to Kurt Miller not only for his always-splendid cover art, but for *his* patience and insight in working with me to create it. Thanks to everyone at Baen books for their never-ending support and enthusiasm.

Thanks, in perpetuity, to my agent, Winifred Golden.

Finally and forever, thanks to Mary Beth for everything that matters.

ABOUT THE AUTHOR

Robert Buettner's best-selling debut novel, *Orphanage*, 2004 Quill Award nominee for Best SF/Fantasy/Horror novel, was compared favorably to Robert Heinlein's *Starship Troopers* by the *Washington Post*, *Denver Post*, Sci-Fi Channel's *Science Fiction Weekly* and others. It has been called the Post-9/11 generation's *Starship Troopers*, and a classic work of modern military science fiction.

Now in its ninth English-language printing, *Orphanage*, and other books in his Jason Wander series, have been republished by the Science Fiction Book Club, and released by various publishers in Chinese, Czech, French, Japanese, Russian and Spanish.

Orphanage has been adapted for film by Olatunde Osunsanmi (*The Fourth Kind*) for Davis Entertainment (*Predator, I, Robot, Eragon*).

Orphan's Triumph, the fifth and final book in the Jason Wander series, was named one of Fandomania's best fifteen science fiction, fantasy and horror books of 2009—one of only two science fiction books to make the list.

Robert was a 2005 Quill nominee for Best New Writer.

In March, 2011, Baen books released *Overkill*, his sixth novel, and in July, 2011, his seventh, *Undercurrents*.

A long-time Heinlein Society member, he wrote the Afterword for Baen's recent re-issue of Heinlein's *Green Hills of Earth/Menace From Earth* short story collection. His own first original short story, *Sticks and Stones,* appears in the 2012 anthology *Armored*, edited by John Joseph Adams. Robert served as the author judge for the 2011 National Space Society Jim Baen Memorial short story writing contest.

Born in 1947 on Manhattan Island, Robert graduated with Honors in Geology from the College of Wooster in 1969, and received his Juris Doctor from the University of Cincinnati in 1973. He served as a U.S. Army intelligence officer, a director of the Southwestern Legal Foundation, and was a National Science Foundation Fellow in Paleontology.

As attorney of record in more than three thousand cases, he practiced in the U.S. federal courts, before courts and administrative tribunals in no fewer than thirteen states, and in five foreign countries. Six, if you count Louisiana.

He lives in Georgia with his family and more bicycles than a grownup needs.

Visit him on the web at *www.RobertBuettner.com.*

AUTHORS PREFACE TO MOLE HUNT

Mole Hunt was originally published electronically, as a Baen Free Library short story, in 2011. The events detailed in *Mole Hunt* occur in the *Orphan's Legacy* series time line before *Balance Point* and after series book 2, *Undercurrents.*

Mole Hunt was written as an experimental standalone short story, and therefore differs radically in style and viewpoint from the rest of the *Orphan's Legacy* series.

Superficial similarities to Shakespeare's *Othello* are purely on purpose.

MOLE HUNT

In the pre-dawn alien twilight, Roald Otman knelt in the mud, and groped until his blood-slick fingers found Rodric's carotid artery. Cold, even in the equatorial heat. First Sergeant Rodric's body lay tangled in death with another bipedal corpse, man-sized and reptilian.

The line wrangler who knelt alongside Otman stared across the ring of cleared ground that separated the two of them from the rain forest. The minefields in that ground protected Downgraded Earthlike 476's human settlement from the rest of this hostile world.

The wrangler shook his head. "Never seen these little ones cross the minefield before."

Otman narrowed his eyes. "But this one did. My cameraman's dead. Why?"

The wrangler pushed his broad-brimmed hat back on his forehead and shrugged. "Bigger pred chasin' after this one probably flushed it across. Coincidence."

Otman frowned. After twelve years as a covert ops mercenary, he disbelieved in coincidence.

The wrangler pointed at the hilt of Rodric's bush knife protruding from the dead beast's throat. It was his turn to narrow his eyes and frown. "For a nature photographer, your friend was good with a knife."

After twelve years in covert ops, Otman also lied easily. He cast his eyes down and pressed his hands to them. The pose was only partly for show. Since his team had hit dirt two days before, he had experienced sharp, momentary headaches. Alien pollen and spores, probably. "It's ironic. My crew and I came to film this uniquely savage ecosystem, and already it has consumed one of us."

The wrangler laid a hand on Otman's shoulder. "Mr. Otman, you seem like a nice fella. Want some advice?"

Otman managed the nicest smile a mercenary killer could, and nodded.

The wrangler, a Trueborn Earthman like the rest of the colonists, rested his hand on the gunpowder revolver holstered at his waist. "Here on Dead End, every man's business is his own."

Otman stifled an eye roll at the prospect of a terracentric rant about liberty and the pursuit of happiness.

"And here every man's business is dangerous." The wrangler pointed into the mist that clung to the distant trees. "But making a movie out there? Call this a preview, a bad omen. Whatever. But Dead End's waiting to eat you alive. The spiders are as big as supper plates. Even the plant eaters are carnivores. They only eat the plants to get the parasites inside. The mid-level predators are like six-legged tyrannosaurs. And on top of the pyramid, the grezzen are eleven tons of speed, guile and meanness. Natural history's not worth what your documentary's gonna cost."

Otman nodded. On that, he agreed with this cowboy. Otman's recon team came here not to film natural history, but to change human history. The prize they sought could win Cold War II for Yavet and lose it for the Trueborns. And that was worth any cost to a Yavi, even one for hire.

Otman said, "Bad omen or not, it's a risk we're prepared to take."

The wrangler looked up at the lightening overcast of his adopted world and sighed. "Well, then, safest time for you all to cross the line is dawn. The nocturnal predators are bedding down. But the day shift's still yawnin' and peein'." He paused. "Sir, I know you're upset. But if you're bound to continue, an early start is safer. I can have the body buried for you."

This civilian had no idea how abhorrent it was to leave a man behind. But Otman the "filmmaker" just swallowed. "That's very kind.

But I would prefer that we return the remains home to Yavet with us. Would it be possible for you to just have Mr. Rodric's remains held at the local morgue until we return in ten days?"

The wrangler raised his eyebrows, just as something huge bellowed from the distant trees. "Sure. Just never thought about the possibility that you'd be returning."

Then, without further discussion or emotion, the man walked back down the trail toward his line cabin. Otman watched him go and felt a strange kinship. This wild outpost and Otman's overpopulated home world shared an indifference to death, though for very different reasons.

Otman stared, arms crossed, at the rainforest's billion billion trees until the Earth man disappeared. Then Otman permitted himself a tear. Rodric had been Otman's non-commissioned right hand for six years. But then Otman blinked, breathed and ground his teeth.

Not at the wrangler's indifference, nor even at Rodric's death, but at his own failure.

As the team's commanding officer, Otman had sent Rodric ahead to recon the vehicle path through the minefield before their "film crew" zigzagged its three vehicles out beyond the perimeter. It was a routine precaution that Otman had delegated a hundred other times in a hundred other places. But this time, Otman had actually wondered, fleetingly, whether predators ever got flushed in across the minefield.

Otman could have—obviously, should have—ordered Rodric to carry a rifle. Otman could have sent two men, not one. But Otman had done neither, because, as the wrangler had just confirmed, this attack was unprecedented.

Coincidence. Bad luck. Bad omens. Otman believed in none of those.

Otman believed in focus on the mission, in discipline and in steel well maintained and accurately aimed.

He zipped Rodric's death into a mental body bag and thumbed his hand talk. No names, no ranks. These Trueborns were frontiersmen, not counterespionage wizards, but a cover worth doing was worth doing to excess. "Bring the vehicles forward. But please don't jolt the editing equipment."

"Yes . . . Mr. Producer. Uh . . . that Trueborn cowboy just passed by on the way back to the settlement. He said Rodric—"

"It's true. But Mr. Rodric went down swinging." Otman looked over his shoulder as three headlight pairs lurched toward him up the trail from the outpost.

He thumbed his hand talk again. "Let's make sure he died for something."

Otman knew that his team, to a man, felt gut-shot at the news of Rodric's death. But he also knew that each man would now seal that loss into his own mental body bag. They would grieve together, but only after the job was done.

Nine hours and fifty miles later, Dead End's hot, humid gray dawn had yielded to its hotter, humider gray afternoon.

Otman peered through the windscreen as he swayed alongside his driver, aboard the second vehicle in a convoy of three. The locally rented, six-wheeled bush cats snaked around tree boles so thick that the biggest arterial uptube in the biggest stack city on Yavet could have easily fit inside one.

Otman drew a breath of local air that went down as thick and hot as breakfast syrup, and smiled. Heat. Humidity. Allergies provoked by a billion billion trees' pollen. Otman loved it all.

Yavi grew up in stacked cities with ceilings for sky. Diagnosed agoraphiles like Otman, who enjoyed open spaces, were aberrant outcasts among Yavi. Fit to fight their society's battles, but ill-suited to more genteel intel assignments.

The feeling was mutual. Otman had despised every moment of his last assignment, a desk job back home on Yavet, combing files to root out deep-cover Trueborn spies within Intelligence Branch. Otman had come to hate the mole hunts, hate the distrust in comrades that they bespoke. In fact, the one and only Trueborn thing that he had uncovered during his year of mole hunting was the expression's origin. Moles were Earth rodents, probably mythical, that burrowed undetected through darkness and eroded structures from within.

The Bush cat bounced, and he grimaced and smiled simultaneously. Here in the fetid jungle, intangible moles were replaced by palpable discomfort and danger, and men he trusted to share those dangers equally. And here his quarry, although also Trueborn, was real.

Otman gazed up through the Bush cat's open roof hatch. Silhouetted against low clouds, man-sized, fork-tailed dragons glided, wheeled and screeched.

Otman shrugged mentally. The wrangler had advised them not to worry, at least not about the gorts. The flying monsters nested and hunted among the treetops, never venturing lower than fifty feet above the ground. Gorts kept their distance because Dead End's top predators, the grezzen, could bound fifty feet into the sky, swat a flying dragon dead with one paw, then swallow the gort whole before touching the ground again. So the suicidally voracious gorts didn't threaten ground-bound humans.

But, in the early colonial days, strikes by attacking gorts had routinely downed human aircraft. For decades now, nothing mechanical had flown above Dead End. Except the impregnably huge chemical-fuel orbital shuttles, like the one that had shuttled Otman's team, posing as a "film crew," down from the interstellar Trueborn cruiser that had borne them out here.

Otman smiled and silently thanked the flying dragons. The Trueborns' inability to fly Dead End's skies, or rather the Trueborns' smug attempt to prove that they could, had created the opportunity that had brought Otman's team here, to the jagged edge of the known universe.

Otman's handtalk crackled with a transmission from Desmond, who was operating the magnetometer in the lead Bush cat. "Captain, I got metal. Big metal."

The film-crew pretense had been dropped as soon as the team passed out beyond Trueborn listening range. The men now wore jungle fatigues and had broken out the team's normal tactical weapons from "photographic equipment" crates, supplementing the "film crew's" Trueborn gunpowder weapons. Recon Scout Team Eight was again full-on field tactical. Bogerd's chest swelled, even as another headache pricked behind his sinuses. Everything out here, even the pollen, was their enemy, but that was the challenge they lived for.

Big metal. Desmond's words raised hair, even on Otman's recently shaved neck. The only metal out here would be a manmade object, and a manmade object was the prize they sought.

"Range?" Otman leaned forward.

"I make it forty-six hundred yards, Captain."

"How big?"

"Sir, the supply weenies disguised this mag as a photo image previewer. But they porked the mass calibration doin' it. Five tons, wild-ass guess."

It would be a dead-on guess. Senior Tech Sergeant Desmond had served with Otman longer even than First Sergeant Rodric had. Desmond's courage and loyalty had saved Otman's missions, and his life, often. Desmond, as the team's sensor wizzo, wasn't cleared to know what their quarry was, much less what it should weigh.

But Otman knew, and the guess worried him. Few Yavi had ever touched a Trueborn Scorpion's hull, much less put one on a scale, but the briefers had predicted thirty-five tons.

Desmond asked, "Sir, should we make for the anomaly?"

Had the crash broken up the Trueborn ship? One bit of debris could lead to another.

Otman thumbed his handtalk. "Is the anomaly moving?"

"Like a rock, Skipper."

Otman rubbed his forehead as the allergy headache spiked, then receded. "Make for it, Sergeant. But maintain present speed." Racing to catch something that wasn't trying to get away was reckless. And if this object was, or led to, their quarry, they were early.

Desmond's voice rasped, "Skipper, that heading's gonna take us past a flat-topped hill a thousand yards short of the anomaly. The hilltop's bald granite, so it should be clear of local bugs."

Desmond, like every soldier in the teams, wore multiple hats. He had just changed hats from sensor specialist to senior non-commissioned officer. Therefore, he was commenting on the enemy situation. Though on Dead End, the enemy was no army, it was the world itself.

Otman traced a finger across his vehicle's flat-screen map display, tapped an oval of enclosed contour lines. "Top elevation six twenty-six?"

"That's it, Sir."

Otman eyed the flat-screen map again, then peered at the darkening sky. Why blunder up onto this unknown object at dark? Desmond, like any good senior non-commissioned officer, was suggesting to his commissioned commanding officer, without suggesting, that they halt short of the anomaly. That would place them on a defensible terrain feature, with daylight left to emplace perimeter sensors and point-defense weapons. It would create a night defensive position impenetrable by Dead End's predators.

Otman nodded and thumbed his handtalk. "Nice catch, Sarge. We'll laager up there for the night."

Four hours later, Otman stood behind his team while they sat, backs to him, in a semicircle on the bald granite summit. The laager position they occupied provided unobstructed fields of observation and fire. Better, three of its sides were hundred-foot cliffs that Otman doubted even the local monsters could scale. The summit was clean of vegetation and the dangerous local pests that sheltered in it. A nice catch by Desmond, indeed.

The team sat cross-legged, eating chow and cleaning weapons. Desmond stood at the semicircle's center point, facing Otman and the men, displaying images on a flatscreen. For this hastily assembled mission, the 'puter to which the screen was hardwired carried virtually all the mission-specific information about this world. Desmond was now transferring the dope to the team on the fly.

Otman himself had known so little about DE 476 that he had purchased a paper local guide when they arrived at the landing strip that passed for a spaceport. He had yet to open the book.

Desmond scratched his gray-fuzzed temple as a bright yellow, fanged spider filled the screen. "The locals call this here a lemon bug. Twelve inches across. Habitat you-*bick*-wit-us. They look mean, but for this ecosystem, they're pussies."

Cassel, the Medic and Grenadier, raised a hand. "Poisonous?"

Desmond shook his head. "This thing's bite'll kill a six-ton local grazing animal in thirty seconds. But our biochemistry's different. Humans just swell up and puke for two days."

Cassel, who was also the team newbie, cocked his head at Desmond, half smiled. "All the bugs here that friendly, Sarge?"

"Nope." Desmond popped a new image. This showed a black bug the length and diameter of a flaccid penis. "Local name, dick bug. These aren't passive."

"Neither's mine." An anonymous comedian.

Laughter.

Desmond waited, stone-faced, for quiet. After Rodric, he had been the team's most senior, and avuncular, noncom. Now he was the acting top kick. "This is the only bug on Dead End that'll kill a human. The sting feels like injected fire, and you die screamin' in ninety seconds. There's no known antidote."

Somebody's boot scraped granite as he squirmed. "Great. Those ubiquitous too, Sarge?"

Desmond swung his hand at the barren plateau. "That's one reason the Captain picked this laager. Dick bugs don't like high ground, rock and open space."

Otman smiled. Desmond had picked this position. But loyal, self-effacing Desmond wouldn't accept credit in front of the men, even if Otman tried to acknowledge him.

Cassel scowled. "What about the grezzen, Sarge?"

Several grumbles of agreement.

Desmond scowled the school master's stone face, again. "Keep your diapers on. There's, like, eleven animals in the food chain before this briefing gets to the top predator. The little one gets chased by the big one what gets chased by the bigger one. Like from you maggots up to me."

Otman smiled in the darkness. He felt like he could hear nine pairs of young eyes roll. Despite the kids' reaction, the human glue that held a merc team—held any tactical-sized infantry unit—together was that every man in the team knew every other man completely, down to the way each rolled his eyes. And every one would lay down his life for the other. Not for flags or against tyrants, but because each man absolutely trusted that his buddy would do the same for him.

Only when the last man had finished chow did Otman crack his own ration. Simultaneously, Desmond's brief got to Dead End's top predators, the grezzen.

Each previous species that Desmond had profiled had been bigger, stronger, faster and meaner than the last. The grezzen, however, were in a figurative and literal class by themselves.

Mature male grezzen resembled, and had been named by the first Trueborn colonists for, a hirsute Earth carnivore called a grizzly. But while Trueborns had occasionally trained grizzlies, no one had ever "trained" a grezzen. At least, no one had survived and told about it. Absent empirical data, it was assumed that grezzen were roughly as intelligent as grizzlies, capable of rolling a large ball or walking on hind legs if stimulated by an appropriate reward. Which was more intelligence than they needed, given their physical gifts.

When Desmond finally put up a grezzen image, someone puckered a low whistle. Grezzen were ten times larger than grizzlies, eleven tons of six-legged muscle. Their carbon-12-based skeleton and integument allowed them to be disproportionately stronger, faster and more durable than species indigenous to normal Earthlikes' ecosystems. And they looked the part of top predator in hell, with three red eyes arrayed across a flat face, and tusks that curved down from their upper jaws like ebony scimitars.

According to Dead End's fossil record, the grezzen hadn't changed in thirty million years. Why would they? They perfectly dominated this world. And dominated the only offworld species who had challenged them for it. Dumb brutes that they were, grezzen had somehow, nevertheless, exterminated the first two Trueborn colonial expeditions. The grezzen had also slaughtered the reinforced Legion battalion that was sent along to protect the colonists of the second expedition. If the third expedition had failed, the Trueborns had planned to carpet bomb the place from orbit. But the current tiny colony had survived the subsequent decades, albeit by cowering behind minefields that discouraged the brutes, as well as the rest of Dead End's unfriendly population.

Desmond finished his brief, repacked the background data 'puter and simultaneously assigned the night watch schedule. Then he stomped the hilltop's crevassed granite with a boot. "Long as the watch stays awake, the sensors and rover mines will keep all the big predators out. You can sleep outside instead of in the vehicles 'cause the dick bugs don't like it up here."

Desmond's offer brought smiles. Most Yavi preferred enclosed spaces, but the vehicle interiors were ovens, especially when left idling as they would be to power the sensor and weapon arrays.

Otman laid out his own bedsack on the smooth-worn rock, trusted the watch to do its job, and fell into exhausted sleep after counting back just six digits.

Screams woke him in the darkness. He sat up, still inside his bedsack, and saw a running silhouette, arms flailing as though on fire. The man leapt into the third vehicle. The Bush cat rocked as the man thrashed inside.

Graunch.

Otman heard the emergency brake release, then the vehicle rolled slowly forward, away from him.

Otman tore free of his bedsack, groped for his night snoops, couldn't find them. He stumbled half-blind toward the vehicle, buckling on his sidearm.

In the darkness, others ran, some also flailing like the man in the vehicle.

The Bush cat lurched along the plateau, then toppled off its edge.

By the time Otman reached and peered over the cliff, the 'Cat rocked, inverted, on the scree below. Metal groaned and echoed, then the wreck burst into flame.

Otman staggered back, crushed something with his bare heel, and looked down.

A dead dick bug. He shuddered. A second bug was already squirming out of an inch-wide joint in the weathered granite. Otman drew his sidearm, reversed it and hammered the bug with the pistol's butt. Then another, and another. He looked around. The black nightmares covered the pale granite like writhing pepper.

Twenty minutes later, someone had thought to douse the rock with spare vehicle fuel, light it and sear a safe zone around the remaining two vehicles.

Otman sat with his seven men on the hoods of the two Bush cats, breathing in the mixed stench of burned kerosene and immolated bugs.

A soldier stared at Desmond. "You said this place had no bugs."

Desmond, hollow-eyed, shook his head. "The 'puter said it."

"The cracks were full of 'em."

Otman knit his brows, said to Desmond, "Let's take another look at that 'puter."

Desmond nodded at the black smoke that still drifted up from the wreck. "It was in that 'Cat."

The eight survivors spent the next hours huddled atop the 'Cats like castaways aboard flotsam. Most dozed. Otman couldn't. All told, four dead. Over the years his units had taken casualties, and every one still pained him. But nothing compared to this debacle. How? Why?

Otman stared at Desmond, who lay on his back on the other 'Cat's rear cargo rack, staring up at the darkness. Otman had never known Desmond to misread a map coordinate, a warning order paragraph, or even a soldier's name when distributing bonus vouchers. If Desmond hadn't erred, then what had happened?

Perhaps local predators had driven the bugs into this non-normal habitat. As Desmond had said, the little ones get chased by the bigger ones, and so on. But that would have been a coincidence, and Otman still didn't believe in coincidence.

So what else could have happened? Otman's year of mole hunting had taught him how easily a 'puter entry could be overwritten. It would've been simple. Reverse the habitat preferences of dick bugs.

Cold grew in the pit of Otman's stomach. Something on this carnivorous planet was eating his team. Was that something eating from the inside out? Had the Trueborns planted a mole in his team? Plenty of Trueborn zealots would sacrifice their own lives to sabotage an elite Yavi covert team.

Otman frowned at the two bodies that lay bagged alongside the opposite Bush cat. If there was a mole among them, who was it? Cassel was the newbie. The man Otman knew least. And as the medic, Cassel had accessed the tech 'puter day in and day out, studying the medical idiosyncracies of this hellhole.

Otman turned onto his side, gazed at Cassel. The kid slept, his face hairless and placid. What better disguise than youthful innocence?

By dawn, the dick bugs had vanished, though they were not supposed to be nocturnal. Nor did the crevasses display any evidence that bugs, or anything else, made a home on this rocky tombstone of a hilltop.

Otman had been too exhausted, too stunned, too pressed by yet another fleeting headache to think of the casualties until Desmond reminded him.

Two soldiers rappelled down to the wreck and roped up their comrades' remains. The team cremated the three bodies, consecrated the ash, and were off the knob's sloping back side and on track again before the gray sky was fully light.

The two remaining vehicles made good time, because the six-legged, six-ton grazers who rumbled across the planet in herds of twenty thousand had recently denuded the area. The grazing herd, which the team's route skirted, was barely visible in the distance, a vast, serene brown line on the horizon.

That morning Otman had placed himself in the lead vehicle, along with only the magnetometer itself and the Bush cat's driver. One way to thwart a mole, if there was one, was to deny him information about the team's next move.

So Otman himself first spotted the objective. The grazers had so recently passed through that the normally green, overgrown landscape was brown stubble.

The "object" proved to be many objects. The largest mass was an unremarkable cargo-truck-sized habitat box, a "sleeper," surrounded by empty food and fuel containers and vehicle spares. The durable effluvia of a long-abandoned campsite.

The trailing Bush cat stopped fifty yards short of the anticlimactic objective to repair a damaged road wheel before it stalled the vehicle altogether.

Otman dismounted the lead vehicle into thick midmorning heat heavy with insect drone, and Desmond walked forward from the following vehicle.

Otman kicked a rusted, empty cartridge box, looked around, hands on hips.

Desmond swore. "Captain, this crap's been here for years. Some Trueborn's idea of a safari. Gone wrong."

Not, Otman thought, as wrong as his own safari had gone already. He stared down at his hands. Normally steady, they twitched, and as he stared he realized that his right eye had begun to twitch. He pressed his eyelid with a fingertip to still it.

"Skipper?"

Otman snapped his head up. Desmond was staring at him.

"Captain? You okay?"

"What's that supposed to mean?"

Desmond drew back. "Nothin', Sir. You just seem a little, I dunno . . ."

Otman didn't know, either. He knew that he disrespected officers who failed to focus on the mission. Who blundered. Who failed to protect their men. Now, for the first time in his career, he was such an officer. Guilt. Shame. These were emotions unfamiliar to him.

Otman breathed deeply, refocused on the reality in front of him. The "sleeper's" corroded shell lay flattened, and scars in the soil revealed how it had been tossed and dragged first in one direction, then another, like a paper scrap, as the herds had grazed, then regrazed the spot over the years.

Desmond pointed at the scars. "This thing was prob'ly whole when the Trueborns abandoned it. Woog herds only regraze an area after it regrows. Two-year intervals."

Otman ground his teeth. This junk heap had nothing to do with a recently missing C-drive starship. A dead end on Dead End. So far he had accomplished nothing except to get four good men killed. Now what?

The Bush cat's driver lowered his window. "Captain? Sarge? You feel that?"

Otman's boot soles vibrated.

The vibration grew until the thatch on the ground twitched.

The driver wrinkled his forehead. "Could it be those woogs we passed?"

"Maybe." Desmond shook his head. "But they won't come this way." He pointed at the barren ground. "No chow left."

Thunder rumbled. The driver frowned. "Well, something's gainin' on us."

Now a thin brown line showed in the distance. A dust cloud boiled, like a tank division at full gas. If the woogs were, for some reason, inbound, they would be lumbering no faster than a soldier could route march.

Otman blinked, and in that instant the brown cloud seemed closer.

He remounted the lead 'Cat while he called to Desmond. "I don't like this. Get back to your vehicle, Sergeant."

Desmond was already on his way at a dead run, shouting to the crew, who remained clustered around the damaged wheel.

Otman tugged optical binoculars from the Bush cat's utility bin and cursed the cover story that denied them the body armor and optics of contemporary battle dress.

He focused on the herd. Even at this distance, the animals loomed as big as Earth elephants, but with corkscrew antlers and six legs.

They weren't grazing. They galloped, crashing into one another in panic and disarray. Leading animals at the front stumbled, fell, then disappeared in the dust as those behind overran them.

Otman turned to his driver. "It's a stampede. Get us out of here!"

Gears ground, and the Bush cat lurched forward.

Thirty seconds later, the vehicle slowed so violently that Otman's head struck the dash. "What the hell?"

The driver was staring at his rear view.

Otman frowned. "Floor it!"

"Sir? The others can't keep up."

Otman twisted in his seat and peered out across the rear rack. A six-wheel could easily move on five, but the trail vehicle limped along, now a hundred yards behind them. It tilted on five wheels, its detached sixth lashed to its roof.

Already the stampede, its front now stretched across their left and right rear as far as could be seen in the dust, had closed to within one hundred yards of the trailing 'Cat.

Within seconds, the stampede would swallow the crippled 'Cat and flatten it beneath a hundred thousand hooves.

Otman shouted to his driver, "Stop! When they catch up, we'll take 'em aboard."

Otman snatched a Trueborn big-game rifle from the 'Cat's dashboard rack. He had seen a Trueborn cowboy holo once where a stampede was split by killing a lead animal.

He stood, head and shoulders out the roof hatch, turned and faced the stampede. Vibration shook the three-ton Bush cat on its suspension, now, and made aim impossible. But the vast target made aim unnecessary. Otman emptied the rifle into the herd, then groped for another magazine.

He reloaded, fired again. His shots no more slowed the stampede than thrown pebbles slowed a tidal wave.

The herd was fifty yards behind the trailing Bush cat when the 'Cat stopped dead, belching black smoke. Men spilled from the vehicle's doors and ran, hopelessly slowly, toward the lead vehicle's dubious sanctuary.

A lone figure scrambled out through the crippled machine's roof hatch, a stubby grenade launcher in hand.

Cassel, the newbie kid, the putative mole, and the team's grenadier, straddled the road wheel lashed to the 'Cat's roof, planted his feet, and fired into the stampede's center.

A heartbeat later, the herd surged across the motionless 'Cat like a wave across a stone. Cassel and the 'Cat cartwheeled through the air in opposite directions, then vanished into the dust.

The lead animals, wild-eyed, mouths agape, overtook and trampled the men running from the demolished Bush cat.

In two heartbeats, the wave would crush the lead 'Cat, too.

Otman aimed his sidearm at the herd, then braced his free hand on the roof against the final impact.

Boom.

The delayed detonation of the grenade that Cassel had fired was muffled by the bulk of the bull woog that he had shot. The bull belched blood, stumbled, and fell a yard short of the lead 'Cat, so close that an antler tip exploded through the Bush cat's rear window, and skewered the driver's chest.

The herd divided, infinitesimally, around the fallen bull. Passing animals pummeled the 'Cat's flanks as they passed, so close that the smell and heat engulfed Otman, and woog hide scraped his shoulder.

Then the animals were gone. The thunder receded.

Someone moaned, then stopped.

Otman lowered himself back down into the 'Cat's passenger compartment, arms aquiver. The dead driver's blood spattered the compartment's floor. Nothing to be done there. Otman staggered out, then limped toward the wrecked 'Cat. Between the two vehicles he found the others, trampled, twisted, dead to a man.

When he reached the crumple that had been the other Bush cat, bleeding fuel, five wheels to the sky, he whispered a curse.

"Captain? Izzat you?" It was Desmond, pinned, but protected, beneath the twisted wreck.

Otman didn't even answer, just nodded.

As the ranking man in the trailing Bush cat, Desmond had waited for the last man, Cassel, to exit the disabled vehicle before he fled himself. Ironically, Desmond's selflessness in going down with the ship had saved his life.

Otman knelt and asked, "How you doing, Sarge?"

Desmond coughed blood. "Been better, Sir."

Otman flattened himself belly down and peered beneath the wreck. Desmond wasn't impaled. Otman had seen enough casualties to triage this as broken ribs, one of which had likely punctured a lung. "Better still if I can get this thing off you."

Otman retrieved the intact 'Cat's meds kit and sedated Desmond, then set a canteen where the man could reach it and returned to the operable Bush cat.

It took Otman twenty minutes to remove the driver's body from behind the lead Bush cat's wheel. First he had to cut the woog's antler with a hand saw, then rend the antler's tip from the driver's back. The dead man's blood had spilled out of the vast wound, coursed down the antler tip, and covered Otman's hands.

At last Otman turned the 'Cat around, rigged its winch cable and shifted the wreck. Once Otman had dragged half-conscious Desmond out from beneath the wreck he inspected him for other injuries. Then he turned Desmond on his side to drain the oral bleeding and covered the injured man with a blanket to mitigate shock.

Then Otman, dazed by the enormity of the calamity, leaned against the intact Bush cat's fender. He stared down at his hands and tried to scrub the blood from them. Blood that his leadership, or lack thereof, had spilled.

Cassel the newbie a mole? Hardly. The kid had sacrificed himself to save his buddies, in the best tradition of the teams. So why, how, had this latest and most total disaster been visited on them?

Otman felt himself all over, and shame rushed hot to his cheeks. He wasn't even scratched.

His fingers touched something hard, rectangular, in his fatigues' breast pocket. Otman tugged out the forgotten tourist guide he had bought at the spaceport a million years ago.

Otman thumbed to the wildlife section. He skipped past the supposedly omnipotent grezzen, of which species not a hair had been seen, to the woogs. Woogs stampeded at the scent of predators. Stripers, the six-legged tyrannosaurs that preyed on woogs, were attracted to, naturally enough, woogs. But they were also attracted to *fire*, kindled on this planet by lightning strikes, because animals slain by the resultant blaze often provided an easy meal.

Otman narrowed his eyes. A mole bent on sabotaging this mission couldn't imitate a striper's scent to force a stampede. But a mole could create a fire, and attract a striper, and achieve the same result.

Otman stared at Desmond, who lay with his eyes closed amid the dust-painted stubble the woogs left behind. Atop the granite hill, it had been Desmond who had reminded Otman about the dead. Which had led to the fire. Which had attracted a striper. Which had caused the stampede.

More than that, Rodric's death had conveniently breveted Desmond to the team's top kick, a promotion that had positioned him to recommend the night in the poison bug nest. And Desmond had no need to tamper with the 'puter. He simply had to lie about what the 'puter said.

Of all the men on this team, Desmond, decorated, plain-spoken, loyal old Desmond was the least likely candidate for a mole. And so who better?

Enough of this! Otman still had a mission. Indeed, now the mission was all he had, all that kept him from sliding away from sanity. He set his suspicions aside, leaned in to the Bush cat's cab, and thumbed on the magnetometer.

His heart leapt. From this new vantage, a new magnetic anomaly had become visible. It glowed onscreen, seven miles away, nestled in a steep-sided valley. The Trueborns' lousier sensors would have missed it. More importantly, the mag computed the anomaly's mass at thirty-five tons. But hadn't Desmond said that the mag's mass function had been porked?

"Captain?" Desmond whispered through bloody lips.

Otman thumbed the magnetometer screen black.

Desmond coughed. "Sir, I'm afraid I can't be much help with the men."

Otman stiffened. "You're suggesting another fire, Sergeant?"

Desmond gathered a shallow breath. "Can't just leave 'em, sir." The sergeant stared up at Otman. "Sir, it wasn't your fault. None of it."

Otman smiled. "Oh, I know that, sergeant. I know that quite well."

"Sir? I mean, you been acting, well . . ."

"First I'll police up the bodies, Sergeant Desmond. Then we'll discuss it."

Desmond tried to straighten to acknowledge the order, grimaced. "Yes, sir. As you say, sir."

Even using the winch, it took two hours to gather the bodies.

Otman, sweat soaking his fatigues, stood panting alongside the rank of corpses.

Desmond inclined his head toward the canteen Otman had left him. "Drink, sir?"

Otman cocked his head. "A toast, Desmond?"

"Sir?"

"To the success of your mission." Otman knelt alongside the open meds kit and tugged out a field dressing.

Desmond squinted. "Sir, I—"

Otman peeled open the dressing pack. "What did they offer you, Desmond? When did you go over? Or were you Trueborn from the beginning, and planted?"

Desmond shook his head, slowly. "Captain, I don't know what you're thinking. Sir, I seen stress casualties before. You're just, uh, troubled by the losses. And you blame yourself."

Otman knelt beside the wounded man. "I blame *you*, Desmond. I don't know how you got Rodric to drop his guard when he was reconning our route. But I know how you whittled us down, one 'coincidence,' one bit of 'bad luck,' at a time."

Desmond kept shaking his head. "Sir, those things just happened. What you got's called traumatic combat paranoia. It's temporary. Let's get you calmed down. Then we'll continue the mission. The two of us."

"The two of us? You think I'll give you another chance to turn this world against me?"

Desmond pointed a quivering finger at the open meds kit. "There's sedatives in there, sir."

"Ah. Yes."

Otman reached down, turned Desmond onto his back, then pressed the field dressing over Desmond's face, covering his nose and mouth. The older man stiffened, screamed behind the wadded gauze.

Desmond's eyes bulged, he kicked both legs and he tore at Otman's forearms with both hands.

Otman shifted his weight, bore down and forced the dressing against the wounded man's nose and lips.

Desmond's struggles weakened.

Otman stared into the traitor's eyes. "Staff Sergeant Terrelle Desmond, as the ranking officer of this duly licensed contractor to the armed forces of Yavet, I have, upon due and diligent investigation, found you guilty of espionage and high treason. Wherefore I have sentenced you to summary field execution."

Desmond stared up at Otman, eyes bulging, and shook his head, mute.

Otman glared down, kept the pressure on, until, finally, the mole choked on his own blood, and his body relaxed.

Otman didn't cremate Desmond, or the rest of the team. Fool me once . . . He left the dead where they lay, to keep the predators busy, and so off his ass.

Then Otman drove the remaining Bush cat off in search of thirty-five tons of metal.

By the time the 'Cat lurched around the tight valley's last bend, twilight shrouded it. But Otman's heart skipped when he saw the object. Sleek as an ebony teardrop, half obscured beneath a ledge, the crashed star fighter lay on its side like a beached fish.

Otman stopped alongside the wreck, then paused with his hands on the wheel.

The self-righteous Trueborns fancied themselves guardians of peace, but fought one another so frequently that they gave wars numbers as well as names. So far, they had dominated Cold War II. Not because they were actually righteous, nor peaceful, but because they alone possessed C-drive, the key to interstellar travel. But it was a key they hadn't earned. They had just stolen C-drive from an alien race, then exterminated them.

Otman smiled. He was about to break the Trueborn monopoly.

He clambered up onto the Scorpion, then ran his hands along the fuselage until he found the latch to the C-drive unit's access panel. The unit inside, just as the tech briefers had predicted, was a stripped, shrunken version of a cruiser's drive. It was so compact that the Bush cat's winch could pull it like a bad tooth. Then Otman would drive it back to the colony, conceal it in a crate that had contained camera equipment and smuggle it off planet under the Trueborns' upthrust noses.

He returned to the Bush cat, bent and grasped the front winch cable in both hands. They were still bloodstained. But the stain was really on the Trueborns' mole. Otman had defeated him, had defeated them, though at a terrible price.

And then Otman felt the allergy headache again, more intensely. He realized this time that it was not a headache. It was a probing. An inquiry. Otman had felt it first before he had sent Rodric out to recon the route, and again and again since.

He turned and stared back down the valley, in the direction he had come. Nothing. The valley's head was also empty.

Otman lifted his gaze, and recoiled.

Twenty feet away, across the star ship's hull, a great beast glared at him. That three red eyes glinted with more intelligence than a simple predator's. The grezzen didn't growl, didn't move. But Otman felt it, he realized now, time and again.

And then it all became clear.

Grezzen so dominated this ecosystem and its lesser prey because they, for want of a better term, read minds.

That was why they had so easily exterminated trained and well-equipped human troops. But when their probing revealed that the vaster human species had both the will and the means to exterminate them, they had feigned simplicity. They had tolerated and contained on their world a tiny human presence.

The grezzen cared less about Cold Wars or about intrahuman affairs of any sort. But Otman had contemplated invading, however slightly, their world, and the grezzen cared about that a great deal. And so they had set out to destroy him, without revealing or exposing their true nature.

The grezzen knew where and when to flush a predator that would kill Rodric because Otman himself had revealed both Rodric's location and his vulnerability. Similarly, they had forced an unexpected army of deadly insects into a place where Otman would not expect them, because he had revealed his plans to them. They had stampeded woogs to a place where, again, Otman would not expect to find them, because he told them. The mole in Otman's team was Otman himself. That was bad enough.

But Desmond's death? That had not been the grezzen's work. It had been the work of Otman himself, of his suspicion, paranoia and hubris. Or his madness. By any name, it could not excuse the monstrous horror that Otman had committed.

Across from him, the grezzen gathered itself like a tusked cat and rumbled a growl. Otman drew his revolver and cocked the hammer. But victory was impossible. And living with himself after what he had done unimaginable.

Otman sentenced himself, pressed the revolver's muzzle to his temple and squeezed the trigger.